THE FAIRY TALES COLLECTION

ELIZABETH KELLY

EK PUBLISHING INC.

VOLUME ONE

BEAUTY

BEAUTY

Mirabelle Vale, library assistant, bookworm, and downright dangerous with a slingshot, knows exactly who sends her a single red rose every year – Bennett Saxby.

After saving her life when they were children, he disappeared, and the yearly rose is the only proof of his existence.

When her childhood crush returns home – all grown up and a positive beast of a man – Mirabelle is eager to have the man of her dreams.

But Bennett's hiding his true nature and wants to keep his "Belle" from discovering the truth.

PROLOGUE

Bennett wanted to shift. He *needed* to shift – it was the only way to defeat them – but thinking that way was madness. Better to take the beating than expose who he really was.

His bear growled at the thought, and for one brief, heart-thudding moment, it nearly broke free of its bonds. He held it back grimly as the boys above him punched and kicked mercilessly. He curled into a ball, trying his best to protect his head, and bit back his grunt of pain when the ringleader delivered a heavy kick to his ribs.

Tears streamed down his face, and his bear howled with rage. It tore through his thin barrier of control, and the shift began. He was losing control. His bear's instinct to survive was too strong, and he moaned helplessly as one of the boys brayed shrill laughter.

"Look, Kevin! He's cryin'! Crybaby! I told you he wasn't so tough!"

Hair began to sprout on his arms and legs, and he growled deep in his throat. The sound was lost in the shouts and laughter of the boys standing above him in a tight circle. His shift was interrupted by the scream of one of the smaller of his tormentors.

Another scream of pain and outrage followed a soft whistling noise, and the tormentor danced away, holding the side of his head as blood dripped through his fingers. The others were looking around cautiously, and he raised his head and sniffed the air. A wonderful scent drifted to him, like books and cinnamon, and his bear whimpered in happiness before retreating.

"What's wrong with you, Tim?" Kevin scowled at the moaning boy.

"Somethin' hit me," Tim said.

"What are you talking about?"

Tim showed him his bloody hand as more blood dripped from his scalp. "Somethin' hit me, I said!"

"What do you -" Kevin made his own scream of pain and grabbed his leg as the other boys backed away uneasily.

Bennett sat up, holding his ribs and panting harshly as the scent grew stronger. It made him feel safe and forget the pain. He watched eagerly as the bushes parted and a girl stepped out.

She was tall – much taller than him – and wore jean shorts and a t-shirt. Her long dark hair hung in two messy braids down her back, and her glasses had slid down to the end of her nose. Her bright blue eyes studied the circle of boys as she pulled back and aimed the slingshot in her hand.

"Well, look who it is – fatty four-eyes! Get out of here!" Kevin sneered.

"Get away from him," she said.

"Mind your own business, dummy!" Kevin said. "Go home before we beat you up too!"

"Kevin, we can't beat up a girl," one of the other boys said. "My mama says you ain't never supposed to hit a girl."

"Shut up, Marty! Besides, Belle ain't no girl. She's a fat pig. Isn't that right, fatty?"

Kevin screwed up his face and made oinking noises. The girl flushed and let the stone fly from her slingshot without saying another word. It hit Kevin in the chest, and the oinking noises cut out with a harsh wheeze as he grabbed his chest.

"That hurt!" he squealed, sounding remarkably piggish himself, as the girl grinned fearlessly at him and deftly loaded another smooth stone into the slingshot.

"Get lost, Kevin. Or I'll knock out your front teeth."

"There's only one of you and seven of us," Kevin said. "And you're just a stupid, fat pig, who don't know -"

He howled with pain when she shot him again. This time the stone hit him in the jaw, and he danced around, shrieking and squealing as tears poured down his face. Quick as a snake, she loaded another stone and shot one of the other boys in the arm. He turned and ran as she popped a rock into the slingshot and aimed it at another.

He took off at a run, and with a wild grin on her face, she aimed and shot him in the ass with the stone. He screamed with pain, grabbing his butt as he disappeared through the trees. She laughed hysterically as the other boys ran, ducking and running for cover.

She aimed her slingshot at Kevin's crotch, and the boy's face paled before he chased after his companions. She watched them go, holding her slingshot with the steady hand of a predator until the noise of their retreat had disappeared.

She lowered her weapon and smiled at Bennett. He stared silently at her as she sat down on the ground beside him. Scrapes and scratches covered her legs, and she itched absentmindedly at a bug bite before pushing her glasses up her nose. "You okay?"

, He nodded, and she patted his arm. "They're jerks, and they don't fight fair."

He remained silent, and she cocked her head and stared at him before smiling. "My name's Mirabelle, but everyone calls me Belle. What's your name?"

He wanted to reply, but he was mesmerized by the gleam of her dark hair, overwhelmed by the perfect blue of her eyes, drowning in her intoxicating scent.

"Hey, what's your name?" she said.

He opened his mouth, and she nodded encouragingly. When there was only silence, she frowned and leaned a little closer. "Can't you talk?"

"Bennett," he said. "My name is Bennett."

"Bennett." She spoke it softly, tasted it on her tongue before grinning. "That's a funny name. I like it, though. It's," she struggled for a moment to find the right word, "unique."

"How old are you?" he asked.

"I'm seven. How old are you?"

"Nine."

He struggled to his feet, holding his throbbing ribs. She popped up beside him, dusting off the seat of her jean shorts with one hand before shoving her slingshot into the front pocket. He was oddly embarrassed to see that she was a foot taller than him and probably outweighed him by twenty pounds. She was big for a girl, but it didn't negate the fact that he was small. Hell, he was small for a human boy - as a bear shifter, he was downright tiny.

His father was worried. Bennett could see it in how he looked at him sometimes and was constantly plying him with raw meat, but his mother brushed off his father's concerns.

"Don't you worry, my love," she always said, "you'll grow big and strong soon enough."

He realized that Belle was speaking to him and cleared his throat. "What?"

"I said I've seen you at school before. You play with that big blond boy. I forget his name."

"Duncan," he said as he rubbed at his ribs. Already the pain was beginning to fade.

"You live in that giant house on the hill, right?"

He nodded, and she grinned happily. "It's kind of a creepy looking house. I live in the trailer park over on Compton Avenue. Do you have any brothers and sisters?"

"No," he said.

"Me neither," she said. "It's just my dad and me."

She lapsed into silence, and he scuffed a bit of dirt with the toe of his sneaker before mumbling, "Thanks for helping me."

"You're welcome," she said. "It wasn't a fair fight."

"Where did you learn to do that?" He pointed to the sling-shot poking out of her pocket.

"From a book," she said. "I like to read. Do you?"

He shrugged, and she grinned again at him. "I go to the library almost every day. It doesn't cost any money to borrow the books, and it's like being in a different world. You can escape, you know?"

"Why do you want to escape?" he asked.

She bit at her bottom lip. "Sometimes being in this world isn't much fun."

He stared at the freckles scattered across her cheeks as she sighed. "I guess I should go. Do you need me to walk you home in case those boys come back?"

He glared at her, his nine-year-old pride roaring to life. "I'm not afraid of them."

"I know, but they might come after you again, and you're not very big."

She spoke in a matter-of-fact tone, but it still made him scowl.

"I'm big enough. They just took me by surprise."

"Right."

She stood next to him, and he hesitated a moment before saying, "You wanna see something cool?"

"Sure! Hold on a sec." She disappeared into the trees before reappearing with a blue backpack. She slung it across her back and grinned at him. "What is it?"

"You'll see."

She followed him deeper into the woods and kept up a steady stream of chatter. He didn't mind. He was naturally quiet, and it was nice to listen to her talk. By the time they had reached the giant oak tree, she was breathless from the quick pace, and he waited patiently as she caught her breath.

"You gotta go through these bushes." He pointed at the large cluster of bushes behind the tree, and she peered at them before glancing around.

"I've never been this deep in the forest before," she said. "Is it safe?"

"I'll keep you safe," he said.

She studied him carefully before nodding, and they squirmed their way past the thick bushes, arms thrown over their faces to protect them from the heavy branches.

"Almost there," he grunted. He wished he could change into his bear form. The thick fur would protect him, but humans had no idea shifters existed, and it needed to stay that way. He'd lost track of how often his father had lectured him to remain in his human form when around humans. If they discovered their existence, they'd take him away from his family to a lab, poke him with needles, and cut open his stomach to look at his insides. He shivered all over at the thought.

"Hey, are you okay?" Belle asked.

She placed her hand on his back, and another shiver went through him at her touch.

"Yeah." He pushed through the last bushes and jerked with surprise when Belle grabbed his hand.

"Help me, Bennett," she puffed.

He tugged, and she popped free of the bushes with a muffled grunt. He hesitated and then pulled out the twigs entangled in her braids.

"Thanks." She grinned cheerfully at him.

He blushed a little before stepping aside. Belle's eyes widened, and the look of pure delight on her face brought a surge of happiness to his belly.

"Oh my gosh, it's so pretty," she whispered.

She took a few steps forward and stared wide-eyed at the rose bush. The bush was large, nearly ten feet tall, and covered from top to bottom in bright crimson flowers. She reached out and touched one of the flowers delicately.

"So soft," she said.

"Do you like it?" he asked eagerly.

"I love it," she breathed. "The flowers are perfect, aren't they?"

He nodded, and when she sank to the ground and stared at the roses, he sat beside her.

"My daddy used to give my mama flowers," she said. "It made her so happy. He gave her flowers almost every week. She would have loved these roses. They were her favourite."

"You could take one back to her," he said.

She shook her head. "Mama died last year in a car accident."

"I'm sorry."

She smiled at him, but he could see tears glistening in her bright blue eyes. "I miss her a lot. Daddy does too. He won't

11

say that he does, but he cries when he thinks I can't hear him, and now he – he drinks a lot."

"I'm sorry," he said again. He felt helpless and stupid. Not knowing what else to do, he leaned forward and tore a rose from the bush, ignoring the thorns that pricked his fingers. He handed it to her, and she brought the flower to her nose, inhaling deeply before smiling at him.

"It smells wonderful."

She smelled wonderful, and he leaned closer, inhaling the warm scent of old books and cinnamon as she held the rose carefully.

"You're bleeding!" There was a note of alarm in her voice, and he stared at the blood dripping from his fingertip.

"You shouldn't have picked the flower," she scolded gently as she took his hand. Using the edge of her t-shirt, she wiped away the blood. Another drop of blood welled up, and she frowned before pressing her shirt against his fingers. "Stupid thorns."

They sat silently for a moment, and she smiled happily when she rechecked his finger, and no blood appeared. His fingertip had healed completely, and she gave him a curious look. "You're a fast healer, huh?"

"Uh, yeah," he said before snatching his hand back.

"Thank you for bringing me here, Ben."

He wondered if he should tell her that it was Bennett, not Ben but decided he liked how she shortened his name. "You're welcome, Mirabelle."

She giggled. "No one calls me Mirabelle, remember?"

"I like Mirabelle better," he said. "It's pretty." He stared at the ground before mumbling, "You're pretty."

"No, I'm not," she said. "I'm too fat to be pretty. My best friend Rowan is really pretty because she's got red hair and is skinny. But me and Ella are too fat."

"Who's Ella?"

"She's my other best friend," Belle said. "She lives in the trailer park where I do. Her mama died when she was a baby, and then her dad died a couple of months ago, but she has a stepmom. She's kind of mean, though. She makes Ella do a bunch of chores and stuff, and sometimes she even makes her go to other people's houses and clean."

She sighed and stared at the rose bush again.

"My best friend is Duncan. He's a li -"

He shut his mouth with a snap, and Belle stared curiously at him. "He's a what?"

"Uh, he's a nice guy."

She frowned but let it go, and he released his breath in a harsh rush. What was wrong with him? He had almost told her that Duncan was a lion shifter.

"I should go. It's getting late," she said before climbing to her feet.

"Will your dad be worried?" he asked.

She shook her head. "No. He was drinking when I left, so he won't even notice I'm gone, but I told Ella I would meet her later."

She stared a final time at the rose bush before squirming through the thick bushes. He followed her, and she smiled at him when they reached the other side. "Thanks again for showing me the rose bush, Ben. I really liked it."

He nodded, and his heartbeat kicked up a notch when she said, "Maybe we could hang out again sometime?"

He hesitated. Although technically, he wasn't forbidden to play with human children, his father strongly encouraged him to stay away from them. He watched as Belle's face flushed.

"Sorry, I shouldn't have said that."

"What do you mean?" He touched her shoulder before she could walk away.

She shrugged and twirled the rose gently between her fingertips. "Boys don't like playing with me. They only like playing with pretty girls."

"I think you're pretty," he said again.

Her eyes sparkled behind her glasses, and she patted his arm. "I think you're pretty too, Ben."

She stared at the oak tree. "Maybe we could hang out tomorrow. We could meet in the forest again if you... what's wrong?"

Bennett lifted his head and inhaled again. His eyes widened at the scent he caught, and he grabbed her hand, squeezing it tightly. "We have to go. Right now."

"Why? What's wrong?"

"C'mon!" Before he could lead her away, a soft growling came from their right, and he froze as his bear made a grumbling noise of warning.

"Ben?" Mirabelle whispered. "What – what is that?"

The growling intensified, and her eyes widened when the cougar stepped out from the trees. Her hand tightened on Ben's, and she moaned in fear as the cougar stalked forward.

"Ben," she whispered. "Wh-what do we do?" She glanced at him, a small squeak of surprise emerging from her throat.

The shift was happening, his bear reacting to the threat, and he dropped Belle's hand as fur sprouted on his face and arms.

"Ben? What's happening to you?" she asked, her face going pale.

His bones cracked, and he fell to his knees as the cougar made a soft hissing noise before yowling.

"Run," Ben growled as his teeth lengthened and his body swelled. "Run, Mirabelle. Run!"

He shifted completely to his bear form, and she backed away before dropping her backpack and the rose and fleeing.

The cougar yowled again and chased after her. Ben roared angrily when the cougar swiped at her. Its claws tore through her t-shirt, and blood welled up on her back as she screamed in pain. She was knocked off her feet, and her glasses flew from her face as she landed on the hard ground. Ben roared again as the cougar crouched over her. He leaped onto the cougar's back, tearing at the back of its neck with his fangs as his claws sank through the thick fur to gouge and tear at its skin. The cougar screamed angrily and shook its large body, dislodging Ben like a troublesome fly. He landed on the ground with a harsh thud and rolled to his feet, growling loudly. The cougar stared at him before crouching. Fear flooded through him, but he growled again. He had to keep the cougar from hurting Mirabelle. That was all that mattered.

The cougar's body tensed, and Ben rose to his hind feet. He was going to die, but maybe Mirabelle could get away while the cougar attacked him. He roared again as the cougar sprang forward. A gunshot rang out, and the cougar's body landed on him with a heavy thud, knocking him to the ground. Blood poured from a crater-sized hole in its head, and he scrambled free of its body, staring wide-eyed at the man standing next to Belle.

"Shift, little bear," he said as he knelt next to Belle.

Bennett shifted with a quiet pop and swiped at the blood smeared across his chest before lunging forward.

"Is she dead?" he cried as he fell to his knees beside Belle. Blood had soaked through her shirt, and he made a harsh cry of dismay. Belle turned her head and blinked blearily at him.

"Ben?" she whispered. "You – you're a bear."

A combination of relief and fear flooded through him as the man touched his arm. "Move back, little bear."

He watched helplessly as the man removed his jacket and

pressed it against Belle's back. She screamed in pain, and Bennett echoed her cry as her eyes rolled up in her head and she slumped against the ground.

"She's dead!" Bennet shouted as his bear surged forward.

"Calm yourself," the man said before reaching out and shaking him roughly. "She's not dead yet."

He shouldered his rifle and Belle's backpack before carefully lifting Belle into his arms. "Go home now."

"No, I can't! I have to make sure she's okay."

The man shook his head. "I'm taking her to the hospital. You need to go home."

"I'm going with you!"

"No. You have no clothes and no control over your shifting right now. Go home. I'll keep her safe."

Bennet stared wide-eyed at him, and the man smiled reassuringly. "Quickly, now. I need to get her to the hospital, or she will die. Go on."

"Do you promise to help her?" Ben asked.

"I promise. Run, little bear."

The man turned and, holding Belle's unconscious body, sprinted through the forest. Tears streaming down his face, Ben watched him disappear before gently scooping up the fallen rose he had picked for Belle. Holding the stem lightly in his teeth, he shifted to his bear form and raced toward home.

———

THE YOUNG MAN KNOCKED TWICE ON THE MASSIVE WOODEN door. It opened after only a few moments, and the woman, who was large and broad through the shoulders like most female grizzly shifters, stared blankly at him.

"Good evening, Mrs. Saxby. My name is -"

"I know who you are, wolf shifter," she said. "Come in."

He stepped into the hallway, and the woman hesitated before hugging him hard. "Thank you for saving my boy."

He patted her back awkwardly as a giant of a man appeared in the hallway.

"Conrad," the woman said, "this is -"

"Rafe Taggert," the bear shifter said. "Your father and I worked together many years ago. Come into the kitchen."

"Would you like a cup of tea, Mr. Taggert?" the woman asked.

He shook his head. "No, and please call me Rafe."

He sank into a chair as the grizzly shifters did the same. Conrad ran his hand through his short dark hair. "Thank you for saving my son."

Rafe nodded. "Honestly, it was pure luck that I was in the forest yesterday."

"Well, we're still grateful you were there," the woman said as she squeezed her husband's hand. Tears dripped down her cheeks, and Conrad leaned forward and pressed a kiss against her forehead.

"He's fine, Annette."

She nodded and wiped at the tears as a low voice spoke from the doorway. "Is she dead?"

Rafe twisted around and smiled at the boy standing in the doorway. "No, little bear. She lives."

His mouth trembled, and Annette held out her arms. "Come here, Bennett."

He climbed into her lap, and she rocked him soothingly, kissing his cheeks as Rafe cleared his throat. "They gave her blood transfusions and stitched up her back. They don't think there will be permanent damage from the cougar's claws beyond scarring."

"Oh, thank goodness," Annette said as she continued to rock Bennett.

"I didn't tell them your son was there," Rafe said.

A look of relief crossed Conrad's face. "Thank you, wolf shifter. We are in your debt."

Rafe shook his head. "There's still a problem, Mr. Saxby."

"What do you mean?" Annette asked.

"The girl is awake. I stopped by the hospital this morning, and the girl was awake, telling anyone who would listen that your son was there and that he turned into a bear."

Annette moaned in dismay, and Bennett clutched at her. "I'm sorry, Mama. I tried not to shift, but I couldn't help it."

"It's okay, my love. It's okay," she said as she gave her husband a frightened look.

"Did they believe her?" Conrad asked.

Rafe shrugged. "I'm not entirely sure. They had given her a lot of medication for pain, so they may believe that she is not thinking clearly."

"For the moment," Conrad said grimly.

"Yes, for the moment," Rafe said. "Still, I don't think there is much to worry about."

"We can't take that risk," the grizzly shifter said. "Annette, we're leaving."

"Conrad, we can't just -"

"We can and we will."

Bennett sat up and stared wide-eyed at his father. "Papa, I will speak with Mirabelle. I will convince her to keep my secret."

Conrad shook his head. "No, boy. Humans cannot be trusted. You know that. She will continue to speak of this, and sooner or later, another human will believe her. We leave today."

He stood and held his hand out to Rafe. "Thank you again, wolf shifter."

Rafe stood and shook it firmly as Bennett slid from Annette's lap. "Papa, I don't want to leave."

"We have no choice!" Conrad snapped. Bennett flinched, and his father's expression softened. "I'm sorry, son. We have to leave."

He turned and strode out of the kitchen as Bennett stared at his mother. "Mama, please."

Her face was pale, and she trembled lightly, but she kissed his forehead and pushed him toward the doorway. "We must listen to your father, Bennett. Go and pack your things."

He burst into tears and ran from the room as Annette smiled wearily at Rafe. "Thank you again, Rafe."

He nodded, and she walked him to the door. "Are you certain you should leave? This may blow over quickly."

"My husband is a good man, but he will never trust the humans. Even a rumour started by a little girl is enough to make him fear for our safety. It's better for everyone if we leave."

"Good luck," Rafe said.

"Thank you. Goodbye, Rafe."

CHAPTER 1

"Ms. Vale? Can you sign here, please?"

The voice was loud and intrusive in the quiet library, and she instinctively made a shushing noise before smiling at the courier. He gave her a bored look and held out the clipboard. "Sign here."

Her hands trembling, she scribbled her name before taking the long, narrow white box. The courier left, his boots clomping loudly on the wooden floor as she set the box on the desk and used scissors to cut the ribbon around it.

She held her breath as she lifted the box lid and unwrapped the tissue paper. A rose, its crimson petals as dark as blood against the white tissue, was nestled in the box, and she lifted it carefully before pressing it to her nose.

"Ms. Vale? I can't find a book."

She placed the rose in the vase of water she had filled this morning and smiled at the little girl. "What book this time, Valerie?"

Valerie studied the piece of paper in her hand. "Little Women."

Mirabelle smiled again. "That's a very good book. I'm glad you're going to read it, Valerie."

"Mama says it's a classic," Valerie said solemnly.

"It is. Follow me."

She moved around the desk and led the little girl to the children's section. She scanned the shelves before pulling the book. "Here, honey. Take it to Mrs. Simpson. She'll check it out for you."

"Thanks, Ms. Vale!" Valerie grabbed the book and scampered back to the desk as Mirabelle followed more slowly. She passed the computers, tugging self-consciously at her cardigan as one of the young men working at the closest computer glanced up at her. His gaze wandered over her plump body with vague disinterest before he returned to staring at the screen.

She adjusted her cardigan again before moving behind the desk. Her glasses slid down her nose, and she pushed them up irritably. Man, she needed to remember to pick up her contacts tomorrow. She supposed she should go tonight, but she was meeting Ella at Gaston's Bar and Grill after work. She'd have to put up with her glasses for another day.

Speaking of which - she glanced at her watch - ten minutes until closing. She hurried around the desk and shelved the last of the books as the head librarian, Mrs. Simpson, announced the closing of the library. She smiled as people gathered their things and headed to the door. She loved working at the library and knew how lucky she was to get the job. The economy was the shits right now, and she was still surprised that she had managed to find her dream job in her small town.

As Mrs. Simpson ushered the last of the patrons out the door and locked it, she returned to the desk and gathered up her jacket and purse. She picked up the vase with the delicate rose, another little beat of pleasure going through her. As the day ticked on, she had worried that perhaps this year would be the year that no flower appeared. For the last eighteen years, on this exact day, a rose had been delivered to her without fail. The scars on her back throbbed suddenly, and she winced before touching the rose's soft petals.

"Belle?"

She smiled at Mrs. Simpson. "It was busy today for a change, huh?"

"Yes." The older woman looked distinctively uncomfortable, and Belle gave her a worried look.

"What's wrong?"

"I'm sorry, Belle, but I'll have to let you go."

Belle blinked at her, certain she had misheard. "I'm sorry?"

"I have to let you go. There isn't enough work to support the two of us, and the town has slashed our budget again. We have to cut costs wherever we can."

Belle sank into the chair behind the desk and stared numbly at the rose she still clutched. "I – are you sure?"

"Yes, I'm sorry," Mrs. Simpson said with a heavy sigh. "I wish we could afford to keep you on. I'm going to miss you."

Belle blinked back the hot tears that threatened to fall as Mrs. Simpson patted her shoulder with one thin hand. "I'm so sorry, Belle."

She nodded and rose unsteadily to her feet. "I guess there's some paperwork I need to fill out."

"It'll only take a minute," Mrs. Simpson said. "If you'd like, you can come back tomorrow and -"

"No," Belle said. "I'd rather do it now."

"BELLE! OVER HERE!" HER BEST FRIEND ELLA WAVED, AND Belle joined her at the booth. She placed the vase with the rose on the table and shrugged out of her jacket, tossing it into the booth before sliding her chubby body into the booth. Ella leaned forward and smelled the rose.

"I see your mystery man sent you your annual rose again."

"He's not a mystery man," Belle said. "I know exactly who he is."

"Are you sure it's Bennett Saxby, Belle? No one has seen his family since that day."

"It's him, Ella," Belle said. "I know it is."

"You met him once when you were seven years old. You're twenty-five now. Do you really think it's been him sending you a flower every year? Eighteen years is a long time, honey."

"I know, but who else would it be?"

Ella shrugged before taking a sip of her drink. "Maybe you have another secret admirer."

Belle rolled her eyes. "You know I don't. I couldn't get a date in this town if I tried. No one wants to date the crazy fat girl."

"You're not fat," Ella protested. "You're deliciously plump." She glanced down at her own chubby body. "It's not your size, Belle. I've had plenty of dates, and we're the same size."

"No, I'm bigger than you," Belle said. "By about three sizes."

Ella rolled her eyes, and Belle sighed. "It doesn't matter. There's still the crazy part."

Her best friend remained silent on the subject of crazy, and Belle couldn't help but grin. "Thanks for your support."

"You're not crazy," Ella said. "But you had a lot of blood

loss that day, and you were attacked by a cougar. It's not surprising that you thought -"

She stopped talking as a group of young men walked by their table. They didn't spare a glance at either of them, and Belle stared intently at Ella. "Bennet Saxby turned into a bear that day, Ella. You're my best friend – you're supposed to be on my side."

"I am," Ella said. "It's just – you have to admit that thinking a person can turn into a bear is, well…."

"Crazy," Belle said.

"You know what's crazy?" Rowan slid into the booth beside Ella, her red hair gleaming in the lights. She jingled the change in her apron. "You dressing like a librarian just because you work in a library."

Belle touched her dark hair that was swept back in a ponytail and pushed up her glasses as Rowan eyed her cardigan and shirt with distaste. "Maybe you could unbutton just one or two buttons, Belle. What do you say?"

Belle smoothed her shirt self-consciously. "Yes, because flashing a bunch of kids and old men at the library is totally professional."

Rowan laughed. "You've got great tits, Belle-baby. There's nothing wrong with showing them off. God, I'd kill to have a rack like yours."

She eyed her small breasts as she stretched out her legs and propped her feet on the seat beside Belle.

"Yeah, well, I'd kill to weigh a hundred and fifteen pounds," Belle said.

Rowan rolled her eyes. "Men like curves. I've got hips like a damn boy."

"Whatever. You're gorgeous, and you know it," Ella laughed.

"Not as gorgeous as you, my sweet," Rowan said before kissing her cheek. "You want your usual, Belle?"

Belle hesitated, tempted for a moment to have something stronger, before nodding. "Yes, please, Rowan."

"Rowan!"

Rowan rolled her eyes as the bartender shouted her name. "Oh God, here we go."

"I'm not paying you to visit with your damn friends!"

"Yeah, yeah, shut your piehole, Kevin! I'm working!" Rowan shouted back before sliding out of the booth. "God, that guy's a douchebag. Do you know he hit on me the other night?"

She walked away, staring at them over her shoulder. "Like I'd ever date an asshole like him. He's got – oh!"

She stumbled back as she ran into the solid chest of the man standing behind her. She stared up at him, and Belle watched, a little amused, as a flush covered her pale, freckled skin.

"Hello, Ms. Jameson."

"H- hello, Mr. Taggert." Rowan's usual brash personality had disappeared completely, and she licked her lips as the man smiled politely at her.

"Rowan! Get your ass over here and serve some goddamn drinks!"

She jumped at Kevin's shout, and the man instinctively reached out to steady her. He stopped just shy of touching her, and they both reddened. Rowan hurried away as Belle slid out from the booth.

"Rafe! It's good to see you again."

"Hello, Ms. Vale." Rafe smiled at her, and she laughed before hugging him.

"How many times have I told you to call me Belle? Will you join us for a drink?"

"I'm afraid I can't. I just popped in for a minute, but I thought I would say hello. How are you?"

"I'm good." She smiled at the man who saved her life as a child. "Are you sure you can't have one drink with us?"

"Unfortunately, no. But perhaps another time?"

"I'd like that. I feel like it's been a very long time since you came to town. Don't you get lonely living out in the woods?"

"I enjoy my privacy," he said.

Rowan returned with a glass of wine, and Belle watched as Rafe's gaze flickered over her face and body before he looked away. "It was good to see you, Belle. Take care."

"You too, Rafe," she said.

He walked away, and Ella leaned forward. "For an old man, he's super hot."

"He's not that old," Belle said.

"He's at least thirty-five," Ella said.

"He's forty," Rowan said absently as she set the glass of wine in front of Belle. She turned to study the retreating back of Rafe as Belle gave Ella a pointed look.

"How do you know how old he is?" Ella asked.

"What?" Rowan craned her neck, trying to get one last glimpse of Rafe as he left the bar, and Ella poked her in the side.

"Never thought you had daddy issues, Ro."

"I have no idea what you're talking about," Rowan said.

"Oh please," Ella scoffed. "We're your best friends. You think we don't notice when you're eye banging someone."

Rowan's blush, which had just begun to fade, flamed back to life. "Just because I'm eye banging Rafe Taggert doesn't mean I have daddy issues, Ella. The guy is incredibly hot, and a good three-quarters of the women in this town have had a crush on him at one point or another."

"That's true," Ella said. "My stepmother hired him last summer to sod the back yard. I had to put up with Ana and Dru for a week because the garage apartment has an unobstructed view of the back yard. Ana hit on him at least once a day. Hell, even my stepmother hit on him."

"Gross," Belle said.

"Yeah," Ella said.

"Did he sleep with either of them?" Rowan asked.

Ella shook her head. "No. Ana was so pissed."

"That's nothing new," Belle said before smiling at Rowan. "You thinking of sleeping with Rafe, honey?"

"Unfortunately, Rafe Taggert has no interest in me," Rowan said. "He used to come into Gaston's all the time, at least that's what Jana said, but about a month after I started working here, he stopped coming in."

"He totally checked you out earlier," Belle said.

Rowan's eyes widened. "Are you fucking with me, Belle?"

"Nope. He might be fifteen years older than us, but I have a feeling he wasn't exactly noticing the age difference when he looked at you."

A small, pleased smile crossed Rowan's face before she shook her long red hair back. "Whatever. The man is a virtual hermit. I couldn't imagine living in the woods in the middle of nowhere."

"Your grandmother does," Ella pointed out.

"Don't remind me. I nearly died of boredom when I was a teen and spent my summer holidays with her," Rowan said.

She paused before saying casually, "Did you hear someone is living in the Saxby place?" Her gaze fell on the rose sitting in the middle of the table.

"What?" Belle's heart knocked in her chest. "Is it – is it the Saxby's?"

"I don't think so," Rowan said. "I was driving by the place on my way to work last week, and some guy was gardening in the backyard. I didn't get a good glimpse of him, but he was huge. I mean, he was the biggest guy I've ever seen."

Belle sank back against the seat. It couldn't be Bennett. Her memory of his appearance had gotten a little fuzzy over the years, but he had been much shorter and skinnier than her. She closed her eyes for a moment and concentrated, trying to bring forth the memory of his face. An image of his eyes, the warm colour of dark chocolate, was all she could conjure, and she sighed and opened her eyes.

"I saw your dad working on the roof," Rowan said hesitantly.

Belle groaned under her breath. "It must be a stranger living there. No one in town will hire him anymore."

"He looked sober...mostly," Rowan said.

"He probably wasn't. He never is," Belle said.

"I gotta get back to work before douchebag over there has a heart attack," Rowan said. She blew a kiss to the both of them before heading back to the bar.

"Belle?" Ella reached across the table and touched her hand. "Tell me what's wrong."

Belle smiled a little. Ella could always read her like a book. "I lost my job today."

"What? You're kidding me?"

She shook her head. "No, they did budget cutbacks, and there wasn't enough for two full-time employees."

"I'm so sorry, honey."

"Yeah, me too. We're barely making ends meet as it is. I'm going to end up living with my father forever at this rate."

Ella squeezed her hand. "I could ask my stepmother to hire you at the cleaning company."

"Thanks, Ella, I appreciate it."

"Mind you, then you'd have to deal with her and my step-sisters, and that's not exactly a picnic in the park," she grimaced. "God, those three – they drive me crazy."

She grinned at Belle. "Of course, misery loves company, so I'd love it if you worked with me."

Belle laughed. "Can I think about it? I actually thought maybe it was time I got the hell out of this town."

"What? You can't leave me!" Ella said. "What would I do without you, Belle? Besides, you love this town."

"I do," Belle said softly. "Plus, I can't really leave my dad, can I?"

Ella squeezed her hand again. "Your dad is a grown man, Belle. You can't take care of him forever."

"I know," Belle said. "But if I left and something happened to him…."

Ella gave her a sympathetic look. "It wouldn't be your fault."

"Maybe not," Belle said before picking up her glass of wine. She drained nearly all of it in one large swallow. "Dad's been off drinking for the last week. I don't even know where he is right now. Probably holed up in some motel somewhere so that I won't yell at him. I guess I know where he got the money this time. God, I hope he at least finished the job before he disappeared."

She finished her wine and smiled at Ella. "I'll get back to you on the job thing, okay?"

Ella nodded. "I know cleaning other people's houses isn't the greatest job, but -"

"A job's a job," Belle said. She touched the rose's soft

petals again as an image of a dark-haired boy flickered through her head.

"It's about time you left that mansion of yours." Duncan clapped Bennett hard on the back and grinned at him. "You know, for a bear shifter, you spend a ridiculous amount of time gardening. It's not exactly manly."

"Keep your voice down." Bennett glanced around them. The street was mostly empty, but Duncan's voice was loud.

Duncan laughed. "Please, the humans only hear what they want to hear."

They walked quickly down the street, their large bodies taking up most of the sidewalk.

"It's good to have you back, Bennett. I've missed you."

"I've missed you too, Duncan."

It was true. He had only spoken to Duncan a handful of times in the eighteen years he'd been gone, but in the two weeks since his return, it hadn't taken long for them to pick up the threads of their boyhood friendship.

"Now tell me why you've come back."

Bennett frowned at him. "I told you, Duncan. The only reason I left was because my father forced me to. When I discovered in his will that he had never sold our home here, I decided to return."

"So, you returned for the house?" Duncan said skeptically. "No offense, man, but it's not that great of a house."

"It's my childhood home," Bennett said. "I have fond memories of it."

"Yeah, but it's falling apart around your ears."

He shrugged. "It can be fixed."

"Is that why you hired that drunk to fix the roof?"

Bennet scowled. "That drunk has a name."

"Yeah, he does, but it doesn't explain why you hired him. Shit, you'll be lucky if the guy doesn't show up drunk, fall off your roof, and break his neck."

"He hasn't shown up for work in a week," Bennett admitted. "I paid him up front and -"

"You what? Man, that was your second mistake. Old man Vale is off drinking himself stupid with your money. You know that, right?"

Bennett nodded. "I know."

"So why the hell did you pay him before he finished the job?"

Bennett just shrugged, and Duncan cocked his eyebrow at him. "It wouldn't have anything to do with who his daughter is, would it?"

"No," Bennett said. He could feel a flush rising up his neck, and he pulled at the collar of his jacket as Duncan grinned.

"Course not. Have you seen her yet?"

"No, why would I?"

"You've sent her flowers every year for eighteen years. Why wouldn't you try to see her?" Duncan said.

Bennett groaned inwardly. Earlier in the week, Duncan had stopped by for beers, and after one too many, Bennett confessed his secret.

"Wait until you see her. Miss Mirabelle Vale has filled out nicely in the last eighteen years. Really nicely."

Duncan held his hands out in front of his chest, and Bennett growled at him. "Don't talk about her that way, Duncan."

Duncan didn't reply, and Bennett glanced at him. "I'm not going to be seeing her. She hates me. I know she does. I almost got her killed."

"Well, you might have a point there," Duncan said thoughtfully. "It's not just the cougar attack thing either. She insisted for years that you turned into a bear, and the whole town thinks she's," he pointed a finger to his head and made a twirling motion, "completely cuckoo."

Bennett groaned, and Duncan patted his shoulder. "Don't worry about it, man. She'll probably still be nice to you. She doesn't have a mean bone in her body."

"I have no interest in seeing her. I send her a flower every year to say I'm sorry."

"Of course you do. Besides, you wouldn't have a chance with her anyway. She's been dating -"

Anger roared through him, and his bear rose to the surface, snarling and growling and ready to battle with whatever idiot dared lay hands on what belonged to him. He grabbed Duncan by the collar. "Who? Who is she dating?"

"Whoa, slow down there, big guy. I'm just kidding. She's not dating anyone – that I know of."

Breathing harshly, Bennett growled at the lion shifter. Duncan's eyes flashed from blue to yellow, and he made an answering growl before yanking free of Bennett's grip. "No interest in her, my ass. What? You telling me the big bad bear has been saving himself all these years for his childhood love that he met precisely once?"

Bennett growled again. "Of course not. I'm not in love with her."

They walked silently down the street as Bennett sighed inwardly. He wasn't in love with Mirabelle. He wasn't. It was just – ever since he had stepped foot in his hometown, his mild obsession with the girl he had met once had grown until she was all he could think about. From the moment he had arrived, his bear had been nearly uncontrollable in its insistence that he find her. He had thought about her often over the last eighteen years but now…

He sighed again, and Duncan glanced at him. "What's wrong?"

"Nothing. Listen, I think I'm going to take a raincheck on -"

"Nope, not a chance. We're going for a drink. It's not healthy to stay cooped up in your big old mansion. Why did you move back if you're just going to hide away in your house?"

Duncan tugged open the door to Gaston's Bar and Grill and grinned at Bennett. "After you."

CHAPTER 2

"I'm just going to the ladies' room. I'll be right back." Ella slid out of the booth before Belle could tell her she was thinking of leaving.

She sighed and traced the rim of her empty wine glass. She was sorely tempted to have another but living with an alcoholic had made her hypersensitive to drinking. No way was she ending up like her father. Rowan appeared and set a glass of water down before taking her wine glass. Belle smiled gratefully at her as the tiny, graceful redhead disappeared into the crowd.

It was busy for a Thursday night. Mind you, she didn't usually stay this late at the bar, not when she had work the next day.

That's not a problem anymore.

She dropped her head into her hands. She was unemployed, and jobs were hard to come by in their small town. She would end up working for Ella's bitch of a stepmother just because she didn't have the balls to leave her hometown. She loved her father but living with him was destroying her. Ella was right. He was an adult and not her responsibility. She rubbed wearily at her forehead and tried to ignore the rising babble of conversation. She had almost succeeded when Ella's sharp scream had her sliding out of the booth and bolting toward the bathrooms.

ELLA SLIPPED PAST THE CROWD OF MEN HOVERING AROUND the hallway to the bathrooms. A drunk woman with lipstick smeared across her face gave her a bleary grin, and Ella neatly sidestepped her when the woman staggered on her feet. She hurried forward, glancing behind her to make sure the woman wasn't going to fall on her face. She grunted in surprise when she ran face-first into a hard, warm wall of flesh.

Rough hands gripped her upper arms, and she stared at the man in front of her. A groan of dismay escaped her lips, and the man's smile widened into a predatory grin as he looked her up and down.

"Good evening, Ms. Cinders."

"Mr. Gillis," she said stiffly.

"You're looking lovely." He still held her arms, and she yanked herself out of his grip, nearly tripping over her own feet in the process.

"Thank you. You're looking," she paused and glanced at his broad chest in the tight, dark red t-shirt, "very clean."

He laughed, and she flinched when he reached out and brushed a lock of her blonde hair back from her face. "Why so twitchy, Ms. Cinders?"

"I don't like having my hair pulled," she snapped.

"Are you still angry about what I did in grade school? I didn't think you were the type to hold a grudge."

"You know nothing about me," she said.

"I know your hair is very soft," he said. "I know you used to wear it in two delightfully adorable braids. I miss those braids."

"Yes, well, perhaps if I hadn't had those braids pulled every single day, I wouldn't have stopped braiding my hair."

"Would it help if I apologized for pulling your hair when I was nine, and you were seven?" he asked.

She glared at him. "You make it sound like you did it once. It was every day for an entire school year."

"Are you angry about the braid pulling or angry because of the day I found you -"

"Be quiet!" she snapped. "God, just shut up for once in your life, Duncan Gillis!"

She tried to dodge around him and squeaked in alarm when he pressed her up against the hallway wall. He placed his hands on either side of her head, trapping her. She had to force her traitorous body not to breach the thin space between their bodies.

"I think it's time we put this decades-old feud behind us. Don't you, Ella?" His warm breath on her face and the sound of his velvet voice saying her given name made her pussy quiver, and she pressed her thighs together to try to ease the sudden ache between them.

"Perhaps you would forgive me if I allowed you to tug something on my body," he said with a wicked grin.

Her mouth dropped open as her gaze fell to his crotch. Shamefully, she could almost see herself reaching into his pants, taking his cock into her hand, and stroking it until he moaned.

"Naughty girl," he said in a low voice. "I know what you're thinking."

She blushed, her pale skin turning the same bright red as his t-shirt, and his grin widened. Embarrassed by her reaction to him, she shoved at his hard chest. He grunted in surprise and stepped back as she glared at him.

"Get lost, pervert! I wouldn't touch any part of you with a ten-foot pole." She walked into the bathroom without looking at him.

She spent nearly five minutes in the washroom, waiting for her hot face to cool down and her stomach to stop churning with an odd combination of anxiety and desire. She hated Duncan Gillis, she reminded herself. She would always hate him, and it didn't matter that the little blond-haired boy who had spent an entire year tormenting her had grown into a golden-haired, hard-bodied, sinfully gorgeous specimen of a man. She hated him.

She took a deep breath and stepped out of the bathroom and into the hallway. Duncan was gone, but she groaned under her breath at the man who hovered just outside the door.

"Hello, Ella."

"Marty," she said coolly. "What are you doing here?"

"I just wanted to talk to you for a minute."

"I'm not interested." She stepped around him, ignoring the niggle of fear in her belly when she saw his friends blocking the far end of the hall. "Get out of my way."

"Ella, just wait. You can't avoid me forever."

"Yes, I can," she said. "Tell your friends to move."

Marty made a harsh noise of frustration, and she spun around and glared at him when his hand touched her back.

"Don't touch me. Ever. Do you understand?"

"Just let me explain, okay? I miss you, Ella. I miss you so much -"

"You miss me?" she said. "Maybe you should give Ana a call."

Marty scowled at her. "Your stepsister came on to me, okay? She was flirting with me for weeks."

"You just couldn't resist, huh?" Ella said.

"I made a mistake. You gonna punish me forever? You know you still love me. Hell, I still love you and, sweetheart, you're not gonna do much better than me. Not with the weight you keep gaining."

"Fuck you, Marty!" Ella turned and stormed toward his friends as he made a harsh noise of frustration.

"We ain't done talkin', Ella."

"Like hell we aren't. Tell your friends to get out of my way, or I'll scream."

She crossed her arms over her ample chest and glared at the men blocking her way. They glanced over her head at Marty, and when she felt his meaty hand wrap around her arm, she screamed shrilly.

He cursed and pushed her up against the wall before clamping his hand over her mouth. "Jesus, Ella, why do you have to be such a drama queen? All I want to do is talk for one goddamn minute, and you owe me the courtesy of -"

There was an angry roar, and Marty's eyes widened as his friends were shoved aside and Duncan stalked into the hallway. Marty's hand tightened briefly on her mouth, and then Duncan ripped Marty away from her and threw him against the wall. He squeezed his hand around Marty's throat, and Ella watched wide-eyed as he growled deep in his throat.

"You dare to touch what is mine?"

His face a bright red, Marty clawed at Duncan's hand.

"Duncan! Look out!" Ella's thin scream came too late, and she watched in horror as Marty's friends jumped on him. They knocked him to the floor and fell on him as Marty staggered away from the wall and grabbed her arm. She slapped him across the face, and he made a hoarse shout of pain as

Belle, her large chest heaving beneath her sensible cardigan, bolted into the hallway.

"Ella! Ella, are you okay?"

"Belle!"

"Son of a bitch!" Belle cried and, without hesitating, jumped on Marty. She drove him to the floor and then punched him in the face. He shouted in surprise before shoving her off of him. Belle hit the floor, her head bouncing off the hard tile and her glasses flying off her face. Ella screamed again as Marty clambered to his knees. Breathing heavily, he touched his bleeding nose and snarled, "You stupid bitch!"

He balled his hand into a fist, and Ella, her legs shaking madly, latched onto his arm and raked her nails down his hairy forearm. He howled with pain and shoved her back into the wall with his other arm before raising his fist again. Before he could drive it into Belle's face, a large hand gripped his wrist.

Marty stared up at the bear of a man standing beside him. "Let go of me, man. Let go of me right now or so help me God, I'll -"

His face serene, the man twisted Marty's wrist, and Ella flinched when the wrist broke with a sharp crack. Marty screamed in agony, and the man grabbed him by his hair and flung him from Belle with effortless strength.

The man leaned over Belle. He put his large hands around her waist and lifted her from the floor as easily as a child. He set her on her feet and wrapped one heavily muscled arm around her waist. He cupped her face as she stared up at him.

"Are you hurt?" he asked.

"You," Belle said. "It's really you."

"Are you hurt?" he repeated as there was a low roar of anger behind them.

She shook her head, and he gently pushed her next to Ella before turning and lifting two of the men from the squirming pile of bodies on the floor next to him. He shoved them down the hallway before shouting, "Leave!"

They turned and ran as Duncan, blood pouring from his lip, knocked the final man off of him and leaped to his feet. He kicked his attacker in the ribs, and the guy squealed once before grabbing his side and curling into a ball. Duncan pushed his way past the man and grabbed Marty's arm. He hauled him to his feet and shoved him back against the wall.

"If you touch her again, I will kill you. Do you understand?" Duncan snarled.

Marty whimpered in pain, and Duncan shook him roughly. "Do you understand?"

"Yes!" Marty screamed as tears and snot dripped down his face.

Duncan released the man with a look of disgust, wiping his hands on his jeans as Marty staggered down the hallway and disappeared. Kevin and one of the bouncers stood at the end of the hallway, and Belle's saviour raised one dark eyebrow at them.

"Everything's fine."

"You need to leave," Kevin said with a nervous glance at his companion. "Or Gaston's gonna call the cops."

The man cocked his head at him. "Kevin, isn't that right?"

"Yeah," Kevin replied. "Do I know you?"

The dark-haired man gave him a hard grin, and Kevin took a step back, his eyes widening. "Do I know you, buddy?"

"I was your punching bag for a brief time when we were children," the man said before stepping closer. "For you and your gang of friends."

Kevin backed away. "That – that was a long time ago."

The man studied him silently before cracking his knuckles. "Indeed. It's good to see you again, Kevin."

"Y-you too," Kevin said.

"Tell your boss we'll be leaving in a moment," the man said as Duncan stalked angrily back and forth in the hallway.

"You need to leave right now," the bouncer said.

"Give us a minute," the stranger growled.

Kevin grabbed the bouncer's arm. "It's fine, Mickey. Give them a minute."

They turned and scurried out of the hallway, and Belle snorted soft laughter before shouting, "Thanks for your help, assholes!"

She slung her arm around Ella. "Are you okay, honey?"

Rowan rushed into the hallway. "What the hell just happened?" She put her arm around Ella from the other side and stared at the pacing Duncan.

When Ella didn't reply, Belle squinted at her before following her gaze to Duncan. Ella watched as he curled his hands into fists before hitting the wall.

"Calm yourself, Duncan," the man said.

"Calm myself?" Duncan snarled at him before wiping the blood from his mouth. Thick golden scruff covered his jaw, and Ella gasped when his gaze fell on them. Duncan's eyes were a glowing dark yellow, and she squeezed Belle's waist as Duncan made an actual growl.

"He touched what is mine and only mine to touch," he growled. "I should have killed him."

"Leave, Duncan," the man said with a mild note of alarm in his voice.

Belle pressed her mouth against Ella's ear. "Is it just me, or is Duncan getting bigger?"

"I – that's impossible," Ella whispered as the seams of Duncan's t-shirt tore with a soft purr.

"Duncan!" the man said. "Control yourself!"

"She's mine!" Duncan snarled again. "Do you hear me?"

"Yes," the man said. "But you need to go before you do something you regret."

"I won't leave her," Duncan snapped.

"I'll see her home safely, my friend. I promise you." The man rested a cautious hand on Duncan's bulging upper arm. "Go home. I'll text you later."

Duncan glanced briefly at Ella before shaking off the man's hand. "Do not touch her. We are friends, but if I find out that you placed so much as a finger on her, I'll tear out your throat."

"I'm not going to touch her," the man said calmly. "You know I won't. Now go. You're scaring her."

Duncan's gaze snapped back to Ella, and he seemed to shrink a little at her pale face and trembling lips.

"Fuck!" Duncan said and stalked out of the hallway.

The man sighed deeply before bending and snagging Belle's glasses from the floor. He handed them to her, and she shoved them onto her face before blinking at him.

"Hello, Ben."

"Hello, Mirabelle."

BELLE STEPPED OUT OF HER CAR. BENNETT HAD INSISTED ON following her home, and she waited nervously by her car as he shut off his truck and climbed out. Belle had driven Ella home, but she'd been quiet and withdrawn. She'd squeezed Belle's hand before climbing the steps to her apartment over her stepmother's garage.

"Mirabelle? Are you sure you're not hurt?" Bennett stood beside her, and she craned her neck to stare at him. He was massive with broad shoulders and a thick neck, and she swallowed down the trickle of lust that went through her.

"You're so big," she said.

I bet he's big everywhere.

Her face flamed, and Bennett stared curiously at her. "I'm sorry?"

"I uh, I said you've grown a lot since the last time I saw you."

He shrugged. "Yeah, I started sprouting up when I was about twelve. Come on. I'll walk you to your door."

They walked silently up the broken sidewalk to the front door of her trailer. She was suddenly ashamed of the state of it. It desperately needed repairs, but they couldn't afford it. Not with her dad spending all of his money on booze. Her librarian salary had barely kept them fed and paid the bills.

"This is nice," Bennett said.

She laughed. "Yeah, it isn't, but what are you going to do, right?"

They stood awkwardly for a moment before she smiled at him. "When did you get back?"

"A couple of weeks ago," he said.

"Are you just visiting or…"

"No, I'm back for good."

A fierce little rush of pleasure went through her. "Good, I'm glad."

"Are you?" he asked.

"Yes, why wouldn't I be?"

"I almost got you killed when we were kids."

"No, you saved my life."

He started to protest, but she touched his arm, and he

44

stopped talking abruptly. "Thank you for the roses, Bennett. I looked forward to them all year."

"You're welcome," he said gruffly.

"So… how did you know I worked at the library?" she asked.

———

SHIT. NOW WHAT DID HE DO? BEN SHOULD HAVE REALIZED she would ask him that, but, of course, he hadn't planned on seeing her again.

Right, because she would have been easy to avoid in a town of twelve hundred people. Idiot.

Pretty confident that Belle wouldn't like knowing he had Internet stalked her for years, he said, "I remembered you liked books. Figured you'd get a job at the library."

She frowned at him. "But how did you even know I still lived here?"

Starting to sweat, he groped desperately for a believable answer. "I kept in touch with Duncan."

"Oh, right. He never mentioned it to me," she said.

He cleared his throat as she smiled up at him. "Why did you come back after all this time?"

"A year ago, my parents were on holiday in Panama and did a sight-seeing tour in one of those smaller planes. It crashed, and they died. I discovered in my father's will that he had never sold our house here. I missed living here, so I decided to move back after the estate stuff was finished."

"Oh, Bennett." She stared sympathetically at him, and his dick twitched when she stepped forward, and her breasts brushed against his arm. She squeezed his shoulder. "I'm so sorry."

His bear made a soft growl of happiness, and Ben was

about two seconds from picking her up and carrying her into her run-down trailer. She could show him exactly how sorry she was in the sweetest way possible. She would be soft and warm, and her lush curves would cushion his body as he took her – again and again until she was his and only his.

He bit the inside of his cheek until he tasted the metallic tang of blood and took a step away from her. Shit, he needed to get control. She was trying to comfort him over his parents' deaths, and he could only think about getting her naked.

"Bennett? Are you okay?"

He nodded, and she squeezed his shoulder again. "I really am very sorry. You must miss them terribly."

"I do," he said hoarsely.

She reached for his hand and linked their fingers together. He squeezed it tightly and cursed inwardly when a grimace of pain flashed across her face.

"I'm sorry."

"That's okay." She smiled at him. "You're pretty strong, huh?"

He shrugged. "Yeah, I work out a lot."

A complete lie, but he had to say something to explain his size and his strength.

"Why did you leave, Bennett?" she asked. "I got out of the hospital, and my dad said you and your parents had packed up and left without saying anything. Why?"

"There was a family emergency," he said. "We had to leave, and it never worked out for us to come back."

"A family emergency," she echoed.

He nodded, and she cocked her head at him, biting her bottom lip in a way that made him want to lean down and nibble at it instead.

"So, it wasn't because I told everyone that you were a bear?"

He cleared his throat again. "Uh, no. Why, uh, why would you think I'm a bear?"

"Because you are," she said.

"I'm not," he said. "That day in the woods, you were injured, scared, and confused."

"No, I wasn't," she said steadily. "I remember everything about that day, Bennett. I remember Kevin and his gang beating you up and that we walked through the forest together. I remember the rose bush."

A small smile crossed her face. "You picked a flower for me and pricked your finger. The bleeding stopped after only a few seconds. Then, you turned into a bear when the cougar attacked us."

"I didn't," he rasped. "Mirabelle, I'm not a – a bear."

She tugged her hand free and gave him a look of such unbearable sadness that it made his chest tighten. "Do you know that this entire town thinks I'm crazy? Even the children at the library know the story of crazy Miss Vale, who thinks people can turn into bears. I spent the first five years desperately trying to convince anyone who would listen to me that you had turned into a bear. I was teased at school. Hell, even adults teased me until I finally stopped talking about it. It was too late, though. People in small towns never forget, do they? I've been laughed at and called crazy behind my back for most of my life. I told myself I didn't care because I knew the truth, and so did you."

She closed her eyes as pain flickered across her face. "Now, eighteen years later, you're back in my life. Only, you're telling me you're not a bear after all. All this time, I really have just been crazy."

"Mirabelle," he whispered. "You're not -"

"MY BONNIE LIES OVER THE OCEAN! MY BONNIE LIES OVER THE SEA!"

Bennett turned and stared at the man staggering up the sidewalk in the dark. He moved instinctively in front of Belle as his bear growled. The man tripped and fell to his knees, his singing cutting out abruptly, and he heard Belle sigh behind him.

"Oh, Daddy."

She ducked around him and walked quickly to the fallen man before squatting next to him. "Dad, are you okay?"

"Just fine, baby Belle! Just fine!" The man bellowed cheerfully.

She winced and squeezed his arm. "Dad, be quiet. It's late."

She helped him to his feet. Bennett rushed forward to help, and she shook her head as the smell of whiskey drifted to him. "It's fine. I've got him."

"I can help him into the house."

"No, don't worry about it. I'm used to it."

"Hey," Belle's father stared blearily at him, "I know you."

"Hello, Mr. Vale."

"Bennett Saxby, what are you doing here?"

Before he could reply, the old man lurched forward and clapped him hard on the back. "How's your new roof doing?"

He grinned at Belle. "Bennett here hired me to fix his roof, didn't you, son?"

"Yes, sir," Bennett said.

Belle wrapped her arm around her father's waist. "Come on, Dad. Let's get you into the house."

She unlocked the door, and her father staggered his way inside. There was the sound of a lamp tipping over, and she winced before giving Bennett an embarrassed look. "You shouldn't have hired him to fix your roof."

He just shrugged, and she said, "Did he even finish the job?"

"Uh, well…"

"He didn't," she said. "How much did you pay him?"

"Two thousand," he said. "It doesn't matter, I -"

"Of course, it matters," she said. "Although you really shouldn't have paid him up front. But how could you have known he would go on a bender with it."

There was another splintering crash and a muffled curse from her father, and she closed her eyes for a moment. "I have to go. I'll get the money from my father and stop by your house tomorrow afternoon with it, okay?"

"Mirabelle, you don't have to -"

"Good night," she said before shutting the door gently.

He hesitated on the doorstep, and his heart sped up when it opened, and she stepped out into the cool night air. She studied him carefully before standing on her tiptoes and pressing her lips against his cheek. "Welcome home, Bennett."

She was gone before he could reply, leaving only her sweet scent of books and cinnamon and a burning warmth where her lips pressed against his skin.

CHAPTER 3

He spent all morning gardening. His father had loved to garden. He used to gently tease his mother that it was the only thing that soothed his savage bear, and he had taught Bennett to love it as well. Eighteen years ago, the back yard had been a lush, colourful garden of brightly blooming flowers, and Ben was determined to return it to that. As he hacked away at the weeds choking out the bed of wild daisies, he sniffed the air before dropping his shears and wiping the sweat from his forehead.

"Hello, Duncan."

"Hey, Bennett."

He grabbed the jug of water sitting on the ground beside him and drank nearly half of it before joining the lion shifter on the small deck.

"Why aren't you painting?" he asked.

Duncan shrugged. "I took a personal day. It's not like I need the money."

"True. Does anyone in this town know exactly how rich you are, Duncan?"

"Nope, and they don't need to know."

"Why not? What's the big deal?"

"You think the people in this backwater town even know what art is beyond a Norman Rockwell painting?" Duncan asked.

"You think they'll treat you differently if they know you're a damn millionaire?"

Duncan scowled. "I don't care what they do. Besides, you're one to talk – how many of the good town folk know you've got money falling out your ass?"

"Point taken," Bennett said, a little taken back by the anger in Duncan's voice.

It wasn't like Duncan to be so angry. The lion shifter had always been easy going with a sarcastic sense of humour, even as a boy. He watched as Duncan reached into the bag at his feet and pulled out a six-pack of beer. He handed one to Bennett and opened another before taking a long swallow.

"Go ahead," he said when Bennett didn't open the can.

"It's not even noon," Bennett said.

"It's almost one," Duncan said. "You've been out in the sun too long. It's fried your brain."

Bennett opened the can of beer. He sipped at the cold liquid as Duncan stared moodily at the back yard.

"You gonna tell me what's wrong or just get drunk on my patio?" Bennett asked.

"Tell me I didn't do what I think I did last night," Duncan said.

"Do you mean when you threatened to kill a man for touching Ella Cinders or announced that she belonged to you right in front of her? Or maybe it was when you nearly shifted in front of her, Mirabelle, and that redheaded waitress. Wait – maybe it's the part where you threatened to tear out your best friend's throat if he touched your woman?"

"Fuck," Duncan said. "I was hoping I had imagined all of that."

Bennett laughed. "Afraid not, my friend. What happened last night?"

"I don't know," Duncan said miserably. "I heard Ella scream, and then I saw that asshole Marty touching her and I... lost control."

He took another drink of beer. "I don't know why I said what I said. Hell, I'm attracted to her – always have been – but the woman hates me. She won't give me the time of day."

He paused before giving Bennett a sheepish look. "Do you know I hired her stepmother's cleaning company to clean my house?"

Bennett shook his head, and Duncan sighed. "I did. I tried to tell myself it wasn't because I wanted Ella in my house, but that's a damn lie. The irony is that it's not even Ella who cleans it. It's her stepsister, Ana. Who, by the way, is a real piece of work. I can't be home when she's cleaning, or she spends the entire time hitting on me. I found a pair of her underwear tucked under my pillow with her cell number written on them."

Bennett burst out laughing, and Duncan gave him a wry grin before staring at his can of beer. "What the hell is happening to me, Bennett? How do I explain what I said to Ella?"

"You probably won't have to. If Ella hates you like she says she does...."

"Yeah, you're right. She'll just completely ignore me like she always does. If she doesn't, if she wants to know what the hell I meant, I'll tell her I was drunk." Duncan rubbed his forehead. "God, I never thought I would fall for a human. Did you?"

"Don't take this the wrong way, Duncan, but I never

thought you'd fall for anyone. You're not exactly the commitment type."

"I meant, are you surprised you've fallen in love with a human," Duncan said.

"What do you mean?"

Duncan rolled his eyes. "You're in love with Belle Vale."

"I am not."

"Oh, please. You look at her and immediately get this puppy dog look like you want to curl up in her lap while she pets you."

"Shut up," Bennett said.

"Try to deny it, but it's ridiculously obvious. You came here for one reason, and one reason only, and that reason has gorgeous blue eyes and a seriously magnificent rack."

Bennett growled at him. "Talk about her rack again, and I'll gut you like a fish, Duncan."

Duncan laughed. "I'm not after your woman. Relax."

"She's not my woman."

"Not yet, she isn't. But I'll bet you a thousand bucks that by this time next week, you two are making the beast with two backs."

"Nice, Duncan," Bennett muttered.

"Yeah, I've never been much of a wordsmith," Duncan said cheerfully. "Now, do we have a bet or not?"

"I'm not betting with you on sleeping with Mirabelle," Bennett said. "Besides, it isn't going to happen. Humans and shifters aren't meant to mate."

"Says who? Your father? Just because he was old-school about keeping separate from humans doesn't mean everyone is. Hell, my cousin in Trenton is married to a human. She's been mated to him for nearly five years now, and no one cares that he's not a shifter."

"Are you serious?" Bennett said.

"I am. Her in-laws don't know she's a lion shifter, but she's pregnant with their first kid, so that'll change soon. It'll be difficult to explain why in a couple of years, their grand-baby is just randomly turning into a lion from time to time," Duncan said.

Bennett couldn't help but grin. Shifters started to change to their animal form when they were toddlers, and it took at least a good two months before they learned to control it. Shifters had learned long ago to keep their toddlers away from humans during the time it took to teach them to control the shift.

"You know what I think?" Duncan said thoughtfully. "I think way more humans know about the existence of shifters than most shifters realize. The High Council are fooling themselves if they believe our existence is as secretive as they want it to be.

Bennett stiffened as a car door slammed, and the faint scent of cinnamon wafted over him. He stood and yanked Duncan to his feet. "You need to go."

"What? Why?"

"Mirabelle is here."

Duncan grinned at him. "She's visiting you at your house? You sure you don't want to bet -"

"Knock it off!" Bennett said. "Hey – how do I, uh, look?"

Duncan laughed. "Seriously, dude?"

Bennett flushed, and Duncan laughed again. "Truthfully, you're pretty sweaty, you've got leaves in your hair and," he sniffed in his direction, "you're not smelling all that great. You want me to distract her while you have a quick shower?"

"Hi there."

Bennett groaned inwardly at Belle's soft voice before raking his hand through his hair. A few leaves fell to the ground as Duncan swung around and grinned at Belle.

"Hello, Miss Belle. How are you today?"

"Good. I heard voices, so I came around back. I hope that's okay."

"It's fine," Bennett grunted.

They stood in awkward silence before Belle smiled faintly. "I'm sorry. You have company, and I'm interrupting. I'll come by later."

"Don't leave," Bennett said. "Duncan was just leaving."

"That's right, I was," Duncan said. "It was lovely to see you again, Belle."

"You as well, Duncan." A devilish gleam appeared in her eyes. "I was just visiting Ella. She's at home if you thought you'd like to continue your discussion with her about how she belongs to you."

Duncan's tanned skin turned bright red, and he cleared his throat. "Uh, I was drunk last night, Belle. Very, *very* drunk."

"Oh, right, of course," Belle said with an innocent smile.

With an uneasy look, Duncan waved at Bennett and left the backyard.

"Do you have a few minutes to talk, Bennett?" Belle asked.

"Yes, why don't you come into the house."

As she followed him up the deck to the patio doors, he was acutely aware of how sweaty and smelly he was. In contrast, she looked cool and crisp in a jean skirt and soft pink shirt. Unlike her clothing from yesterday, the shirt dipped low at the neckline, revealing a deliciously pale hint of cleavage. He clenched his fists and tried not to notice how her long hair fell down her back like a dark waterfall. God, she was gorgeous.

"The back yard is starting to look good," she said as she followed him into the kitchen.

"Thanks. I like to garden," he said.

She smiled but didn't reply, and he poured them both a glass of water. He handed one to her, and his bear growled happily when their fingers brushed. "You're not wearing glasses."

She self-consciously touched her face. "Yeah, I normally don't anymore. I just hadn't picked up my contacts yesterday, so, you know...."

She took a small sip of water. He searched for something to say as silence filled the large kitchen. "How's your dad feeling today?"

She closed her eyes briefly before smiling at him. "Hungover, but that's nothing new. I," she paused and gave him a heartbreaking look of shame, "I spoke with Dad about your money. He hasn't spent all of it but refuses to give me the rest."

"That's okay," he said.

"It isn't," she insisted. "It's not okay at all, but I - the thing is - I lost my job yesterday and don't have much extra money on hand."

"Mirabelle, it doesn't matter. I don't need you to pay me back the money."

She glared at him. "I don't need your charity, Bennett."

"That's not what I meant," he said. "I just meant that -"

"I thought," she said, "that maybe I could pay my father's debt to you in some way other than money."

An image rose in his mind, one that was darkly inviting and utterly intoxicating. Mirabelle, naked in his bed, moaning and gasping as he buried his face between her pale thighs. He drank the glass of water in four giant gulps. Somehow, he didn't think Mirabelle would accept his proposal of bringing her to orgasm repeatedly in exchange for her father's debt. The coolness of the water did nothing to drown the fire in his belly for her, and she took a nervous step back when he raised his gaze to hers.

"What did you have in mind, Mirabelle?" Even he could hear the dark desire in his voice, and he watched as she flushed and the heady scent of her arousal filled his nose.

Oh fuck, she wanted him just as badly as he wanted her.

She made a nervous sound in the back of her throat, and his desire deepened when he glanced at her breasts. Her nipples had hardened. He could see them clearly through her bra and thin shirt, and it made his cock stiffen until it rubbed painfully against the front of his pants.

He turned around quickly, staring out the window over the sink and ignoring his bear's demands that he take Mirabelle to his bed and fuck her repeatedly.

"Bennett?" she said.

"Sorry," he said hoarsely. "You don't have to do anything."

"I want to," she said. "I thought maybe I could do some cleaning for you. This house is huge, and I'm sure after eighteen years of sitting empty, it could use a good cleaning. I could come by every day in the morning and -"

"What will you do for money?" he asked. "While you're paying back your father's debt, how will you buy groceries and pay your bills?"

"I... well, that's nothing you have to worry about," she said. "I'll be fine. What do you say, Bennett? I'll clean your house from top to bottom in exchange for the money my father owes you."

He didn't reply, and she took a step closer. "I realize that won't cover the entire amount, but I'd be willing to do regular housecleaning until you feel the debt is paid off. I could come by once a week if you don't mind me scheduling it around my new job."

"Where are you working?"

"Ella's stepmother owns a cleaning business. I'm meeting her this afternoon about a job, but I'm pretty confident she'll hire me, and I'll probably see if I can get some work at the Food Market. As a teenager, I worked there as a cashier, and I'm still pretty friendly with Victor, the owner."

He whirled around and glared at her. "How friendly?"

She blinked at him in surprise. "What?"

He clenched his hands into fists and swore inwardly at his bear. The damn thing had come roaring forward when she mentioned another man's name, and he hadn't been able to stop his outburst.

"Nothing. Never mind," he said. "I don't need a housekeeper."

Her face fell. "Right. Okay, well, maybe we could work out a payment plan then? I could give you fifty dollars a week," she bit at that deliciously full bottom lip before finishing hurriedly, "with interest, of course."

He shook his head again, and he could almost taste her frustration. "Bennett, I can't afford to pay you back the money in full right now. Please, can't we -"

"Come with me," he said.

"Where are we going?"

"I have something to show you."

———

OKAY, SO HE HADN'T AGREED TO HER PLAN, AND SHE WAS maybe panicking a little about how she would pay him the money he was owed, but despite her panic, she was still fascinated by the size of Bennet's house as she followed him.

"Gosh, this place really is a mansion," she said.

He shrugged but didn't say anything. She stared at his

broad back. His t-shirt stuck to him with sweat, and she wondered what he would say if she lifted his shirt and licked his back.

Belle! Knock it off!

Right, focus. She needed to focus. Still, that look he had given her in the kitchen and the way he had asked what she had in mind... good Lord, if it hadn't made her panties soaking wet. What was it about him that made her act like a sex fiend?

Oh, I don't know. Maybe it's the fact that he's, like, eight feet tall with more muscles than Thor? Maybe it's the deep voice, dark eyes, or how he looks at you like he wants to throw you over his shoulder and carry you to his bed.

She should be so lucky. She had never once had a man lift her off her feet – they'd probably put their back out if they tried.

Bennett wouldn't. He's strong, remember?

She remembered. She could still feel the imprint of his arm around her waist, the touch of his hand when he cupped her face. A shiver went down her back, and fresh moisture dampened her pussy. What the hell was happening to her?

They were still walking, and she realized she was already hopelessly lost. Ridiculous that someone could get lost in a house, but she'd always had a lousy sense of direction. She wondered where exactly he was leading her. Any deeper into the house, and no one would ever find her again.

No one would hear her screams of pleasure as Bennett pushed that large body between her thighs and finally took what was his. She'd be at his mercy, her body his to do whatever he wanted with and –

Belle!

Sweet mother of Mary, she was frackin' losing it. Bennett wasn't leading her to his bedroom. He wouldn't demand sex in exchange for her father's debt. Technically she'd known him less than twenty-four hours, but she knew instinctively he wasn't dangerous, nor would he ever make her do something she didn't want to do.

What about something you want to do?

Shut up!

Lost in her thoughts, she didn't realize Bennett had stopped until she ran into his broad back. She squeaked in surprise, her hands gripping his narrow waist as she took a deep breath. He smelled good, like a wood fire and crisp autumn days, and she was helpless to stop from burying her face into his damp t-shirt and inhaling again.

"Mirabelle?" His voice was hoarse, and his entire body had stiffened against her.

Her face flaming, she stumbled back. "I'm so sorry."

"That's okay," he muttered before opening the door. "Hang on a minute."

He walked into the room, and she blinked when he drew back the heavy curtains, and the sunshine flooded the room.

"Oh – oh my God," she whispered.

The room was a library – the most magnificent library she'd ever seen. Floor-to-ceiling bookshelves covered every wall, and they were crammed full of books. There was a mezzanine, accessible by a narrow spiral staircase, and more shelves of books lined the second level. The forest green walls and the dark wooden floor gave the room a cozy and secretive feel. A gas fireplace was at one end with a few pieces of furniture, hidden by dusty sheets, in front of it.

"Bennett, this is – this is amazing," she said.

He smiled. "My mom collected books. She loved to read – like you."

"How many books are in here?" She traced her fingers across the spines of the books closest to her as he shrugged.

"I don't know. That's where you come in."

"You want me to count the books?"

"Sort of. What I'm looking for is someone to catalogue the books in a spreadsheet, as well as assess and research their value. Some of these books are old and worth a lot of money, and I need an accurate monetary value of the library for insurance purposes."

"You're asking me to go through every one of these books and find out what they're worth?" she asked.

"Yes, although I imagine there will be some that you'll know right away aren't worth anything."

"Bennett, this – this will probably take at least a year," she said.

"That's fine."

She stared thoughtfully at him. "So, if I do this, we're even-Steven for the money my dad owes you?"

"No. There's more work here than the two grand your father owes me. I'll pay you an hourly wage. What did you make as a librarian?"

"I was a library assistant and made fourteen bucks an hour."

"What would you make working for the cleaning company?"

"Uh, I'm not sure. Probably about eleven dollars an hour."

"I'll pay you twenty-five an hour," he said.

Her mouth dropped open, and she blinked at him. "To catalogue books?"

He nodded. "Yes. I'd like it if you worked eight hours a day, five days a week, but you can decide when you want to work those eight hours. I sleep pretty soundly, so if you're a night owl and want to work at night, I'm fine with that."

"What about the money my dad owes you?" she asked.

"Maybe I could work for the cleaning company the first couple of months until I can pay you back and then work here full time."

He waved his hand impatiently. "I'll take a hundred bucks off each paycheque until it's repaid. What do you say? Will you help me?"

She took a deep breath, inhaling the much-loved scent of old books, before holding out her hand and grinning happily at him. "When do you want me to start?"

CHAPTER 4

"So, are you and Bennett knockin' boots yet or what?"

"Rowan!" Blushing furiously, Belle glanced around the diner. "Keep your voice down."

Rowan grinned and stuck another forkful of eggs into her mouth. "Answer the question, my sweet Belle."

"No, we are not knocking boots," Belle said in a low voice.

"Why not? You've been at his place every day for the last three days," Rowan said.

"Because I'm working for him. You know that, Ro," Belle said.

"Working at getting into his pants. Am I right, or am I right, Ella?" She elbowed the chubby blonde in the side and wiggled her eyebrows.

Ella looked up from her coffee mug. "Sorry, what?"

Belle frowned. Ella was pale with dark circles under her eyes. "Ella, what's wrong, honey?"

"Nothing, I'm fine. I just haven't been sleeping well lately. What were we talking about?"

"Belle and Bennett having sex," Rowan said cheerfully.

Ella's eyes widened. "You had sex with Bennett?"

"No!" Belle said. "I'm cataloguing the books in his library, that's it. I haven't even really seen him the last three days."

Much to her dismay, that was entirely true. Ben greeted her Monday morning, made some polite small talk, and gave her a house key. Since then, she'd only seen him when she'd peeked out the library windows to watch him working in the backyard. She decided she wouldn't admit to her best friends that she kept peeking all day, hoping he would take off his shirt. Sadly, he had kept on all of his clothes.

"You haven't seen him at all?" Rowan asked.

"Not really. He's been letting me do my own thing. I asked if he wanted to approve the spreadsheet created to catalogue the books, but he just said he trusted me."

She glanced at her cell phone. "Crap! I need to go. I wanted to be at Bennett's by nine this morning."

"I need to go too," Ella said. "My stepmother added two more houses to my schedule today, and I have no idea how I'll get everything done."

She slid out of the booth and smoothed down her shirt. "I'm fairly certain she's trying to kill me."

Rowan gave her a sympathetic look. "Did you hear back from the bank yet about the business loan?"

Ella smiled ruefully. "I forgot to tell you – I was turned down."

"What? Why?" Belle asked.

"They don't think I have enough experience as a massage therapist to run a successful business. They have a point – working for three months at the Magic Spa Retreat doesn't exactly give me strong work experience."

"It's not your fault the spa closed down," Rowan said.

"No, but it was the only place in town that offered

massage therapy. Unless I start my own business, the money I spent earning my massage therapy certificate will be completely wasted."

"You could always find a position in a city," Rowan said gently.

"I love it here. You know I don't want to leave," Ella said.

"I know. But you don't have to leave forever. Gain some experience, save some cash, and then move back and start your own business."

"I keep telling you," Belle said, "you've got a massage table and the other supplies. Just start your business with that. You can have people come to your apartment, or you could go to them. You could be the travelling massage therapist. Just make sure people know it's therapeutic massage. Most of the guys in this town would kill to have your hands on them in a decidedly non-therapeutic sense."

Ella rolled her eyes. "That's an exaggeration."

"Like hell it is," Belle said.

"It doesn't matter," Rowan said with a grin. "You're both forgetting that Duncan Gillis has vowed to murder anyone who touches our sweet Ella."

Ella flushed to the roots of her blonde hair before slinging her purse over her shoulder. "I have to go."

She hurried out of the diner as Rowan gave Belle an odd look. "What was that about?"

Belle shook her head worriedly. "I'm not sure. She's been acting weird ever since that night at the bar. We shouldn't tease her about what Duncan said. I know she says she hates him, but I'm not so sure she's telling the truth. She always gets awkward and nervous when she sees him, you know? Besides, Duncan told me he was drunk that night."

"Bullshit," Rowan said. "He'd only been there maybe fifteen minutes, and I'd served him one beer. Anyway, you have to go, and I'm headed to Nana's place. It's been a couple of weeks since I visited her. I'll talk to you later, okay?"

"Okay," Belle said. She added her share of money to the bill and followed Rowan out the door.

BELLE STRETCHED AND GENTLY MOVED HER HEAD FROM SIDE to side. She had been hunched over for most of the day, inputting books into the spreadsheet on the laptop Bennett had provided, and she felt stiff and sore. She stood and walked across the library to look out the window. The back-yard remained empty, and she sighed loudly. Bennett had been gone when she arrived this morning and hadn't returned. She hadn't taken the job specifically to spend time with Bennett, but she'd considered it a job perk. Last week she was positive he was attracted to her, but now doubt crept in. Would he be so obviously avoiding her if he was?

No, she decided, he wouldn't. She sighed again before unzipping her hoodie and tugging it off. It left her in just a thin tank top which wasn't exactly work appropriate, but it was hot in the library, and besides, Bennett wasn't around.

Your nearly twenty-year crush on a guy you met once is kind of ridiculous. You know that, right?

Yeah, she did. But dammit, did he have to grow up to be so big and handsome? She was itching to touch him and taste him. The idea that he would feel the same way because he'd looked at her once in a way that suggested he might want to lick her all over was ridiculous.

She stretched again and then froze when there was a sharp inhale behind her. She turned around, and butterflies flickered to life in her stomach when she saw Bennett standing in the library.

"Hi," she said as his gaze drifted down her body. She crossed her arms nervously over her torso and glanced at the hoodie she had draped across the table. "I didn't hear you come in."

He strode forward, the floor shook lightly beneath his feet, and she twitched in surprise when he grasped her upper arms and gently turned her around.

"Bennett, what -"

Her voice died out when he traced the top of the four ragged scars on her upper back.

"Mirabelle, I'm so sorry," he said. His deep voice made her nerve endings sing with anticipation.

"It's not your fault," she said.

"Are they painful?" he asked as she shivered delicately.

"No," she said. "Just ugly."

"Nothing about you is ugly," he murmured.

She couldn't stop the soft moan when she felt his lips brush against the scarring on her back. His hands grasped the edge of her tank top, and she cleared her throat. "Bennett, what are you doing?"

"Lift your arms. I want to see all of it," he said in a low but demanding voice.

Like a woman in a dream, she raised her arms and allowed him to pull the tank top over her head. He dropped it to the floor, and she dug her fingers into the windowsill in front of her. She could see his reflection in the window and watched as a look of sorrow crossed his face.

"Bennett, it's fine," she said. "Really."

"This is my fault."

"It isn't," she insisted. "Don't think that – oh my God."

His fingers had flicked open the clasps of her pale pink bra, and she automatically clamped her hands over her breasts as the fabric loosened. He dipped his head, and she arched her back when he licked the length of one scar. The scars ran from her upper back to the waistband of her pants, and she didn't object when he placed one arm around her waist and drew her back against him before licking a second scar. His t-shirt was warm from the sun, and he smelled so good that she felt nearly faint from his closeness. His hand curled around her hip and held her as he placed a row of soft kisses across the top of her shoulder.

"Bennett, please," she whispered before turning her head to stare at his mouth. His eyes darkened until they were almost black, and she made a soft, pleading noise. He bent his head and pressed his mouth against hers. She was surprised by his gentleness. She wasn't exactly sure what she had expected, but it wasn't this feather-light touch of his warm lips against hers. She parted her lips eagerly, and he brushed the tip of his tongue against her upper lip like he was tasting her. Even that light touch was enough to set her on fire, and she ground her ass shamelessly against his growing erection.

She licked his lip in return, and he growled softly against her mouth before sliding his tongue between her lips to dart and flick lightly at hers. She moaned again and returned his kisses eagerly. When his hand slid up her round stomach, she dropped her arms and thrust out her chest. He raised his hand without touching her aching breasts, but her groan of disappointment ended when he pulled off her bra and dropped it to the floor as well.

He studied her breasts over her shoulder – she could feel his heart pounding against her back – before cupping the right one in one big hand. He held it firmly, testing the weight in his hand, as her nipple pebbled against his palm. Her back arched again when he used his thumb and finger to pull lightly on her stiff nipple.

"Oh my God," she said.

"I've dreamed about seeing you like this," he rumbled into her ear as his second hand cupped her left breast. He kneaded and rubbed them as he pressed his pelvis rhythmically against her ass. "Do you have any idea how much I want you, Mirabelle?"

"I want you too, Ben," she said

His hands tightened on her breasts, and then he kissed her again, this time hard and deep, his tongue pushing past the barrier of her lips to claim her mouth. She returned his kisses, their tongues stroking and sliding against each other as he reached down and unbuttoned her jeans. He slid his hand into her panties and cupped her aching core.

"You're so wet, little Mirabelle," he said against her lips before pushing one finger deep inside her. She rose on her tiptoes at the unexpected invasion, and he cupped and squeezed one breast soothingly before easing his finger out of her. He rubbed her clit lightly and placed hot, wet kisses against her neck and shoulder.

"I want to fuck you," he said. "I want that so much. It's all I can think about."

"Me too," she said breathlessly.

"Good," he muttered. "But first, I want to watch you come all over my fingers."

She inhaled sharply, her hand latching onto his wrist and squeezing tightly as he rubbed roughly at her clit. It was already swollen and throbbing, and she bucked her hips against his hand as he stroked lightly, then roughly. The need was a fevered pitch inside of her, and she closed her eyes and arched her back, soft cries spilling from her lips as he brought her closer and closer to her release.

"Ben, oh, Ben, oh God," she moaned. "It feels so good. It feels so -"

Her body stiffened, and she rode the wave of her orgasm

as he growled again in her ear and rubbed his cock against her ass. She collapsed against him, and he sucked lightly on her earlobe before turning her around and yanking her jeans and panties down her legs. She stepped out of them. Her legs were still weak from her orgasm, and she gave him a shy look as he studied her body in the sunlight.

"You're so beautiful," he said hoarsely.

"You're beautiful too," she said.

Belle mourned the loss of his hard body when he suddenly took a step back and pulled his t-shirt over his head. She studied his broad chest, and he inhaled sharply when she ran a trembling hand through the layer of dark hair that covered it.

"Fuck, I'm going to come in my pants if I don't take you right now," he muttered.

He pulled his wallet out of his back pocket and took a condom from the billfold. He unbuttoned his jeans, shoving them and his briefs down his legs, and her eyes widened at his size. She pushed away the thin trickle of apprehension as he kicked off his shoes and finished removing his clothes.

He reached for her, and she gasped in surprise when he pushed her to the floor. He rolled the condom onto his cock and lowered his heavy body onto hers, his thighs pushing hers apart.

"Ben," she said nervously. "You – you'll be gentle, right?"

"Yes," he said before kissing her lightly. "I won't hurt you, Mirabelle."

She doubted that was true. There was no way he couldn't not hurt her – not with a cock that size – but her anxiety disappeared when his mouth dropped to her breasts, and he sucked one nipple into his mouth.

"Oh!" She arched against him, his cock rubbing against

her pussy, and threaded her hands through his thick, dark hair as he pulled lightly on her nipple with his teeth. He nipped it lightly before switching to the other breast. When she was panting and wiggling beneath him, he reached between them and guided his cock to her wet opening.

As the head breached her opening, she tensed and gripped at his broad, smooth back. "Ben, I -"

She cried out, her hands digging into his hard flesh as he pushed completely into her in one smooth motion. The flare of pain brought tears to her eyes, and his groan of pleasure trailed off as he stiffened above her.

"Mirabelle?" he said hoarsely. "Have you had sex before?"

Her face flushed bright red, and she clung tightly to him when he tried to withdraw. "Don't stop, Ben."

He propped himself up on his hands and stared down at her. "Are you a virgin?"

She hesitated and then nodded, blinking back the tears when a look of dismay crossed his face.

"Fuck!" he muttered. "What have I done?"

"Don't be angry," she said.

"I'm not angry." He stroked her dark hair. "But I've hurt you."

"It doesn't hurt anymore," she said.

It was true. The pain had faded. She moved experimentally beneath him. His breath hissed out, and she gasped when he made a slow thrust in response.

"Mirabelle," he moaned, "I think we should stop."

"No!" She wrapped her legs around his waist. "Please don't stop, Ben. I want this so much."

She pushed her pelvis up and felt a thrilling sense of power when he thrust against her with a look of almost helpless need.

"I don't want to stop," he groaned.

"I know," she said. "I don't want you to stop either."

He groaned again before moving within her in long, slow strokes. She braced her feet on the floor and met each of his strokes as she watched his face carefully.

"You feel so good, my sweet Mirabelle," he said, and she smiled at him as the pace of his thrusts increased. The pain was gone now, leaving just warmth and an odd feeling of fullness, and she thought she could stay connected to him like this forever. It didn't matter if she ever came again. It was enough to feel him inside of her, to watch his face as he found pleasure in her body.

She touched his dark beard with her fingertips as he closed his eyes and pushed harder and deeper. A slight frown crossed her face – did he have a beard before? She couldn't remember. He must have. He couldn't grow a beard in a matter of minutes and –

Her internal musing was forgotten when Bennett reached between them and rubbed one rough finger against her clit. It brought her nerve endings screaming back to life, and she bucked her hips against him as tension coiled in her belly.

"Come for me again, Mirabelle." His deep voice made her pleasure grow. "I want to feel your pussy squeezing around my cock when you come."

"Ben," she gasped as she dug her nails into his back. "Oh my God, Ben."

"Can you do that for me, little Belle?" he whispered into her ear. "Can you come all over my thick cock?"

The sound of her nickname being said in his rough voice, the touch of his warm fingers against her clit, and the dirty things he was whispering brought a surge of wetness between her legs and a shot of pleasure straight from her crotch to her toes.

"Yes," she gasped. "Yes, Ben."

"Then do it," he growled. "Come all over my cock, little Belle."

She arched her back as his fingers tugged at her clit, and she came with a screaming, roaring rush of pleasure that blotted out everything but the feel of Bennett's hard body, his hot breath blowing in her ear and the exquisite feeling of fullness as he drove into her a final time and climaxed.

Her eyelids fluttered open as he roared his pleasure, and she stared mutely at the sharp fangs that protruded from his mouth. She blinked, and they were gone. His big body trembled above hers before he collapsed against her, his heavy body making her gasp for oxygen.

"Ben, I can't breathe." She pounded on his back, and he rolled off of her with a harsh groan. They lay panting on the hard floor of the library, and her tentative smile died on her face when he sat up and looked at her. The look of regret on his face chilled her to the bone, and she sat up, drawing her knees up against her chest.

"Mirabelle, we shouldn't have -"

"Don't, Ben. Don't say it," she said as she blinked back the hot tears.

"Why didn't you tell me you were a virgin?"

"Why did it matter?" she asked.

His eyes widened. "You should have told me."

"It's not that big of a deal," she said defensively.

"Not that big of a deal?" He gave her an angry look. "I was rough with you. I... I hurt you. If I had known you were a virgin, I wouldn't have," he looked around the library in dismay, "taken you on the floor of my goddamn library. Hell, I wouldn't have taken you at all."

Hurt flooded through her, and she reached for her pants and underwear, yanking them over her legs and hips before buttoning her jeans. "You sure know how to ruin a moment, Bennett Saxby."

"Mirabelle," he protested as she struggled into her bra, "there are other reasons for why this was a mistake."

Her body stiffened, and he groaned loudly. "Wait, that didn't come out right. I just mean that -"

"It's fine, Bennett," she said. "What girl doesn't like to hear a guy tell her that sleeping with her was a mistake."

She slid her tank top over her head and grabbed her hoodie before stomping to the library door. "I'm suddenly not feeling very well. I'll make up the time I miss today if that's okay?"

"Don't leave. We need to talk about -"

"Fuck it," she suddenly snapped. "If you're not fine with it, you can fire me."

She stormed out into the hallway and slammed the door behind her.

"WAIT, LET ME GET THIS STRAIGHT." ROWAN CROSSED Ella's tiny apartment and collapsed in one of the armchairs. She folded her legs under her and took the glass of wine from Ella with a nod of thanks. "You finally gave up your v-card to Bennett Saxby, of all people."

"What's that supposed to mean?" Belle asked.

"Belle, honey, I know you've spent the last eighteen years romanticizing the boy who nearly got you killed by a cougar, but what do you really know about him? You've seen him, what – half a dozen times in the last week and had maybe three conversations with him?"

"Just this morning, you wanted to know if I was

'knocking boots with him' remember? Now suddenly, it's the worst thing I could have done?"

Rowan sighed. "I know I was teasing you, but I didn't think you would sleep with him, Belle."

"Why not?"

"Because that's not you. You don't sleep with men you barely know. That's my department."

Belle rolled her eyes. "Maybe I'm changing. I don't see what the big deal is."

Rowan gave Ella a pointed look. "Help me out here, Ella."

"Honey, what Ro's trying to say is that sleeping with Bennett might not have been the smartest idea."

"It was a great idea," Belle protested before rubbing her forehead. "Fine, I know. It felt right at the time but his whole 'I made a mistake' thing kind of killed that feeling."

"He said it was a mistake?" Rowan gave her a look of indignation. "Why that giant asshole. The next time I see him, I'm going to -"

"You're not going to do anything," Belle said. "Besides, it was kind of my fault. He was upset that I didn't tell him I was a virgin."

"You didn't tell him!" Rowan stared wide-eyed at her. "Belle, you should have told him."

"Why? Are you telling me that you told Ricky Jarwin that you were a virgin?"

"Damn straight I did. And Perry Mosen and Bobby Taylor. Oh, and Jim -"

Ella burst out laughing as Belle stared wide-eyed at Rowan.

"What?" Rowan shrugged. "Guys like thinking they're a girl's first."

"Bennett didn't like it," Belle said. "He said if he had known I was a virgin, he wouldn't have taken me at all."

Ella squeezed her arm sympathetically. "I'm sorry, honey."

They sat silently for a moment before Rowan drank the last of her wine in one large swallow. "Okay, enough wallowing in self-pity. When you fall off a horse, you dust yourself off and climb back on, right?"

"Are you suggesting that Belle climbs onto Bennett Saxby again?" Ella asked with a small grin.

"Nope. Obviously, that ship has sailed. Sorry, sweetie," Rowan said when Belle winced, "but if the guy is showing regret immediately after sleeping with you – it's not exactly a lasting relationship. But that doesn't mean there aren't plenty of guys in this backwater town to ride."

Belle laughed and shook her head. "Not interested, thanks."

"Of course you're interested," Rowan said. "You've finally had sex! You can't tell me you don't want more. Sex is better than chocolate and wine and amusement rides put together. Sex is a gift from the gods!"

Ella nodded solemnly. "She has a point."

Belle didn't reply, and Rowan leaned forward and patted her knee. "Sweetheart, don't judge sex from the first time alone. It always hurts, and it's awkward and forget having an orgasm. It's just too -"

"I had an orgasm," Belle said. "I had two."

"Damn," Rowan said, "nicely done, Bennett Saxby."

Belle flushed, and Rowan patted her knee again. "Still, I think you need to forget about your boyhood crush and start sampling what this town has to offer. You don't just eat one thing off the menu, you know?"

Ella laughed, and Rowan winked at her. "We'll have her dating someone by the Centennial Ball."

"It's not a 'ball'," Ella said. "It's the Centennial Celebration."

"Whatever," Rowan said. "The whole town will be there, there will be music and dancing, and we'll dress up fancy. It's a damn ball, and I, for one, am looking forward to it. Anyway, the three of us are going out tonight, and we're getting Belle laid again."

"I don't want to get laid again," Belle said. "Honestly, Ro, I don't. Besides, you know how people see me in this town. They all think I'm a lunatic. If I haven't found someone to date me by now, I never will."

"Not with that attitude." Rowan eyed Belle's jeans and t-shirt. "Or that outfit. Listen, you don't have to actively try to get laid tonight, but can we at least go out and do some flirting? I finally have a night off and want to live a little."

"I have to work in the morning," Belle said. "I think. I mean, there is the possibility that Bennett is going to fire me. I did kind of storm out earlier this afternoon."

"C'mon, Belle-boo," Rowan wheedled. "Ella and I don't want to go without you."

"I'm not going," Ella said.

"Like hell you're not!" Rowan said.

"I don't want to go to Gaston's. Not after what happened the last time I was there," Ella said.

"We're not going to Gaston's. You think I want to hang out at my place of employment?" Rowan said. "We're going to The Woodsmen Pub."

"That place is practically out in the damn forest, and it's full of loggers and cowboys," Ella replied.

"Save a horse, ride a cowboy, sweetheart," Rowan said.

CHAPTER 5

"Remind me again why we're here and not at Gaston's?" Bennett asked irritably.

"I told you," Duncan said, "I don't want to run into Ella again, not after what happened the last time."

"So now I'm forced to drive an hour for a beer because you've got a hard-on for a woman?"

"Oh, please, you'll fit right in with the rest of the rednecks," Duncan said as he grinned at the waitress who approached their table. "I'll take a beer, whatever you have on tap."

She nodded and gave him a slow look of appreciation which, Bennett was amused to see, Duncan took no notice of. He had only been back a few weeks, but even he could see that Duncan wasn't acting normally. The lion shifter loved women, and if he was to be believed, the women loved him.

"I'll have the same," Bennett said. The waitress nodded before smiling at Duncan. "You sure you don't want something to eat? I can get the cook to make you something special."

Duncan shook his head as he glanced at his phone. "No, thanks."

A look of disappointment crossed her face, and she walked away as Bennett elbowed Duncan. "What was that about?"

"What?" Duncan asked.

"Our waitress, who is lovely, by the way, was practically offering herself on a platter to you."

Duncan blinked at him before glancing at the retreating waitress. "I didn't notice."

"Yeah, that was obvious. What's up with you?"

"Nothing," Duncan said. "What's up with you?"

"Nothing."

"Bullshit. You've been acting weird since you got in my car. Plus," he sniffed at Bennett, "I can smell Belle all over you. You two finally had sex, and you're acting like your dog died. Was she terrible in the sack?"

"Keep your voice down, Duncan," Bennett growled at him. "It'll be a cold day in hell before I discuss Mirabelle's bedroom abilities with you."

"Fair enough," Duncan said. "But her scent is ridiculously strong – you must have gotten her really hot and bothered – so, well done?"

"Please be quiet, Duncan," Bennett said.

Duncan laughed. "Hey, I'm just saying that…." His eyes widened as he sniffed the air. "Oh fuck, it can't be."

"What? Oh shit," Bennett muttered as the scent of cinnamon drifted to him. "Are you kidding me?"

They both turned and stared at the pub entrance. Belle, Ella, and Rowan walked through the door, and he and Duncan shrank into the shadows as the three women walked by.

"Time to leave," Duncan said. "Right now." He was

holding his hand over his nose, and their waitress gave them an odd look as she set the beer down in front of them.

"That'll be eight fifty."

Bennett gave her a ten and shook his head when she held out the change to him. She made it disappear into her apron and gave Duncan another appreciative look before leaving.

"Let's go, Bennett," Duncan said.

"The wolves are here, Duncan."

Duncan followed his gaze to the group of men standing near the two pool tables at the back of the pub. A pack of wolf shifters had lived for years in the woods outside of town. Rafe Taggert's pack, actually, until he had done the unthinkable and left them.

"So what?" Duncan said. "Let's go."

"They like human females. You know they do," Bennett said. "Unless this group differs from every other pack of wolf shifters I've met?"

"They're not," Duncan said. "But there are dozens of women here. The odds of them going after Belle or Ella is...."

He trailed off as four wolf shifters broke off from the others and headed toward Belle, Ella, and Rowan. The three women had snagged a table near the dance floor, and Duncan growled when the wolves took the table next to them. The biggest of them, who had long dark hair and a thick beard, smiled at Ella, and she blushed and glanced at the table.

"Oh, hell no," Duncan growled again. "That fucking asshole touches her, and he'll find my claws in his intestines."

"Keep it together," Bennett said. "He hasn't even said anything to her."

Duncan glared at the wolf shifter, his large hand squeezing compulsively around his beer as Bennett glanced around uneasily. Duncan would lose his cool if the wolf shifter went anywhere near Ella, and Bennett needed to do something to distract the lion shifter. He caught a glimpse of a familiar face, and he half-stood before waving. With a slight smile, the man crossed the pub before holding out his hand.

"Bennett Saxby. I heard you were back in town."

"Hello, Rafe. It's good to see you." Bennett shook his hand firmly. "You remember Duncan Gillis?"

"I do. Hello, Duncan," Rafe said politely before taking a swig from the beer bottle he held in his left hand.

"Hey," Duncan grunted. He was still staring at Ella, and Rafe followed his gaze. He jerked and took a step back as Bennett gave him a curious glance.

"What's wrong?"

"Nothing," Rafe said. "But I should probably get going. It was good to see you again, Bennett. We should -"

"Don't leave," Bennett said. "Let's get caught up. It's been a long time."

He pulled the chair out, and Rafe hesitated before sinking into it. His large body blocked Duncan's view of Ella, and Duncan glared at him as Bennett placed his hand on his arm. "Relax, Duncan."

"Maybe you should tell your pack over there to stay away from Ella Cinders," Duncan snapped irritably at Rafe.

"They are no longer my pack and haven't been for many years," Rafe said calmly. "I would have about as much sway with them as you do, lion shifter."

Duncan scowled at him, and Rafe folded his arms across his chest. "Perhaps it would be best if you and your friend left, Bennett."

"I'm not leaving her here alone," Duncan said. "No fucking way."

"Then perhaps you should heed your friend's advice and

relax," Rafe said. "You don't want to be on the wrong side of a wolf pack."

"I don't give a shit about that," Duncan said. "Besides, I can tear them apart easily."

"One or two, perhaps," Rafe said. "But there are at least eight here tonight, and that isn't even half of the pack. Injure a member of the pack, and the rest will go after you."

"You think I'm afraid, old man?" Duncan snarled. "Is that what you think?"

"Duncan! For God's sake, just relax," Bennett said. "Sorry, Rafe. He's got a, uh, thing for Ella Cinders."

Rafe's eyes, which had flared to the colour of jade at Duncan's insult, faded to his usual hazel. "Then might I suggest that, instead of threatening to kill the wolves, you claim Ella as yours before one of my former pack mates does."

"Easier said than done," Bennett said. "She kind of hates Duncan."

"She doesn't hate me," Duncan said heatedly. "She's just mad because I pulled her braids in school."

"For an entire year," Bennett said.

A slight grin crossed Rafe's face, and Duncan scowled again at him. "You're one to talk. You think we can't smell your lust for Rowan?"

The smile dropped from Rafe's face, and his hand clenched around the table. "I feel nothing for Rowan Jameson. I barely know her."

"Whatever," Duncan snorted. "Maybe you should take your own advice instead of dishing it out to me."

Rafe didn't reply, and Bennett sighed loudly before taking a drink of beer. "Can we all just admit that we're attracted to the humans and be done with it?"

Rafe's nostrils flared slightly, and he stared pointedly at

Bennett. "It would seem Ms. Vale is receptive to your advances."

Blushing, Bennett looked away from the wolf shifter's steady glare. The man was only thirteen years older, but he suddenly felt like his father was chastising him. "She's working for me – cataloguing my mother's library. She's been in my home all week, and that's why you can smell her on me."

Duncan snorted, and Bennett glared at him as Rafe made a low chuckle. "I am not a fool, Bennett."

"I know," Bennett said. "It's kind of complicated at the moment."

"Love always is," Rafe said.

"Oh my God," Duncan suddenly groaned. "Is she trying to kill me?"

Bennett took a quick look at the three women. They were out on the small dance floor, and he watched, desire flooding through him, as Belle shimmied and shook her body to the fast beat of the music.

The smell of his lust was being overpowered by Duncan's, and he forced himself to look away as Duncan groaned again. "Jesus, I am going to lose my shit in a minute. I swear to God."

His eyes were glued to Ella's ass as she swayed to the music, giggling and bumping her hips against Rowan's.

Bennett glanced at Rafe before he stared at the people sitting at the table next to theirs. He sighed in relief that they weren't paying any attention to them and nudged the wolf shifter. "Maybe you should leave, Rafe."

The wolf shifter's eyes glowed bright green, and a dark beard covered his jaw. He watched Rowan with a fierce intensity, and his hands were in tight fists on the table. As Rowan raised her arms and rocked her hips, the wolf shifter made a low growl and a nearly overwhelming scent of lust radiated from his body.

"Rafe," Bennett repeated, "you should go."

Rafe blinked at him before shaking his body and standing abruptly. "Yes, I believe you're right, Bennett. Good night."

He stalked away as the music ended and a slow song began. Bennett sat back in his chair as Duncan shoved his chair back and stood.

"No fucking way," he snarled and yanked his arm out of Bennett's grip before hurrying toward the dance floor.

"Shit," Bennett said. Two of the wolf shifters had joined the women on the dance floor. The largest of the wolf shifters was about to pull Ella into his arms to dance, but Bennett's concern that Duncan would rip him apart ended the moment he saw Belle smile at a second wolf shifter and nod. The wolf grinned happily and put one thick arm around her waist as she took his hand, and he pulled her up against his body. His hand rested familiarly at the top of her ass, and Bennett growled before standing and following Duncan to the dance floor.

"GOOD GRAVY, ELLA," ROWAN MUTTERED, "THAT GUY IS SO hot for you I can practically see the lust rising off of him."

Ella blushed before grinning at her. "You know, Rowan, I'm starting to think your idea of coming here was brilliant."

She smiled at the large, bearded man, who gave her a slight nod and a slow look of approval as Rowan laughed.

"Of course, it was. I know exactly how to turn those frowns upside down. Now, let's show those handsome boys some of our moves."

She took Belle's and Ella's hands and led them to the dance floor. Belle moved her body to the music. She was a terrible dancer, but she loved to dance anyway, and she shook her hips with abandonment as Ella bumped her hips against Rowan's. Rowan laughed and raised her arms before rocking her hips, and Belle grinned at her.

"I really need to take dance lessons," she shouted above the music.

Rowan shook her head. "Nah, you got the moves, honey. Trust me."

Belle winked at her as the music ended and a slow song started. She turned and squeaked in surprise when she bumped into the broad chest of one of the men who'd been sitting at the table beside them.

"May I have this dance, beautiful?" He held out his hand, and she hesitated before nodding.

"Sure."

He grinned, and she twitched when he wrapped his arm around her waist and pulled her up against his large body.

Not as large as Bennett's, her mind whispered. *Or as hard and warm. And those blue eyes of his are doing nothing for me.*

Her smile faltered, and the man squeezed her hip. "What's wrong?"

"Nothing," she said.

She stared over his shoulder, and her mouth dropped open in surprise. Duncan Gillis, his face grim, stalked across the dance floor toward Ella.

"CARE TO DANCE?"

Ella smiled tentatively at the man standing in front of her. "I'm not a very good dancer."

He grinned, showing even white teeth before holding out

his hand. "Neither am I, so perhaps you'll forgive me when I step on your foot?"

She laughed and reached for his hand. Before she could take it, there was a low growl behind her. She gasped when her arm was taken in a firm grip, and she was spun around.

"Duncan? What are you doing here?" She gaped in surprise at the blond man.

Ignoring her, he glared at the man standing in front of her. "The woman is mine."

"Oh, for the love of God, Duncan Gillis. This is ridiculous!" Ella said as he wrapped his arm around her waist, yanked her up against his body, and steered her away from the man.

"You're holding me too tightly," she said.

He responded by pulling her even closer, his thick arm like a band around her waist and his free hand wrapping around the back of her neck to hold her firmly.

"What are you even doing here?" she asked as he swayed lightly to the music.

"What are *you* doing here?" he said.

"Trying to have fun with my friends," she said. "And I was succeeding until you showed up."

Hurt crossed his face, and she ignored her guilt.

"That man you were about to dance with is dangerous, Ella."

"Do you know him?" She tried to turn her head to stare at the man who had returned to his table, but Duncan's grip prevented her from looking.

"Not exactly."

"Then you can't possibly know he's dangerous," she said. "Duncan, I don't want to dance with you."

Another one of those oddly hurt looks, and her guilt increased. "Duncan, I -"

"Just one dance, Ella," he suddenly said. "Please."

She bit at her bottom lip before nodding. "Okay. One dance."

He dropped his hand from her neck and put both arms around her waist. Trying to ignore the butterflies in her stomach, she draped her arms around his shoulders and made a low startled noise when he pulled her body against his until every part of them touched. She stared over his shoulder as his warm breath stirred her hair.

***

"So, what's your name, beautiful?" The man rested his hand on the top of her ass, and Belle reached behind her to move it up to her lower back.

"My name is -"

"Excuse me," the low familiar voice spoke behind her, and she froze in surprise as the man she was dancing with scowled.

"Can I help you, buddy?"

"You can take your hand off my woman's ass."

"And if I don't?" the man said.

"I'll break it," Bennett said.

The man gave him a long, assessing look, his nostrils flaring as he sniffed the air before releasing Belle and taking a step back. He held his hands up and shrugged carelessly. "She's all yours."

"That's right. She is," Bennett said.

He pulled Belle into his embrace as the man turned and walked off the dance floor.

Belle stared up at Bennett as he took her left hand in his right and slung his arm around her waist. He let his hand linger low on her hip as he glared at the man's retreating back.

"What the hell, Bennett Saxby?" she said.

"What?" He still stared over her head, and she poked him lightly in the chest.

"Suddenly I'm your woman? Sleeping with you once doesn't make me your woman."

He didn't reply, but his hold on her hip tightened, and he swung her in a tight circle until she clung to him.

"What are you and Duncan even doing here?" She peered around Bennett's wide body. Ella, every inch of her curvy body pressed against Duncan's, had her eyes closed as Duncan moved her slowly across the dance floor. She didn't object when Duncan nuzzled his face into her blonde hair.

"Well?" Belle demanded. "Are you following me?"

"No," Bennett said. "Duncan wanted to go here instead of Gaston's and dragged me with him. Thank God he did. Do you have any idea what kind of guy that is you were dancing with?"

"No. I don't even know him," Belle said.

"You were dancing with him, letting him touch your ass," Bennett said.

"I wasn't *letting* him touch my ass," Belle said. "And even if I was – it's none of your damn business, Bennett Saxby. Let me go. I don't feel like dancing anymore."

He gave her a look of frustration but refused to release her. "Mirabelle, I'm sorry about earlier today. Truly I am."

"Yes, I know," she said. "You've already made it clear that I was a mistake."

"No!" Bennett nearly shouted. He took a deep breath and made his voice low. "I mean, I'm sorry for what I said, not what happened between us. I was a complete idiot."

"Yes, you were," Belle said.

"I was just – well, surprised that you hadn't had sex before," he said.

She blushed and stared at his broad chest. "It's not that big of a deal, Bennett."

"Yes, it is," he insisted. "A woman's first time shouldn't be on the floor of a goddamn library."

"The library is my favourite place," she said.

He grinned, and she blushed again. "Well, it is."

"Why haven't you slept with anyone, Mirabelle?" He asked as they swayed to the music. "A woman who looks like you must have men doing everything they can to get her into bed."

She didn't reply, and he gave her a hesitant look. "Were you... were you saving yourself for me?"

She stared up at him, and it was his turn to blush. "Sorry, that was a stupid thing to ask."

Belle closed her eyes for a moment before taking a deep breath. "Everyone in this town thinks I'm crazy, Bennett. Guys don't want to date me, and if they do, it's because they want bragging rights for bedding the crazy girl who believes a boy can turn into a bear."

He winced, and she gave him a solemn look. "At least that's what I told myself for years. Only, I think a part of me was waiting for you. Waiting for you to come back and tell me that you had thought about me as much as I thought about you for the last eighteen years. Waiting to give you a gift that you didn't even want."

She sighed and dropped her gaze to his chest again. "What an idiot I was."

"Don't say that," he said. "You're not an idiot, Mirabelle."

"I am," she said. "I was an idiot to think that you would

be happy that I had a crush on you. Happy that I waited for you. Instead, you were upset that you were my first."

"No," he said before stopping at the edge of the dance floor and cupping her face. "I wasn't upset about that."

"Yes, you were," she said. "I saw it in your face."

"What you saw was regret for taking you the way I did," he said. "Your first time should be special, and I feel horrible that it wasn't."

"It was," she said. "Despite how it ended up, it was special, Bennett. I wouldn't have wanted it any other way."

He studied her closely for a moment before taking her hand again and moving her slowly around the dance floor.

"A relationship between us wouldn't work," he said.

"Why not?"

"It just wouldn't. We're from two different worlds."

"I suppose we are," she said with a note of sadness that made his chest tighten. "I know you're rich, Bennett. It doesn't take a genius to figure that out. I don't blame you for not wanting a relationship with an unemployed library assistant who lives in a single wide trailer with her alcoholic father."

"That isn't what I meant, Mirabelle. I don't care if you're -"

"It doesn't matter," she said. "You're right."

"I'm sorry," he said.

"Me too," she said.

He held her a little closer, and she rested her head on his broad chest for a moment before staring up at him. "But just out of curiosity, what would you have done differently if you'd known I was a virgin?"

His heart pounding, he lowered his mouth to her ear. "I would have given you multiple orgasms first so that your sweet pussy was soaking wet and completely ready for me."

She inhaled sharply, and he bit back his groan when her pelvis pressed against him. "I had an orgasm before we had sex."

"You should have had more than one," he murmured. "I should have taken you to my bed, undressed you slowly, and touched every inch of your warm body before I buried my face between your legs and licked your pussy until you were begging me to fuck you."

"Oh," she whispered and then gasped when he ground his erection against her stomach.

"Have you had your pussy eaten before, little Belle?" he asked before licking the curve of her ear.

"N-no," she gasped.

"I want you in my bed so much, sweet Belle," he groaned. "I want to touch every part of your body. I want to taste your pussy and hear you scream my name. You have no idea how hard it is not to take you away from this goddamn place and drive you straight to my house."

"Yes," she said.

"What?" he said.

"Yes," she repeated. "Let's go back to your place. Right now, Bennett."

"Mirabelle, we can't," he said. "We just said that we can't have a relationship."

"I'm not asking for a relationship," she said. "I'm asking you to take me home so we can have a do-over."

"A do-over?"

She smiled sweetly at him. "You feel bad about how you took my virginity, right? So, take me home and spend tonight showing me what you wish you had done."

"Mirabelle, I can't…."

"Just for tonight, Ben," she said. "I won't ask you for anything more after tonight. I promise."

"This is a very bad idea," he groaned.

"No, it isn't," she said before standing on her tiptoes and pressing a kiss against his mouth. "It's a very good idea. Will you take me home, Ben? Will you take me to your bed?"

He stared at her sweet face before nodding. "Hell, yes."

"Good." She took his hand and tugged him toward Duncan and Ella.

ROWAN EASED OUT THE PUB'S BACK DOOR AND TOOK A DEEP breath of the warm summer air. She glanced around guiltily before pulling the pack of cigarettes from her pocket and lighting one. She took a deep drag, holding the smoke in her lungs before blowing it out.

She checked her phone before sticking it in her back pocket. Technically, she had quit smoking six months ago, at least, that's what she had told Belle and Ella, and she wasn't exactly lying. She really didn't smoke that much anymore, but something about being at the pub and having a beer made her crave a cigarette. She took another drag of the stale cigarette and blew a couple of smoke rings before staring at the sky. Faintly glimmering stars dotted the darkness, and she smiled to herself. Bennett and Duncan were pursuing Belle and Ella. They could deny it all they wanted, but it didn't make it less true. She was ridiculously happy about it. They deserved love, both of them.

So do you.

Yeah, she did. But the men in this town weren't exactly stellar quality.

Didn't stop you from fucking half of them.

Her smile widened. Her inner voice had a point, but hell, she loved sex. Just because she didn't want to marry or date any town boys didn't mean she had to deny herself a little fun.

Maybe it's because it's not a boy you want but a man.

An image of Rafe Taggert's face flickered in her head, and she took another puff of her cigarette before pushing Rafe's image from her head. Thinking she had a chance with him was idiotic. The guy was fifteen years older than her. That didn't bother her in the least, but despite what Belle had said earlier about him checking her out, she was confident that Rafe Taggert had zero interest in her. Why would he? She was just the short little redhead who served him beer at Gaston's. It was best to ignore the fact that she'd been crushing on him since she hit puberty and ignore the butterflies she felt on those rare occasions that she saw him and –

The door to the pub opened, bringing a wave of fried-onion-scented air and a blast of music. She dropped her cigarette to the ground, crushing it with her heel before swinging around guiltily. Her relief that it was neither Belle nor Ella was short-lived when the dark-haired man grinned at her.

"Hey there, pretty lady."

"Hello," she said.

"I saw you dancing in there. You got some good moves."

"Thank you." She started forward and stopped abruptly when two more men came out of the bar.

"You're beautiful," the man said. "Did you know that?"

"Yes, I do know," she said shortly. "Excuse me. My friends are waiting for me."

"Now, hold on. We thought that maybe you would like to get to know us a little better," the man said softly.

Rowan studied him silently. He was good looking in a frat-boy kind of way, and his khaki pants and crisp white shirt stuck out like a beacon among the more casual dress of the other pub patrons.

"No thanks," she said.

The man blinked at her before glancing at his friends. "You're turning me down?"

"I am."

He scowled at her. "My friends and I are new to town, but we know who you are."

"Who am I?" Rowan asked.

"You're the slutty little waitress who'll open her legs for any man who looks twice at her," the man said. "You're nothing but a little whore."

Rowan rolled her eyes. "I get that you think calling me a slut and a whore is an insult, but it really isn't. I like fucking, and I'm not ashamed of it."

"You like fucking so much, but you won't even give me a chance?" the man said sullenly.

"Because I prefer real men between my legs, not pretty boys like you. Boys like you are a dime a dozen. I know you think your dick is God's gift to women, but I've got standards, sweetheart."

She dropped her gaze to his crotch. "Anything less than eight inches, and I'm not interested, so I'm afraid the four and a half inches you're so proud of just isn't going to do it for me."

The man's mouth dropped open, and he glared at her. "You got a real smart mouth for a slut."

"Sluts can be smart, too," Rowan said cheerfully. "Now you and your little friends go back inside before you do something you'll regret."

"You smart-mouthed little bitch," the man snarled as he darted forward and reached for her. "I'm about to teach you a lesson you'll never -"

He stopped, his face paling and his breath rushing out of his mouth in a loud groan as Rowan punched him in the right side, her fist driving under his ribs. He bent over and Rowan, grinning widely, delivered two quick, hard blows to his face. His nose broke with a sickening crack, and he howled loudly before staggering back and falling to the ground. Blood gushed down his face, and he cupped his wounded nose before staring wide-eyed at her.

"What the fuck did you just do?" One of his friends said.

"Well, first I punched him in the liver, and then I broke his nose," Rowan said. She smiled at the two men and spread her feet slightly before raising her fists to chest level. "Which of you would like to be next to have his ass kicked?"

The men started forward, and another rush of adrenaline went through Rowan. She took a deep breath and frowned when the men stopped abruptly. The one gave the other a look of fear, and moving jerkily, they dragged their fallen friend to his feet and pulled him toward the door of the pub. They yanked the door open and stumbled inside, slamming the door behind them

Rowan lowered her hands before snorting, "Pussies."

She shook her aching right hand and eyed the already-swelling knuckles. "Fuck, that hurts."

Movement flickered on her left, and she turned her head, her breath escaping from her mouth in a soft little wheeze. A wolf, his dark grey fur rippling in the light breeze, stood beside her.

"Oh shit," she whispered.

The wolf was so big he would have been taller than her if he had stood on his hind legs. He stared silently at her. His green eyes glowed in the moonlight, and Rowan, her legs feeling weak and useless as cooked spaghetti, stumbled back. Her lower back hit the front bumper of a truck, and she made another quiet moan as the wolf started toward her. He stood in front of her and blocked her path to the pub before she could even think of running. She sank to her butt, holding her injured hand in front of her, with the vague idea that perhaps she could slide under the vehicle. She started to inch down, and the wolf growled low in his throat. She froze, her mouth trembling and tears sliding down her cheeks as the wolf bent its massive head.

"Good puppy," she whispered. "Please don't eat me."

She shrieked when the wolf brushed his wet nose across her cheek. His tongue licked her skin, and he whined quietly before sitting on his haunches. Even sitting, he towered above her, and she stared wide-eyed at him, her breath heaving in and out of her lungs in harsh pants as the wolf whined again before dipping his head and licking at her wounded hand.

"Good puppy," she whispered again. The wolf stared steadily at her, and she raised one badly trembling hand and brushed his cheek's thick fur. He didn't move, and she trailed her hand down his neck before patting him tentatively on the white patch of fur on his chest.

"Good boy," she said. "Um, that's a good wolf."

He suddenly grinned at her, and at the sight of all those enormous sharp teeth, she pressed her body back against the truck, her head banging painfully against the bumper. The wolf cocked his head before leaning forward and licking her cheek again.

She brushed her hand along his chest again, and he nudged her face with his head. He stood and glanced up at the moon before barking once. She flinched, and the wolf gave her a weirdly embarrassed look before loping across the parking lot and into the woods behind the pub.

"What the fuck just happened?" Rowan asked. The low

sound of the wind was her only reply, and, her legs still shaking, she climbed to her feet and staggered toward the pub.

———————

"YOU'RE GOING HOME WITH BENNETT SAXBY?" ELLA GAVE her a look of disbelief, and Belle nodded.

"Yes. Are you ready to go home? If you aren't, I'll pay for your Uber."

"Belle, what are you doing?" Ella asked.

"I'm going home with Bennett."

"I know that. I just wonder if you've thought this through. Earlier this evening, you were convinced he was finished with you, remember?"

"What are you two talking about?" Rowan joined them, and Belle wrinkled her nose at the faint scent of cigarette smoke.

"Were you smoking, Rowan?"

Rowan gave her a guilty look. "Just one, Belle."

"Rowan," Belle said with a frown, "smoking is terrible for you, and you quit six months ago, remember?"

"Yeah, I know," Rowan said.

Belle studied her closely before saying, "What's wrong?"

"Nothing."

"There's something wrong. Tell me."

"Stop changing the subject, Belle," Ella said. "Ro – our girl just told me she's going home with Bennett Saxby."

"Oh yeah?" Rowan said distractedly. "Good for you, honey."

"Rowan!" Ella said. "Don't encourage her."

"Why not?" Rowan said. "What's wrong with a woman having a night of sex with a man she's into?"

"There's nothing wrong with it." Ella's gaze flickered to where Bennett and Duncan were standing.

Rowan followed her gaze and smiled a little. "Maybe you should leave Belle's decision making to her and find your own fun tonight with Duncan."

"I am not interested in Duncan Gillis," Ella said heatedly. "I hate that guy."

"Yeah, so you keep saying," Rowan said. She brushed her hand through her hair, and Belle frowned when she winced.

"What's wrong with your hand?"

She grabbed Rowan's wrist and studied her swollen knuckles as Bennett and Duncan started toward them. "What happened?"

"I was out in the back parking lot, and a few frat boys decided they wanted me to show them a good time. I changed their minds when I broke the lead frat boy's nose."

"You broke someone's nose?" Standing so close to Ella that his arm brushed against her shoulder, Duncan glanced at Rowan's hand. "How the hell did a little thing like you break someone's nose?"

Rowan glared at him. "I'm not a fragile little girl, jackass."

"Never said you were, Ro," he said with an easy grin. "Just curious, that's all."

"My grandmother taught me to box when I was a teenager," she said.

"Damn, I need to meet your grandmother," Duncan said.

"Are you ready, Belle?" Bennett took her hand and squeezed it lightly.

"Yes. But I drove Rowan and Ella here, so I need to give them some cash to take an Uber home. Does this place have an ATM?"

"I can drive them home," Duncan said. He smiled at Ella,

and she stepped away from him before putting her arm around Rowan's shoulders.

"We'll take a cab home."

"I'm fine with Duncan driving us home," Rowan said.

Ella gave her a pointed look. "It's not polite of us to keep Duncan here longer than he wants to."

"I'm ready to go home," Rowan said. Her pale skin was even whiter than usual, and she looked tired and a little melancholy.

"Rowan? Honey, are you okay? Those guys didn't hurt you, did they?" Ella asked.

Rowan shook her head. "Nah, didn't even get close to me. But I need to put some ice on my hand, and I'm suddenly exhausted. We'll get home a lot faster if Duncan drives us. Do you mind, Ella?"

"Of course not, honey," Ella said before kissing her forehead. She turned to Duncan and gave him a stiff smile. "If you're sure you don't mind, we'll get that ride home from you now."

"I don't mind at all, Miss Ella," he said before holding his hand out to her. "Ready?"

She nodded and, ignoring his outstretched hand, walked past him toward the door.

CHAPTER 6

Belle stepped into Bennett's house and slipped out of her heels before placing her purse on the small side table. Bennett dropped his keys next to it and smiled at her.

"Thank you for the ride home, Mirabelle."

"You're welcome," she said. She was suddenly feeling nervous and unsure. Bennett had been quiet the entire ride, and while she was pretty sure that being quiet was just a part of his personality, she couldn't help wondering if he had changed his mind about sleeping with her again.

"So, uh, did you want to, uh…oh!" She gasped when Bennett suddenly bent and scooped her up.

"Bennett!" She clung to his shoulders as he strode down the dark hallway toward the staircase. "Put me down. You'll hurt yourself."

He laughed. "I won't. You're light as a feather."

"Oh please," she said. "We both know that isn't true."

He held her tighter as he started up the stairs, and she patted his back. "Seriously, Bennett put me down. You really shouldn't be climbing the stairs with my entire weight."

He shrugged. "I like carrying you, and I'm certain if I put

you down, you'll bolt for the front door. You're nervous, Mirabelle."

Now how the hell did he know that? She thought she was doing a remarkably good job of hiding her sudden case of the jitters.

"I'm not going to run," she said as he crested the top step and took a left down the hall. "This was my idea, remember?"

"I remember," he said. "But you are nervous, and I know it's because I hurt you earlier."

"No, it isn't," she said. "Honestly, Bennett, you need to let that go. It really didn't hurt that much, and you're kind of, um, large, so the odds are it's always going to hurt a little, right?"

He shook his head. "No, it won't. I promise you, Mirabelle."

He carried her into his bedroom, and she stared at his bed. "My God, that's the biggest bed I've ever seen."

He set her on her feet, and she shivered delicately when he put his arm around her and caressed her stomach with his warm hand. "I'm a big guy."

"I remember," she said.

"I won't hurt you again," he said.

"I know." She twisted in his embrace and put her arms around his neck. "Kiss me, Bennett."

"My pleasure," he said before pressing his mouth against hers. Like before, the kiss was soft and infinitely gentle, and she leaned against him as he rubbed her back and explored her mouth with long, slow licks and light nips.

He pulled down the zipper of her dress, and they broke apart so he could ease it down her body. She felt a little self-conscious and uncertain as he studied her body, but it disappeared when his hot gaze lifted to hers.

"Bennett?" she asked. "Are – are you okay?"

His nostrils flared, and he reached out and traced the swell of her breast. "Better than okay, Mirabelle."

He stepped forward and kissed her again. This one had more than a little heat to it, and she moaned into his mouth as her core ached. She suddenly felt feverish and restless and tugged impatiently at his shirt. He stripped it over his head, and she traced her hands across the broadness of his chest, smiling when his breath hissed out between his teeth.

She suddenly needed him with a primal desire that overpowered her nerves, and she boldly took his hand and pushed it between her thighs. "I need you right now, Ben."

His eyes flashed, and he pressed his fingers against her for one brief, heart-stopping moment before he pulled his hand away.

"Bennett," she pouted, and he grinned at her.

"We're going slow, remember, Mirabelle?"

"I've changed my mind," she said before reaching down and stroking his thick cock through his jeans. "I don't want it slow. I like it hard and fast."

He muttered a curse before taking her hand and pushing it to her side. "Let's try slow first before you make your decision."

"I can't wait," she complained as he reached behind her and unfastened her bra. She helped him remove it and smiled smugly when he made a low groan. "And you can't either."

She brushed her breasts against his naked chest, and he made another harsh groan. "Let's do what we both want, Bennett."

His big hand covered her breast and kneaded it roughly before shaking his head. "No, little Belle."

She wanted to smack him. She knew she was being irrational, but dammit, her body was practically on fire, and he knew it. Before she could complain again, Bennett lifted her, and she automatically wrapped her legs around his waist. He kissed her throat as he carried her to the bed, and she giggled when he dropped her, and she bounced on the firm mattress.

Her giggles dried up when he stripped off his jeans and briefs, and she had her second look at his cock. It was bigger than she remembered, and she sat up and studied it carefully.

"Can I touch it?" she asked.

"God, yes," he said with a touch of amusement in his voice. She blushed softly before wrapping her hand around him. He was hard steel encased in velvety soft skin, and she pumped him experimentally with her hand as his hips thrust forward.

"Does that feel good?" She couldn't look up at him. She felt shy and nervous again and worried she was doing something wrong.

"You have no idea how good," he muttered.

She risked a glance upward, her breath caught in her throat, and her hand tightened around him. The look on his face sent an ache straight to her core, and before she could lose her nerve, she bent her head and slid her mouth over his cock.

His reaction was hot and immediate. He moaned hoarsely, and his big hand cupped the back of her head as he pumped his hips. His cock filled her mouth, stretching her lips and making her feel like she was going to choke, and she immediately retreated.

"Fuck!" he snarled. "I'm sorry, Mirabelle."

"It's fine," she said. "It just took me by surprise. Hold still, okay?"

His hand was still cupping the back of her head, and he twisted his fingers into her hair before giving a clipped nod. "Right. Hold still."

She smiled a little at the tight desperation in his voice

and, this time, wrapped her fingers around the base of him to help hold him steady. She sucked at the head of his cock as he groaned loudly. He had a slightly salty taste that she liked, and she licked around the ridge experimentally as his hand tightened almost painfully in her hair. She stroked him with her hand as she sucked again, this time taking more of him, and lifted her gaze. He was staring at her, his eyes dark and the strong line of his jaw covered by his dark beard.

Beard? He didn't have a beard before. Girl, something isn't right.

Her inner voice was a distant annoyance. She didn't give one fuck about his facial hair at the moment, and she shut the voice out as she sucked firmly. He sucked in his breath, and she made a startled squeak when he pushed her away from his cock.

"Ben? Did I – did I do something wrong?"

"No," he said in a tight, dark voice. "You were doing everything right. I just – I was losing control."

She smiled happily, delighted that her first blowjob was a success and leaned forward again.

"Fuck," he said and stepped away before she could suck his cock into her mouth.

"I want to try again," she said.

He shook his head. "Not right now, sweet Belle."

"Why not?"

He gave her a half-grin tinged with desperation. "Because you have no idea how you affect me."

"But it's my first time doing this, and I need to practice," she said with a cheeky grin.

It was the wrong thing to say. Bennett snarled softly, and he had her flat on her back, her legs spread wide, and his large body nestled between them before she could even blink.

His fingers curled in her hair in a tight grip, and when he

bit her lightly on her throat, her pelvis arched, and she gasped at the erotic combination of pleasure and pain it brought forth.

"Practice?" he said in a dangerously soft voice. "Who are you practicing for, Mirabelle?"

"Ben, I -"

"Do you really believe that I'll allow you to touch or taste or," his eyes glittered angrily, "fuck any cock but mine?"

A hard thrill went down her spine. She hated the possessive, macho bullshit act that men put on, so why was she suddenly so turned on by it?

Because it isn't an act. You belong to Bennett Saxby now, Belle. You know that. Don't you?

"No," she whispered. She wasn't entirely sure if she was answering her inner voice or Bennett, but a smug look of satisfaction crossed his face.

"That's right, little Belle. You're mine."

He kissed her before she could protest, and was she really going to protest belonging to the man she had loved for eighteen damn years, anyway? She sucked on his tongue as he cupped her breast and tugged at her nipple. It hardened, and she gasped into his mouth before he pulled away and trailed kisses down her chest. When his mouth closed around her nipple and pulled, she arched her back and wound her hands into his thick hair. He teased her nipples with his lips and teeth until she was crying his name and squirming beneath him.

"Oh please, Ben, please," she said. "I want you."

"I want you too, Mirabelle," he said before licking the hollow between her breasts.

She moaned in dismay when instead of fucking her like she wanted, *needed*, he moved down her body, kissing and licking her smooth skin as she twisted and pleaded.

"Soon, baby," he said. "I want to taste you first."

He was between her legs now, his broad shoulders forcing her thighs wide, and she gave him a nervous look as he pulled her panties down her legs and dropped them on the floor. He pressed a kiss in her dark curls before massaging the crease between her left thigh and her pussy with his thumb and smiled up at her.

"Don't be nervous, little Belle."

"I'm not," she lied.

He grinned at her, and her pleasure skyrocketed when he rubbed the ball of his thumb against her swollen clit. She arched off the bed, and he pressed her down with one big hand across her stomach.

"Hold still, Mirabelle," he said with another small grin as he rubbed her clit again.

She glared at him. "Stop teasing."

He brushed his beard against the wet lips of her pussy, and she jolted against him.

"Holy fuck!" she moaned. His beard was slightly scratchy and weirdly soft at the same time, sending tingles of heat from her pussy to her toes. He licked her wet lips before kissing them, and she jerked again. "That feels so good."

He laughed, "You haven't felt anything yet, little Belle."

"What do you mean?" she panted as he spread her open with his thumb and forefinger.

His reply was a long, slow lick across her clit. She screamed, arching against the hand that still held her firmly to the bed and felt more than heard his low chuckle.

"Fuck!" The word exploded from her mouth in a harsh puff of air, and she pulled hard on his hair. "Do that again. Right now."

He licked her repeatedly, his tongue caressing her clit, and she ground her pelvis shamelessly against his face. His tongue was fucking magic, she decided rather hysterically. Fucking magic and –

Her breath caught in her throat, and her back arched again when he slid his tongue into her tight entrance. He fucked her with his tongue, his fingers rubbing her clit roughly, and she clenched her hands into the quilt below her and pleaded uselessly for him to make her come. He licked her clit again, and she squealed with pleasure when he brushed the tips of his fangs against her wet lips.

Fangs?

The errant thought disappeared when he sucked firmly on her clit and slid one thick finger inside her. She screamed again, her body rising off the bed as her climax exploded within her in a dizzying rush of bone-shattering pleasure. She pumped against his finger, her pussy squeezing rhythmically around it, and she was only dimly aware of his loud curse before he moved off of her.

Her legs shaking from the force of her orgasm, she watched through half-closed eyes as he hurriedly rolled on a condom before pushing on her legs. She spread them wide, presenting herself to him like a trophy for the taking, and he growled loudly before kneeling between her legs and thrusting into her.

There was no pain, just a feeling of stretching and fullness, and she clutched at his waist as he propped himself on his hands above her.

"Okay?" he said hoarsely.

"So good, Ben," she moaned.

His head fell back as he pushed past the contractions of her pussy and buried himself deep inside her. He moved in long, tantalizing strokes, rolling his hips in and out as she braced her feet on the bed and gripped his hard ass.

"Little Belle," he whispered raggedly, "I'm so close already."

She smiled at him. "I want you to come, Ben."

He muttered a curse and dropped onto his forearms so that his chest pressed against her breasts, and he could plant hard and frantic kisses against her mouth. She returned his kisses, bumping her hips against his as his strokes turned fast and quick.

She squeezed him experimentally with her inner muscles, and he groaned into her mouth before his pace quickened, and he was driving into her with hard, furious thrusts that bounced her on the mattress. She watched in utter fascination as his head fell back, his mouth dropped open, and he roared so loudly that the picture frames rattled on the wall. He pumped feverishly within her as his orgasm overtook him, and she clung to him as he collapsed against her. He rolled off her before she felt completely squished, and she curled up against him, resting her head on his chest. He stroked her bare back with the tips of his fingers as she listened to the rapid beat of his heart.

"I'm sorry, Belle," he said.

She lifted her head and touched the dark stubble on his chin before pressing a kiss against his mouth. She could taste himself on him, bringing an unexpected lust throb to her belly.

"For what?"

"Multiple orgasms, remember?" he said with a disgruntled sigh. "God, I couldn't wait any longer to be inside of you."

She laughed and nuzzled his throat affectionately. "I couldn't wait either, and, besides, it didn't hurt at all this time."

"Are you sure?" He scanned her face anxiously, and she nodded.

"Yes. It felt amazing, Ben."

"Good."

"Also," she traced her fingers across the dark hair on his chest, "the night is young, so there's plenty of time for multiple orgasms."

He didn't reply, and she gave him a tentative look. Her sudden worry that he would ask her to leave ended immediately. Bennett was giving her a look of smoking-hot need, and she squealed in surprise and happiness when he covered her with his large body and nuzzled her throat.

"That," he licked her soft skin, "is a very good idea, little Belle."

BELLE WOKE AT EIGHT-THIRTY THE NEXT MORNING, HER EYES widening as she slithered out from under Bennett's heavy arm and scurried into the bathroom. She wasn't exactly sure what her job status was with Bennett, but if she was still employed, she had only half an hour to get to her job on time.

That brought a snort of giggles as she rummaged under the sink and, with a triumphant grin, found a new, unwrapped toothbrush. Even with taking the time to shower, she wouldn't be tardy. The benefits, she supposed, of sleeping in her employer's bed. She brushed her teeth quickly and then hopped into the shower. Like everything else in Bennett's home, the shower was older and needed some repairs. The water turned tepid after only ten minutes, but she didn't mind. She loved Bennett's home, and as run-down as it was, it was still in better shape than the trailer she shared with her father.

She felt a moment of guilt as she wrapped the towel

around her wet body. She had never not come home before, and she wondered if her father was worried about her. Not likely. He would have gotten drunk like he did every night and would be sleeping it off. He wouldn't have noticed she was even missing.

She tiptoed out of the bathroom and padded across the bedroom toward the closet as she glanced at Bennett's sleeping form. It didn't seem necessary, Bennett hadn't been kidding when he said he was a deep sleeper, but she didn't want to wake him. They had been up for most of the night – her entire body shivered with pleasure as she thought of all the ways Bennett had made her climax – and she rubbed absently at her aching thighs. He needed sleep.

Is that it, or are you just trying to avoid an awkward conversation?

She sighed. There wouldn't be an awkward conversation. She and Bennett had agreed on one night only, so there was no point in hoping that he wanted to continue. She opened the closet door. To her surprise, it was a large walk-in, and she slipped inside. A pile of neatly folded t-shirts was on a shelf at the very back of the closet, and she selected one before sliding it over her head. It was like a tent on her, and she smiled to herself. Lord, Bennett Saxby was a big man. She smoothed the soft fabric with her hand. When he woke, she would ask him if she could use his washer and dryer. Wearing just his t-shirt wasn't the most work-appropriate outfit, but she didn't want to spend the entire day in the same clothes she had worn yesterday.

As she turned to leave, a flash of red caught her eye. She turned toward the dresser shoved against the wall, and her eyes widened. A dried rose, encased in a protective glass dome, sat on top of it, and she traced her fingers over the glass.

It's not the same rose, Belle.

It was. She knew that without a doubt. Even after eighteen years, she recognized the perfect fullness of its dark red petals, the slight bend of its stem where a nine-year-old Bennett had pulled it free.

Her heart beat frantically in her chest, and a few hot tears slid down her cheeks. He had kept it. He had kept it all this time. She took a deep breath and wiped the tears away before walking slowly out of the closet. She avoided looking at Bennett as she crept out of the bedroom, closing the door quietly behind her, and headed for the library.

It doesn't mean anything, Belle. He told you a relationship wouldn't work, remember?

She remembered.

BENNETT OPENED THE LIBRARY DOOR. IT WAS JUST AFTER eleven, and he had woken to find himself alone in his bed. He had panicked for a moment before spying Belle's clothing in a crumpled heap on the floor. She wouldn't have left without her clothes. The thought had brought a surge of relief, and ignoring it, he had used the bathroom, brushed his teeth, and showered quickly before making his way downstairs. His stomach was growling, but instead of going to the kitchen, he had walked quickly to the library. He was confident that Belle was still here, but he had needed to confirm it with his own eyes.

He caught her scent in the room, and his bear made a low grumble of happiness as he scanned the large room. He would make her lunch and, his stomach tightened unpleasantly, talk to her about the future. Not that they had a future. They didn't, and the thought filled him with a mindless sort of despair, but as much as he cared for Belle, he couldn't risk her finding out what he truly was.

Humans can never know about us.

His father's words rang in his head, and he sighed harshly. No, they couldn't, which is exactly why it had been a mistake last night to take Belle to his bed. But he couldn't regret it. He had wanted her too much for too long and –

He caught sight of Belle, and all thoughts fled from his mind as lust, immediate and delicious, coursed through him. She was at the far end of the library, bent over a box of books sitting on the floor in front of one of the large windows, and his bear made a low noise of need as he stared at her ass. It was covered, just barely, by his shirt, but he had seen her panties still lying on the floor next to the bed. Unless she carried an extra pair in her purse, she would be completely bare beneath his shirt.

And wet and tight, his mind whispered. *So fucking tight.*

He growled softly as the last vestiges of self-control dropped away and strode quickly across the room. Belle hummed quietly as she rummaged through the box and screamed, her body jerking when he wrapped his hands around her hips.

Without straightening, she turned and glared at him. "You scared the hell out of me, Bennett Saxby."

He didn't reply, and her eyes widened when she saw the look on his face. "Bennett?"

"Hello, Mirabelle," he said in a harsh growl.

She started to straighten, and he placed his big hand on her back, stopping her.

"No," he growled again. "Don't move."

"Ben, I – I'm working," she moaned as he hiked his shirt up around her waist and smoothed his hand over her naked ass.

"Spread your legs," he demanded.

When she didn't immediately obey him, he grunted in displeasure and pushed her thighs apart with one jean-clad thigh.

"Oh!" She winced slightly and then made a startled noise of surprise when he cupped her pussy and rubbed deftly at her clit. She rose on her toes and her back arched as she ground her pussy against his hand.

He grinned, already his fangs had descended, and she grumbled loudly when he moved his hand. He stripped off his shirt and unbuttoned his jeans, pulling his cock out and pressing it against her pussy as he thrust lightly back and forth. It rubbed along her clit, and she moaned excitedly.

He grabbed her shirt and yanked it over her head. She tried to straighten again, and he pressed her back down. "No, hold onto the windowsill."

She grabbed the sill, her body trembling with anticipation, and he spent long torturous moments rubbing his cock back and forth over her clit until both her pussy and his cock were drenched in her moisture.

"Ben, please," she moaned.

He reached under her and tweaked her nipple. She gasped, her fingers tightening on the windowsill until they went white, and he pulled and tugged at both of her nipples as he stroked her with his cock.

"Ben, you fuck me right now!" she demanded before hissing at him like a cat.

He grinned – God, he loved how demanding she could get – and guided his cock to her entrance. He pushed in to the hilt, his balls slapping up against her ass. She was warm and wet, and her pussy clung to him as he thrust back and forth. She cried out, and he gathered her damp hair in one fist and held it tightly as he rocked in and out of her.

"Touch your clit," he demanded hoarsely. A tinge of pink rose in Belle's cheeks, but she moved her hand between her legs and rubbed at the swollen button. Her pussy tightened around him, and he groaned as he pushed in and out with deep upward strokes.

"Oh, oh, oh," she moaned quietly as her fingers worked her clit.

He couldn't remember the last time he'd gone bareback in a woman, and the feel of her warm pussy sealing around his cock without any barrier was like heaven. She was starting to get close. After a night spent pleasuring her, he could read her signals easily and slowed down his thrust to a gentle, slow-paced motion.

She squirmed and pushed back against him furiously as her fingers caressed and tugged her clit, and he bared his fangs triumphantly when she came all over his cock, her pussy squeezing him in a relentless rhythm that made him want to come too.

He gripped both of her hips and pounded into her. She braced herself against the windowsill and made small noises of encouragement as her body trembled from the aftershocks of her orgasm, and her pussy continued to milk his cock with hard rhythmic squeezes. He was going to climax, it was impossible not to with her wet tightness, and a dim part of his brain pushed past his lust-fueled haze.

You're not wearing a condom, idiot!

She's ours! Put our cub in her belly, and show her she belongs to us, his bear immediately growled in reply.

The idea of Belle carrying his cub was intoxicating, and he pumped faster as his orgasm began.

What are you doing?

With a truly heroic effort of willpower, he pulled out of her warm pussy and wrapped his hand around his cock. He rubbed furiously as he came, his seed spilling on the floor at his feet. He stared at it as Belle straightened and pulled his shirt over her head.

"Ben?"

"I'm sorry," he said. "I'm infection free, but I should have used a condom."

She stared at the puddle of his seed on the floor, her cheeks a bright red, before shrugging. "You didn't come in me. It's fine."

"I wanted to," he admitted hoarsely.

"I'm not on the pill, so it's a good thing that you didn't," she said.

His bear roared in anger, and it was all he could do to stop from picking up Belle and carrying her back to his bed. He would take her repeatedly, fuck her until she was pregnant with his cub and then she'd be his forever. No one could take her away from him. She would be –

"Ben?"

He realized he was reaching out for her, and he dropped his arms and gave her a guilty look. "Sorry."

"It's okay. Are you all right?" she asked.

"Yes," he said.

"Well, I'll just, um, get some paper towels and clean this up," she said awkwardly.

He blushed and shook his head. "I'll clean it up. C'mon, we'll go to the kitchen, and you can decide what you want for lunch, okay?"

She bit at her lip before nodding. "Sure, but you don't need to make me lunch. I can just go out and grab something."

"Wearing nothing but my shirt?" He buttoned his jeans and held out his hand, feeling relief when she took it without hesitating, and led her toward the library door.

"Right, I kind of forgot about that. Would it be okay if I used your washer and dryer?" she asked.

He nodded and squeezed her hand. "I didn't hurt you, did I?"

"Not this again," she said before rolling her eyes. "No, it didn't hurt, Bennett."

"You winced," he said.

"My God, does nothing get by you?" she said irritably. "My thigh muscles are a little tight and sore probably because I'm not used to this particular type of workout. Stop worrying, Bennett. I'm not a fragile little flower."

She gave him a peculiar, almost guilty look, and he frowned. "What?"

"Nothing," she said quickly.

They were in the kitchen now, and he grabbed some paper towels and the bottle of Lysol. She giggled and said, "Kills ninety-nine percent of sperm germs."

He gave her a mock scowl before leaning down and kissing her lightly. "I'll be right back."

"THANK YOU FOR LUNCH, BENNETT. IT WAS DELICIOUS," Belle said.

"You're welcome," he said as he cleared the dishes.

She stood and pulled at the hem of his shirt. "Well, I guess I'll just put my clothes in the wash and then get back to work."

"We need to talk, Belle," he said.

"No, we don't."

"We do," he insisted.

"No, we don't," she repeated. "Bennett, we were both

119

very clear last night about what this was. We don't need to rehash it, okay? I'm a big girl, and I'm perfectly fine."

"I'm sorry," he said.

"You don't need to be. I'm not sorry at all. What happened last night and this morning were wonderful and amazing, and I'll never forget that. Thank you for being so sweet and gentle and just, well… you." She gave him a sweet smile that made his chest tighten.

"Thank you," he said. "It was amazing for me too."

For a moment, her smile faltered, and he thought he saw tears in her eyes before she cleared her throat. "You're welcome, Bennett Saxby."

He laughed, and she grinned at him. "Are you home for the rest of the day?"

He nodded, and she headed toward the kitchen door. "Okay, I'll check in with you before I leave."

She left the kitchen, and he finished loading the dishwasher before staring blankly out the window at the backyard. Belle seemed fine with not having a relationship and sticking to their agreement that it be a one-night only thing between them, which was a good thing. So why was he feeling such a crushing surge of disappointment?

CHAPTER 7

B elle unlocked the door of the trailer and stepped inside. Her nose wrinkled at the smell of stale beer, and she crossed to the kitchen and pushed open the window.

"Dad? Dad, are you home?"

There was no reply, and she set her purse on the table, wondering briefly if she should call Gaston's and see if he was there. It was only five-thirty, but he would have slept off the worst of his hangover by now and gone looking for a faster cure. She sighed and headed down the narrow hallway toward the bathroom, barely noticing the peeling wallpaper or the water stains on the ceiling. The door was partially open, and she frowned when she pushed on it and met resistance.

She stuck her head through the narrow opening, and her eyes widened with horror. "Dad!"

Her father was lying on the bathroom floor with his legs blocking the door. She pushed frantically against it until the opening widened, and she could squeeze her body through. She fell to her knees beside him, panic yammering at her brain, and shook him roughly.

"Dad! Wake up! Dad, look at me!"

He didn't move. His face was pale, and the heavy bags under his eyes were a dark mottled purple.

"Daddy?" she whispered. Her fingers trembling, she pressed them against his neck and started to cry when she felt the faint beat of his pulse. She stumbled out of the bathroom and hurried back to the kitchen, grabbing her purse from the table and yanking out her cell phone. She called 9-1-1 as adrenaline pulsed through her veins.

Bennett stumbled down the stairs as the doorbell rang again. It was half-past seven in the morning, and he scrubbed his jaw irritably.

"I'm coming!" he bellowed. "Hold your fucking horses!"

He had slept terribly last night, reliving in his dreams the day the cougar had attacked Belle. The cougar attack had been interspersed with images of her in the library. Her face was happy as he held her close and whispered that he loved her.

The doorbell rang for the third time, and he snarled before reaching for the door handle. Whoever was on the other side was about to be very sorry.

"Bennett?"

He stared blankly at the woman standing on his front porch. "Ella? What are you doing here?"

Terror suddenly gripped him, and he squeezed the door frame so hard that the wood cracked. Ella took a step back as he stared wide-eyed at her. "Is Belle okay?"

"She's fine," Ella said hurriedly. "Well, physically, she's fine."

"What's wrong?"

"Her dad. Her dad had a heart attack yesterday morning and is in the hospital."

"Shit," he said.

She nodded and rubbed at the logo on the front of her shirt. It said "Cinders Cleaning" in bright yellow lettering, and she traced the letters absentmindedly.

"When Belle got home last night, she found him unconscious on the floor. The doctor said he would have died if she had been even an hour later."

She gave him an anxious look. "Belle called me, and I spent the night at the hospital with her, but I needed to go to work. My stepmother, she," a fleeting look of anger crossed her face, "she wouldn't give me the day off and threatened to fire me if I missed work. Belle's all alone at the hospital, Bennett. I couldn't get a hold of Rowan, but she worked last night and is probably sleeping. Belle shouldn't be alone right now."

She glanced at his naked chest. "I'm sorry. I know it's early, but I didn't have your cell number, and Belle wouldn't give it to me. She said I shouldn't bother you and would call you later to explain why she missed work. But she needs you, Bennett. I know she does."

"I'll go over there right now," he said.

"He's in room 115," she said with relief. "Thank you, Bennett."

She started down the porch steps, looking over her shoulder when he called her name.

"Thank you for telling me," he said.

"You're welcome."

BELLE RUBBED AT HER FOREHEAD AS SHE LEANED BACK IN the chair. Her head throbbed, she was nauseous, and her eyes were swollen from crying. She stared at her father sleeping soundly in the hospital bed. They had moved him from the ICU at two thirty this morning, after he had woken and, surprisingly, asked for something to eat. The heart attack had been mild, but if she hadn't gotten home when she did...

Her entire body shuddered, and she began to cry again. She was crying for her father and, selfishly, for herself. Despite what she had told Bennett, she had hoped that a relationship would develop between them. Her father nearly dying had proven to her that it was impossible. He couldn't take care of himself, and she should never have left him alone last night. He had almost died because of her.

Once he was settled in his room, she repeatedly apologized while crying softly and steadily. Her father had also cried and tried to reassure her that it wasn't her fault. He promised her he would never drink again, but she knew it was a lie. How many times had he made that promise? A hundred? A thousand? He had been an alcoholic for nearly twenty years, and although this had scared him badly, the need for alcohol was too strong. The doctor had given him brochures about different rehab facilities during his early morning rounds, and her father had looked through them, but she could already see his need for a drink on his face.

She tried to stop crying as her head throbbed and pulsed. Her father needed her help, and her wish for a life with Bennett was pointless. She couldn't leave her father, and even if Bennett changed his mind and wanted a relationship, her constant care and worry for her father would eventually drive a wedge between them. She couldn't fully invest in a relationship with someone when she couldn't leave her father's side.

"Mirabelle?"

His low voice snapped her head up, and she stared in disbelief as Bennett walked into the room.

"Wh-what are you doing here?" she whispered.

"Ella dropped by the house on her way to work," he said.

"She shouldn't have done that."

"Yes, she should have." He crouched in front of her and placed his hands on her knees. "How are you holding up, honey?"

Her face crumpled, and he pulled her into his embrace. She clung to him, sobbing softly into his throat as he rubbed her back and made soothing sounds. After nearly five minutes, she pushed away and snatched a tissue from the box on the tray next to her father's bed. She wiped her face and blew her nose before giving him a watery smile.

"I'm sorry."

"You have nothing to be sorry about," he said. "How's your dad doing?"

"Better," she said as she glanced at the sleeping man. "All things considered, he's pretty lucky."

"You should have called me, honey."

"Why?" She asked, her lips trembling. "What good would that have done?"

He winced and brushed back a strand of her dark hair caught in her mouth. "Because I care about you, Mirabelle."

"Do you?" she said.

"Yes. Honey, I was wrong about what I said earlier. I want a relationship with you. I realize this isn't the best timing, but knowing that you were here at the hospital, worried and afraid, and didn't think you could call me, made me realize what a fool I've been. I want to be with you, Mirabelle."

THE LAST THING BENNETT EXPECTED WHEN HE TOLD Mirabelle he wanted a relationship was for her to burst into sobs.

Panic gripped him, and he rubbed her arms. "Honey, don't cry, please."

"It's too late," she sobbed.

"Don't say that," he said. "It isn't too late."

"It is," she cried. "Don't you understand, Bennett? My father almost died because I wasn't there. I had a moment of selfishness, and it nearly killed him. I can't – I can't be with you. I have to take care of my father. I'm all he has."

"I'll help you take care of him," he said.

She barked bitter laughter. "No, that isn't fair to you."

"I don't care," he said. "I'll do whatever it takes to be with you, Mirabelle. I mean that."

"I can't ask you to do that," she said. "Eventually, his disease will take over our lives, and you'll resent me for it. I don't want that."

"It won't happen that way," he said. He cupped her face and pressed a kiss against her mouth. "Let me be there for you."

"No. You deserve better than me."

"Mirabelle," he said in frustration, "I'm a grown man. I can make that decision for myself."

"You're blinded by your lust right now," she said. "That will fade, and you'll see I'm right."

"It's not just lust," he said. "It's more than that. It's lo -"

"No!" She stood and gave him an angry look. "Don't you dare say it, Bennett. Not now. Not after I've just told you that we can't be together."

She bent and pressed a kiss against her father's forehead. "I'll be back later, Daddy."

"Mirabelle, wait," Bennett said.

"I'm exhausted, and I have a throbbing headache, and I need to go home and have a hot shower and a nap. Please, stay away from me, Bennett. Don't make this harder than it already is."

She started to cry again before running from the room. He collapsed in the chair and stared numbly at his hands. He had lost her. He had lost her because he had waited too long to tell her how he felt.

"Well, I really fucked up this time, didn't I, son?"

The gravel-rough voice made his bear growl, and Ben stared at Belle's father as the man pushed a button, and the head of his bed rose with a soft hum.

"You're awake," Bennett said.

"Yes. Heard everything that just happened."

The old man sighed and rubbed briefly at his chest before staring at the IV in his arm. "I've destroyed my girl's life. There was a time when she was the most important thing in my world, and now I've hurt her so much she'll never forgive me."

"Yes, she will," Bennett said, the anger seeping in. "Don't go feeling sorry for yourself, Maurice. You have Mirabelle doing exactly what you want her to do."

Maurice glared at him. "You think this is what I want for my child? You think I don't want her to be happy, to find love and raise a family?"

"You can't see past a bottle," Bennett said. "You don't care about Mirabelle. All you care about is when you'll get your next drink."

Maurice's face fell, and he gave Bennett a look of shame. "You're right."

Bennett stood, but before he could leave, Maurice said, "Why didn't you want a relationship with Belle until now?"

"It doesn't matter," he said. "Goodbye, Maurice."

He stalked toward the door, his body stiffening when Maurice said, "Is it because you're a bear shifter?"

He turned his head, the tendons in his neck creaking, and stared at Belle's father. "What did you say?"

"Sit down. Just for a minute, would you?" Maurice asked.

Bennett closed the door before returning to the chair. "Why do you think I'm a bear shifter?"

"Because my girl said you were, and she's not a liar," Maurice said.

"There is no such thing as a shifter," Bennett said.

"No?" Maurice cocked his eyebrow at him. "Well, that seems mighty strange to me considering I was married to one."

Bennett's mouth dropped open, and a small smile crossed Maurice's face.

"You – Mirabelle's mother was a shifter?"

Maurice nodded. "A tiger shifter."

"But Mirabelle, she's human ...."

Maurice nodded. "Yes, she got my genes, not her mother's."

"She doesn't know," Bennett said.

"No. Her mother and I decided we would wait to tell her when she was older - when it was easier for her to understand - but then her mother died."

"You should have told her anyway," Bennett said. "Why didn't you?"

"I meant to," Maurice said. "But then that business with you started up, and I saw how the townfolk looked at my girl."

"They thought she was crazy," Bennett said. "You could have told her she wasn't, could have helped her understand that -"

"Don't you think I know that?" Maurice snapped. "I

128

should have told her. Hell, there are many things I should have done when it came to her, but I started drinking, and nothing else seemed to matter after that."

Bennett stared numbly at him. "Did my parents know?"

"About my wife?"

He nodded, and Maurice shook his head. "No. My wife was a stay-at-home mother, and she didn't much like to socialize with other shifters. You know how the tiger shifters are."

Bennett sat silently. He wasn't surprised by that. Tiger shifters were loners and rarely had anything to do with shifters outside of their kind.

"I've fucked up a lot of things in my life, and most of it has hurt Belle terribly," Maurice said. "I'm asking you - no, I'm *begging* you - to not give up on her. That girl has loved you since she was seven years old. Even a drunk fool like me could see that."

"She won't have anything to do with me," Bennett said. "You heard what she said."

"I did." Maurice grabbed one of the rehab brochures with a trembling hand and stared fixedly at it. "If she knew she didn't have to worry about me, if she knew that I was finally taking care of myself, I bet she'd change her mind."

"You want to go to rehab?" Bennett asked.

"I'm an old man, and I've ruined most of my life and my daughter's life, and I'm afraid that it's too late for me to change, but, yeah, I want to go to rehab."

"I'll pay for it," Bennett said. "If you're serious about this, I'll cover the costs."

Maurice frowned at him. "That's generous of you, but I can't accept it."

"You won't be able to go if you don't," Bennett said. "I'm not trying to get rid of you, Maurice, I'm not. I want you to get healthy so you can be a part of Belle's life, a part of *our* life, instead of being a burden to her."

Maurice winced and then sighed deeply. "Well, that stung a little, but I can't say I didn't deserve it."

He studied the brochure again before holding out his hand. "You have yourself a deal, Bennett Saxby. Now, go to my daughter and tell her the truth."

"That I'm a bear shifter?"

Maurice smiled a little. "You can start with that – don't say anything about her mama yet, I'll tell her before I go to rehab – but that's not what I was talking about. Tell her the truth about your love for her."

"I do love her," Bennett said hoarsely. "I've loved her for eighteen years."

"Then tell her," Maurice said.

BELLE TIGHTENED THE BELT ON HER ROBE AND STARED INTO the fridge. She should eat something, she knew she should, but even though her headache had subsided, her stomach was rolling with nausea and the thought of eating made her want to vomit. She would have a nap and then try to eat before going back to the hospital.

She closed the fridge and turned, shrieking and staggering back when she caught sight of Bennett through the screen door, his hand raised to knock.

"Mirabelle!" He opened the door and hurried inside as she leaned against the counter and rested her hand against her pounding heart.

"Oh my God, Bennett. Stop doing that to me!"

"I'm sorry, honey," he said. He reached out to touch her, and she shrank back.

"Don't, Bennett."

Hurt crossed his face, and she gave him a pleading look. "Please don't look at me that way. I – I don't mean to hurt you. I really don't. We can't be together. Why can't you accept that?"

He turned and started for the door, and her heart sank despite what she had said. Fuck, she couldn't live without him. She really couldn't. It felt like her heart was being ripped out of her chest, and she stared in confusion when he closed the inside door and locked it. He went into the living room and closed the curtains.

"Bennett? What are you doing?"

"I have something to tell you and show you, honey," he said.

He started stripping off his clothes, and she closed her eyes. "Bennett, I'm not in the mood to be seduced."

Why not? What better way to forget your problems than having Bennett Saxby in your bed? C'mon, Belle, do this for me.

He chuckled, and her eyes flew open. "What's so funny?"

He just smiled, and she stared greedily at his cock when he pushed his briefs down and stepped out of them.

"Stop looking at me like that, Mirabelle, or I won't be able to stop myself from fucking you," he said warningly as he stood completely naked in her living room.

She tore her gaze away from his crotch and scowled at him. "Bennett, this isn't the time to…."

Her voice died off in a whispery moan as Bennett closed his eyes. His body swelled, and dark fur sprouted across his body and face. His nails lengthened and thickened before turning black, and fangs extended from his mouth with a soft pop. In less than ten seconds, Bennett Saxby was gone, and a massive grizzly bear stood in his place. She stared unblinkingly at the bear as it dropped to all fours and moved slowly to her.

He sniffed at her hand before nudging it with his giant head. Numbly she raised her hand and scratched the side of his face, digging her fingers into the thick fur as he made a chuffing noise of pleasure and leaned his cheek against her hand.

"Holy shit," she said, and the bear chuffed again before shuffling back.

Ben shifted to his human form and said, "Are you okay, Mirabelle?"

"I knew it!" she shouted. "I knew you were a fucking bear!"

He winced and held up his hands. "Honey, shh."

She glanced at the closed front door. "Shit. I'm sorry."

She dropped her voice and whispered, "I knew you were a fucking bear."

His smile disappeared when she stalked forward and whacked him in the stomach. "That's for lying to me!"

He acted like he'd barely felt the blow, but she cursed under her breath and held her throbbing hand. He took it and massaged it gently. "I'm sorry I lied to you, Mirabelle."

"Why did you?" she asked.

"My father had it drilled into me from a very young age that I couldn't ever let humans know what I really was. That I would be taken away from him and Mom and dissected in a lab."

"Oh, Bennett," she said softly. She took a step toward him, and he put his arm around her waist and pulled her into his embrace.

"I wanted to tell you," he said. "I begged my father to let me talk to you, that I could convince you not to tell anyone, but he was afraid. He made us pack up our things and leave the day after the attack."

"I won't tell anyone," she said. "I promise you."

"I know," he said. "I trust you, Mirabelle. I just wish things could have been different."

"Me too," she said as he rested his forehead against hers. "You said you had something to tell me and show me. What did you want to tell me?"

He pulled his head back and studied her carefully. "You just found out that shifters exist. You're being remarkably calm about it."

She shrugged. "I always knew, Bennett. Even after you came back and denied it, there was a part of me that just knew." She paused, "Are there other kinds of shifters?"

He nodded, and a small smile crossed her face. "Other shifters in our town?"

He hesitated before nodding again, and she squeezed his arms gently. "You don't have to tell me who. But I want to know what you wanted to tell me."

He took a deep breath and said, "I love you, Mirabelle. I've been in love with you since I was nine years old."

"I love you too," she said.

He smiled and bent to kiss her. She pulled her head back and said, "But it doesn't change anything. I still can't be with you."

"Your father is going to rehab."

"What?"

"Your father was awake while we were talking and heard everything. After you left, we talked, and he said he knew how much he had messed up and wanted to go to rehab."

"Oh my God," she said. "Are you being serious?"

"I am," he said. "I'll pay for him to go to rehab."

"Ben, I can't let you do that," she said.

"You can and you will," he said. "Besides, it's not up to you. I've already discussed it with your dad, and he's agreed to let me pay for it."

He leaned down and kissed her, igniting a spark of hope deep in her belly. "I love you, Mirabelle, and I'm not letting you go. Ever. Your dad will get help, he'll get better, and if he doesn't – we'll handle it together. Okay?"

She started to cry, and he wiped at her tears with his thumbs. "Don't cry, honey."

"I love you," she said again. "I love you so much."

He lifted her and hugged her tightly as she buried her face in his neck. After a few minutes, she raised her head and smiled at him. "Take me to bed, Bennett."

"You do look pretty tired," he teased.

"Keep talking like that, and I'll take away the honey for a week."

He growled at her, and she giggled. "You don't scare me, little bear."

He kissed her again, his tongue slipping into her mouth as his hands moved to her ass and squeezed. "I love you, Mirabelle Vale."

"I love you, Bennett Saxby."

Keep reading for Ella's and Duncan's story in "Ella".

VOLUME TWO

ELLA

ELLA

Ella Cinders is looking for a fresh start. Tired of working for her stepmother's cleaning company and anxious to start her massage therapy business, she'll do anything – even accept Duncan Gillis as a client.

She hates the arrogant, golden-haired playboy who pulled her braids when they were children and witnessed her most humiliating moment, so why does his touch make her blood burn?

Why does his insistence that she belongs to him make her want to join him in his bed?

And why does *her* touch make him purr?

PROLOGUE

She fought bitterly against them as they dragged her toward the closet. She tried to scream, but the sound was muffled against a palm. She tried to punch and kick, but the girls were older and stronger than her. They shoved her into the closet, their girlish laughter shrill and unpleasant and slammed the door behind her.

"No!" she screamed and pulled uselessly at the door handle before pounding on the door so hard it made her hands throb. The door didn't budge, and she backed away, sobbing and panting. She screamed again when her back hit the metal shelf, and small paint tubs and boxes of coloured pencils tumbled down onto her. She twisted to her left and banged into the wall before sliding to her butt and clutching her chest.

It was recess, and she had snuck into the art room, telling herself she wanted to admire the work of the older boys and girls, not hide from her stepsisters and their gang of friends. It was partially true. Although she didn't have any skill in drawing or painting, she was fascinated by those who did. Still, if she was completely honest, she had wanted just one recess where she wasn't tormented and figured the art room was the perfect place to hide.

She was wrong, terribly wrong. The older girls had entered the room giggling and laughing, intent on taunting her. She had tried to dodge past them, but they had caught her. It was easy to do when it was five against one. It was her stepsister, Ana, who had suggested they lock her in the art supply closet. She knew of Ella's fear of the dark and enclosed spaces. Of course, she did. It was Ana who had shoved her into the tiny closet in her bedroom and locked her in there for hours when Ella was only three.

She screamed again, and one of the girls pounded on the door. "Be quiet in there, or we'll never let you out!"

Her seven-year-old brain panicked at the thought of being trapped forever, and she staggered to her feet and ran forward blindly. She banged into the shelf again, and more bottles tumbled down to strike her in the face. She slammed her fists repeatedly on the door, sobbing loudly as terror knifed through her. She was trapped like a rat in a cage. As fresh panic filled her body, her bladder let go, and warm wetness flooded her crotch.

She shrieked again. Her voice was hoarse and her throat raw. When the door opened unexpectedly, she pitched forward onto her knees in the bright classroom.

"You okay, Ella?"

His voice sent fresh embarrassment through her, and her cheeks, red from crying, turned brighter. Why did it have to be him? Her hair hung in her face, and she stared at him through the golden strands. Duncan Gillis, his hair as blond as hers and his blue eyes filled with worry, stared back at her.

Tears streaming down her cheeks, snot dripping from her nose, she cried out like a wounded animal when his hand gripped her arm and pulled her gently to her feet. He had freed her from her cage, but at this moment, she was almost tempted to run back into it. She hadn't told anyone, not even her best friends Belle and Rowan, that she had a crush on the boy who pulled her braids nearly every day. She would never admit that she liked the attention of the handsome nine-year-old. For him to see her now was almost more than she could take.

"Ella, are you okay?" he repeated.

"She's fine," her stepsister said with a shrill laugh. "She's just a big baby who…."

Ana suddenly screamed laughter and pointed to Ella's crotch. "She peed her pants! She peed her pants!"

The other girls stared and joined in the laughter, pointing and giggling as Ella cried harder.

"Shut up, all of you!" Duncan snapped. "Ella, don't cry. It's okay. Just don't cry, please."

He glanced at the wet spot on the front of her jeans, and her fragile control broke. She yanked her arm from his hand and fled for the classroom door, her stepsister's cruel laughter echoing down the hallway.

CHAPTER 1

"**E**lla? You okay?"

Ella Cinders jerked wildly and took a step back as her best friend Rowan grabbed her arm.

"Hey, what's wrong?"

"Nothing," she said quickly. She stared at the closet in Belle's bedroom, well, technically, it was Belle's and Bennett's bedroom now, holding onto the stack of Belle's shirts like it was a lifeline.

It was a large walk-in closet, but even the thought of going in there filled her with panic and brought on the painful childhood memory of being locked in the dark.

"Here, give them to me," Rowan said abruptly.

"It's fine. I'm just acting like a baby," Ella said.

"It's no big deal, honey." Rowan plucked the stack of shirts from her grip and walked into the closet. She set them on a shelf and returned to Ella, closing the door behind her. "Come downstairs with me. Belle's making us lunch."

Ella followed Rowan down the maze of hallways.

"God," Rowan said, "I don't know how she doesn't get

lost in this place. We're going in the right direction, aren't we?"

Ella laughed and pointed to the hallway that snaked to the left. "That way leads to the stairs."

Rowan grinned at her and hooked her arm around Ella's. "I'm so happy for Belle. Aren't you?"

"Yes," Ella said. "She deserves this."

Three weeks ago, her best friend Belle started dating Bennett Saxby. Bennett had just moved back to their small town after being gone for eighteen years. Ella knew better than anyone how much Belle missed him.

Belle had only met him once as a child, but he'd saved her life that day, and she'd never forgotten him. After his return, things had started a bit rocky between them, but Belle and Bennett officially became a couple within a couple of weeks.

They walked into the kitchen, and Ella plopped down into a chair as Belle stirred the pasta salad. There were cold cuts, cheese, and crackers on a large platter on the table, and Ella helped herself to some cheese as Belle grinned at her and Rowan.

"Thank you again for helping me move into Bennett's. I owe you."

"No problem," Rowan said. The slender redhead sat in the chair next to Ella's and ate a piece of cheese. "You sure you're ready to be living with someone, Belle-baby?"

Belle nodded. "Yes. I know it's quick, but I love Bennett and hate staying at the trailer alone. Besides, with Dad in rehab, there's no need for me even to stay there."

"How's that going?" Ella asked.

"Good. Bennett and I went up yesterday to visit him. It's the first time we've seen him since he left. The center cautioned against family visiting the first two weeks, so we waited until Dad asked us to come. He's twenty-five days sober."

"That's awesome," Rowan said.

"It is," Belle said happily. "I know it's been difficult for him. He was honest with us about how much he was struggling, but he still seemed to be in a better place. Once his sixty days are done, he's thinking of moving to a sober-living facility for a while. He says there will be too much temptation if he comes back home, at least at first."

"Where is Bennett anyway?" Rowan asked.

"He's over at Duncan's. Duncan bought a new TV, and Bennett is helping him mount it to the wall," Belle said.

"Don't take this the wrong way, Belle," Rowan said, "but does Bennett even work? He seems to have plenty of money, but what exactly does he do?"

Belle laughed. "Well, he has family money, but he also is a bit of a genius in investing. He's increased his family wealth substantially with some smart investment decisions. It's allowed him to retire early, as he puts it."

"I'll say. The guy's twenty-seven and retired already. That's like my damn dream," Rowan said. "Maybe I should get him to teach me some investment shit. I'm getting tired of working at Gaston's."

She nudged Ella, "Maybe you should talk to him about investing too. It could help you with your business."

"Yeah, maybe," Ella said.

"Ella? What's wrong?" Belle said.

"You mentioned Duncan, that's what's wrong," Rowan said cheekily. "You know she gets all hot and bothered just hearing his name."

"Cork it, Ro," Ella said. "How many times do I have to tell you I hate that guy before you believe me?"

Rowan leaned forward and pinched her cheek affectionately. "At least a thousand more times, sweet Ella. Actions speak louder than words, you know."

"What's that supposed to mean?" Ella said.

"It means I can practically see your hooch go into over-drive whenever Duncan Gillis is near. I'm surprised you don't start dry humping him whenever you're near him."

"Rowan!" Ella said as Belle burst into laughter.

"What? It's nothing to be ashamed of. Duncan Gillis is a good-looking guy," Rowan said.

"Yeah? Then why aren't you sleeping with him?" Ella asked.

"Because I know you like him," Rowan said. "Plus, he's never shown any interest in me. He likes the girls with the big boobs and booties."

"I don't like him," Ella said through gritted teeth. "He tormented me as a child and -"

"Yeah, because he liked you," Rowan said.

"And," Ella glared at her, "he saw me at the worst possible moment of my life."

"Honey, you were seven years old and had just been locked in a closet. You're claustrophobic. Of course it was going to upset you."

"I wet my damn pants, and he saw it!" Ella said.

"So what? You were seven," Rowan said with a shrug. "You remember last year when the fair came to town? I told Jim I didn't want to go on that damn roller coaster, but he insisted. I peed my pants because I was so freaked out."

"You did not," Ella said.

"I totally did," Rowan said.

Laughing so hard her face was red, Belle said, "What did you do?"

"I made Jim take me home, I had a quick shower, and

then I fucked his brains out," Rowan said cheerfully. "He didn't care that I had just wet my pants."

"It isn't just the whole 'pants wetting' thing," Ella said. "The guy's a playboy, and I'm so not interested in becoming another one of his conquests. How many notches do you think he has on his headboard?"

"Probably as many as I do," Rowan said with a grin.

Belle laughed again as the front door slammed, and Bennett called, "Mirabelle? I'm home."

"We're in the kitchen!" she shouted.

He strolled into the room and planted a soft kiss on Belle's mouth before smiling at Ella and Rowan. "Ladies."

"Hey, big guy," Rowan said. "How's it going?"

"Good," he said.

"You're finished earlier than I thought," Belle said. "The girls and I are finished unpacking, and I was going to work in the library this afternoon."

"It didn't take long to get the TV set up, and Duncan had a few errands to run." Bennett grabbed a handful of crackers.

"Well, you're just in time for lunch," Belle said as Ella stood. "Ella? You're leaving?"

Ella nodded. "Yes. I need to stop at the post office. My new business cards have arrived. I want to drop off some of them at Dr. Mitchell's office before I have the weekly Friday night dinner torture with my stepmother and stepsisters."

"Ella's starting her own massage therapy business," Belle said to Bennett.

"Nice," Bennett said. "Do you have a space in town?"

She shook her head. "No, I'm going to do it out of my home, or I can go to the person's home."

"Have massage table, will travel," Rowan said with a grin. "It's a brilliant idea, Ella."

"You should book an appointment with Ella." Belle

nudged Bennett. "All that gardening you do - it's bound to affect your back."

"Uh, yeah, sure," Bennett said with a remarkable lack of enthusiasm.

Ella smiled briefly. "Anyway, I'm going to go. Are we still on for coffee on Sunday morning?"

Belle and Rowan nodded, and she waved to them before leaving.

BELLE GAVE BENNETT A GENTLE POKE WHEN SHE HEARD THE front door close behind Ella. "What was that about?"

"What?" he asked.

"You could have shown a bit more excitement about hiring Ella for a massage," she said. "I've had a few of her massages, and trust me, they're amazing. She finds tense muscles I didn't even know I had."

"Sorry," Bennett said, "but I'm not into having my best friend beat the crap out of me. If he found out I touched Ella, he'll have my head on a pole."

"Technically, Ella will be touching you," Rowan said, "so you should be safe from Duncan's fists of fury."

"Yeah, well, Duncan isn't exactly level-headed regarding Ella."

"God, I wish those two would hurry up and fuck already," Rowan said. "It's obvious they both are attracted as hell to each other. Why torture themselves?"

"Do you think Duncan will cause trouble with Ella's new business?" Belle said worriedly. "I mean, his obsession with her is somewhat adorable, and it's cute in a bar scenario when he tells any guy in the place that she belongs to him. But if he starts trying to beat up men who book her for a massage appointment, Ella really will hate him. She can't keep working for her stepmother forever, not with how that bitch treats her. She's damn good at massage therapy. It's her dream to have her own business."

"I'll talk to him," Bennett said. "I can't guarantee it will help, but maybe if he knows how important this is to her, he'll cool it with the caveman behaviour."

"Thank you, honey," Belle said before planting a kiss on his cheek.

"You've got two packages," Karen said.

"Two?" Ella stared in confusion at the short, silver-haired woman who'd run the post office for as long as she could remember.

"Yep." Karen had her sign a form before handing her the large envelope and the brown paper-wrapped box.

She took them with a nod of thanks and sat down on the low wooden bench that flanked one wall of the post office. She tore off the paper and peeled back the tape before opening the box. A smile crossed her face as she pulled out the glittery, silver shoe with the narrow, tapered heel. She had forgotten that after too much wine and Rowan's encouragement, she had ordered these for the Centennial Celebration. She touched the shoe's fabric before setting the box on the bench beside her. The bell jingled over the door, but Ella didn't look up at Karen's low murmur of greeting. Her fingers trembling, she ripped open the top of the envelope. She reached in and pulled out one of the stacks of cards held together with a rubber band.

She stared happily at the business cards before taking the band off and fanning them out in her hand. She'd ordered them online and was ridiculously happy to be holding them. It made her business seem more real, and a little thrill of excitement, mixed with a tinge of anxiety, went through her. She would take some to Dr. Mitchell's office and maybe a few other businesses in town. Hell, she'd ask Karen if she could leave some here. She needed to do as much marketing as she could.

"I like the shoes."

Her eyes widened, and she glanced up as Duncan Gillis, his thick blond hair gleaming in the sunlight from the wide front window, picked up the box of shoes and sat distractingly close to her. He studied the shoes as she scowled at him.

"What are you doing here?"

"Mailing a parcel?" He raised one eyebrow at her, and she blushed furiously as Karen made a decidedly girlish giggle before lifting the large paper-wrapped parcel off the counter and carrying it into the back room.

"Great shoes," he said again.

"Thanks," she said.

"Buy them for something special?"

She sighed and tried not to notice how the blue of his shirt matched the blue of his eyes perfectly. "The Centennial Celebration."

"So, you're going to that, are you?" he asked.

"Everyone in town is going," she said.

"True. Would you like to go with me?"

She gave him a blank look of surprise. "What?"

"Would you like to go to the Centennial Celebration with me?" Duncan said. "You already know I'm a great dancer."

He set the box of shoes on his right side and slid closer until his hard thigh brushed against hers. She tried to move away subtly but was at the end of the bench, and unless she wanted to fall off the end, she was trapped.

"Well, what do you think?" Duncan said in a low, persuasive voice.

"I," her throat was dry, and the heat of his body made her brain malfunction, "I already have a date for the Centennial."

His eyes changed, the blue around his pupil gradually lightening to a strange yellow. She unconsciously leaned a little closer to him. Was he wearing some kind of contacts? But what contacts changed colour seemingly at will?

His eyes were completely yellow at Gaston's. Remember?

Before she could overthink that, Duncan cupped her face with one hard hand and pulled her so close she could feel his warm breath on her lips.

"Who, Ella?"

"What?" She couldn't seem to look away from his rapidly changing eyes. Were his pupils narrowing into slits?

"Who's the asshole taking you to the Centennial? Tell me."

She swallowed heavily as his thumb stroked the curve of her jaw. "Tell me who will be," his eyes dropped to her cleavage, and her nipples hardened against her bra, "touching you. Kissing you. Taking you to his bed."

He said the last word on a growl, his hand tightening around her jaw, and she squeaked, "Rowan."

Now it was his turn to stare. "What?"

"Rowan is my date for the celebration. We're going together. I won't be, uh, kissing her or, um, sleeping with her though," she finished stupidly.

He dropped his gaze for a moment, and when he looked at her again, his eyes were their usual blue, and his pupils were round. "Good. Well, I'll be there, so save me a dance."

"I'm not dancing with you again," she said.

He grinned at her before plucking one of the cards from her hand.

"Hey! Give that back." She tried to reach for the card, huffing angrily when he held it out of her reach as he read it.

"Healing Hands Massage Therapy. Owner, Ella Cinders. You're a masseuse?" He gave her a decidedly wicked grin.

"It's therapeutic massage, pervert," she muttered.

He stared thoughtfully at her. "You worked at the spa before it closed, right?"

"Yes."

Even though he'd never once come into the spa in the three short months she worked there, she wasn't surprised he knew. There were no secrets in their small town.

"I didn't realize you were doing massage," he said. "I would have stopped by. I've got some tight muscles."

An image of Duncan lying naked in her bed as she straddled him and rubbed oil all over his hard body made her blush to her hair roots. His nostrils flared lightly, and he grinned at her. She had a feeling he knew exactly what she was thinking, and she scowled again at him.

"Give me my card back, please."

"Are you starting your own business?"

"Yes," she said stiffly.

"Where's your office?"

"I don't have one," she said. She was suddenly nervous that he would think her idea of using her apartment or going to a client's home was stupid. "I'm doing something a little different. I'll be travelling to a client's home to give them a massage. It'll be easier for my clients and may help them relax more if they're in their own home."

He didn't reply, and she cleared her throat. "I can also do a massage therapy session at my home. It'll be whatever the client prefers."

"It's a good idea," he said.

"Do you think so?" she asked tentatively.

He nodded. "Yes, I think you'll get a lot of business that way."

"Thanks."

"In fact," he brushed the card against the tip of her nose, "you just got your first client."

"What?" She shook her head. "No, I told you – it's therapeutic massage, not...."

Her face flushed again as he laughed. "I get it, sweetheart. I'll be on my best behaviour."

He slipped her business card into his pocket as he stood. "How about Monday evening at seven?"

"Duncan, I..."

"I'll email you tomorrow to confirm it. See you later, Ella Cinders," he said with a small wink before strolling out of the post office.

Ella stared blankly at the cards still in her hands. She had just gotten her very first client. Why the hell did it have to be Duncan Gillis?

CHAPTER 2

"You're late, Ella." Her stepmother gave her a disapproving look over her glasses. She was a coldly handsome woman with silver-streaked hair and a tall, slender figure.

"I'm sorry, Mother." Ella tried to keep her voice pleasant. "The pipes under the kitchen sink are leaking again, and I had some clean-up to do."

Her stepsister, Ana, tapped one finger against the kitchen counter. "You always have an excuse for everything."

She turned to her younger sister, Dru, who was stealing a piece of beef from the platter on the counter and poked her viciously in the side. "If you keep stuffing your face with food like that, you'll be as fat as Ella."

"Shut up, Ana!" Dru whined. "Mom, make her shut up!"

"Be nice to your sister, Ana," Edith said as she set the salad bowl on the table.

"She started it," Ana said sourly.

Ella could barely stop from rolling her eyes. Ana was two years older, and Dru was her age, but both still lived with their mother. They also worked at the cleaning company, but,

155

unlike Ella, neither had aspirations to do something different. The three women had a disturbing codependent relationship, and Ella doubted the two sisters would ever marry or leave the nest.

"Mother," Ana said as the four of them sat at the table. "I need next Friday off."

"Of course, my pet," Edith said as she pulled the bowl of roasted potatoes from Ella's grip and handed her the salad. "No carbs for you, Ella."

Ella smiled stiffly. "How was your day, Mother?"

"Fine, busy," she said. "You'll have to cover Ana's houses on Friday."

"It's my day off," Ella reminded her.

"So?" Ana snapped. "You don't have any plans. You never do. You'll just sit in your stupid apartment like you always do."

Ignoring her stepsister, Ella said, "Speaking of apartments – can you have a plumber come in and look at the pipes under the sink? The leak is getting worse, and some weird noises are coming from the pipes."

"It's not my responsibility," Edith said as she passed the potatoes to Dru. "Eat up, my love."

"It kind of is. You're my landlord," Ella said.

Her stepmother immediately bristled, and Ella groaned inwardly. She knew better than to provoke the woman, but the pipes did need to be looked at, and she couldn't afford it. Her credit card was maxed out thanks to the purchase of her massage table and other supplies for her business.

"I let you live in that apartment at a very reasonable rent, and still you complain. Where else are you going to live in this town where you only pay three hundred for your place, Ella?"

"Nowhere," Ella said.

"Exactly! Do you know how much money I could make if I rented the apartment to a stranger? Rentals are in high demand, and your little apartment is charming and in a great location."

Ella bit her tongue to stop her sharp retort. The apartment did have its charms – if you liked living in a bachelor suite barely three hundred and fifty square feet, cold in the winter, and every morning when her stepmother started up her car in the garage below, it smelled a little like car exhaust fumes.

"You're costing me money, Ella, but do I complain?" Her stepmother was on a roll now, and Ella knew from experience that it was best to let her get all her vitriol out. "No, I don't. Not even my child, and yet I've clothed you, sheltered you, worried about you from the moment your father died and left me saddled with a child who wasn't even mine. I could have sent you off to foster care, Ella, I had enough troubles of my own, but I didn't, did I?"

She waited for an answer, and Ella, hating that she felt guilty, said, "No, you didn't."

"No, because I'm not the monster you think I am. Anyone else in this town would have washed their hands of you. For years I've treated you like you were one of my own daughters, and this is the thanks I get. You're going to sit at my table, eating my food, and complain to me that the apartment I so generously allow you to live in isn't good enough?"

Edith's face was pale with fury now, and Ella, her guilt and the decades-old need to try to please the only mother she'd ever known pulsing through her, shook her head. "I'm sorry, Mother. I didn't mean to complain."

Her stepmother, chest heaving and eyes cold chips of blue, stared silently at her before giving a slight nod. "That's better. I swear I don't know what gets into you, Ella. You're the most ungrateful child I've ever met."

Dru took a few noisy gulps of wine. "Mom, I need to borrow a couple of hundred bucks."

"For what?" Edith said sharply.

Dru flinched at her tone. "I need to get my make-up and hair done for the Centennial Celebration."

Her mother softened, "Oh, of course, my darling. We need you looking your loveliest. The whole town will be there."

Dru smiled at her, and Ella snorted inwardly. While Ana was gorgeous with her slender figure, shiny dark hair, and light blue eyes, Dru was short and a little, well, unfortunate looking. Her dark hair was almost straw-like, and her bulbous nose and acne-riddled face wasn't doing her any favours. It would take much more than make-up and a new hairstyle to fix her looks.

Unkind, Ella!

She flinched a little. Yes, it was unkind, and another bout of guilt blossomed inside her. She smiled at Dru. "Who are you going with to the Centennial Celebration?"

Dru glared at her. "None of your business, Ella. God, you're so nosy."

"I'm going with Duncan Gillis," Ana suddenly announced, and Ella's heart dropped to her stomach.

"You – he asked you to go with him?" Ella said. "When?"

"He hasn't asked me yet, but he will," Ana said.

"Of course, he will, my pet." Edith patted her oldest daughter's hand. "You're so lovely. How can he resist?"

"He's resisted so far," Dru snickered and shrieked when Ana hit her on the back of the head.

"Shut up, Dru!"

"Mom!" Dru wailed indignantly as she rubbed her skull.

"Girls, be nice to each other," Edith said.

"I ran into Duncan earlier this morning, and he could

hardly keep his eyes off me," Ana said with a pleased smile. "He's so handsome, don't you think?"

Relief coursing through her, Ella couldn't help herself. "I'm surprised you're not going with Marty."

Ana rolled her eyes. "Are you still upset about me sleeping with Marty? God, get over it, Ella. He came on to me, and besides, it's not my fault the men you date find me more attractive. Try hitting the gym occasionally, and maybe you'll be able to keep your man."

Ella's face turned a brilliant shade of red, and she clenched her hands into tight fists. She wanted to reach across the table and punch Ana in the face. Instead, she forced her gaze to her plate of untouched food.

Let it go, Ella. It doesn't matter.

She took a few deep breaths as Ana smiled at her mother. "On Friday, Duncan plays basketball with a few other men at the rec center. I'm just going to happen to be there in that new red dress. When he sees me in it, I won't be surprised if he asks me to the celebration right then and there."

"Why the sudden interest in Duncan Gillis?" Ella asked.

"It's not sudden, Ella. The man's gorgeous and the most eligible bachelor in the whole damn town. I'm tired of playing the field. It's time to settle down with the right man, and I've chosen Duncan. We're perfect for each other."

She gave Edith a dreamy little smile, "Can you imagine how beautiful our children will be, Mother?"

They would be beautiful, Ella thought sourly. Her stomach was a knot of anger at the thought of Duncan sleeping with her stepsister, but she tried to ignore it. Ana had set her sights on Duncan, and what Ana wanted, Ana got. Duncan wouldn't be able to resist her for long. She did not doubt that Ana's charms would win him over. She wasn't as confident as Ana seemed to be that she would end up as

Duncan's wife, but he would sleep with her. They always did.

He says you belong to him, remember?

Yeah, so what? The guy was known for his considerable charms when it came to women. It was just a pick-up line and a rather brilliant one at that. Well, at least when it came to Ella. Every time he said those words in his raspy voice, it sent a weird and rather violent tingle of pleasure through her. She'd never been into men who were over-the-top jealous and possessive, but the thought of belonging to Duncan Gillis was an undeniable turn-on.

"We'll be married at the little church on Roven Street," Ana said to her mother. "Navy blue and cream will be my colours, and it will have to be a spring wedding. I want the entire church filled with tulips and -"

"Don't you think it's a little early to plan your wedding?" Ella asked. "You haven't even been on a date with him."

Ana glared at her. "Shut up, Ella. Unlike you, I have no intention of dying a spinster. I actually go after my dreams, and there's nothing wrong with that."

"Ella's going after her dreams," Dru said. "Michelle told me that Karen told her that Ella's started a massage therapy business. She left business cards all over town this afternoon."

"Oh, Ella," her stepmother said with a sigh. "Are you still pursuing that silly dream? I held my tongue when you wasted all that money taking your little massage courses, and I never complained when the girls and I had to cover a few of your shifts but trying to start your own business? This town isn't big enough for that type of business. If it were, the spa wouldn't have closed down, would it?"

Ana poked Dru in the side with her elbow. "Ella's just so desperate to touch a man that she'll probably pay them to let her massage them. How many *happy endings* are you going to hand out, Ella?"

"It's therapeutic massage," Ella said through gritted teeth. "Get your mind out of the gutter, Ana. Therapeutic massage is well-known to help people with chronic pain and -"

"Whatever," Ana said. "No guy will want to be massaged by a fat-ass like you. They want skinny, pretty girls to touch them."

Ella pushed back her chair. Her head was throbbing, her stomach was rolling with nausea, and she'd had all she could take of her family.

"Where are you going?" Edith frowned at her.

"I'm not feeling very well," Ella said. "Thank you for dinner, Mother."

She turned and hurried out of the kitchen.

ROWAN DROPPED THE BANANAS INTO HER BASKET AND wandered out of the produce section. She turned down the first aisle and stared appreciatively at the ass bent over in front of her.

Rafe Taggert. Delicious.

She flushed, a little embarrassed that she could recognize the man by his ass alone, but it didn't stop her from staring eagerly at it as he straightened and placed the can of tomato paste in his cart.

Now's your chance, girl. Go.

She hurried forward as Rafe's body stiffened and his head lifted. He almost seemed to sniff the air before striding forward, pushing the cart in sudden, jerky movements.

"Mr. Taggert?"

Nice, Rowan. Maybe seducing the man would be easier if you called him by his first name. What do you think?

He stopped and cleared his throat as she stood next to him. "Hi."

"Hello, Ms. Jameson," he said politely.

"Please," she said, "we've known each for years. Call me Rowan."

He gave her a stiff smile, and she waited for him to tell her to call him Rafe. Her smile faltered a little when he didn't, and she glanced at his cart. "Doing some grocery shopping?"

Smooth, you idiot.

"Yes," he said.

"Me too," she said. "So, how are you?"

"Very well, thank you. How are you?"

"I'm good. I haven't seen you at Gaston's lately."

He hesitated. "I've been going to the Woodsmen Pub as of late. It's closer to my home."

"I was there a few weeks ago," she said.

"Oh?" he said.

"I saw a wolf."

"A wolf?" He raised his eyebrow at her, and she blushed lightly.

"Yeah, in the parking lot."

"Interesting," he said.

After a moment of awkward silence, he gave her a small smile and started walking. She kept pace with him. "So, what's on the menu for tonight?"

"Risotto," he said.

"I've never had risotto before. Is it good?"

"I like it," he said. There was more silence before he gave her a quick look. "Have you been to visit your grandmother lately?"

She shook her head. "No, but I'm planning on going there this weekend. I'll hear it from Nana when I get there."

A rare grin crossed his face. "Your grandmother has some strong opinions."

"You're telling me," Rowan said. "Do you know her well?"

"Her cabin is close to mine."

"Oh really? I had no idea. Nana never told me."

"Well, I suppose close is relative. I'm about a mile from her place. I drop by every few days to make sure she's doing okay and, secretly, to eat a piece of her delicious apple pie."

Rowan laughed. "She does make amazing pie. I talk to her almost every morning, but the conversation usually centers around how I need to visit her more."

"You used to go there every summer, didn't you?"

"I did. My mom sent me there for a few weeks every July. Between you and me, I think she just wanted a break from me."

He laughed, and she said, "I couldn't imagine why. I was a perfect angel as a teenager."

He laughed again, and she gave him a mock scowl. "Are you doubting my angel claim?"

"Not at all," he said with a slight grin. His gaze drifted over her hair before dropping briefly to her small breasts. That brief look brought butterflies fluttering to life in her stomach. She took a deep breath and threw caution to the wind.

"Mr. Taggert – Rafe – would you like to have a drink with me sometime?"

She rested her hand on his arm, very aware of the hard muscle below her fingers, and he immediately stiffened before pulling away.

"I cannot, Ms. Jameson."

"Why not?" she asked.

"I need to go," he said. "It was nice to see you again, Ms. Jameson. Take care."

He walked away, and she groaned inwardly before turning and walking in the opposite direction. Dammit, why the hell was she so taken with a man who didn't want anything to do with her?

"YOU HAVE YOUR FIRST CLIENT?" BELLE SAID IN DELIGHT. "Honey, that's wonderful! Congratulations!"

"You did hear the part where I said it was Duncan Gillis, right?" Ella said as the waitress set an order of dry toast in front of her.

"What's with just dry toast for breakfast?" Belle asked.

Ella shrugged. "I'm trying to lose some weight."

"Ella, you're the one who's always telling me that beauty comes in every size," Belle said. "Since when have you felt the need to diet? You're perfect just the way you are."

"My blood pressure was a little high at my last check-up, and so was my cholesterol. I'm doing it for health reasons."

She stared at her plate, knowing that Belle and Rowan would see the lie on her face if she didn't. She'd gotten a perfect bill of health at her last doctor's visit. She might have some extra weight, but she exercised regularly and, for the most part, ate a balanced and healthy diet. She was just one of those women with curves, which had never really bothered her. Until that was, Ana had made that comment about people not wanting a fat woman to massage them. What if it was true? She couldn't have her business fail just because of how she looked.

164

"That's weird, isn't it?" Belle said. "You've always been really healthy."

"I guess the extra weight is just catching up to me," Ella mumbled.

"Ella, what -"

"Rowan, you're being quiet," Ella said. "What's up with you?"

"I asked Rafe Taggert out on a date," Rowan said.

"What?" Belle stared wide-eyed at her. "That's awesome!"

"No, it was decidedly not awesome," Rowan said. "I bumped into him at the grocery store yesterday, and we were having a pretty good conversation. Usually, the guy gives a polite hello and moves on, but I thought we were connecting, you know?"

"What happened?" Ella asked.

Rowan propped her chin in her hand. "I asked him if he wanted to have a drink with me, and he couldn't get away from me fast enough. The look on his face…."

She groaned and sipped at her coffee. "I made a fool of myself."

"I'm sure you didn't," Belle said. "Besides, Rafe is interested in you. I know he is."

"He's definitely not," Rowan said. "Seriously, Belle, the guy ran like his ass was on fire."

"I'm sorry, Ro," Ella said.

Rowan shook her head. "It's fine. I tried, he said no. No big deal."

"It seems like a big deal to you," Belle said.

"It isn't," Rowan said. "I don't want to talk about it anymore. I'm getting embarrassed all over again just thinking about it."

She took a bite of her oatmeal before smiling at Ella.

"Congratulations on getting your first client. I'm personally not surprised that it's Duncan. Are you itching to get your hands on that hard body of his or what?"

Ella blushed. "It's therapeutic massage, Ro. I'm going to be professional."

"I know you will, honey," Rowan said. "I'm not trying to suggest that you won't be. I'm just saying that in this particular case, your new career has some added benefits. Plenty of women would love to get their hands on him."

"Plenty of women have, remember?" Ella said dryly.

Belle laughed. "That's true. Duncan does love the ladies. Although, I haven't seen him dating anyone in months. Have you?"

Rowan shook her head. "Now that you mention it, no. He comes into Gaston's regularly, and women hit on him all the time, but he hasn't left with any of them in," she thought back, "at least six months."

"That can't be true," Ella said.

"It is," Rowan said. "I swear it."

"Ana's going after him. I mean, really going after him. She's convinced he'll ask her to the Centennial Celebration, and she's already planning their wedding," Ella said.

"Shocker," Belle said. "I'm surprised it took this long for her to try to sink her claws into him. Don't worry, honey. Duncan won't be interested in someone like her."

"She'll get what she wants," Ella said morosely. "She always does."

"Maybe you should take what you want first," Belle suggested.

"I don't want Duncan Gillis," Ella said. "In fact, if Ana wants him, she can have him."

Rowan glanced at Belle. "Have you ever heard a woman more in denial than our Ella?"

"Nope," Belle said cheerily.

"Subject change," Ella said. "What are you doing after this, Belle?"

"Going home and boinking Bennett's brains out," Belle said.

Ella and Rowan burst out laughing, and Belle gave them a sweetly innocent look. "What? The man's got mad sex skills."

"I'm surprised you can even walk," Rowan said.

Belle laughed before shrugging. "Honestly, if it keeps up the way it is, I'll probably have to book Ella for weekly massage appointments. I need to stay limber."

Ella grinned at her before biting into her piece of toast. "If you book weekly appointments, I'll give you a discount."

"Sweet," Belle said happily. "What time are you going to Duncan's tomorrow?"

"Seven, but he's coming to my place," Ella said. "I was a little surprised because he said my idea of going to clients' homes was a good one."

"Weird," Rowan said. "Maybe he's messy and doesn't want you see his place."

Ella shrugged. "Ana cleans his house every week."

"Really?" Belle said.

"Yeah, didn't I tell you that? He hired Cinders Cleaning a few months ago. Ana insisted on getting his house to clean. I guess she was already putting her marriage plans in motion."

A wave of jealousy, so intense it surprised her, washed over her. Three months ago, she hadn't given a rat's ass that Ana was cleaning Duncan's house, but that was before Duncan had started talking about how she belonged to him and nearly beat the crap out of Marty for touching her. His occasional flirty behaviour had been turned up to full volume, and she tried to ignore the ripple of excitement in her belly.

She wasn't interested in being another notch on his bedpost. She wasn't.

As her two best friends dug into their food, Ella took another bite of her toast and tried not to think about tomorrow night. She was nervous and excited about her first official client booking for her new business. She reminded herself firmly that it was not because she now had an excuse to touch Duncan Gillis.

CHAPTER 3

Duncan glanced at his watch before rapping lightly on the door. It was ten to seven. He was a little early for his appointment with Ella, but he couldn't pace at home any longer. He took a deep breath as he heard Ella's footsteps.

Behave yourself, Duncan. Don't make a fool of yourself just because Ella is touching you.

The door opened and Ella, wearing a white shirt and a pair of dark pants, smiled tentatively at him. "Hello, Duncan."

"Hi. I'm a bit early," he said.

"That's fine. Come in," she said.

Duncan followed her into her apartment, slipping off his boots as he glanced curiously around. She lived in a bachelor apartment over a garage, and although it was incredibly tiny, it had a warm and cozy feel. To the right was the kitchen, which consisted of a narrow counter with a smaller-than-average fridge and stove and a row of cupboards above the counter. A round café table with two wooden stools was crammed into the spot at the end of the counter. Directly in front of him was her massage table. A wooden tray at the head of the table held a variety of bottles. Beyond that was her double bed covered in a green checkered quilt. His mouth went dry as he pictured Ella lying naked in it.

Stop it, Duncan.

There were two doors to the right of the bed. He assumed they were the bathroom and a closet, and he studied them briefly before his eyes wandered again to her bed. He had half-hoped that he would be lying on Ella's bed for the massage and his inner voice berated him.

You're kind of an idiot. You know that, right? Ella is a professional, and this is her damn job. Stop acting like this will end with the two of you having sex.

He dragged his eyes from her bed and stared at her living room. It was too small for a couch, but there were two worn, comfortable-looking chairs in front of a small television sitting on top of a bookshelf. A small desk to the right of the bookshelf held a laptop and a few books.

"Oh, um, you're not allergic to cats, are you?" she asked as a fat grey tabby emerged from under one of the chairs.

He shook his head, stupidly pleased that she had a cat, and she smiled with relief. "Oh, good. Gus won't bother you, he doesn't like strangers, but I'd feel terrible if…."

Gus, no doubt recognizing one of his kind, rubbed against Duncan. He bent and petted the cat as it purred loudly.

"Oh my God," Ella said. "He never goes near strangers."

Duncan grinned at her and couldn't resist. "Pussies love me, Ella."

She blushed furiously, and his grin widened before the collage of frames hanging on the wall over the desk caught his attention. He grunted in surprise. "You're into art?"

She nodded and didn't protest when he moved to the art wall and studied it carefully. "Yes, I love it. I have no artistic ability, but I'm fascinated by people who do."

The art in the frames was all by the same artist, and he stared at the familiar pieces. "Is this guy your favourite or something?"

"He is." Enthusiasm replaced the nervousness on her face. "Have you heard of him?"

"No," he lied.

"His name is Samuel, and his work is just amazing. He's a local artist, and there's a rumour that he's from Newport. I've been following his work for years. He's a bit of a mystery, actually." She leaned forward and traced one of the pieces of art. "He's very well-known in the art world, but no one knows what he looks like. He never does interviews, and he doesn't go to his exhibitions. Even the fact that he goes by one name is a little mysterious, don't you think?"

He didn't reply, but she didn't notice. "There's also a rumour that Samuel is a woman, but I don't think he is. The paintings have the bold brushstrokes of a man." She blushed a little. "I know that sounds strange, but I've studied art since I was a teenager, and there usually is a difference in the work between male and female artists. Plus, a good ninety percent of his paintings are of females."

"Which one is your favourite?" he asked.

"This one." She pointed to the frame in the middle. A little girl, her blonde hair in two long braids down her back, swung on a tire swing hanging from a large oak tree planted in the middle of a vast field.

"Why?" he asked.

She shrugged. "I don't know. I guess I love that even though it looks like she should be lonely – she's in a middle of a field and completely alone - you get the feeling that she isn't. Like this is her favourite place in the whole world. There's no one around to bother her, no one to make her feel bad about herself."

She blushed again. "Sorry, that's not a very good explanation. Our high-school art teacher, Mr. Jillin – do you remember him?"

He nodded, and she smiled softly. "Mr. Jillin told me once that what made a person drawn to a particular piece of art or artist was different for everyone. He said it was what made art so amazing."

He stared at her lovely face. She nearly glowed from her enthusiasm, and he had to bite back his overwhelming urge to kiss her. Instead, he turned away and studied the art again. "Did you print these?"

She nodded. "Yes. I want to purchase one of his paintings, but his work is incredibly expensive. Still, they made me happy, so I printed some photos of his work using my computer and framed them. I feel a little guilty about enjoying his work without paying for it, but it's not like Samuel will come knocking on my door, is it?"

He cracked his knuckles. "No."

"He has a sale and show tomorrow night in Newport," she said with a tinge of excitement. "It's the first time his work will be shown in his hometown, and he's revealing his latest work. Belle and Bennett and I are going to it."

He jerked in surprise. "You are?"

"Yes," she said. "Are you kidding me? I wouldn't miss it. I won't be bidding on any of his work, but I can't wait to see it in person."

A grin crossed his face, and she blushed. "Sorry, here I am going on and on about art, and I'm supposed to be giving you a massage."

She walked toward the massage table. "So, with a full-body massage, you'll need to remove all your clothing. You can place your clothes here," she pointed to the wooden chair at the end of the massage table, "and lie on your stomach. I'll start with your upper body, so drape this sheet over your lower half." She patted the sheet folded neatly on the end of the table. "I'll wait in the bathroom. Just call me when you're ready, okay?"

He nodded, and she smiled nervously before disappearing into the bathroom and shutting the door. His own nerves a tangled jumble, he stripped quickly before climbing onto the massage table and draping the sheet over his lower body. She emerged from the bathroom when he called her name, and he watched as she turned on two small lamps before shutting off the overhead light.

The room turned comfortably dim, and she moved to her laptop and clicked a few buttons. Soft music played, and he tried to relax as she approached the table and picked up a bottle of oil from the tray. "Is vanilla scented oil good with you?"

"Yes." His voice was hoarse.

"Is there something wrong?" she asked.

"No," he said before clearing his throat. "Maybe a little nervous."

She smiled at him. "There's nothing to be nervous about. If you don't like a particular touch or it hurts at any point, just let me know, and I'll stop, okay?"

"Sure," he said.

She rubbed oil into her hands, and he jerked wildly at the first touch of her soft hands against his back. "Duncan? Are you okay?"

"Yes," he gritted out. His cock stiffened painfully against the table, and he closed his eyes. Jesus, this had been a terrible idea.

As her hands rubbed and massaged his muscles, he tried desperately to control himself.

"You're very tense," she murmured. "It's good that you booked an appointment."

He made a low mutter of acknowledgement and tried not to jerk again when her hands drifted over his shoulders and rubbed firmly. She was quiet as she worked, and he breathed in the combined scent of vanilla and her own personal one. She always smelled slightly of cleaning supplies - pine and lemon - and his cock stirred again. Jesus, only he would be turned on by the smell of cleaning supplies.

For thirty torturous minutes, she rubbed and kneaded his back and arms. When her strong hands moved to his hands, he made a soft moan. His hands were generally quite sore. In his line of work, it was nearly impossible for them not to be, and for the first time, he relaxed a little.

"That feels really good," he rasped.

"People don't realize how much tension they carry in their arms and hands," she said quietly.

She finished his hands, and he shifted uncomfortably against the table. He had a raging erection, and his lion was about five seconds away from trying to claim Ella.

Enough, he muttered inwardly, and his lion made a low hiss of disapproval.

Ella moved down to his lower body. She shifted the sheet upward until it covered only his hips and ass, and he couldn't stop the loud purr when her hands touched the back of his thigh.

She paused, "Duncan? Are you okay?"

"Yes," he rasped again. Fuck, he had never purred in front of a woman before. Even during sex, he had always managed to contain it, and now he was fucking purring like a kitten just because Ella touched his damn leg. As her hands gripped his thigh just below his ass, his lion made a roar of need and panic soared in him. He needed to leave right now. He had been a fool to think he could have Ella touch him and resist the urge to take her to bed. He had made a terrible mistake.

"Ella, stop!" he said.

She immediately released her grip and took a step back. "Did that hurt?"

"No." He shook his head and sat up with his back to her, awkwardly clutching the sheet around his middle. His erection was painfully evident against the thin sheet, and he hopped off the table, keeping his back to her.

"Duncan, what's wrong?"

"I have to go," he said.

"But you paid for a full body massage," she said. "I'm not finished."

"I'm sorry," he said. "I need to leave."

He grabbed his clothes and ran for the bathroom, slamming the door behind him.

ELLA STARED BLANKLY AT THE CLOSED BATHROOM DOOR. HER very first booking, and somehow, she had fucked it up royally. She should have known it wasn't going well. Duncan's body was unbelievably tense when she started. Shamefully, it had only worsened as she worked on him. He should have been limp and relaxed, but he had tensed up more and more the longer she massaged. She started for the bathroom door before turning and moving into the kitchen. She turned on the faucet and ran her oil-soaked hands under the tepid water.

There was a loud grinding noise from under the sink, and she cursed under her breath before squatting and opening the cupboard door beneath the sink. The pipes rattled, and another horrible grinding noise, this one louder than the first, made her clap her hands over her ears. Gus, who had wandered over to investigate with her, made a sudden hiss and sprinted under the bed. With a loud bang, the biggest pipe burst, and water sprayed out. She screeched and fell onto her butt, sputtering and choking on the water that soaked her head and body as she struggled to her knees and tried to reach past the spraying water to find the shut-off valve on the pipe.

Hard hands grabbed her arms and yanked her away, and she pushed her dripping hair from her face as Duncan, wearing only his jeans, reached under the sink. The water stopped abruptly, and she lurched to her feet as Duncan stood gracefully.

"Are you okay?" Duncan asked as they stood in the lake of water on her kitchen floor.

"Yeah." She wiped at the water clinging to her eyelashes before wringing the hem of her shirt. "Fuck. I'm really sorry."

"For what?"

"You're soaking wet," she said. Her gaze drifted down his body and her breath caught in her throat. Water dripped down his naked chest and – *oh good lor*d – his six pack.

His chest was hairless, but a narrow trail of golden-coloured hair snaked from below his belly button to disappear beneath the waistband of his jeans. She bit her bottom lip as she imagined unbuttoning his jeans and following that delicious trail of hair.

"So are you," he said hoarsely.

"What?" she said.

"You're soaking wet as well," he said.

She tore her gaze from his body and glanced down at her own. Her white shirt was now transparent and clinging to her, and her hardened nipples were visible through her bra and shirt.

Like a woman in a dream, she watched as Duncan's big hand reached out, and he traced her nipple with the tip of his index finger. A moan escaped her mouth, and he made a harsh growl when her back arched.

He stepped closer, his arm snaking around her waist, and pulled her against his wet chest. He claimed her mouth roughly, pushing his tongue past her lips to taste and tease. She moaned again and melted against him as he wound his hand into her wet hair and held her tightly. The touch of his mouth sent waves of pleasure through her lower body, and she cried out when he ground his erection against her.

His hand cupped her breast and squeezed. She gasped and dug her nails into his back when he kissed her throat with an open mouth and roving tongue. He nipped her sharply, the rough rasp of his beard scraping red marks against her skin, and she made a soft moan of submission.

He took her mouth again, forcing it wide as he took what was his. His fingers plucked at her nipple, sending a bolt of pleasure straight to her crotch. Her pussy throbbed and pulsed as he pressed her up against the counter.

"I want you, Ella," he muttered against her mouth. "Will you give me what I want?"

Fuck, she wanted to say yes. Duncan's hard mouth and rough hands had driven away all of her doubts, and she couldn't remember why it would be so wrong to take him to her bed. The last person she'd had sex with was Marty, and it hadn't exactly been thrilling. His touch had never made her feel like she would explode if he didn't fuck her and fuck her right now.

She opened her mouth to say yes - to say *hell, yes* - and they both jerked when there was a loud knock on the door.

"Ella? I know you're in there. Open up. I need the keys to

your car. Mine's dead again." Ana's shrill voice made her cringe, and she tried to pull away from Duncan.

"Ignore her," he muttered almost pleadingly. "She'll leave."

"She won't," she whispered. "Besides, she has a key, and she'll -"

She pushed away from him just as the lock turned and the door opened. Ana walked into the tiny apartment, her mouth dropping open as she stared at Duncan and Ella. "What the hell is going on?"

"The pipe under the sink burst," Ella said.

Ana's gaze narrowed as she stared at Duncan's half-naked body. "What are you doing here?"

"Duncan booked a massage appointment," Ella said hurriedly. "Then the pipe exploded, and he was just helping me with it."

Ana ignored her completely. She crossed the room, sloshing through the water on the floor, and grasped Duncan's upper arm with one smooth hand. "Duncan, if you wanted a massage, you should have called me. I'm excellent with my hands," she trailed her fingers up and down his bicep, "and I certainly wouldn't have charged you to do it."

She let her gaze land briefly on Ella before smiling at Duncan again. "It's so nice of you to help Ella with her burst pipe, but she's so clever I'm sure she can repair it on her own. On the other hand, I am positively useless when it comes to mechanical things. Do you think you could take a brief look at my car before you leave?"

"I should help Ella clean up," Duncan said.

"Oh, Ella doesn't mind," Ana said sweetly. "She's used to doing things for herself. Aren't you, Ella?"

"Yeah," Ella muttered. Ana's sudden appearance had

killed her lust for Duncan, and she watched as Ana tightened her grip on Duncan's arm.

"Please, Duncan?" she pleaded. "I would so appreciate it."

"I don't know anything about cars," Duncan said.

"Well, then, maybe you could give me a ride downtown?" Ana said.

He sighed. "I can't leave this mess for Ella to clean up."

"I told you, she doesn't mind. She wants you to help out her sister." A hint of impatience had appeared in Ana's voice. "Tell him, Ella."

She gave Ella a pointed look, one that suggested she would make Ella's life a living hell if she disagreed, and Ella smiled stiffly. "I don't mind at all."

She hated the thought of Duncan being alone with Ana but what had almost happened between them was a mistake. If he didn't leave, she'd be apt to let him talk, or more likely kiss, his way into her bed, and while that would be one hell of a fun night, his interest in her would wane, and where would that leave her? Pining for a guy she couldn't have.

Better to forget that she wanted him and just let Ana have him. She would get him eventually, and if Ella defied her now, she'd never hear the end of it from Ana or her step-mother. The thought made her shudder, and she looked away from Duncan's steady gaze.

"I'd appreciate it if you'd give Ana a ride, Duncan." She nearly choked on her words as an image of Ana riding Duncan in his bed flooded through her.

"Fine," Duncan said before running his hand across the stubble on his face. She wondered if she imagined the hurt in his voice as he stomped into the bathroom. He returned fully dressed and placed some money on the end of the massage table.

"Thanks for the massage, Ella," he said and was out the door with Ana before she could tell him to keep his money.

———————

"DUNCAN?" BENNETT'S VOICE ECHOED DOWN THE HALLWAY as the front door slammed.

"I'm up here!" Duncan shouted.

The floor shook as Bennett tromped up the stairs and stuck his head into the room. "Hey, what's up? Your text seemed urgent."

"Why didn't you tell me you were going to the exhibit tonight with Belle and Ella?" Duncan didn't look away from the large canvas in front of him as he added black to his paintbrush and jabbed the canvas with hard, heavy strokes.

Bennett shrugged. "I didn't think about it."

"Didn't think about it?" Duncan said. "You're taking your girlfriend and her best friend to my show, and you didn't think about it?"

"What's gotten into you, man?" Bennett asked as he crossed the room and lowered his body into the paint-flecked chair near the window.

"Ella is into art. Did you know that?" Duncan pointed his paintbrush at Bennett.

"No, why would I?"

"She's especially into Samuel's work," he said. "He's her favourite artist."

A wide grin crossed Bennett's face. "That's great."

"No, it isn't," Duncan said.

"The woman you're in love with happens to love your art. I don't see the problem," Bennett said.

"One – I'm not in love with her, and two – what if she finds out I'm Samuel?" Duncan said.

"What if she does? Honestly, I've never understood why you've kept it such a secret anyway," Bennett said.

"Because if people knew I was Samuel, I'd live under constant scrutiny," Duncan said. "Shifters are supposed to keep a low profile, remember? How long do you think it would take for people to figure out I was a goddamn lion shifter?"

"How would they find out?" Bennett said. "It's not like you'll start shifting in front of them."

Duncan sighed before adding more strokes of black to the canvas. "The High Council would lose their shit. Shifters need to fly under the radar and not bring attention to themselves in the human world. Besides, I like my privacy and have no interest in having damn art groupies pounding on my door day and night. It'll happen, Bennett. You have no idea how insane people in the art world are."

"Just relax, Duncan. No one's going to find out you're Samuel," Bennett said. "Least of all Ella. Just because she likes your art doesn't mean she will figure out it's you. She doesn't even know you're an artist."

"I'm going with you tonight," Duncan said.

"What? No way, man. You can't go to your exhibit."

"Of course, I can. No one knows what Samuel looks like, remember?"

"Duncan, I don't think it's a good idea. Ella was over earlier today, and I overheard her telling Belle what happened last night."

Duncan glared at him. "Nothing happened."

Bennett gave him a dry look, and Duncan dropped his paintbrush on the stool beside him and wiped his hands with a towel.

"I should never have asked Ella to give me a massage,

Bennett. Jesus, just having her touch me got my damn lion so worked up I could barely contain him."

"Apparently, you didn't contain him," Bennett said with a grin. "At least not according to Ella."

"Yeah, well, she didn't exactly appreciate it."

"What do you mean?" Bennett asked.

"Her stupid stepsister barged into her apartment, and when she asked me for a ride downtown, Ella couldn't wait to get rid of me. She practically handed me to that bitch Ana on a damn platter. Ana manhandled me the entire ride. I had to knock her hands away from my crotch at least half-a-dozen times."

Bennett's laugh cut out at Duncan's loud growl.

"Sorry, it's not funny, I know," Bennett said. "Listen, I don't know a lot about Ella's relationship with her stepmother or stepsisters, but from the little bit Belle told me, their relationship is pretty awful. They've done some horrible things to her. I get the feeling that Ella just does what they want because it's easier for her."

"Yeah, well, I'm not some prize she can hand over to her stepsister," Duncan said.

"Tell me what's really bothering you, Duncan."

Duncan stared moodily out the window. "I want Ella Cinders so badly I can barely think straight, and my lion is driving me fucking crazy with his constant demands to take her. I mean, I've always wanted her, but ever since I saw that shithead Marty with his hands on her...."

He rubbed at his forehead. "My lion has claimed her, and I don't know what the fuck to do about it. She doesn't want anything to do with me."

"I don't think that's true," Bennett said. "Things were getting pretty hot and heavy between the two of you last night."

"Yeah, before she decided just to let her stepsister have me," Duncan said. "It was a moment of insanity for her, nothing more. She's hated me since we were kids, and just because I turn her on doesn't mean that's going to change her feelings. Hell, plenty of people fuck someone they hate."

Bennett shook his head. "I don't think that's true."

"Whatever," Duncan said. "What time are you picking me up tonight?"

"Duncan, why do you even want to go? If Ella makes you so crazy, why torture yourself?"

"You couldn't stay away from Belle, could you?" Duncan said.

Bennett hesitated before shaking his head. "No, I guess I couldn't. So does this mean you're going to tell her you're a lion shifter?"

"Of course not," Duncan said.

"Why not? I told Belle I was a bear shifter, and it didn't even faze her."

"Yeah, well, didn't you tell me her mother was a tiger shifter? She's predisposed to accept it, even if she's fully human. Ella wouldn't understand, and besides, just because my lion has claimed her and wants to fuck her doesn't mean I'm going to start a relationship with her. I only need to get her out of my system, give my lion what he wants, and then it's done."

"That's romantic."

"I don't do romance, and you know that, Bennett," Duncan said.

"Yeah, well, you've never freaked out over a woman like this before."

"I'm not freaking out over her," Duncan said. "And you were gone for eighteen years. You have no idea about my relationships with women."

"True." Bennett raised his eyebrows at him. "But you honestly don't consider threatening to tear out the throat of any man that goes near her, freaking out?"

"That's my lion, not me," Duncan protested. "Besides, once I've slept with her, that will stop."

"Sure, it will," Bennett said.

Duncan gave him a dirty look. "What time tonight, Bennett?"

Bennett stood and headed toward the door. "We'll pick you up at five-thirty."

CHAPTER 4

"Why are we stopping here?" Ella peered out the passenger window of the truck. Her eyes widened when the door to the modest cream-coloured bungalow opened, and Duncan stepped out.

"What the hell?" She reached forward and grabbed Belle's shoulder. "Why didn't you tell me Duncan Gillis was coming with us?"

"I found out right before we picked you up," Belle said.

"You should have told me," Ella said.

"You wouldn't have come if I did, and you've been looking forward to this for months," Belle said. "It'll be fine, Ella. It's cool that Duncan is also into art, don't you think?"

Ella groaned and sat back in her seat. She stared at the back of Belle's head as Duncan approached the truck.

It's fine, Ella. You'll have to see him sooner or later, and this will give you the chance to apologize and return his money.

Her stomach twisted at the memory of last night. Her first client booking, and she had fucked it up terribly. She could only hope that once she apologized and returned his money,

Duncan would keep the disaster of an evening to himself. She'd never be taken seriously if clients found out that she practically threw herself at them after a massage.

It's only because it was Duncan. Chill out, girl. If you'd just do what you want and fuck him, you could finally get him out of your damn system and return to your normal life.

The door opened, and she smiled tentatively at Duncan as he climbed into the backseat of the truck next to her and buckled his seat belt. "Hi, Duncan."

"Hello, Ella," he said briefly before staring out the window.

Her stomach dropped to her ankles at the coldness in his voice, and she looked away as Bennett started the truck and drove down the street.

"Well, that drive was awkward as hell," Belle said to Ella.

Bennett and Duncan were checking their coats, and Ella grimaced. "I'm sorry."

"For what? It's not your fault Duncan's all awkward and weird tonight."

"It is," Ella said. "He's upset about last night. I can't believe I practically attacked him in my apartment. What kind of massage therapist does that?"

Belle squeezed her arm. "From what you told me, it sounds like Duncan started it."

"It doesn't matter. I'm supposed to be a professional."

Duncan and Bennett were approaching them, and Ella took a deep breath. "Can you give Duncan and me a minute? I'm going to apologize and return his money, and maybe that'll help."

"If it doesn't, I'll kick his ass," Belle said. "I'm not letting him ruin a night you've been so excited about."

"He hasn't ruined it," Ella said. "Even if he's still upset, I'll feel better after apologizing. It's a big gallery. I can give him his space for the evening."

Belle reached for Bennett's hand as the two men joined them. "C'mon, honey, let's go check out the artwork."

She tugged on his hand, and after a glance at Duncan and Ella, he followed her. Duncan gave Ella a stiff smile and started after them.

"Duncan?" she asked. "Can I speak to you for a moment?"

He hesitated and, staring over her shoulder, said, "What is it?"

"I want to apologize for last night. I did a terrible job with the massage, you were more tense after than before I started, and I – well, what happened yesterday was inappropriate. I made a fool of myself, and I'm very sorry."

She fumbled in her purse before holding out the money he had given her. "Here."

He frowned. "What is that?"

"It's your money from last night. You didn't enjoy the massage, and I'm not going to charge you for something you hated."

"I don't want the money," he said.

She tried to press it into his hand. "Please, Duncan. I'd feel much better if you let me return it. As well, I know this is a lot to ask, but if you didn't mind not mentioning to others what happened last night, I would appreciate it. I'm usually very good at massage, and if other people find out that you didn't enjoy it, it'll sink my business before it even gets started."

"You think I didn't enjoy the massage?" he said slowly.

"Obviously, you didn't," she said. "And that's fine. It's all my fault, and I feel awful that I didn't do my job properly. I want to offer to try again free of charge if you're interested."

She gasped when he stepped toward her and cupped the back of her head, ignoring the other people's looks as they stepped around them. "Let's get something straight. I enjoyed the massage, and I'm not taking my money back."

"You didn't," she protested. "You were incredibly tense, and you made me stop halfway through, and -"

"I made you stop because I was so turned on I was ten seconds away from tossing you onto that damn massage table, tearing off your clothes, and fucking you until you were screaming my name. If I'd let you touch me a minute longer, I wouldn't have been able to stop myself."

Her bottom lip dropped, and he stared at it before groaning softly. "Jesus, Ella, do you have any fucking idea what you do to me? I want to bury myself in your sweet pussy so badly I can hardly think straight."

"Duncan, that – that's not a good idea," she said shakily as her limbs trembled and her pussy throbbed.

"You thought it was a good idea last night," he muttered as his gaze lingered on her mouth. "We both know I would have been balls-deep inside of you with those hard nipples of yours in my mouth if your stepsister hadn't shown up."

"It was better that she did. It stopped us from making a mistake."

Hurt crossed his face. "So that's why you served me to her like a pig on a spit? Because I'm a mistake?"

"What are you talking about?" she asked. "I didn't serve you to her. She needed a ride, and I was trying to be nice."

"No, you were trying to avoid what you know will happen between us eventually. You want me, Ella Cinders." He inhaled deeply as his fingers tightened around her skull.

"I can smell it on you. I want you too, and I will have you."

Her throat was bone dry, and she was so unbelievably aroused that her knees were weak. Duncan meant every word he said. For a moment, she could see herself in his bed. She could imagine lying on her back with her legs spread obscenely wide. She could feel her nails clawing his back as he thrust his cock into her and gave her what she wanted, what she *needed*.

"You're mine, Ella. The sooner you realize that, the better," he said in a low murmur.

"A mistake," she choked the words out. "It's a mistake, Duncan."

His eyes flared bright yellow for one heart-stopping moment, and then he took a step back and released his grip on her head. "Let's go."

"Go where?" An image of Duncan leading her to Bennett's truck, of him opening the door and bending her over the seat as he tugged her dress over her hips and unbuckled his pants, sent another overpowering wave of lust through her.

He would fuck her right there, and to hell with anyone walking by. She didn't care if they saw her, didn't care if they knew she was being fucked in a parking lot. All she cared about was having Duncan's cock, having that ceaseless empty ache between her legs filled by him.

He inhaled deeply before he muttered an obscenity and gave her a sharp look. "Fuck, Ella. Are you trying to kill me?"

"What do you mean?" she whispered.

"Whatever you're thinking about? Stop right now. I only have so much goddamn willpower."

He headed deeper into the gallery, giving her an impatient

look when she didn't follow him. "Are we going to look at the damn art or not?"

She nodded and, keeping a safe distance from Duncan, followed him into the gallery.

"WHAT ARE YOU DOING HERE?" HIS AGENT SPOKE INTO HIS ear, and Duncan glanced at the others who had wandered ahead. He drifted to a stop, waiting for them to round the corner before turning to his agent.

"Hello, Reva."

"What are you doing here, Duncan?" Reva, a slender woman with long, flowing hair, glanced around the gallery before saying in a low voice, "You never come to your shows."

He shrugged. "Just thought I'd check one out."

"Well, it's good to see you. Did you get my email about the show in London?"

He nodded. "Yes. Go ahead and book it."

"I will. Your new painting is turning heads, you know."

"Is it?" he asked.

"Yes. We've already had twelve bids on it, and it's only an hour into the show." She gave him a pleased look. "I was thinking maybe you could paint a few more of this woman."

Duncan had tried repeatedly to capture Ella's beauty in his paintings, but as hard as he tried, he didn't think he would ever come close. He thought his new painting was the closest he'd ever gotten to truly capturing her beauty. It was the reason he had sent it to Reva. It was too good to languish in his art studio with the other portraits of Ella.

Reva was waiting for his reply. He shook his head. "I don't think so."

"Why not?" she asked. "Duncan, you could make a lot of money from this. Seriously, it's your best work yet. I don't know who this mystery woman is, but it's obvious she's your damn muse. Why not capitalize on that?"

"I said no, Reva," he snapped and then sighed when she frowned at him. "Sorry, I'm a little on edge tonight."

"Understandable," she said before patting his arm, "but unnecessary. It's going very well. You'd realize that if you came to more of your shows."

He laughed. "Next, you'll tell me to reveal myself to the art world."

"Oh God, no," she said. "Part of your allure is the mystery. People are dying to know who this Samuel is and I, for one, am hell-bent on keeping them guessing."

"That makes two of us." He bent and kissed the woman's cheek. "Thanks for all of your hard work, Reva. I don't say thanks enough."

"No, you don't," she said with a grin. "But I'm used to working with artists, so I don't even notice anymore. It was good to see you, Duncan."

"You too, Reva. Listen, has there been any interest in the tire swing painting?"

She nodded. "Yes. Three bids so far."

"Put a sold sign on it, would you?"

"What? Why?"

"I'm taking it off the market. I'll email you an address. After the show can you package it and send it by courier? It's imperative the person doesn't know you've sent it."

She nodded. "I can do that. But, Duncan, it's got some high bids on it. Are you certain you want to do this?"

"Yes. Thanks, Reva. Take care, okay?"

"I always do," she said with a small smile. He watched her walk away before heading after the others.

"HOLY SHIT," BELLE SAID. "I DON'T KNOW MUCH ABOUT ART, but this is amazing, right?"

Ella nodded slowly. They stood in front of Samuel's newest painting, and she couldn't tear her gaze away from it. A blonde woman, her long hair drifting down her naked back in soft waves, sat in the vast empty plains of Africa. She was turned at a slight angle, her face completely hidden, but the heavy curve of one pale breast and the swell of her belly hinted at with soft strokes of the paintbrush.

A lion, his fur a slightly darker shade than the woman's hair, sat on his haunches beside her. The woman's head leaned against his shoulder and her left arm curved around his back, her fingers disappearing into the heavier brown of his thick mane. The lion's tail curled entirely around the woman's waist like a belt, the end brushing against her full hip. The thick, brownish-yellow grass concealed her naked backside and legs, and her other hand gently pulled on the strands of grass.

Belle leaned closer. "The lion is amazing. How someone can create something so life-like with a brush and some paint is incredible."

She poked Ella gently in the side. "The woman reminds me of you."

"What?" Ella said.

"The woman in the painting looks like you."

"No, she doesn't."

"She does," Belle insisted. "Her hair is the same length and colour as yours, she has the same body shape as you do, and," she leaned even closer until her nose almost brushed the painting, "she has an almost identical scar to yours on her upper arm."

Ella stared at the crescent-shaped scar on the woman's arm, feeling an odd little prickle in her scalp. It wasn't almost identical - it was exactly the same. The only difference was that it was on the woman's left arm, and hers was on her right.

"Bennett? Don't you think that woman reminds you of Ella?" Belle said.

"Um, yeah, maybe," Bennett said as Duncan joined them. "If you squint."

Belle laughed. "You don't have to squint to see the resemblance. Duncan, look at this woman – doesn't she remind you of Ella?"

Duncan shook his head. "No, not really."

Belle gave the men an exasperated look. "Both of you are nuts."

Ella studied the painting as Duncan cleared his throat. "Do you like it, Ella?"

He sounded anxious, and she glanced at him before nodding. "I love it. It's so," she struggled to find the right word, "incredible."

"Good. I'm glad you like it." Duncan's face relaxed, and he gave her his first genuine smile of the evening.

She studied him for a moment, wondering what the look in his eyes meant before her gaze was drawn back to the painting in front of her. She stared at it for another five minutes as the others waited patiently. She smiled at them. "Sorry, we can move on now."

"We can stare at it as long as you want," Belle said.

Ella laughed. "There's a crowd gathering behind us. Besides, I want to look for my favourite painting. I heard it was finally up for sale."

She moved down the hallway, stopping at each painting to study them carefully. Her favourite was around the corner, and she couldn't stop her sigh of disappointment when she saw the 'sold' sticker on it.

"It's sold," she said.

"Sorry, honey," Belle squeezed her arm. "I know you wanted to buy this one."

"I could never have afforded it, Belle."

She knew it would never be hers, but there'd been a small part of her that often daydreamed she would have an original Samuel art piece in her possession. She would love any of them, but this was the one she'd wanted the most.

"Really? How much do these paintings sell for anyway?" Belle leaned forward and studied the small, discreet price tag hanging from the frame's lower edge.

"Holy fuckballs," she said in a quiet voice. "This thing costs a hundred grand!"

Bennett laughed. "That's just the starting price. Samuel's paintings go to the highest bidder."

"Really?"

"Yes," Ella said. "A person will put in a bid for the starting price. In this case, it's a hundred grand. If other people are interested, they can put in higher bids. Each person who bids is notified of the price hike and can decide if they want to counteroffer. The highest bidder takes the painting home. One of Samuel's paintings went for nearly half a million last year."

"No way," Belle said in a faint voice. "I mean, I get that the guy is good but who has that kind of money to spend on a painting?"

"Lots of people," Ella said. "Art like Samuel's is priceless, really. I'm surprised that this one has a sold sign on it already. I thought the bidding wouldn't have ended until the show was over."

She reached out and lightly traced the heavy wooden

frame it was encased in. "I hope she goes to a good home. Someone who loves her as much as I do."

Ella took one last look at the painting before glancing at her watch. "If you guys are ready, we should probably go. I have a busy today tomorrow."

Belle took Bennett's hand and squeezed it lightly. "We're ready whenever you are, Ella."

ELLA STARED AT THE UNFAMILIAR NUMBER ON HER CELL phone before shutting off her car. She was already running late for her appointment but answered the phone anyway.

"Ella Cinders, speaking. How can I help you?"

"Ms. Cinders?" The man's voice was vaguely familiar. "This is Henry Treating."

"Hello, Mr. Treating. How are you?" Henry owned the only car repair shop in town.

"Oh, can't complain. Well, I could but ain't no one around who would listen."

She laughed politely as he cleared his throat. "So, Duncan Gillis was in the shop today, and he mentioned that he got a massage from you the night before last? Said you had started up your own business where ya come to a person's house?"

"That's right," she said. "Healing Hands Massage Therapy."

"Right," he said. "Well, Doc Mitchell says I got problems with sciatica, and Duncan said that your massage fixed his lower back pain right up. He gave me your number and said to call you. Does massage help with sciatica?"

"It does," she said as excitement brewed in her belly. "Massage therapy has been proven to be very effective in relieving sciatica pain."

"Good, good," Henry said. "Do you think I could book you for an appointment then? Some days it's so bad I can barely work on the cars."

"Of course," she said. "What day were you thinking?"

"Well, I can't do it during the day. Most of the time, I'm the only one at the shop, you know."

"That's fine. Evenings work better for me," Ella said.

"Good, good. How about tomorrow night, then? Say around six?"

"Perfect," Ella said.

"Good, good. I'll text you my address then."

"You text?" she said with a touch of amusement.

"O'course. Don't everybody text these days?" Henry said. "I gotta run. Someone's in the shop. See you tomorrow night, Ms. Cinders."

"Yes, thank you, Henry."

"Ayuh," he grunted before hanging up.

Ella stared at her cell phone. She had another booking, and it was all thanks to Duncan Gillis. Why on earth would he recommend her? She didn't have a clue, but holy hell – she had another client.

Her phone rang again, and she made a little shriek of surprise and nearly dropped it. Another unknown number and her hands trembling lightly, she answered it. "Ella Cinders speaking. How can I help you?"

"This is Marjorie Wilkins calling!"

Ella winced as the old woman's cracked and shrill voice bellowed into her ear. "I'm Duncan Gillis' neighbour."

"Hello, Mrs. Wilkins. How can I help you?" Ella asked.

"What's that?" Mrs. Wilkins shouted.

"How can I help you?" Ella shouted into the phone.

"All right, dear, no need to shout," the old woman said irritably. "I've got arthritis something bad in my hands, and this morning when Duncan took out my trash, he said that you did massage. He said he's got sore hands and that he had you massage them, and it helped a tremendous amount. I told him that was all fine and dandy for someone like him who didn't have a bum leg and had a driver's license, and he said that you would come to my house. Is that true?"

"Yes, ma'am," Ella said.

"What was that? Speak up!" the old woman said.

"Yes, ma'am," Ella hollered. "I can come to your house."

"Good. I'll expect you at my house Friday morning at seven. Don't be late. I cannot stand lateness," the old woman shouted. She recited her address, and Ella hurried to write it on a napkin she found in her purse.

"Seven am," the old woman shouted again and hung up before Ella could reply.

"Holy shit," Ella said. She stared at the address on the napkin before stuffing it into her purse. "Dammit, my appointment."

She tucked her phone into her purse, climbed out of her car and walked quickly toward her accountant's office. Three years ago, the town's council voted in favour of building a new high-rise building in the downtown core. It was only twelve floors but compared to the rest of the downtown buildings, it was considered a high-rise. There had been a petition sent around in protest of the buildings. The town's older residents had seen the new buildings as a blight against the town's rather picturesque appeal, but it hadn't gained much steam, and the construction had gone ahead. The town council had planned on building two more, but funding had fallen through, and now the building stood out like a sore thumb among the smaller, older buildings of the downtown core.

She pushed open the lobby door and crossed the dark tile

to the elevator. She pressed the button, feeling that familiar low tinge of panic in her belly. She usually avoided elevators, but her accountant was on the twelfth floor, and she was already running late. It would take her forever to climb the twelve flights of stairs, and she'd be sweaty and out of breath if she did.

Ignoring her fear, she stepped into the elevator and pushed the button before taking a deep breath. She could do this. It was less than a three-minute ride. She bit her bottom lip and swallowed heavily as the doors started to slide close. She was fine. She was perfectly fine.

A hand slid between the nearly closed doors, and they bounced open immediately. Duncan Gillis, dressed in his usual t-shirt and jeans, slipped into the elevator and grinned at her.

"What are you doing here? Are you following me?" she asked as he pushed the button for the tenth floor.

"No. I have an appointment with my lawyer." He stared at her work shirt, his eyes lingering on the logo over her right breast, and she had to fight her instinct to cover her breasts with her arms.

"Didn't realize Cinders Cleaning worked on commercial buildings as well," he said.

"We don't. I'm on my lunch break, and I have an appointment with my accountant," she said as the elevator doors closed.

She fiercely suppressed her immediate panic as Duncan stiffened before sniffing in her direction. "What's wrong?"

"Nothing," she said as the elevator moved upward.

"You're afraid," he said and moved toward her.

"No, I'm not." She backed away until her butt hit the wall of the elevator.

"Yes, you are," he said with a frown. "Why are you -"

There was a terrific jolt, and she screamed breathlessly as the elevator shuddered to a stop with a grinding noise that made fear blossom in her belly. The lights went out, plunging them into darkness, and she screamed again as panic flooded her nervous system.

CHAPTER 5

Ella tried to take a deep breath, but there wasn't enough oxygen, and she panted harshly as she began to cry. She was trapped, trapped in the dark, and she couldn't breathe, and she –

"Ella," Duncan's low voice came out of the dark, and when his hands touched her shoulders, she threw herself forward and clung to him with panicky tightness.

"Ella, you're hyperventilating, sweetheart. Slow your breathing down," he spoke into her ear, his hard hands rubbing her back soothingly.

"Can't breathe," she gasped, "not enough air."

"There is," he said. "There's plenty of air, sweetheart. Breathe like I am."

He pressed his forehead against hers, and she felt his warm breath puffing against her face. She could hear him inhaling and exhaling in a steady rhythm, and she tried to mimic it, concentrating on nothing but the sound of his breathing.

"Good," he said. "Keep breathing just like that, Ella."

He started to step away, and she made a harsh cry of fear. "Don't leave me!"

"I'm not," he said immediately. "I'm not going anywhere, sweetheart. I promise. I just want to find the phone and -"

There was a low buzzing noise, and the emergency light clicked on, bathing them in dim red light. Duncan cupped her face and smiled at her. "There, that's better, isn't it?"

She nodded but moved with him when he crossed the small space and opened the door on the button panel. He lifted the black phone handle and waited patiently.

"Hi," he said after a moment. "Two of us are stuck in your elevator."

He listened, and she closed her eyes and concentrated on her breathing, one hand clutching the back of his shirt as panic fluttered through her. He hung up the phone and gave her a reassuring look.

"They're sending maintenance to fix it right now. Nothing too serious, just an electrical malfunction. They think it won't take very long."

"How long?" she whispered.

"An hour, maybe two."

"Oh my God," she moaned as fresh panic poured in. "Duncan, I can't be in here. I can't …."

She was hyperventilating again, and she didn't protest when Duncan pulled her into his embrace and rubbed her back. "Deep breaths, sweetheart. No passing out on me, okay?"

She inhaled through her nose, blowing her breath out through her mouth as she stared at Duncan's face.

"We'll run out of oxygen," she said.

"No, sweetheart, we won't."

"Do you promise?"

"I promise. Why don't we sit down?"

Without waiting for her reply, he sat down on the floor and pulled her into his lap. She was still panicking, despite the reassuring bulk of Duncan underneath her, and he rubbed her back slowly as he pushed her face into his neck.

"Just close your eyes and breathe, sweetheart."

"I'm so sorry," she said.

"You don't need to be sorry. Having a panic attack isn't your fault."

"There isn't enough air," she repeated.

"Yes, there is," he said. "Nice deep breaths for five minutes, Ella. You'll feel better after that, I promise."

She closed her eyes and tried to ignore how the walls were closing around her as she did what he said. After five minutes, he squeezed her thigh and murmured, "Better?"

She was surprised to realize that it was a little better. She didn't feel quite as panicky, and while her heart still pounded, it no longer felt like it was going to explode in her chest.

"A little," she said.

"Good." He continued to rub her back.

She raised her head to stare at him. "At least I didn't wet my pants this time."

He gave her a look of sympathy before pressing a kiss against her forehead. "You were seven years old and locked in a closet when you're claustrophobic. You couldn't help what happened."

She wiped the tears on her face before resting her head against his broad shoulder. "I was so embarrassed that day."

"I know, sweetheart," he said. "I'm sorry you had to go through that."

"It could have been worse, I guess. For some reason, my stepsisters and their friends never told anyone that I wet my pants, and they didn't make fun of me either."

He didn't reply, and she sat up again as understanding dawned. "Duncan, did you ask them not to say anything?"

"That depends. Is threatening to tie them up in the forest and leave them for the cougars and bears if they said anything about what happened considered asking?"

Her mouth turned up in a trembling smile. "I – thank you. That was really nice of you."

He stroked her blonde hair back from her face. "You deserve to have nice things happen to you."

She leaned against him again, watching as his big hand slowly stroked her thigh. "I booked two more massage appointments today."

"Oh yeah?" he said.

"Both because of you and your recommendations," she said. "Thank you, Duncan. You didn't have to do that."

"You're good at what you do, Ella. I mean that. Just because I'm too much of a damn horndog when it comes to you doesn't mean that others won't benefit from your massages."

"Thanks," she said. "How much longer do you think?"

He squeezed her thigh. "Try not to think about the time, okay?"

She nodded and closed her eyes. "Right."

She sat quietly until the feeling of the walls closing in became too much to bear. She needed a distraction. "Hey, Duncan?"

"Yes?"

"What do you do for a living?"

"Oh, uh, I'm in investing."

"Like Bennett?"

"Yes," he said.

"Do you enjoy it?"

"It pays the bills," he said. "Why do you still live with your stepmother?"

"I don't live with her," she said. "I rent the apartment above her garage."

"Why?"

"She cuts me a break on rent. I'm trying to save money for the business, you know?"

"She makes you pay rent?" The disgust in his voice was apparent.

She shrugged. "I don't mind. Although I wish she'd fix the damn pipe under the sink. I still don't have running water in the kitchen. She says it's my responsibility because she doesn't charge me much rent."

"Sweetheart, you need to get away from her and those two hags she calls daughters. They're not good for you."

"They're my family, Duncan."

"No, they're not," he said.

She sighed. "Fine, they're the only family I have left since my dad died. Ana and Dru are walking nightmares, but Edith isn't that bad. She could have given me up to foster care when my dad died, and she didn't. I know she seems harsh around the edges, but a part of her loves me. She wouldn't have taken care of me if she didn't."

"Forcing you to clean other people's houses when you were a child isn't taking care of you, Ella," Duncan said.

She jerked in surprise. "How did you know that? I didn't tell anyone but Belle."

"People talk in small towns," he said.

She made a bitter sound in the back of her throat. "Yeah, there are no secrets in this damn town."

He didn't answer, and she shifted against him. "Why didn't you leave with your parents when they moved?"

"I was eighteen and old enough to do my own thing. My

parents were moving to the Bahamas because they love the heat, but I had grown up in this town. I love it here and don't want to leave," he said.

"I love it here too. Belle and Ro keep telling me I should leave for a couple of years." She winced when his arms tightened around her. "Duncan, too tight."

"Sorry." He eased his grip around her.

"That's okay. Anyway, they keep telling me I should leave and get a job as a massage therapist in a bigger city."

"Are you going to?"

She wondered if that was worry she heard in his voice.

"Not right now. Belle suggested I do this traveling massage therapy thing, and I decided to try it. Although if it doesn't work out, I'll probably be forced to leave. I don't want to clean houses forever, and I enjoy doing massage therapy. I want to make a difference for people in chronic pain instead of just cleaning their toilets."

She leaned against him, trying to fight back the still-lurking fear. "Has it been an hour yet?"

"No," he said gently. "Not yet."

"Thank you, Duncan. If you weren't here with me, I would have gone crazy," she said.

"No, you wouldn't have," he said. "You're strong, Ella."

"Not when it comes to this." She fanned herself with the front of her shirt. "It's sweltering in here."

"Yes," he said.

"Not much oxygen."

He squeezed her thigh again. "There is, sweetheart."

She fanned herself again before touching the front of his shirt. It was nearly soaked through, and she straightened. "Oh, Duncan, I'm sorry. You're much too warm with me leaning against you."

"It's fine," he said.

"It isn't," she said. "I'm too heavy to sit on your lap. Your legs must be numb."

"They're fine," he repeated. "You don't need to move, Ella."

She hesitated and touched his shirt again. "You're soaked with sweat."

He grabbed the hem of his shirt and pulled it over his head before she knew what was happening. "There, that's better."

She stared silently at his chest, and he rubbed her thigh. "Ella? Are you okay? Remember to breathe, sweetheart."

"You're so pretty," she said in a whisper.

"What?" He leaned forward and then inhaled sharply when she traced her fingers down his chest.

"Ella, you should stop touching me," he said in a low growl.

She lifted her gaze to his face. "I – I don't want to."

He groaned and leaned forward, pressing his mouth against hers. She returned his kiss immediately, licking at his mouth with her tongue and sliding it between his lips when he parted them.

He let her control the kiss as he gently turned her body until she straddled his thighs. He rubbed her thighs through her pants as they repeatedly kissed, slow and gentle brushes of their mouths that drove her nearly crazy with need.

She moved her mouth to his throat, tasting the saltiness of his skin with the tip of her tongue. He groaned and cupped the back of her head. She licked his neck again before kissing her way to his earlobe and sucking.

"Fuck," he muttered as his pelvis thrust against her.

She gasped and pushed back against him, tearing another groan from his throat. He cupped her face and kissed her repeatedly until she was rocking against him and rubbing her breasts against his chest. He slipped his hand under her shirt and cupped her breast through her bra, rubbing her nipple through the lace fabric until it hardened.

"I want to see your beautiful breasts, Ella," he murmured against her mouth.

She nodded and helped him pull her shirt over her head.

"So gorgeous," he said before placing a soft kiss against the upper swell of her right breast.

He traced the front clasp with his finger, and when she didn't object, he unclipped it and peeled back the cups. Her breasts spilled out into his hands. He groaned and cupped them. "Look at your beautiful pink nipples."

He gently lifted her breasts, bent his head, and sucked one nipple into his mouth.

"Oh God," she moaned. She clutched at his hair and arched her back, silently asking for more.

He switched from nipple to nipple, sucking and nipping until her pelvis thrust helplessly against him. He slid his right hand inside the waistband of her pants, and she grabbed his wrist.

"Duncan, I'm not sure if this is a good idea," she said hesitantly.

"I need to touch your pussy," he whispered hotly into her ear before tracing the curve with his tongue. "Please, sweetheart. Please."

She released his wrist, and he purred into her ear.

"What was that?" she asked as she pressed one hand against his chest. "Duncan, did you – did you just purr?"

He pushed his hand under her panties and cupped her pussy, running his fingers through the soft curls before rubbing her clit, and she cried out, her question forgotten.

"You're so wet for me, sweetheart," he moaned.

"Please, Duncan," she begged, and he rubbed her clit again.

She clutched at his thick neck and arched her back when he slid his index finger deep inside her. Her pussy clenched around his finger, and he groaned harshly. "I want to fuck you, Ella."

"I want that too," she panted into his ear. "So much."

He rubbed her clit with his thumb. She moaned when he said, "You're going to come first while I watch, and then I'll take what's mine. Do you understand, Ella?"

"Yes," she gasped out.

"I want you to come for me right now," he rasped.

"Yes," she whimpered. "Oh God, yes."

He rubbed harder before tugging on her clit. That sound he made – the one she could swear was purring - loudened at her cry of pleasure, and he cupped one breast and kneaded it roughly. "That's right, sweetheart. Show me how good it feels. Show me -"

The elevator lights flickered, and Ella cried out when the entire elevator shuddered. There was another rough jolt, the sound of a motor starting, and the lights came on with a brightness that made them both blink.

"Shit," Duncan snapped. He yanked his hand out of her pants and helped her fasten her bra. Ella climbed to her feet and pulled on her shirt as he slipped into his own. The elevator stopped, and the doors slid open. A maintenance man stood in the lobby, and he grinned at them.

"Sorry about that, folks. Everyone okay in here?"

"Just fine," Duncan said as Ella ran out of the elevator.

He hurried after her. "Ella, wait!"

"I'm sorry," she called over her shoulder. "I have to go. My lunch break is over, and I have to get back to work."

"Let me get this straight." Rowan grabbed another handful of carrots and plopped into the armchair. Gus, who sat on the arm of it, hissed at her and jumped down before stalking toward the bed. He jumped onto the bed and glared at her as Rowan laughed. "Oh, Gus-Gus, why do you hate me?"

"He hates everyone," Ella said as she poured a glass of water for Belle. "Except Duncan Gillis, apparently."

Rowan crunched down a carrot. "So, this morning, you got two more massage clients, were trapped in an elevator, didn't wet your pants, and made out with Duncan. Is that what you're saying?"

"Yes," Ella said.

"Nice." Rowan held her fist up, and Ella bumped it before sitting in the second armchair.

Belle sat in the chair next to the computer desk and sipped at her water. "So now what?"

Ella shrugged. "I don't know. I shouldn't have made out with him, but I was terrified, and it was a good distraction."

"Ouch," Belle said. "Maybe don't say that to Duncan."

"I wouldn't," Ella said.

"You're telling me that the only reason you made out with Duncan was to distract you from your claustrophobia?" Rowan asked.

"Yes?" Ella said.

"I call bullshit," Rowan said cheerily. "If they hadn't gotten the elevator fixed with such horrible timing, would you have fucked him?"

"Rowan!" Ella blushed furiously.

"Answer the question, honey," Rowan said before popping another baby carrot into her mouth.

"Yes," Ella said. "I was actually disappointed when the elevator started working again. I was feeling awful and afraid, and then Duncan and I started kissing, and I could have stayed in that stupid elevator forever."

"Huh, kiss Duncan Gillis and cure your claustrophobia. We should try to market that. We'd make millions," Rowan said with a grin.

Ella scowled at her. "I'm not letting anyone else kiss Duncan Gillis. He's mine and…."

She trailed off and gave Belle a horrified look as Belle snorted. "Sounds like Duncan Gillis is rubbing off on you."

"Oh, I'm sure he'd love to rub off on her," Rowan said.

Belle laughed so hard that water sloshed out of her glass and spilled onto the floor. She jumped up and, still giggling, grabbed some paper towels from the kitchen and mopped up the spill.

"Oh my God, what is happening to me?" Ella said. "I'm losing it."

"Nope, not losing it, just really horny for Duncan, and I couldn't be happier about it. He's perfect for you," Belle said.

"He's not perfect for me," Ella said before hesitating. "Something kind of weird did happen when we were, uh, making out."

"Ooh, I like weird," Rowan said. "What was it? Did he want to call you mommy and have you spank him? Was his dick curved?"

Belle's mouth dropped open. "They can be curved?"

"Hell, yes," Rowan said solemnly. "Perry's dick looked like a banana, I swear to God. It took us a good ten minutes to figure out a position where it wouldn't come poking out my belly button."

"You're lying!" Belle said. "There's no way that's true."

"Hand to God," Rowan said. "I'm guessing that Bennett's is as straight as an arrow, then?"

Belle blushed. "Yes."

"And big, yeah? Very, very big?"

"It's the only one I've seen, but yes, I think it's pretty big."

Rowan winked at her before turning back to Ella. "So, is his dick straight or curved?"

"I don't know, I haven't even seen it or – or touched it," Ella said.

"You need to get on that," Rowan said solemnly. "In more ways than one."

Belle snickered. "What was weird, Ella?"

"When we – and I know this sounds crazy – were making out, Duncan was…purring."

"Purring," Rowan said.

"Yes."

Rowan glanced at Gus. "Purring like a cat?"

Ella nodded. "Again, I know it sounds crazy, but I swear it was actual purring."

"Well, I can't say that I've heard a guy make a sound like purring when we're having sex, but they make a hell of a lot of strange noises from time to time," Rowan said.

"No," Ella said. "It didn't *sound* like purring. It was purring. He sounded exactly like Gus, just louder." She glanced at Belle and frowned. "Belle? What's wrong?"

"Uh, nothing," Belle said.

Ella studied her carefully, but her cell phone chimed before she could say anything. "Sorry to kick you out, ladies, but I need to get going. My appointment with Henry Treating is in an hour, and I need to pack up my stuff and load it into the car."

"Do you need help?" Rowan asked.

She shook her head. "No, go out and have some fun, honey. How often do you get a Wednesday night off?"

"Not very often," Rowan said. "Of course, it would have been better if it was Friday night, but Kevin's been a real dick since I rejected his offer to have sex. I'm supposed to get at least one weekend off a month, and if that dirtbag tries to change the schedule, so I don't, I'm going to punch him in the nuts. I hate that Gaston put him in charge of scheduling."

"You still have next Saturday off, right?" Ella said with a frown.

"I do," Rowan said. "Gaston's closing the bar that night. The whole frackin' town will be at the celebration anyway, so there's no point in keeping it open. Don't worry, Ella-Lou, I'm still your sexy date. Unless," she gave Ella a wicked grin, "you've changed your mind and accepted Duncan's invitation to go with him?"

"Of course, I haven't," Ella said. "I wouldn't abandon you like that and -"

"I don't mind," Rowan said. "I have no problem going to the Celebration solo."

"No," Ella said. "We made plans, and I'm not changing them."

"Fine," Rowan said before standing and planting a kiss on Ella's cheek, "but I'm telling you right now that if you expect me to put out at the end of the night, you'll have to buy me at least one drink."

Ella grinned as there was a knock on the door. She opened the door and stared at the courier holding the large rectangular box. "Can I help you?"

"Delivery for Ella Cinders," he said.

She stepped back, and he placed the box on the floor before holding out a clipboard. "Sign here, please."

She signed and shut the door behind him as Belle studied the box. "What's this?"

"I have no idea," she said. Belle handed her a pair of scissors, and she slit the tape on the box before opening it. She pulled off the bubble wrap as Rowan and Belle stood over her.

"Oh my God," she said as the painting was revealed.

"That's cool looking," Rowan said.

Her hands shaking, Ella carefully picked up the painting from the box.

"Hey," Belle said, "isn't that the painting from the gallery? One of Samuel's?"

Ella nodded numbly. "Yes, but it has to be a replica."

"It looks exactly like the one from the gallery," Belle said. "It's in the same frame and everything."

Ella stared at the painting, her heart beating fiercely in her chest as she realized Belle was correct. "I – it is. It's the original."

"Holy shitballs," Belle said.

"What?" Rowan asked. "What's the big deal?"

"This painting costs a hundred grand. It had a sold sign on it when we looked at it in the gallery," Belle said.

Rowan's mouth dropped open. "A hundred grand?"

"Yup." Belle bent and picked up a small white envelope. "There's a card."

"Open it," Ella said faintly. She leaned the painting against the wall. Her hands still shook, and she was afraid she would drop it. She stared at the little girl on the tire swing as Belle pulled out a plain light-blue card.

"For the prettiest girl in the gallery." She flipped the card over. "That's all it says."

"Someone has a secret admirer," Rowan said.

Ella shook her head. "It's impossible. I didn't know anyone except Belle, Bennett, and Duncan at the gallery."

She looked up at Belle. "You and Bennett didn't buy this for me, did you?"

Belle shook her head. "Where would I get a hundred grand?"

"Bennett has lots of money. That's what you said," Ella said.

"True, but we didn't buy it for you, honey. I swear."

"Maybe it was Duncan," Rowan said. "What does he do for a living?"

"He's in investing like Bennett," Ella said.

"So, he has lots of money then?"

"No, I don't think so. Besides, he wouldn't buy this for me."

"Why not? Maybe he thinks it'll get him into your pants," Rowan said with a grin.

Belle laughed. "Ella's amazing, and Duncan is obsessed with her but buying her a hundred-thousand-dollar painting in the hopes that she might sleep with him? That's a little crazy. Besides, I don't think he's rich like Bennett. His house is small, and he doesn't drive a flashy car or anything."

Ella continued to stare at the painting as Belle kissed her on the cheek before shrugging into her jacket. "Are we still on for breakfast at the diner before work tomorrow?"

Ella nodded. "I'll be there."

"Me too," Rowan said.

She and Belle left, and Ella reached out and traced the painting with her fingertips as a soft smile crossed her face. She didn't know who had sent her the painting, but at this very moment, she didn't care.

CHAPTER 6

E lla slid into the booth at Snow's Diner. She was early. Neither Rowan nor Belle had arrived yet, but she had slept terribly last night. Her appointment with Henry Treating had gone well. He even commented on booking her again next week, and she returned home happy and excited. She spent over half an hour staring at her new painting and grinning like an idiot. But once she crawled into bed, she couldn't stop thinking about Duncan and that moment in the elevator.

She'd tossed and turned restlessly for nearly three hours, and when she finally fell asleep, her dreams were filled with images of Duncan, his hard hands and warm body, and his raspy voice whispering naughty things that had set her body on fire. Erotic images of them in her bed with their naked bodies entwined so closely she could hardly breathe, of his warm mouth kissing and caressing her skin as he purred loudly. She had woken around five. Gus sat on her chest, and she realized the purring in her dreams had been him. Ella had pushed him off, and he'd hissed angrily before flouncing into the living room. She stared at the ceiling for a while as her entire body throbbed and pulsed for relief. She'd masturbated and brought herself to an oddly unfulfilling orgasm before taking a decidedly cold shower.

Not that it helped, she thought grumpily as another wave of painful lust throbbed in her lower body. She was so hot for Duncan that she could masturbate into a coma, and it wouldn't be good enough. Why did he have to be so damn hot? Why did he have to –

"Good morning, sweetheart."

She jerked when Duncan slid into the booth beside her. He crowded up against her and rested his hand on her thigh. He caressed it, and she shivered violently before trying to tug it away.

"What are you doing here?" she asked.

"Thought I'd have some breakfast. You can imagine how happy I was when I saw you here, too," he said.

"Move your hand," she said in a low mutter.

"Sure," he said, and her eyes widened when he easily pulled her thighs apart and cupped her pussy through her jeans. His fingers pressed against her rhythmically, and she clamped her legs around his hand.

"What are you doing?" She licked her lips and looked nervously around the busy diner. She froze when a heavy-set man walked by their booth.

"Moving my hand," Duncan said innocently.

"Stop that," she whispered when his hand tightened, and he put delicious pressure on her already swollen clit.

"Ohhh," she moaned softly, her pelvis thrusting against his fingers.

He grinned wickedly at her. "Doesn't feel like you want me to stop. How did the appointment go last night?"

He pressed her clit again before rubbing it firmly. She gripped the table and willed herself not to squirm against his fingers.

"Ella?" he prompted.

"What?" she gasped.

"Your appointment? How did it go."

"Uh, fine, uh, good. He might book me for another."

"That's great," he said cheerfully.

Their server stopped next to the booth. "Hey guys, what can I get you to drink?"

"I'll take an orange juice, please," Duncan said as his fingers rubbed circles against Ella's clit.

"And for you, hon?" The server glanced at Ella.

"Sweetheart, she asked you a question," Duncan said.

Ella looked up from the table and croaked, "Coffee."

"Coming right up," their server said with a strange look at Ella before walking away.

Duncan leaned in and breathed into her ear, "I didn't sleep last night. All I could think about was how wet your pussy was, how hard your little nipples turned when I sucked on them, and how you moved when I touched you."

"Duncan, please," she whispered.

"I almost came to your house last night." His tongue darted out and probed her ear, and her pelvis jerked against his fingers. "I want to see you come, Ella. You have no idea how much."

"Oh my God," she whispered. "Duncan, you – you have to stop. I'm so close."

"Is that right?"

The dim murmuring of the other diners faded, and she was barely aware of Duncan's warm breath in her ear. The only thing she could feel, the only thing that seemed to matter, was Duncan's fingers rubbing and circling against her jeans in a delicious friction that made her want to scream with pleasure. She clamped her mouth shut, her nostrils flaring as she dragged in desperately needed oxygen.

Fuck, she couldn't come in a goddamn diner full of people. She couldn't. She absolutely, positively could not.

"I can smell how wet you are, sweetheart," Duncan rasped. "It would be so easy to fuck you right now, wouldn't it? So easy to just slide that wet little pussy over my dick and watch you ride me to your climax. Would you like that? Would you like to -"

He stopped, a low growl erupting from his throat as Ella's body stiffened, and she made a soft, hoarse cry. Her nails dug into his wrist, and he eased the pressure of his hand between her legs.

Ella stared fixedly at the table as Duncan's hand slowed to a stop, her heart slamming against her ribcage, and her legs shaking from the force of her orgasm. Holy fucking shit, she had just climaxed in a fucking diner.

"Here's your juice and your coffee." Their server was back, and Ella closed her eyes as the woman placed her coffee in front of her. "You like lots of sugar, right, hon?"

Ella nodded, and there was the soft clunk of a plate as the waitress placed the cream and sugar next to the coffee. She walked away, and Duncan leaned in again.

"Do you know how beautiful you look right now, Ella?"

"Duncan, I…"

"I could watch you come again and again," he muttered. "In fact, why don't we go back to my place right now and -"

"Morning." Belle plunked down in the seat across from them. "Hey, Duncan, I didn't know you were joining us."

Neither he nor Ella replied, and Bella stared at the two of them. "Ella? Honey, what's wrong?"

"Nothing," Ella said. "Move, Duncan. I have to use the ladies' room."

He slid out, and, her legs trembling violently, she hurried

across the restaurant and down the hallway to the ladies' room. She pushed the door open and stumbled to the counter, gripping it tightly as she stared at herself in the mirror. The two stalls behind her were empty, and she said a silent prayer of thanks. She took a deep breath. Duncan Gillis had just made her climax in a fucking restaurant with nothing more than his hand and some dirty talk. Her pussy throbbed at the memory. Already it wanted more - it wanted Duncan's cock - and she glared at it.

"Stop it!" she snarled and then rubbed her hand across her forehead. Jesus Christ, now she was talking to her own damn crotch. Duncan Gillis was driving her insane.

The bathroom door banged open, and she squealed in surprise when Duncan strode through. He took her arm and pushed her against the wall beside the sinks.

"Duncan, this is the ladies' room!"

He kissed her roughly, pushing her arms above her head and pinning them to the wall as he rubbed his crotch almost desperately against hers.

"Spread your legs," he muttered in a harsh growl against her mouth. When she hesitated, he nipped her bottom lip until it stung. "Spread them now, Ella."

She moaned and did what he asked. He groaned and wrapped his arms around her waist. He lifted her, and she automatically hooked her legs around his waist. He pushed her back against the wall, his hips pumping furiously against her, and she gasped with every brush of his jean-clad erection against her pussy.

He kissed her again, swallowing her protests. She gave up at the feel of his warm tongue and returned his kiss with wild abandonment. He rubbed harder as his loud purring echoed in the small room, and she met each of his thrusts with a short pump of her pelvis.

Holy shit, she was dry-humping Duncan Gillis in the bathroom, and, God help her, she was going to come again.

"Fuck," he groaned. "I'm about to come in my goddamn jeans, Ella."

"Do it," she said breathlessly. "Do it, Duncan. I want to see it."

His purring rose another notch. It was all she could hear now, and she watched as his pupils became dark slits, and their colour changed from pale blue to a blazing golden yellow.

"Duncan, what's happening to you?"

She should have been afraid, but she wasn't. Duncan would never hurt her, she belonged to him, and he would never –

"Oh my God!"

The woman's shrill voice made Duncan's purring cut out with an abrupt and jagged cough. He glared over his shoulder at the older woman, and Ella groaned in dismay when she realized it was Marlene Bison, the biggest gossip in town.

"Get out!" Duncan snarled.

"I'll do no such thing, Duncan Gillis!" Marlene snapped. "This is the ladies' room and no place for your – your sexual depravity! The two of you should be ashamed!"

Her gaze narrowed in on Ella. "Just wait until your step-mother hears about this, Ella Cinders!"

Duncan growled at her, and Marlene puffed herself up to her full height. "Did you just growl at me?"

"Duncan put me down," Ella said. She dropped her legs, and he lowered her to the floor before grabbing her hand and tugging her toward the door.

"You keep your mouth shut about what you just saw," he growled to Marlene. She glared at him in return, and he stomped past her, dragging Ella with him out of the bathroom.

"Duncan, stop!" Ella pulled at his hand as he hurried her toward the diner door.

"Come home with me, Ella. Right now," he said.

"I can't," she said. "I'm having breakfast with Belle and Rowan."

His look was almost desperate with need. "Ella -"

"No," she said. "I'm sorry, but I have to work today. I can't just drop everything and go home with you."

Frustration crossed his face, and he released her hand. "Fine. I'll see you around, Ella."

He stormed out of the diner and her face pale and hands shaking, Ella walked slowly to the booth. Rowan sat next to Belle, and they gave her twin looks of concern.

"Honey, what was that about?" Belle asked as Ella slid into the booth and dropped her head into her hands.

"Marlene Bison just caught Duncan and me dry-humping in the ladies' room," she said.

Rowan's mouth dropped open, and she gave Ella a look of pure delight. "Oh my God, you are fucking kidding me."

"I'm not," Ella groaned. "She flipped out and yelled at us and...."

Marlene walked by their booth. She glared at Ella and muttered, "For shame, Ella Cinders."

"Get lost, Marlene," Rowan snapped.

Marlene sniffed loudly and walked away as Belle reached out and took Ella's hand. "Don't worry about it, Ella."

"Don't worry about it? By tomorrow, everyone will know that we were...oh, fuck." She raised her head and stared at her two best friends. "Duncan's really mad at me."

"Why would he be mad at you?" Belle asked.

"Because he wanted me to go home with him, and I said no. I have to work," she said.

"He'll get over it," Rowan said. "Don't worry, honey."

"Yeah," Ella said. She stared at the menu in front of her, ignoring Belle and Rowan's worried looks.

ELLA PARKED HER CAR IN FRONT OF DUNCAN'S HOME. SHE didn't see his car parked in the driveway, and she scanned the street before climbing out of her vehicle. She grabbed her cleaning supplies from the backseat and headed slowly up the driveway.

She had spent last night hiding in her apartment, waiting nervously for her stepmother or Ana to come barging in and demand to know what happened at the diner. To her surprise, they hadn't shown up, and Ella finally went to bed just after nine, another part of her wondering if Duncan would show up. That didn't happen either, and he hadn't replied to her apology text.

She left her tiny apartment early this morning for her massage appointment with Marjorie Wilkins. Duncan's car had been in the driveway when she arrived. She half-expected him to be waiting in his front yard when she left Marjorie's place at around quarter to eight, but his house was quiet and still with the curtains drawn against the sunlight.

She picked through the ring of keys Ana had given her earlier in the week and located the one with Duncan's initials. She knocked and waited. A pointless gesture since he was, at this very moment, playing basketball and being seduced by Ana in her red dress, but she knocked anyway. After a few moments, she entered the house and slipped out of her shoes. She had never been in Duncan's home. Ana had laid claim to cleaning his place the day he hired Cinders Cleaning. Ella was intensely curious about what it looked like. She was very tempted to go directly to his bedroom and maybe lie on his bed or sniff his clothes. She berated herself internally before grabbing her cleaning supplies and looking for the kitchen. She would start there and finish up in his bedroom. The kitchen would be the messiest if Duncan were like eighty percent of their clientele.

Nearly an hour later, she wandered down the hallway. Duncan was surprisingly neat for a bachelor, and she wondered why he even wanted a weekly cleaning service. He seemed to pick up after himself, and his home wasn't that large. Expensive furnishings, though, she thought distractedly. The man had good taste. That was obvious.

There were three closed doors in the hallway, and she tried the first one. It was locked, and she shrugged and moved on to the second. This one revealed a bathroom, and it took her less than twenty minutes to clean it. Swiping the sink one last time, she headed toward the final door. This one led to his bedroom, and her heart sped up when she stared at his rumpled sheets and the pair of jeans lying crumpled on the floor.

"Keep it together, Ella," she muttered. She took a quick peek in his closet, stopping herself from actually sniffing the neat rows of clothing that hung on the metal rod before she dusted the nightstand and the top of the dresser. There was a picture of Duncan and his parents sitting on the dresser, and she picked it up, tracing her finger over Duncan's face before returning it to its spot. She picked up his jeans and laid them on the bed, studying the smears of coloured paint before sweeping and mopping the hardwood.

The door to the connecting bathroom was open, and a grin crossed her face when she entered the small room. As tidy as the rest of his house was, here was actual evidence that Duncan was a bachelor. A pair of his briefs and a couple of towels were on the floor and the mirror over the sink had water spots. Blobs of toothpaste and shaving cream were in the sink.

An image of Duncan shaving, maybe standing there naked as he waited for the shower to heat, went through her and her nipples hardened immediately. She sighed and returned to the bedroom to pick up her bucket of cleaning supplies. Duncan's house was her last house of the day, and she shouldn't linger. She wasn't sure when he would finish playing basketball, but she had no wish to run into him. What if - her stomach churned with jealousy - Ana was with him? She sighed and pushed the image of Ana in Duncan's bed out of her head before starting to clean the bathroom.

DUNCAN TOSSED HIS KEYS ON THE HALLWAY TABLE BEFORE kicking off his shoes. He stopped in the kitchen for a drink of water and then jogged to his bedroom. Basketball at the rec center had been a damn nightmare. Ella's stepsister, Ana, had shown up in a skin-tight red dress that left nothing to the imagination. His teammates were stupidly distracted by her, but he'd ignored her grimly. He'd even slipped out the back door of the locker room, hoping to avoid her, but she'd been waiting for him at his car. His polite smile had turned into a grimace when she pressed her body against his and asked him to go for drinks. At his polite but firm refusal, she pouted like a little girl – God, why did so many women think that was attractive – and then asked him to go to the Centennial Celebration with her.

He nearly laughed in her face, swallowing it down at the

last moment as she rubbed her hand across his chest. At his second refusal, a look of frustration and anger crossed her face, and he mumbled a quick goodbye before sliding into his truck. She'd still been standing in the parking lot when he drove away, looking more than a little shocked at his quick exit.

He pulled his t-shirt over his head and dropped it into the laundry basket. He couldn't get Ella Cinders out of his head, and if he had to listen to his lion grumble at him one more time to claim her, he would go mad. He shouldn't have ignored her text this morning. She had nothing to apologize for, but he was so worked up that he probably would have tried to get her to sext with him if he had returned her text. He had no self-control when it came to her.

There was a noise in the bathroom, and he froze while pulling off his gym shorts. His lion roared happily when Ella wandered out of the bathroom, tugging a pair of rubber gloves off her hands and carrying a bucket of cleaning supplies.

She wore her red work shirt with a pair of worn jeans, and – holy fucking hell – her long blonde hair hung in two neat braids down her back. At the sight of those braids, his control snapped like a twig, and his lion pushed to the front.

***

"DUNCAN? I THOUGHT YOU WERE PLAYING BASKETBALL." Ella stared at the man standing in the middle of the bedroom. He wore just a pair of gym shorts, and she studied his lean body as lust danced to life in her belly. He made a low growl. Her pussy throbbed at the sound as he stalked toward her.

"Duncan," she said as he pulled the bucket of cleaning supplies from her hand and threw them on the floor.

ELIZABETH KELLY

"Mine," he said and yanked her into his embrace. He kissed her hotly as the purring started, and she put her hands against his chest. She meant to push him away and tell him that they couldn't do this, but she moaned at the feel of his warm skin and threw her arms around him. They kissed eagerly, their tongues battling for control before he tore his mouth away and grabbed the front of her shirt. He ripped it in half and yanked it down her arms before fumbling for her bra clasp. He released it, and her bra was gone before she could even blink.

He tore at the button on her jeans and then raked them down her legs along with her panties. When she was naked, he made a low growl of approval before picking her up and carrying her to the bed. He dropped her roughly onto the mattress, and when he shoved down his shorts, she stared eagerly at his cock. It was erect and standing straight up from his body, the tip of it brushing against his lower abdomen. Wetness flooded her pussy as he ripped open the nightstand drawer and grabbed a condom. He rolled it on hurriedly, and she lifted herself to her elbows as he placed his hands on her knees.

"Open," he growled.

She spread her legs immediately, and he glanced at her glistening sex before pushing his lean body between her thighs. The head of his cock bumped against her clit, she cried out, and then he slid into her tight entrance. She threw her head back and moaned. Nothing had ever felt so good, so right, as the feel of his cock stretching her inner walls to the limit. She repeatedly moaned as he pushed again until he was buried completely inside her.

"Fuck!" Desperation coloured his voice as he propped himself up on his hands above her. "Fuck, Ella, I can't wait."

"Don't," she panted. "I'm good."

She slid her hand between their bodies and rubbed at her clit as he thrust back and forth. Her pussy tightened around him, and he muttered another curse before moving in hard and furious strokes. She pressed her other hand against his chest, feeling the reverberation in her hand as his purring started.

He thrust and retreated, their hips slapping together in a quick rhythm as her pussy sucked eagerly at his cock. She caressed her clit, pinched it lightly with her fingers and then rubbed it again as his purring turned deafening. His eyes glowed bright yellow, and a heavy beard covered his lower jaw. She touched the coarse hair, and he turned his head and captured her fingers in his mouth, sucking heavily on them as he fucked her roughly.

She made a sudden cry, her fingers slowing to a stop against her clit and her body shuddered as her orgasm rushed through her. Duncan pumped furiously back and forth and then climaxed with a roar that brought forth images of a large jungle cat. She squeezed her legs around his hips and dug her nails into his back as he jerked, trembled, and moaned above her before collapsing.

She rubbed his back as he licked her neck repeatedly and listened to the sound of his purring. She loved that sound, she realized with soft wonderment. When it began to die out, she stroked her fingers through his thick, blond hair and smiled when the purring immediately started again. He rolled off of her, and she mourned the loss of his cock and his body.

"I'm sorry," he said.

"For what?"

"For being so rough, so impatient," he said. "Plus, I kind of smell."

She laughed softly. "I was impatient too, and I smell like cleaning supplies."

"I like your scent," he said.

She sat on the side of the bed, knowing she needed to leave but not wanting to. He sat up beside her and tugged lightly on one braid. "I like your braids."

"Thank you," she said. "I guess I should probably get going."

He cupped her face and turned it toward his before pressing a gentle kiss against her mouth. "Stay the night with me, Ella."

Happiness flooded through her. "Okay."

"Really?" His grin lit up the room.

"Really, really," she said. "But you'll have to feed me at some point. I'm starving."

He laughed and kissed her again. "I can do that."

CHAPTER 7

"Ella, you don't have to do this."

"I want to," she said as she hopped out of Duncan's bed. He had ordered them pizza for dinner, and she had shamelessly eaten three pieces. She hadn't had much of an appetite for the last few days, but apparently, sex with Duncan brought it roaring back to life. She'd watched in amazement as he polished off the rest of the large pizza.

"How on earth do you stay that lean?" she'd finally asked.

He'd shrugged and patted his stomach. "Good metabolism, and I play a lot of sports."

Duncan grabbed her hand as she reached for her pants. She had borrowed one of Duncan's shirts, but her massage supplies were in the car, and she couldn't very well go outside in just his shirt.

"Where are you going?"

"I've got my massage oil in the car. I worked on Mrs. Wilkens this morning before I started cleaning houses."

"You don't have to give me a massage, Ella," Duncan repeated. "There was nothing wrong with the first one."

She laughed. "You were so tense it was like torture. Let me try again, Duncan, please."

He grinned at her. "Okay, but you don't need to go to your car." He reached into the nightstand and grabbed a bottle before tossing it to her.

She studied the label before arching her eyebrow at him. "Why do you have edible cherry-flavoured massage oil in your nightstand?"

"Why do you think, sweetheart," he said without a hint of shame.

"It's half-empty."

"I masturbate a lot?"

She burst into laughter before patting him on the thigh. "Roll onto your stomach."

He pulled off his shorts and tossed them over the bed before smiling at her. "Take off your shirt."

"Why?"

"I'll be honest with you – when I booked that first massage session, I might have been holding out hope that it would be in your bed and you would be straddling me naked," he said.

She laughed again before whipping off his shirt and striking a pose. "Well, tonight's your lucky night then, handsome. Better?"

"Sweetheart, you have no idea," he breathed. Already his cock was starting to stiffen, and she stared at him in disapproval.

"You need to behave, Duncan."

He grinned at her before flipping to his stomach. "Yes, ma'am."

She straddled him and poured oil on her hands before rubbing his shoulders. He groaned happily, and she smiled a little as she massaged and kneaded the large muscles in his back. When she rubbed his lower back, he moaned loudly, and his pelvis pressed into the bed.

"Fuck, that feels amazing."

"Good," she said. She tried to ignore how her pussy dampened as she stroked and worked the muscles. He had some tight muscles, especially in his upper back, and she worked them until they were loose and pliant under her hands.

She scooted her body down to his thighs and admired his ass for a moment before slapping it lightly. "Turn over, Duncan."

She lifted herself, and he moved to his back. His eyes were closed, and a look of bliss was on his face. Smiling, she rubbed his chest for a few minutes before pinching one flat nipple. He grunted, and his eyes flew open. His gaze immediately latched onto her breasts, and he reached out and cupped her left one, his thumb rubbing at her pebbled nipple.

"Behave," she reminded him before pushing his hand away.

His cock was standing straight up between them, and he took her hands and pushed them toward it.

"Please, sweetheart," he said in a low voice.

"Therapeutic massage, Mr. Gillis, remember?" she said tartly.

He scowled at her, and she grinned before rubbing his ab muscles. Fuck, he had a fantastic body. He moved restlessly beneath her and tried to cup her breasts again. With a teasing grin, she pushed his hands away and traced his v-line with her fingers. It made him jerk and moan loudly, and he clenched his hands around the sheet.

"You're killing me, sweetheart."

"This is supposed to be relaxing you," she said.

His muttered curse turned into a loud moan when she

gripped his cock with her oil-slicked fingers and stroked it firmly.

"Oh shit, yes," he sighed happily as he arched his pelvis into her hand. She wiggled back a little more and stroked him with her hand. His hips rose and fell as his eyes closed, and his hands gripped her thighs.

"Do you like this, Duncan?" she asked.

"Very much," he said hoarsely.

She bent and licked the head of his cock. He made a decidedly unmanly-like yelp of pleasure and thrust his hips upwards. She smiled at him, and he reached down and wrapped a hand around each of her braids. He tugged firmly, guiding her mouth to his cock, and she slid her mouth around his cock and sucked.

He moaned her name as she rubbed the base of his cock with hard strokes and bobbed her head up and down. The combination of cherry and his taste was intoxicating, and his soft groans of pleasure made her pussy throb. She traced his thighs with her fingers before gently cupping his balls. She licked the length of his cock and then sucked on the head before pressing firmly on the smooth spot just behind his balls. He cried out, his body arching and his hands tightening painfully in her braids as precum coated her mouth.

"Ella, please!" He twisted and squirmed beneath her and groaned in dismay when she released him and straightened.

"No!" He growled, and she laughed as she used both hands to stroke his dick.

"Something wrong, handsome?"

"Don't stop," he muttered. "Please."

"I like it when you beg," she said.

"Please," he said again, "Please don't stop."

She stroked his abdomen before leaning over and opening

the nightstand drawer. She smiled in triumph and pulled out the condom.

"Sweetheart," he rasped again, "please."

"I want to fuck you," she said with a sweet smile. "Is that a problem?"

His hands clamped onto her hips, and he thrust against her. "God, no."

He grunted in frustration when she couldn't rip open the foil with her oil-covered hands. "Give it to me."

He ripped it open, and she carefully rolled the condom onto his cock, spending a little longer than necessary smoothing it down, and he growled at her.

"No growling," she chastised before giving his cock a hard squeeze. It never occurred to her that admonishing him not to growl was more than a little odd. Already the purring, the growling, the way his eyes lightened to yellow seemed almost normal to her. They were a part of who Duncan was, and everything about him fascinated her.

She crouched over him, gripping his cock and guiding it into her pussy. She was very wet, and they both moaned as she sank to her knees, sheathing him entirely within her. He started to purr, and she leaned over and brushed her breast against his mouth. He sucked her nipple into his mouth, laving it with his tongue before biting it gently. She cried out, her hands sinking into his hair and clutching tightly as he cupped her breasts and kneaded them before sucking on one nipple and then the other. His hips were thrusting against her in short, hard strokes and she straightened and rubbed his hard chest.

He raised his legs and rasped, "Put your hands on my knees."

She did as he asked, and he stared at her naked body for a

long moment. She would have been embarrassed if the desire, the need for her, hadn't been so evident in his gaze.

"Ride me," he said hoarsely.

Using his knees for leverage, her back arching, she rode him slowly. His eyes were glued to her pussy, and he purred loudly before saying, "You have no fucking idea how good your pussy looks sliding up and down my cock, sweetheart."

She cried out when his fingers traced the soft blonde curls at the top of her sex before moving lower. His thumb massaged her clit, and she jerked against him, bringing a moan of pleasure from his throat.

"That's good," he breathed. "Squeeze me again, sweetheart."

She concentrated on squeezing him as she moved up and down, and he rumbled his approval before tugging on her clit. She cried out with pleasure and rode him harder as he rubbed her clit hard.

Her orgasm started, waves of breathtaking delight that started in her throbbing pussy and went crashing down her legs, and she moaned, "Duncan, I'm going to come!"

He pinched her clit again in reply, and she shrieked softly as she rode him furiously to her climax. He sat up abruptly, throwing his arms around her waist and thrusting his hips as he kissed her hard on the mouth. She could feel his purring reverberating against her breasts, the vibration of his chest making her nipples tingle with pleasure, and she clung to him as he pumped furiously into her. He threw his head back and shouted her name as he came, and she rubbed his back when he buried his face against her throat and panted.

With a soft groan, he collapsed on his back, dragging her down with him. She tried to move, and he shook his head, "No, stay right where you are."

She rested her head on his chest, listening to his purring

as his cock softened within her and his warm hands traced circles on her naked back.

"Hey, Duncan?"

"Yeah?"

"The sex is good with us, isn't it?"

"Yes. Best sex of my life, sweetheart."

She raised her head and gave him a slight grin. "I bet you say that to all the girls."

He stared solemnly at her. "No, I don't."

His intense look made her feel weird, and she stroked his fingers through his thick hair. He immediately began to purr, and she smiled again. "Do you always purr during sex?"

The low rumble of his purr cut out, and he gave her an uncomfortable look. "I don't purr, Ella."

She laughed. "Yes, you do."

She touched him again, petting him like he was a cat and grinned delightedly when the now familiar purring rewarded her. "See. You're like a big old kitty-cat."

He cleared his throat and looked away. "It's not purring. It's just a – a sound I can make, that's all."

"How do you do it?"

"I don't know. It's not that big of a deal. Don't make it into a thing."

She rolled her eyes. "I'm not making it into a thing, Duncan. I'm just curious. I like it."

Stop being such a dick to her.

Ella was studying him, and Duncan smiled tentatively at her. "You like the sound?"

She nodded and rested her cheek on his chest. She rubbed his side and hip, and he was helpless to stop the purring.

Fuck, at this point, all she had to do was look at him, and he had the urge to purr.

Knock it off, he snarled at his lion. It ignored him and continued to purr happily. It wanted him to shift. His lion wanted to feel Ella's soft hands in his mane, wanted to rub up against her and mark her and get her to scratch that one spot on his back that he could never quite reach.

Shift so we can mark our mate, his lion rumbled.

Have you gone insane? I can't shift in front of her. It'll give her a damn heart attack!

His lion hissed angrily, and Duncan's eyes widened when it tried to force the change. His hands tightened around Ella's waist, and he fought bitterly against the shift. His lion roared and tried again, and he muttered a low curse as his body stiffened.

"Duncan?" Ella tried to raise her head, and he cupped the back of her skull and kept it pressed against his chest. He had managed to successfully keep his fangs in check whenever he was around her, but they were out now, large, white, and wickedly sharp, and he knew she'd be terrified if she saw them.

"Duncan? What's wrong? Your heart is going a mile a minute," she said.

"I'm fine," he said.

She wiggled against him. "Let me up."

He released her reluctantly as, with incredible willpower, he forced his lion back. It snarled but retreated, and his fangs retracted with a soft pop.

"Your lip is bleeding," Ella said. She touched his bottom lip and showed him the blood smear on her finger.

"I must have bitten it," he said. "It's fine."

He licked the blood away, and she frowned at him.

"Come to the bathroom, and I'll put a dab of antiseptic on it. It's quite deep."

He followed her into the bathroom and let her fuss over his lip before he turned on the shower and urged her to join him. They washed each other's bodies carefully, and it was tempting to take her again right there, but he was worried that he was pushing her too much. Not many women could match his enormous appetite for sex. He tamped down his libido and kept it strictly non-sexual with control he hadn't thought possible.

They'd dried off quickly, and he'd led Ella back to his bed, holding her hand tightly, a little afraid she might try to leave despite her promise to stay the night.

They made themselves cozy in his bed, turning and changing positions until he was the big spoon to her little spoon.

"Someone sent me one of Samuel's paintings," Ella said quietly.

He studied her carefully. It was after eleven and dark, but he could see as easily as a – well, cat – in the darkness, and he rubbed her hip. "What do you mean?"

"The day before last, a courier brought a parcel to my house, and it was my favourite Samuel painting. It's the original."

"I thought it was sold at the show," he said.

"It was. There was a card, but all it said was 'for the prettiest girl at the gallery'." She hesitated. "You didn't buy the painting for me. Did you, Duncan?"

"No," he said. Technically he wasn't lying. He couldn't buy something that belonged to him already.

He watched as a soft glow of embarrassment covered her face. "That was a stupid thing to say."

"No, it wasn't." He kissed her cheek and cupped her

breast, pushing his half-erect cock against her ass. "Someone must have seen you admiring it at the gallery and bought it for you."

"That doesn't make sense," she said. "Who would buy such an expensive painting and give it to a woman they've never met?"

He shrugged. "Maybe Samuel was at the show and liked your enthusiasm for his work. Maybe it was his way of saying thanks."

She giggled and elbowed him lightly. "Samuel never goes to his shows. Everyone knows that. Besides, as much as I love the painting, I would rather he had just introduced himself if he had been there and noticed my love for his work."

"Really?"

"Yes," she said. "Not that I'm not incredibly happy to own one of his paintings – I am, stupidly so – but it would be a dream come true to meet Samuel. I've admired his work for so long, and he's so," she paused, "inspiring to me, I guess."

She laughed softly. "It's probably better that I'll never meet him. I'd make a total fool of myself if I did."

"You wouldn't," he said before cupping her pussy and rubbing his fingers over her clit.

"Ohhh," she sighed and arched her back. "I would. I'd stutter and stammer and not even be able to express how much his work means to me. God, Duncan that feels so good."

"I like making you feel good," he said as he continued to caress her clit. "Do I need to be jealous of this Samuel guy?"

She shook her head. "No. Unless Samuel is super hot and insists that I'm his muse and he must paint me."

He growled and bit her lightly on the neck, and she

grinned cheekily. "What? It's a dirty job, but someone has to do it."

He cupped her face and turned it toward his before kissing her possessively. "You're mine, Ella Cinders. Say it."

She squinted at him, and he slid one finger deep into her pussy. She gasped, her nails digging into his arms, and he said, "Be a good girl and tell me you belong to me."

"I belong to you," she said in a soft little moan.

"That's right, you do," he growled again before kissing her. "It's time to show you what good girls get, Ella."

"I like the sound of that," she said breathlessly, and he laughed before pushing her onto her back and pulling down the covers. He kissed across her body, taking his time and finding all the spots on her luscious curves that tickled. She squirmed and moaned and dug her nails into his scalp.

"Stop teasing, Duncan."

He was lying between her legs, pressing wet kisses across her lower abdomen, and he gave her an innocent look. "What do you mean?"

"Give me what I want." She scowled at him and pushed on his head, and he laughed before sliding his hands under her ass.

"Yes, ma'am." He studied her lovely pussy before sliding his tongue across her. His lion growled happily at the taste of his mate, and he licked her again, cleaning away her sweet cream as she moaned and sighed.

"Mine," he muttered again before spreading her open with his thumbs and licking her clit. She gasped, her hands pressing against his scalp, and he licked and teased and tormented the sweet little bud until it was swollen and peeking out from between her lips.

He sucked on it, and when he growled, the vibration of his lips sent her over the edge. She shrieked his name, her thighs clamping around his head and holding him firmly in place as warm wetness covered his lips and cheeks. He licked her clean again as her body shuddered with little aftershocks of pleasure before sitting up and rubbing her thighs. He stared at her regretfully, wanting so badly to fuck her that he could barely stand it, but he made himself lie beside her. He had already taken her twice, and she would be tender and sore. The thought of hurting her made him feel sick to his stomach.

"Duncan?" She frowned at him. "Aren't we going to have sex?"

He shook his head. "No, you need to rest. I know you're sore."

"Is that why you didn't fuck me in the shower?"

He nodded, and a look of relief and frustration crossed her face. "God, Duncan, I thought you were getting tired of me already."

He scowled at her. "I'll never get tired of you, Ella. You have no idea how much I want to fuck you again."

She smiled happily and spread her thighs wide. "Good."

She tried to tug him on top of her and smacked him lightly on the chest when he refused to move. "Don't make me tie you to the bed and have my way with you, Duncan Gillis."

"We should wait," he moaned when she reached down and gripped his cock.

"No," she said. "I'm not sore, and if it starts to be too much, I'll tell you."

"Are you sure?" he asked, but he was already reaching for a condom.

"Positive. Unless," she gave him a cheeky grin, "it's too much for you? Totally understand if you're unable to, and I won't judge you at all."

He growled at her and nipped her collarbone. "Keep

talking like that, and I'll fuck you until you can't walk, Ms. Cinders."

"Promises, promises," she said before kissing his chest. "Come on, Mr. Gillis. Show me what you've got."

———

ELLA SQUIRMED UNHAPPILY AND TRIED TO SHIFT AWAY FROM Duncan. She was much too warm. He felt like a damn furnace against her, and she was pretty certain his entire body was draped across her abdomen.

"Duncan, get off," she muttered.

He didn't move, and she opened her eyes, blinking in the bright light from the window as she stared blankly at the ceiling. She yawned and reached down to push Duncan away. "Duncan, you're too heavy. You need to…."

She trailed off as her hand touched soft fur and – holy fucking hell – a wet nose. She looked down, and adrenaline flooded her veins as a low moan of fear escaped her lips. A lion, an enormous and horrifyingly real lion, was in bed with her. His giant head was resting on her stomach, and she snatched her hand away from its face as her limbs began to shake.

"You're dreaming, Ella," she whispered and closed her eyes. After ten seconds, she opened them, and the tears slid down her cheeks. If this was a dream, it was terrifyingly realistic. Her breath tore in and out of her throat in harsh gasps, and she froze when the lion stirred against her. He raised his head and yawned, his teeth the size of her goddamn hand, before blinking sleepily at her.

He immediately began to purr, and she yelped in terror when he butted his face against hers and rubbed his forehead on her chin. His large and painfully scratchy tongue licked her neck, and she moaned again in fear,

The lion raised his head and blinked again as an almost human-like look of confusion crossed his broad face. He sat on his haunches, and Ella lunged to the left as little cries of fear burst from her throat. She fell out of bed, banging her hip hard against the wooden floor and scrambled to her feet before turning to face the lion.

"G-good kitty," she whimpered, holding her hands in front of her like a shield. "Stay, kitty. Stay."

The lion stood on the bed, and she screamed and backed away, almost tripping over her own feet. Her eyes widened, and her mouth dropped open as the lion's body began to ripple, and there were soft cracks and pops. His fur receded, his fangs retracted, and in less than ten seconds, the lion was gone, and a naked Duncan Gillis was on his hands and knees on the bed. He slid off the bed and started toward her. "Ella, honey, take a deep breath. It's okay."

"You're a fucking lion," she said.

"Ella, honey, don't panic. I'm not going to hurt you," he said.

"Don't – don't come near me," she said.

Her ears rang, and the room went blurry. She swayed on her feet, only dimly aware of Duncan rushing forward. Her eyes rolled up in her head, and she fainted for the first time in her life.

CHAPTER 8

"Ella? Honey, wake up. Open your eyes."

Belle's voice dragged her out of the darkness, and she stared blearily at her best friend. "Belle?"

"Hi, honey." Belle smiled at her in relief. "How do you feel?"

"Uh, fine, I think. My hip hurts." She took a deep breath. "I had the craziest dream, Belle. I dreamt that I was in Duncan's bed, and a lion was sleeping with me. A crazy-ass big one. And then it – it turned into Duncan."

She sat up and rubbed her forehead. "It was so real. I can still remember the way his fur felt and how he…."

She stared blankly at the room before glancing down at herself. She was wearing Duncan's shirt again, and she touched it lightly. "Belle, I'm in Duncan's room."

"Yeah, honey, you are," Belle said gently.

"I – it wasn't a dream," she said.

"Ella, listen to me carefully, okay?" Belle took her cold hands and rubbed them with her warm ones.

"It wasn't a dream, was it, Belle?" Ella could hear the panic in her voice, and she took several deep breaths.

245

"No, it wasn't. Duncan is a lion shifter. He can change from human to lion."

"That's impossible," Ella said.

"I know how it sounds, but, honey, it's true. I swear to you it is."

"H-how did you know that Duncan was a…."

She couldn't make herself say the words 'lion shifter'.

"I didn't. At least not until Duncan called Bennett this morning in a panic. I had suspicions after you mentioned the purring, but I didn't know anything for sure."

"Why did Duncan call you and Bennett?" Feeling slow and unbelievably stupid, Ella couldn't quite grasp what she was missing.

"Well, he called us because Bennett -"

"Is a shifter," Ella finished as understanding dawned. "He's a bear shifter, isn't he?"

Belle nodded solemnly, and Ella pulled away from her hands. "Why didn't you tell me?"

"I couldn't, honey. Shifters don't, for the most part, want humans to know of their existence. I can't blame them for that. You know what humans would do to them. Experiments and…"

She shuddered lightly before taking Ella's hands again. "I'm sorry, honey. I wanted to tell you and Ro, but Bennett asked me not to. He never even told me that Duncan was a shifter."

Ella stared at their clasped hands. "This isn't real. There's no such thing as shifters, Belle."

"It's real, Ella," Belle said.

There was something in the tone of her voice and the look on her face that brought home the truth to Ella.

"Oh my God," she said. "Why – how can you be so fucking calm about this?"

"Well," Belle said, "Bennett did shift into his bear form when we were kids, so I'd already seen it. After my dad's heart attack, Bennett told me the truth and shifted to his bear form. Honestly, I wasn't that surprised."

She stopped and gave Ella a nervous look. "And there was something else."

"What?"

"Before my dad left for rehab, he told me my mother was a tiger shifter."

Ella stared in shock at her. "You're a tiger shifter?"

"No," Belle said. "I'm as human as my dad. When a shifter and a human mate, their offspring is either fully human or a shifter. I didn't get any of my mother's shifter abilities."

"Fuck, how many types of shifters are there?" Ella asked.

"I don't really know. Bennett doesn't like to talk about it much, and I haven't pushed him on it."

"If it's such a secret, why did Duncan shift to his lion form when I was in his bed?"

"I don't know," Belle said. "You'll have to ask him."

Ella paled and rubbed compulsively at her lips. "Where is he?"

"In the living room with Bennett. He's pretty upset."

"He's upset? I'm the one who woke up with a fucking lion sleeping on me, Belle," Ella said.

Her eyes widened. "I had sex with a lion!"

"No, you had sex with Duncan." She squeezed Ella's hands. "You should talk to Duncan, honey."

"I'm afraid," Ella said.

"You don't need to be. Duncan would never hurt you."

"You don't know that. What if he was starving one night and lost control and shifted? His lion would tear me apart and eat me for supper."

Belle snickered. "Honey, that isn't going to happen."

"This isn't funny," Ella said.

Belle winced. "I know. I'm sorry, honey. I didn't mean to laugh. I know how weird this is, but I think you'll feel better once you talk to Duncan."

"I don't want to be alone with him."

"I'll stay right there with you, and so will Bennett. Nothing's going to happen, honey, I promise. Come on, get dressed, okay?"

HER HEART POUNDING, ELLA FOLLOWED BELLE INTO THE living room. Duncan wore his gym shorts again and stood by the window with Bennett.

He started toward her. "Ella, sweetheart, I'm sorry. I didn't mean to -"

He stopped, pain crossing his features, when she made a low moan of fear and skittered away from him. He glanced at Bennett, and the bear shifter gave him a sympathetic look as Belle rubbed Ella's arm.

"It's okay, honey."

"Ella," Duncan said, "I'm sorry for frightening you. I swear I didn't -"

"Shift," she said.

He gave her a wary look. "What?"

"Shift," she said. "I want to see it."

"That's not a good idea," he said. "Belle, tell her it isn't a good idea."

Ella shook her head. "I'm not even sure I believe any of this is real, so if you want me to believe that I'm standing in front of a man who can turn into a lion, you need to prove it to me."

Duncan hesitated before grabbing the waistband of his shorts. He turned to Belle, and she said, "Oh, right, sorry."

She turned around and faced the wall as Duncan shoved his shorts down. He took a deep breath and closed his eyes, and Ella watched in a combination of terror and fascination as he shifted into a lion.

He sat on his haunches and stared unblinkingly at her as Belle peeked over her shoulder before turning around. There were a few moments of silence as Ella studied the giant lion. His fur was the same colour as Duncan's hair, the thick mane surrounding his head a darker brown. He was massive in size, and she stared for a long moment at the thick, sharp claws on his feet.

"Ella?" Belle said. "Why don't you touch him."

She didn't want to, she was still terribly afraid despite both Belle's and Bennett's presence, but she stumbled forward on legs that felt like wooden stilts. She clutched Belle's hand like a lifeline as she stopped a few feet in front of the lion. Even sitting on his haunches, he was taller than her, and her hand trembled badly as she stretched her arm toward him. She caught a glimpse of his fangs and dropped her hand before backing away.

"No. No, I can't do this," she said before turning and running from the room. She fumbled her car keys out of her pocket and opened her door, ignoring Belle when she called her name. She started the car and drove away without looking back, hot tears streaming down her cheeks.

What the actual fuck was happening?

———

ELLA WAS BARELY IN HER APARTMENT BEFORE EDITH AND Ana burst through the door.

"Where have you been?" Edith demanded as Ana glared daggers at her.

"None of your business," Ella snapped.

"You little whore," Ana spat. "Did you think we wouldn't find out?"

For a moment, Ella thought she was talking about Duncan being a lion shifter and fear curled in her belly. "What are you talking about?"

"The whole town knows that you and Duncan were having sex in the bathroom at the diner. Marlene told everyone! How could you do this to me?" Ana snarled

"I didn't have sex with Duncan in the bathroom," Ella said. "Although I did have sex with him multiple times in his bed last night."

"You fat bitch!" Ana screeched. "Duncan's mine, you know that!"

"Duncan is a human being, not some possession you can own!" Ella shouted at her. "I'm sorry he's not attracted to you, but get the fuck over it, you spoiled little brat."

"How dare you!" Ana shouted before looking at her mother. "Mother! Are you going to allow her to speak to me that way?"

"Apologize to your sister. Immediately," Edith demanded.

"She's not my sister, and I won't apologize," Ella said.

"You think you have some kind of future with Duncan Gillis?" Ana said. "He may have felt sorry for your fat ass and thrown you a pity fuck, but it's me he's going to be with. Stay away from him, Ella. I mean it!"

"Fuck you, Ana," Ella said wearily.

Edith stormed forward and slapped her across the face. Ella staggered back and stared at her stepmother as Edith glared at her. "Don't you ever speak to my daughter that way again."

"Get out," Ella said. "Get out of my house."

"Your house?" Edith's eyes widened. "You live here because of my generosity. Everything you have, everything you ever will have, is because of me and don't you ever forget that. If it weren't for my generosity, you would have grown up in some foster home where they didn't give a shit about you."

"Your generosity?" Ella laughed bitterly. "I spent my entire childhood cleaning your house and other people's houses while you made money from it. You have a funny idea of generosity."

"You ungrateful cow!" Edith shouted. "I've given you more than you deserve. What more could you want?"

"What more could I want?" Ella stared at her in disbelief. "Are you kidding me? You were the only mother I ever knew. All I wanted was your love. But I'll never get that, will I?"

"No," Edith said. "No one will ever love you, Ella Cinders."

Ella blinked back the hot tears as Ana gave her a look of triumph.

"You will stay away from Duncan Gillis. Do you hear me, Ella? Ana wants him, and she's going to have him," Edith said.

"Are you going to make me stay away from him?" Ella said softly.

"As long as you're living under my roof, you'll do exactly what I say," Edith said.

"Fine. Then I'll leave." Ella crossed the apartment and grabbed Gus's crate and a small suitcase from the closet.

"What are you doing?" Edith said.

"Leaving," Ella said.

"You have no place to go," Edith said. "You need me."

Ella laughed. "No, I don't. Oh, and I quit. I'll never clean another toilet for you again, Edith. Now get out. Both of you."

She stuffed clothes into the suitcase and didn't look up when Edith and Ana left the apartment and slammed the door behind them.

———

"CAN I ASK YOU A QUESTION, BELLE?"

"Sure." Belle placed the stack of books in her hand on the table and dropped into a chair.

Ella stared at the shelves of books in Bennett's library. She had driven to Bennett's house after packing a suitcase and Gus. Belle had welcomed her with open arms, and she and Bennett had returned with her the next day to her apartment to pack up the rest of her things. For the last three days, Ella had been hiding in one of the many bedrooms in Bennett's home with no one but Gus to keep her company.

She smiled at Belle. "Thank you again for letting me stay with you and Bennett."

"Honey, it's no problem. You can stay for as long as you want. Bennett's place is so big there's plenty of room. Hell, the three of us could live here and never once cross paths if we tried hard enough."

"You're sure Bennett doesn't mind?"

"I'm positive. It's about time you cut the cord with those horrible bitches. They weren't good for you, Ella."

"Yeah, I know," she sighed.

"What's your question, honey?" Belle asked.

"You're not afraid of Bennett, are you?"

"No," Belle said. "He would never hurt me."

"He's never just lost control and shifted?" she asked.

"No. Bennett says shifters have excellent control when it comes to that."

"Do they? I'm pretty sure Duncan didn't mean to shift while we were sleeping. Has Bennett ever done that?"

"Once or twice," Belle admitted. "It usually happens when he doesn't get enough sleep. One morning I woke up, and he was in his bear form, and I was sprawled on top of him like he was my personal bear rug that breathed."

She laughed at the memory as Ella said, "What if... do you think about what would happen if he shifted while you were having sex?"

Belle blinked at her before a small grin crossed her face. "No, I can't say that I have. I don't think that would ever happen, honey. I mean, when we have sex Bennett's fangs do come out, and he usually grows a beard and, good Lord, the growling," she grinned at Ella, "but he would never fully shift."

"Duncan purrs loudly when we're, uh, having sex," Ella said.

"That's kind of adorable," Belle said.

"Actually, he purrs just when I touch him."

"Even more adorable," Belle said.

Ella sighed. "I miss him so much, Belle."

"I know you do, honey. You should talk to him. He wants to be with you. I know he does."

"I want to be with him too."

She suddenly stood, and Belle grinned delightedly at her. "Are you going to see him?"

"Yes."

"Yay!" Belle clapped her hands excitedly. "You want me to go with you?"

Ella shook her head. "No, I want to go alone. I'm not afraid of him anymore."

"What are you going to say to him?" Belle asked.

"I'm not entirely sure. I know I'm going to apologize for freaking out the way I did, and I think – I think I'm going to ask him if he wants to, I don't know, date or something. I really like him, Belle."

"He likes you too," Belle said. "He's going to be so happy when he sees you."

"I guess we'll find out. Wish me luck," Ella said.

"Good luck, honey. If you decide to stay at Duncan's and have a marathon sex session, text me, so I know to feed Gus."

Less than thirty minutes later, Ella stood in Duncan's doorway. She took a deep breath and knocked, smiling tentatively at Duncan when he opened the door. "Hi, Duncan."

"Hi, Ella."

"Can I come in?"

He nodded, and she followed him down the hallway and into the kitchen.

"Can I get you something to drink?" he asked politely as he kept a careful distance from her.

She shook her head. There was something different about him, something she couldn't quite place her finger on, and she studied him silently for a moment before saying, "I came to say I'm sorry."

"You have nothing to apologize for," he said. "I need to say I'm sorry. I never meant to shift like that in front of you."

"Why did you then?" she asked.

A look of embarrassment flickered across his face. "My lion wants you as his mate. When I was sleeping, he took control and shifted so that he could mark you with his scent."

"You want me as your mate?" she said.

"My lion does."

"And you?"

Her stomach dropped when he said, "No, I don't."

"So, your lion wants me as a mate, but you just wanted me for a few rounds of fucking?" She couldn't hide the hurt in her voice.

He hesitated before dropping his gaze to the floor. "That's right."

"Well, I guess you got what you wanted." She blinked back the tears.

"I'm sorry, Ella," he said in a low voice.

"Gosh, knowing you're sorry makes me feel so much better. You said you'd never get tired of me. Remember?"

He swallowed hard. "I was wrong."

"Apparently," she said. "You know, I came over here thinking you wanted something more from me. All that talk about how I belonged to you, the flipping out when other guys went near me – I was flattered by it, thought it meant you liked me. But it was just a game to you, wasn't it?"

"Ella," he said, "I'm truly sorry."

"You've made a fool out of me, Duncan Gillis, and I will never forgive you for it."

She turned to leave, pausing when Duncan called her name.

"Stay away from me, Duncan. You and your stupid lion," she said before walking out of the room.

"OPEN THE DAMN DOOR, DUNCAN!" BENNETT POUNDED ON the front door of Duncan's house. "I know you're home."

Duncan yanked open the door. "What do you want, Bennett?"

Bennett pushed past him, and Duncan slammed the door shut. "I'm tired, and I don't feel like company."

"This isn't a social call, you jackass," Bennett said. "What the hell is wrong with you?"

"What do you mean?" Duncan said.

"What do I mean? I've got one sobbing woman and one extremely pissed-off woman at my house right now, Duncan. Belle's ready to murder you."

"It's none of your business, all right? Let it go, Bennett." He shouldered past the giant bear shifter and stalked into the kitchen, growling lightly when Bennett followed him.

"I'm your best friend, Duncan, and I know better than anyone how you feel about Ella Cinders."

"I don't feel anything for her," Duncan lied.

"Bullshit!" Bennett snapped. "You're in love with the woman, and, according to Belle, she's in love with you too. Why the fuck did you tell her that you were using her? Have you lost your goddamn mind?"

"Shifters and humans aren't meant to be together," Duncan said.

"What the hell are you talking about?" Bennett said in astonishment. "You were the one who told me to go after Belle. You have a cousin who's married to a human! What is going on with you, Duncan? You want Ella, so why the sudden change in heart?"

"Because she's afraid of me!" Duncan suddenly shouted. He slammed his fist onto the counter and glared at Bennett. "You saw the look on her face, Bennett. She's terrified of what I am."

"She's not afraid of you, Duncan. It was just a shock to her, that's all. You can't blame her for her reaction."

"Belle was never afraid of you," Duncan said. "She didn't act like you would rip her apart when you shifted in front of her."

"Ella isn't Belle, all right? Belle's mother was a tiger

shifter, and Belle saw me shift when we were children. It was much easier for her to accept that shifters were real. You need to give Ella a chance."

"I can't do that," Duncan said. "The look on her face in the bedroom… it fucking destroyed me."

"She came to your house alone yesterday. She was doing it because she wanted to be with you. If she were still afraid of you, she wouldn't have gone anywhere near you, Duncan."

"She wouldn't even touch me when I was in my lion form," Duncan said. "What happens the next time we're sleeping, and I accidentally shift? What happens when we're having sex, and my fangs pop out, or my eyes start to glow? I can't always control that around her, Bennett. Fuck, all I have to do is think about her touching me, and I start purring. When it happens, and it will, she'll freak out again. I know she will. It's too much for her, and I can't spend my life trying to suppress my lion. We have to shift - you know that. The longer we don't, the less control we have over it."

"Give her a chance to get used to it, Duncan," Bennett said. "You can't expect her to accept it right away. She's spent her entire life believing that humans were the only species on the planet. It's a big adjustment to learn that shifters exist."

"It's too late," Duncan said. "I broke her heart yesterday, and she'll never forgive me. She hates me now."

"She might forgive you," Bennett said. "The Centennial Celebration is in two days. Belle's convinced Ella that she needs to go, and I think you should go too and talk to her. She'll be less likely to punch your lights out if a crowd of people is around."

Duncan shook his head. "I'm not going anywhere near the celebration."

"So, you'll let your mate dance with whichever male asks her?"

Duncan's eyes glowed, and he growled fiercely as his claws extended. Bennett stared steadily at him, and after a moment, Duncan's eyes returned to their normal colour, and he shook his head. "Yes, because she's not my mate."

Bennett clapped him on the shoulder. "She is, Duncan. You can deny it all you want, but deep down, you know the truth."

"I can't be with her," Duncan said.

"If you believe that, then you're as big of a fool as Ella says you are." Bennett squeezed his shoulder and left.

CHAPTER 9

"Ella, you look gorgeous," Rowan squealed with delight when Ella opened the door.

She stared at the pale-blue ball gown before touching the silk fabric. "You look like a princess. This dress is amazing, and I love your hair."

Ella touched her hair. "Thank you. It took me forever to get it up in this stupid French twist."

"It looks fantastic," Rowan said.

Ella grinned at her before standing back a little. "You're looking pretty damn hot yourself."

The slender redhead wore a long, form-fitting green dress, and she grinned at Ella before turning around. "Think the back is too much?"

"Damn," Ella said. "What back?" The dress was completely backless, the green material stopped just above Rowan's ass, and Rowan twisted her head to look at her.

"Is my ass showing?"

Ella shook her head. "No, but you might want to go easy on the dancing."

Rowan laughed. "I've got about eight strips of clothing tape stuck on there. It shouldn't move."

She turned around, and Ella eyed her small breasts. "Do you have any idea how jealous I am of your boobs? They're so damn perky even without a bra."

"Yes, well, the boys would be much happier if they were about two cups bigger. You ready to go?"

"I am." She closed the door, and Rowan grabbed her arm when she stumbled a bit.

"Whoa, princess, you're not supposed to start drinking until we get to the ball."

"I'm not drunk. It's these damn shoes." She lifted her gown so Rowan could see the silver, glittery shoes. "These heels are impossible to walk in."

"You'll be dancing, not walking, so it's fine," Rowan said with a laugh.

They walked slowly toward Rowan's car. "Did Belle and Bennett already leave?"

Ella nodded. "Yes. Wait until you see Belle. She's wearing a bright red mini-dress with matching heels. She looks incredible."

As they climbed into the car, Rowan gave Ella a thoughtful look. "Honey, are you sure you want to go? I know you're still sad about what happened with Duncan, and if you'd rather stay home and watch sappy romance movies, I'm down with that. I'm a super easy date."

Ella shook her head. "Nope. We're going. You've been looking forward to this, and hell, so have I. I'm not going to let Duncan Gillis ruin it. I hate that guy."

"Do you, though?" Rowan asked.

"No," Ella sighed. "But Bennett said he wouldn't be there anyway, and I need to move on with my life. He made it clear that I was just a fling for him. I shouldn't be so surprised or hurt by that. I knew what he was like, you know?"

"I'm sorry," Rowan said. "I wish it was different."

Ella shrugged. "Me too, but it is what it is, right? I don't want to even think about Duncan for the rest of the night. I'm going to eat a little, drink a lot, attempt to dance with these ridiculous shoes, and find a prince to kiss at midnight."

ROWAN STEPPED OUT INTO THE COOL NIGHT AIR AND STARED at the sky. The Centennial Celebration was in full swing, and even with the door closed, she could hear the loud music and the babble of hundreds of people as they mingled in the ballroom.

The Centennial committee had applied for and received permission to hold the celebration at the oldest home in town. The massive mansion had been turned into a historic land-mark in the late eighties, and the town council had spent over ten years returning it to its former glory. It held twice-daily tours for school children and tourists and was the perfect setting for celebrating the town's birthday.

She swept her hand along the porch railing. A terrace ran across the front of the house, supported by the soaring white porch columns, and she could hear people laughing and talking above her as they nibbled on the catered food.

She hesitated before slipping off her shoes and rubbing her aching feet. She had been dancing most of the night – God, she loved to dance – and she felt warm and a little tipsy from the wine she drank.

The moon was out and shining brightly in the sky. She admired it for a moment before her attention was caught by the figure standing in the middle of the well-kept front lawn. He stared up at the moon, and her pulse began to pound. She knew exactly who it was, even in the dark, and she was stupidly happy to see him. She could admit that she had looked for him several times during the evening before finally deciding he'd skipped the celebration. He was as much of a hermit as her grandmother, and it had been too much to hope that he would join the town in celebrating. But… here he was.

Leaving her shoes on the porch, she walked silently down the porch steps and crossed the lawn. The grass was cool on her bare feet, and she tried to move as quietly as possible. God, it was like she was trying not to spook a wild horse, which, she supposed, she kind of was. She needn't have bothered. He didn't move a muscle as she approached him. He stared at the moon with an almost rapturous look of pleasure and jumped when she touched his arm.

"I'm sorry," she said. "I didn't mean to scare you."

He stared silently at her, and her breath caught in her throat when his gaze travelled over her body to stop at the sight of her bare toes peeking out from under her dress. When his gaze returned to her face, she gasped softly. His dark eyes were full of a dark lust that her body responded immediately to, and she was pretty sure she had just ruined her damn panties.

"Mr. Taggert?" she said. "Are you okay?"

"Fine," he said hoarsely. A tight mask of control slipped over his darkly handsome face, and he resumed his usual stare-over-her-shoulder expression. "Enjoying the party, Ms. Jameson?"

"I am," she said. "I'm a little surprised to see you here."

He cleared his throat. "Occasionally, I enjoy the company of others."

She smiled at him. "So does my grandmother, but I couldn't convince her to come tonight. She insisted she was much happier in her pajamas and slippers at home."

"Indeed," he said. "It was nice to see you, but I should -"

"You're looking very handsome tonight," she said. "I don't think I've seen you in a suit before."

She studied the charcoal-coloured suit, her eyes lingering on his broad chest. He did look good, she thought dimly. He looked good, and he smelled good and fuck, had she ever wanted anyone between her thighs as much as she wanted him?

"Thank you," he said stiffly. "You're, uh, looking very pretty." His eyes flickered briefly to her hair. She had straightened it, and it hung halfway down her back in a smooth waterfall of red.

It had taken forever to straighten, but she was suddenly very glad she had made the effort when he said, "I like your hair."

"Thank you," she said.

There was a moment of awkward silence as the music drifting out from the building in front of them died out. As a new song began, one with a slow beat, he said, "I need to go. It was nice to -"

She touched his arm, ignoring how he stiffened, and said, "Will you dance with me?"

"That's not a good idea," he said.

"Please, Rafe," she said softly. "Just one dance. That's all I want."

He paused and then made a brief chopping motion, suggesting a nod. As he turned and started toward the house, she tightened her hand on his arm. "No, right here."

"Outside?" He frowned at her, and she nodded.

"Yes, in the moonlight."

He glanced at the moon, that weird look of pleasure crossing his face again before he nodded. She stepped closer to him, a shiver running through her body when he put his arm around her and rested his hand against her lower back. The heat of his hand against her naked skin sent shockwaves of lust through her, and she bit back her moan of delight as she placed her hand on his broad shoulder. He held her other hand in a loose grip and smiled politely at her before swaying to the music. They moved in small circles as he kept a healthy distance between their bodies, and she tried to hide her frustration. She wanted to be pressed against him, wanted to fit her soft curves against the hardness of his body, but he kept a firm grip on her and made it impossible to breach the space between them.

"You're a good dancer," she said.

He gave her another polite smile. "Thank you, Ms. Jameson."

"Rowan," she said.

He nodded but didn't say anything. She lifted her head to stare at the moon, and he followed her gaze. After a few seconds, his grip eased, and she quickly stepped closer to him, pressing her body against his and slinging her arm around his shoulders. She held the back of his neck tightly, stroking the feather-soft hair she found there as he made a low noise of panic.

"Ms. Jameson, what are you doing?"

"Dancing with you, Mr. Taggert."

He started to push her back, and she clung to him. "No," she breathed into his ear, "don't push me away. Not tonight."

He groaned, the sound sent more shivers down her spine, and then he nearly crushed her against him, his arm a band of steel around her waist as he buried his face in her hair and breathed deeply.

"You smell so good," he said.

"So do you," she said.

His hand stroked her naked back, moving higher in slow circles as he rasped, "I like your dress."

"Thank you."

His hand was in the middle of her back now, stroking the area where her bra should have been, and when his hand slid to her ribs and slipped under the fabric of her dress, she held her breath. She had no genuine belief that he would go any further, it was too fucking much to hope for, so when his hand moved again and she felt his hard palm slide across her nipple and his long fingers cup her breast, her knees buckled.

He held her up easily. They had given up all pretense of dancing, and she pressed her stomach against his erection as he gently squeezed her breast. His fingers played with her nipple, tugging it into an aching hardness, and she moaned before dropping his hand and throwing her other arm around his shoulders. He immediately moved his free hand to her ass, cupping and kneading it with a roughness that made her head spin.

"I love your breasts," he rasped into her ear. "You have no idea how badly I want to know what they look like." He toyed with her nipple. "How many freckles are on them, and what colour your nipples are."

"Take me home, and I'll show you," she breathed into his ear before sucking on his earlobe.

He groaned harshly, his hand tightening on her ass until she made a squeak of pain. He ground his erection against her stomach, his breath warm against her cheek.

She leaned back and smiled up at him. "Leave with me. Right now."

"Ms. Jameson, I can't."

"Rowan," she said. "Say my name, Rafe."

"Rowan," he said. The sound of her given name in his deep voice sent a fresh flood of wetness to her panties, and she bit her bottom lip.

"Take me home, Rafe. Please."

"I can't, Rowan. It isn't -"

She stood on her tiptoes and kissed him, licking at the seam of his lips until he groaned and parted them. She pushed her tongue into his mouth and gasped with surprise when he immediately took control of the kiss. His hand moved from her ass to the back of her skull, and he wound her red hair in his hand and pulled tightly.

"I've dreamed about fucking you," he muttered against her mouth. "Of having you in my bed and under me. This," he tugged on her hair, "amazing red hair spread out like flame on my pillow."

His fingers pinched her swollen nipple again, and she made a sharp cry of need that he quickly swallowed when he slammed his mouth down onto hers. The gentleness was gone now. He was all hard power and desperate need, and she returned his kiss frantically as he sucked on her tongue. She was intoxicated by the hint of scotch she could taste in his mouth and the hard scrape of his teeth against hers, and she moaned when he sucked roughly on her bottom lip.

"I need to fuck you, Rowan. I need to fuck you right now," he growled.

He dropped to his knees, dragging her down with him and pushing her onto her back on the soft grass. He covered her body with his, his knee shoving her thighs apart as he kissed her neck with hard, wet kisses.

Rowan stared at the moon. Her body throbbed with need, and she couldn't believe that Rafe Taggert was about to fuck her right here in the open with hundreds of people less than a hundred feet away. She should have been telling him to stop, should have been asking him to at least take her to his damn car or something, but she realized with utter sureness that this was how it was supposed to be. It felt incredibly right to have Rafe, the man she had fantasized about since she was fourteen years old, fuck her outside with the low whisper of the wind and the bright light of the moon surrounding them.

"Yes," she muttered. "Oh God, yes."

His eyes seemed to glow in the moonlight, their usual hazel colour a bright, vivid jade, and a stronger, nearly uncontrollable jolt of lust went through her.

"Fuck me, Rafe. Please, fuck me," she whimpered.

He reached between their bodies, his hand unbuckling his belt and yanking at the zipper. She grasped for her dress hem, wanting to pull it up and make it easier for him to take her, when a cloud drifted across the moon and plunged them into darkness. He froze, his head lifting as he searched for the moon, and she cried out harshly when he pushed away from her.

"What the fuck am I doing?" he said before reaching down and yanking her to her feet with one hard tug.

"Rafe, no. Don't stop," she pleaded. She tried to kiss him and wrap her arms around his neck, but he gripped her arms and held her away from him.

"Rowan, stop."

"No!" she nearly shouted.

"I shouldn't have done that. I have to go."

"No," she snapped. "Don't you dare leave me like this. I need you, Rafe."

"I'm sorry," he said hoarsely. "This was a mistake. I'm so sorry, Rowan."

He turned and ran across the yard, disappearing down the

dark street, and she clenched her fists and pressed her lips shut against the scream of anger trying to escape. She lowered her head and breathed harshly until a little of the pulsing need had dissipated, and she felt somewhat normal again. She stared at the sky as the moon reappeared before placing her hand over her mouth.

What the hell had just happened? She was not just about to fuck Rafe Taggert in the middle of the Centennial Cele-bration.

Hell, yes, you were.

She groaned and, her heart pounding and her entire body aching with need, turned and walked slowly toward the front porch.

DUNCAN SLIPPED INTO THE BALLROOM AND LEANED AGAINST the wall. He scanned the crowd, his lion growling anxiously when he didn't see Ella.

Just relax, he said to his lion. *She's here. We'll find her.*

And then what? She hates you, remember? Why did you even come here in the first place?

He ignored his inner voice. He knew why he had shown up three hours late to the celebration. He could no longer stand to pace at home - his *lion* could no longer stand it - while Ella was here, maybe dancing with other men, maybe allowing them to touch her.

Find my mate! His lion roared angrily.

He continued to scan the crowd. He saw Bennett and Belle dancing at the edge of the crowd. Bennett shuffled his feet awkwardly as Belle giggled and twirled around him. He still couldn't see Ella - God, where could she be – and as the song ended and the music turned slow, his lion snarled again.

He paced back and forth as people danced by him, their brightly coloured clothing flashing in the light from the massive chandelier above them.

A hint of green caught his eye, and he turned to see Rowan Jameson moving past him. He grabbed her arm and tugged her to a stop. "Rowan, is…"

He paused and gave her a careful look before inhaling deeply. His nose wrinkled a little. Rafe Taggert's scent covered her, her cheeks were flushed, and underneath Rafe's overpowering scent, he caught a faint whiff of her own lust. "Rowan, are you okay?"

"Fine," she muttered before crossing her arms over her chest. "What are you doing here?"

"Is Ella here? Did she come to the celebration with you?"

Rowan eyed him warily. "You thinking of poaching my date, Gillis?"

He shook his head. "No, I was worried about her."

"Why? According to Ella, she was nothing more than a fuck for you."

"I lied, Rowan."

"Why?"

"It's a long story. But I should never have said that to her, and I want to apologize."

"And you chose tonight to do it?"

He just shrugged, and she sighed before pointing to their left. "She's dancing."

He followed her finger, and a growl burst from his throat before he could stop it. Ella, looking beautiful in a pale blue gown that hugged her full breasts, was dancing with Henry Treating. He started forward, his lion snarling for him to show Henry what happened to men who touched his mate and growled at Rowan when she grabbed his arm.

She gave him a disdainful look. "Chill out, Duncan."

He blew his breath out. "I'm sorry."

"Don't worry about it. Believe it or not, you're not the first man who's growled at me tonight."

He didn't reply, and she smiled dryly at him. "I'm not suggesting that you don't talk to Ella. I'm suggesting that you don't flip out because she's dancing with a guy twenty-five years her senior and rein in the jealousy. You'll just end up pissing her off. Go out to the terrace and get some fresh air. I'll send her out to you as soon as the song is over."

"Thank you, Rowan," he said gratefully.

"Yeah, don't mention it. Go on, Duncan."

He crossed the room to the terrace. A couple stood at the end of it, kissing passionately. When they saw him, they gave him identical embarrassed grins before leaving. He leaned against the railing and waited impatiently for the song to end. The door opened behind him, and he turned, the smile on his face dying.

"Duncan Gillis," Ana said softly. "I'm so happy to see you."

She wore a bright yellow dress and ran her hand seductively over the low-cut neckline before moving toward him. "I didn't think you were going to show."

"What do you want?" he asked.

"You know what I want," she said.

"Not interested," he snapped as she tried to drape her arms around his neck. "Get lost, Ana. I mean it."

He groaned when tears welled in her eyes and spilled down her cheeks. "Why are you so mean, Duncan? I don't deserve such cruelty."

He staggered back when she threw herself into his arms. She sobbed, and he patted her back awkwardly. "Stop crying, Ana."

"I know you had a thing with my stepsister, but I don't care," she sobbed. "She's not right for you, Duncan. I am."

"You're wrong," he said as she lifted her head and pouted at him. "Listen, I'm sorry, but I'm not -"

He made a muffled curse when she pressed her mouth against his, and her tongue pushed at his lips. His lion snarled in disgust, and he groaned inwardly. Fuck, could this night get any worse?

CHAPTER 10

"Ro," Ella gave Rowan a confused look, "why on earth do I need to go out to the terrace?"

"Just do it, Ella. Trust me, okay?" Rowan said.

Ella nodded before giving her an uncertain look. "Are you okay? You're really flushed."

"Just fine," Rowan said before giving her a gentle push toward the terrace. "Go, Ella."

With one last look at Rowan, Ella headed to the terrace. As she pushed open the door, she heard soft sobs, and her eyes widened when she saw Ana, her slender body pressed against Duncan, kissing him on the mouth.

Jealousy flooded through her, and she stalked forward as Duncan pushed Ana away. "I said no, Ana."

"Duncan," Ana whined, "You don't – oh!"

She staggered back as Ella grabbed her by the shoulder and whipped her around.

"What the hell, Ella!" Ana shouted. "Get away from me, you crazy bitch!"

"Duncan belongs to me," Ella said in a low voice. "Don't ever touch him again."

Ana's mouth dropped open, and she brayed loud laughter. "As if Duncan would ever want you for anything more than a quick fuck. You're fat and ugly and -"

Her face calm, Ella balled her hand into a fist and punched Ana in the face. Ana stumbled backward. Her legs hit one of the metal tables set up on the terrace, and she went ass over teakettle, landing on the stone floor of the patio with a harsh thud. She stared wide-eyed at Ella as she touched the blood trickling from her lower lip.

"You – you hit me," she said.

Ella stood over her. "Stay away from him, Ana. This is your last warning."

She turned away and glared at Duncan when he tried to take her hand.

"Asshole!" she shouted before stomping toward the door. Her heel caught in a deep crack in the stone, and she cursed and grabbed the doorframe to stop herself from falling.

"Ella!" Duncan rushed forward, and she shook him off angrily.

"Dickhead!" she shouted and limped into the ballroom, leaving her shoe wedged in the terrace when she couldn't pull it free.

DUNCAN WATCHED ELLA LIMP BACK INTO THE BALLROOM, HIS mind whirling and his lion purring loudly at just the sight of her.

"Duncan?" Ana whined. "Help me up."

He ignored her and yanked Ella's shoe free before running into the ballroom. He caught sight of her halfway across the room and ran after her, muttering apologies as he bumped into people.

"Ella, wait!"

"Stay away from me, Duncan Gillis! You – you stupid lint licker!" she shouted over her shoulder and limped faster.

He caught up and pulled her to a stop before turning her around. She kicked him in the shin, and he cursed before simply hoisting her over his shoulder. She shouted in outrage and pounded on his back as he pushed through the crowd of people who stared at them with their mouths open.

"You put me down right now, Duncan Gillis! Put me down or so help me God, I'll kick you in the nuts!" Ella shouted.

As he stalked past Belle and Bennett, he clamped his free arm over her legs just in case she decided to make good on her threat.

"Belle! Help me!" Ella said.

With a grin on her lips, Belle shook her head. "Sorry, honey. I think you and Duncan need to talk."

"Traitor!" Ella shouted and shook her fist at Belle.

"Sorry! I love you!" Belle called after her.

He left the ballroom and opened the first door he came to. It was a small parlour room with an old-fashioned writing desk in one corner and a daybed in the other, and he dropped Ella to her feet and slammed the door shut.

She glared at him. "So now you're kissing my stepsister?"

"She kissed me," he said quickly. "I told her I wasn't interested, she started crying, and then she threw herself at me. I swear, sweetheart, I have no interest in her."

He handed her the shoe he still held in his left hand, and she snatched it from him before chucking it at his head. He ducked, and the shoe hit the wall with a loud bang.

"If I ever catch you kissing another woman again, I'll cut off your balls!" she shouted.

He grinned, he couldn't help it, and she gave him a look of seething anger. "You think this is funny?"

"No, sweetheart," he said. "Well, the part where you punched your stepsister in the face was kind of funny."

Her mouth twitched, and she looked away before smoothing down her dress. "Why are you even here?"

"I came to apologize," he said. "I'm sorry. What I said earlier wasn't true. I'm crazy about you. You're all I think about. I can't sleep, I can't eat – I need you."

"Then why did you say those awful things?" she snapped. "Why did you break my heart?"

"Because when I saw how afraid you were of me, I thought it was better for you not to be with me. You were so afraid of my," he lowered his voice, "lion, and I couldn't stand the thought of trying to make you be with me when you were that terrified."

She blinked at him. "You drove me away because I was a little freaked out."

"You were more than a little freaked out, Ella," he said.

"Oh, well, excuse me for being weirded out by the fact that my boyfriend can change into a damn lion whenever he wants!" she said in a low voice.

A wide grin broke out on his face. "You think of me as your boyfriend?"

She paused before shaking her head. "It was a slip of the tongue."

"No, it wasn't," he said in delight. "You do think of me as your boyfriend. You told Ana I belonged to you. I heard you."

She rolled her eyes. "So what? You say that all the time, and it apparently doesn't mean shit. I danced with seven different guys tonight, and you didn't do a damn thing about it."

"I just got here," he protested. "The only guy I saw you

dancing with was Henry Treating, and the only reason I didn't go over there and tear him away from you was because Rowan convinced me not to. She said it would piss you off if I did."

"It would have," she said. "I'm not your possession, Duncan."

"I know. But you are mine," he said.

"Oh my God," she said. "You know, you're awfully smug."

He pulled her into his embrace and kissed her firmly on the mouth. She smacked him on the back before returning his kiss eagerly, and his lion purred with excitement and need at the touch of her soft mouth.

He kissed her repeatedly until she was breathless and clinging to the front of his suit jacket. "I miss you, Ella," he said. "Please forgive me. Give me another chance."

"I miss you too," she said. She rested her head on his chest and stroked his arms. He purred loudly, and she laughed. "I've missed this as well."

"Do you forgive me?" he asked

She nodded. "Yes. Of course, I do, Duncan. I'm crazy about you, too, and I've been miserable without you."

He hugged her tightly and pressed soft kisses all over her face. "Thank God."

They stood quietly for a few minutes before she raised her face to his again. "I moved out of my apartment."

"I heard," he said.

"Right," she said. "Nothing's a secret in this town. Well, almost nothing."

"Move in with me, Ella," he said.

She twitched in surprise. "What?"

"Move in with me. There's plenty of space, so why rent an apartment you'll never sleep in?"

"Why wouldn't I sleep there?" She stared at him in confusion.

"Because the only bed you're sleeping in from now on is mine."

She gave him a considering look, and he flushed. "I won't shift again, Ella. I promise. I won't ever shift around you."

She frowned at him. "I don't want that, Duncan."

"You don't want to live with me?"

"No, I don't want you not shifting because you think I'm afraid. I'm not, I swear."

"We'll talk about it later, okay?" he said. "Please, will you move in with me, Ella?"

"What about Gus? I'm not leaving him behind."

He grinned. "I like cats."

"Yeah, I guess you do," she said with a small smile.

"Well? What do you say?"

"Before I say yes, are there any other secrets you're hiding from me?" she asked.

He hesitated, and she stared at him. "Oh my God, there is."

"Just one," he said, "and it isn't bad, I promise."

"What is it?" she asked.

"Come home with me. It's easier to show you," he said before grabbing her shoe. He bent and slipped it onto her foot, then straightened and took her hand. "Are you ready, Ella?"

"Ready when you are, Prince Charming," she said.

He gave her a strange look, and she giggled before shaking her head. "Never mind. Let's go home, Duncan."

"Duncan, wait," Ella said.

They were standing in his house, and she tugged him into the living room.

"What I need to show you is upstairs," he said.

"Okay, but first, I want you to shift."

"No, that's not a good idea."

"It's a great idea," she said. "And I'm not budging until you do."

"Ella," he said. "I don't want to shift."

She shrugged. "Either shift, or I don't move in with you."

"That's blackmail, Ella Cinders. I had no idea you were capable of that. You seemed so sweet," he said.

She smiled at him. "Shift or we're done, Duncan Gillis."

He sighed loudly and stripped off his clothing. She made a low whistle of appreciation and wiggled her eyebrows at him. "Just as pretty as I remembered."

He rolled his eyes before giving her a hesitant look. "Ella, are you sure?"

"Very," she said. "Shift, Duncan."

He dropped to his hands and knees and closed his eyes.

Ella watched as Duncan's body swelled, his nails turned to claws and fur sprouted on his body. She stared in fascination as he switched to his lion form and gave her a very human look of apprehension.

"Hello, Duncan," she said.

He made a low purring noise, and she smiled before walking forward. He stayed perfectly still, and she buried her hands in his mane and scratched. He purred again, the sound rumbling out of his throat with every exhale, and she grinned delightedly at him before rubbing his broad nose.

She cupped his large face and lowered her face to his until they were only inches apart. "I'm not afraid."

She pressed her hand against his mouth, and when he opened it, she traced his large fangs with her fingers before stepping to the side and running her hands along his back. He stood, and she smiled when he rubbed his head against her hip. She scratched his back, and his purring grew to an almost deafening volume as he arched his back into her hand and rubbed his face against her again. She laughed when he almost knocked her over and gave his back a final scratch before moving away from him.

He shifted to his human form and gave her an anxious smile. "Are you okay?"

"Yes. I told you, I'm not afraid. It was just a little strange at first. I don't want you stopping yourself from shifting when you're around me. Promise me you won't."

"I won't," he said. "I promise."

"Good." She kissed him lightly on the mouth before squeezing his naked ass. "Now, show me your secret."

He picked up his pants and fished out his keys. He led her down the hallway, stopping in front of the locked room. He unlocked the door and, smiling nervously at her, opened the door and stepped back. She stepped into the room, staring curiously at the canvas on the easel near the window.

"You paint?"

"I do," he said.

She moved closer, studying the canvas with her head cocked before turning to look at him. "This work is – it's…."

She trailed off as she caught sight of the canvases propped up against the wall in a neat row. She inhaled sharply before walking to them and studying each one. Each was of the same blonde woman, her face always obscured, and a large, golden-coloured lion.

"You're Samuel," she said.

"Yes," he said. "My full name is Duncan Samuel Gillis, but I paint under one name – Samuel."

"This girl in the paintings… she's me, isn't she?"

"Yes."

"The little girl on the tire swing – was that me too?"

"Yes. I painted that one a few years ago. These latest ones have all been in the last six months or so."

He moved forward and touched her back through the silk fabric of her gown. "Ella? Are you okay?"

"Am I okay?" she repeated.

"I know it's a bit of a shock, but I needed to keep Samuel a secret. It's too dangerous for shifters to be noticed by humans, so I've kept my identity a secret. Only Bennett, my parents, and my agent know I'm Samuel. I should have told you. I'm sorry that I didn't."

He rubbed her back lightly when she didn't respond. "Sweetheart? Are you okay?"

She turned and grinned with pure delight. "I'm better than okay. I'm sleeping with Samuel, and he's painted pictures of me!"

He burst into laughter as she threw herself at him and kissed him. "I'm so proud of you, Duncan. Your work is amazing."

"Thank you, sweetheart," he said. "You have no idea how happy it made me when I realized that you liked my paintings."

"Not just liked," she declared, "loved. I love them. You gave me the painting, didn't you?"

"Yes. I wanted you to have it."

She blinked back the tears and kissed him again. "It's the most wonderful gift anyone has ever given me. I love you, Duncan."

He didn't hesitate. "I love you too, Ella."

She could feel the waterworks really trying to start now. God, how did she get so lucky?

He pressed his forehead against hers. "Does this mean you'll move in with me?"

"Hell, yes," she said emphatically. "Will you let me watch you paint?"

He nodded, and she squealed with delight before hugging him tightly. "Can I tell Belle and Rowan that you're Samuel?"

"Yes, but you can't tell Rowan I'm a shifter, okay? I'm sorry, I don't want to make you lie to your friend, but it's vital humans don't know about us."

She nodded. "I know. I won't say anything to her."

She reached down and squeezed his ass. "Now, what do you say we go to your bedroom, and I show Samuel just how much I appreciate his creative talents."

He grinned wickedly and scooped her up. "That sounds like an excellent idea, sweetheart."

Keep reading for Rowan's and Rafe's story in "Red".

VOLUME THREE

RED

RED

Rowan Jameson knows what she wants, and what she wants is local landscaper and the sexiest man in the whole damn town - Rafe Taggert.

He might be fifteen years older than her, and he might have an odd obsession with the moon and strolling naked through the woods, but she's had a crush on him for years and she's determined to have him.

She's delighted when she discovers Rafe's hidden desire for her and, with the help of her friends and her grandmother, Rowan will take exactly what she wants.

PROLOGUE

"**P**retty," the toddler whispered.

She watched the butterfly fly from flower to flower, her small hands clasped in front of her chubby body and her red hair gleaming in the sunlight. Her Nana had gone inside to answer the phone and told Rowan to stay in the yard.

She meant to obey her Nana, really she did, but when the butterfly floated into the woods behind the house, she couldn't resist following it. She climbed over logs and skirted bushes, keeping her eyes on the butterfly as it flitted in the rays of light poking through the trees.

"Pretty," she repeated. When the butterfly landed on a dark green bush, Rowan crept closer and reached out with one chubby hand. She wanted to touch it and feel its feather-soft wings even though Nana always said not to. She said it would hurt the butterfly. But if she was very gentle, maybe she could –

The butterfly flew up into the air just as her fingers were about to touch its wings. She pouted in disappointment, squinting as the butterfly disappeared, before staring at her surroundings. The trickle of fear that started in her belly vanished when she saw the chipmunk.

"Chipun!" she shouted happily and chased after it when it scurried away. Giggling, she pushed through some dense underbrush and stared at the wolf drinking from the river that ran through the trees.

"Doggie!" She clapped her hands, and the wolf lifted its dripping snout and stared at her. He was on the larger side, with dark gray fur, jade-coloured eyes, and a patch of white on his chest.

She pushed forward, holding out her chubby hands. "Here, doggie, doggie."

The wolf walked toward her and chuffed in surprise when she buried her tiny face in his chest and scratched him with her fingers. He sniffed her red hair, and she giggled when she felt his breath on her forehead.

"Hi, doggie," she said.

The wolf peered around the woods before stepping away from her. Rowan's eyes widened when he shifted to his human form.

"Doggie?" She cocked her head at him.

RAFE TAGGERT STUDIED THE FOREST AS THE TODDLER STARED up at him. He couldn't smell another human, so what the hell was a baby doing in the woods by herself? He rubbed his hand through his dark hair. What did he do now? He could hear his pack and feel them, not far from the river, but he couldn't take a baby to them. His father would straight up kill him if he brought a human baby to their den. But, Christ, he couldn't leave her either. The woods were full of bears, cougars, and regular wolves, and the thought of them ripping into the defenseless little baby in front of him made his stomach curl.

Her tiny hands patted his naked thighs, and he realized she had toddled forward until she stood before him.

"Up?" she asked hopefully before holding up her arms.

He bent and lifted her into his arms, patting her back when she slung one chubby arm around his neck and rested her head on his shoulder. Maybe she could tell him where she lived.

"What's your name, baby?" he asked.

"Rowan." She smiled at him, and he kissed her soft cheek.

"Hi, Rowan. I'm Rafe."

"I'm fhwee," she suddenly announced before struggling to hold up only three chubby fingers.

He grinned at her, and she giggled and patted his cheek before peering around them.

"Doggie gone," she shouted. "Here, doggie, doggie!"

"Shh, baby," he said. The last thing he needed was a hungry cougar hearing her voice.

She yawned and rested her head on his shoulder again. He jiggled her a little to keep her awake. "Rowan, where do you live? Can you tell Rafe where you live?"

"Nana," she said cheerfully.

"You live with your Nana?"

"Nana," she said again.

"Where does your Nana live? Can you tell me?"

She pointed vaguely into the trees, and Rafe sighed. Thinking a three-year-old would be able to give him directions to her grandmother's house was beyond stupid. He rubbed her back absently as he tried to think what to do. He really had no choice. He needed to take her back to his pack. He would grab some clothes, get his father's truck, and drive the baby into town. He could always say he was out hiking and stumbled onto her.

"Rowan, you're going to come with me, okay?" he said.

"Otay," she said happily.

"We'll find your Nana and -"

"ROWAN!"

The woman's voice echoed through the trees, and Rowan sat up in his arms and clapped her hands before shouting, "Nana!"

She bounced in Rafe's arms and gave him a delighted look. "Nana, nana, nana!"

"Rowan! Where are you? Rowan!" The woman's voice grew closer, and Rafe breathed a sigh of relief. He scanned the trees and opened his mouth to shout.

Have you forgotten you're naked?

Shit! He glanced at his body as Rowan hollered for her grandmother again. Okay, he could explain this away.

Oh yeah? You don't think the woman will freak out when she sees a naked teenager holding her granddaughter?

Fuck! His inner voice was right.

He set Rowan down on the ground, and she scowled at him before holding up her arms. "Up, Rafe."

"No, baby, I need to go," he said quietly. "You stay right here and wait for your nana, all right?"

"Otay," she said.

"Don't move, okay?"

"*Otay,*" she said with a scowl, and he grinned at the annoyance in her voice.

"That's a good girl," he said.

He jogged away from the river and behind a cluster of bushes. He shifted to his wolf form and waited impatiently for the woman to find her granddaughter. He watched as

Rowan stood quietly for a few seconds and then groaned when she turned and walked toward the river.

"Froggie," she said happily.

His eyes widened, and he chuffed nervously when she knelt by the side of the river. It was high and fast flowing this time of the year, and when she leaned forward, he rushed out from the bushes and grabbed the back of her shirt with his teeth as she toppled forward.

She shrieked laughter, dangling and kicking her feet when he lifted her and backed away from the river before setting her on the ground.

"Doggie!" she shouted and jumped to her feet. She flung her arms around his chest and hugged him tightly. "Hi, doggie."

He nudged her with his big head, trying to get her to release him as a woman, her hair was red like the baby's but streaked with silver, ran out of the trees.

"Rowan! Rowan, are you…."

She trailed off, and Rafe swallowed the trickle of fear when she raised the shotgun she held and aimed it at his head. He had healing abilities, all shifters did, but they wouldn't be much use to him if she blew off his damn head.

"Rowan, come here, baby."

"Doggie, Nana!" Rowan said happily.

"I see the doggie," the woman said. "Come to me right now, Rowan. Quickly."

Rafe was impressed by how steady both her voice and her hands were. He stood perfectly still as Rowan grabbed his face, her fingers digging into the fur of his cheeks and pulled down his head.

"Bye, doggie," she said before kissing his nose.

He heard the sharp inhale of the woman behind them, and he remained still as Rowan kissed his nose again and then toddled toward her grandmother. When she was in arm's reach, the woman snatched her up with one arm and kept the shotgun aimed at him.

"Ow! Too tight, Nana!" Rowan complained.

The woman backed away, keeping her gaze on Rafe as she picked her way through the trees. He didn't move a muscle until she and the baby had disappeared, and then he collapsed on the ground, panting harshly and his muscles trembling. After a while - a *long* while - he stood and trotted into the trees.

CHAPTER 1

"Dammit, Rowan, what the hell has gotten into you today?"

The man's voice was muffled by the mouthguard he wore, and he pushed his protective headgear back before glaring at her. She grinned around her mouthguard, and he muttered a curse before raising his gloved hands.

Rowan moved cautiously around the boxing ring, ducking back when the man jabbed at her. She countered with her own jab, hitting him just above his solar plexus and finding her boxing glove's solid thud against his flesh to be delightfully pleasing.

He winced and stumbled back. Smelling victory, she danced forward and threw two hard and rapid punches to his face. He fell to the mat, and she stood over him, panting heavily, before raising her eyebrow at him.

"I'm done," he said sullenly.

"Chicken," she taunted, and he flushed before scrambling to his feet.

"You're being a total bitch today, Ro," he snapped.

She blew him a kiss before ducking between the ropes

and dropping to the floor. An old man stood next to the ring, his bald head gleaming in the lights and his body still straight and strong despite his age. She held her gloved hands out to him.

"The last week, you've been a real firecracker in the ring, Red. Got some aggression to work out, it seems like," the old man said as he unlaced her boxing gloves and pulled them off her hands.

He unwrapped her left hand as she used her right hand to take out her mouthguard. She dropped it into the bag at her feet and held out her right hand for unwrapping.

"Any particular reason?"

Rowan shook her head, and the old man lowered his voice. "Wouldn't have something to do with Rafe Taggert, would it?"

She stiffened and pulled her hand free of his before hurriedly unwrapping it. "Don't know what you're talking about, Joey."

"No? I saw you at the Centennial Celebration." He folded his arms across his barrel-like chest and grinned at her. "Seems like you two were gettin' real close."

"I don't know what you thought you saw, but what you thought you saw wasn't what you thought you saw," Rowan said as she pulled off her headgear and smoothed her hair.

Joey laughed so loudly that the other men milling about the gym glanced over at them. "Horseshit, Red."

Rowan glared at him. "Be quiet, Joey."

"It's my gym," he said with a grin. "I can say what I want to say."

Rowan glowered at him before stuffing her gloves and the wraps into her gym bag. Joey Fanton had opened the gym long before she was born, and while it had been her grandmother who had taught her the basics of boxing, it was Joey who had taught her how to succeed at it.

"Why don't you come by the house tonight, and you can hear what Martha thinks she saw. She was getting into the car with me when you and Mr. Taggert were," he paused before winking at her, "dancin' on the front lawn."

Her face, already red from her exertion in the ring, turned brighter. "I think I'll pass. Thanks, Joey."

He gripped her arm, his callused hand warm on her skin. "In all seriousness, Red, you should come by the house. Martha's been missin' you."

"I will," she said. "I promise. But I'm going straight from here to Nana's. I'm spending the weekend with her."

She slung her gym bag over her shoulder as Joey smiled at her. "Tell Lydia I said hello, and tell her Martha plans to drop by next week for some help with her knittin' project."

"I will," Rowan said. She planted a kiss on Joey's cheek, and he squeezed her waist affectionately. "Joey, don't say anything about what you saw, okay?"

He frowned at her. "O'course I won't. You know I'm not much for gossip, Red."

"I know." She kissed his rough cheek again before heading to the ladies' locker room to shower and change.

"RAFE?" BENNETT GAVE THE WOLF SHIFTER A SURPRISED look as he stepped out onto the back deck. Belle followed him out of the house and pressed a kiss against Bennett's cheek.

"I'm leaving, honey."

"Okay, you and Ella have fun at the movie."

"We will." She smiled at him, and he tugged her head down and gave her a long kiss that made her flush.

"Tell Ella I'll be waiting naked in bed for her when she gets home," Duncan said before taking a drink of beer.

Belle laughed and patted the lion shifter's shoulder. "Since I'd like to actually get her into the theatre, I think I'll divulge that little tidbit *after* the movie."

"Smart move," Duncan said solemnly. "She can't get enough of this."

He glanced down at his lean body clad in shorts and a t-shirt, and Bennett snorted before grabbing a beer from the cooler and handing it to Rafe.

"Sit down, Rafe. Bye, honey."

"Bye, Bennett." Belle gave him a little wave, and Duncan elbowed the bear shifter in the ribs when Bennett leaned back in his chair to get a better look at Belle's ass as she walked into the house.

Bennett growled softly at Duncan before smiling at Rafe. "It's good to see you, Rafe. How are you?"

"Good. Sorry to drop in unannounced, but I was hoping to talk to you about something."

"Sure."

Rafe glanced at Duncan. The lion shifter grinned at him and took a long swallow of beer before putting his feet up on the splintering deck rail.

Rafe sighed loudly. "I need your help, Bennett."

"With what?" Bennett asked.

"Rowan Jameson."

Bennett glanced at Duncan, who shrugged and took another drink of beer. "Christ, Rafe, you're older than us, and you're not in bad shape for an old man. I doubt you need help in getting into Rowan Jameson's pants."

"Shut it, Duncan," Bennett said with a slight grin.

"I need help staying out of Rowan Jameson's pants," Rafe said with a grimace.

Bennett gave him a startled look. "You and Rowan are…"

"No, not really."

"Not really?" Duncan said. "Either you are, or you aren't."

"The night of the Centennial Celebration, I was outside. Rowan came out, and she asked me to dance. I tried to say no, but she insisted, and as soon as I touched her, I…."

He drank half his beer in three big swallows. "I lost control."

"So, you did sleep with her," Duncan said.

"No! I managed to resist, but if the moon hadn't gone behind the clouds, I would have taken her on the goddamn lawn."

"The moon?" Duncan asked.

"Wolf shifters have a harder time controlling their urges when the moon is full," Bennett said.

"Was the moon full that night?" Duncan said.

"No," Rafe said in a low voice. "But it was close enough, and you saw the dress she wore that night. She stood there in that damn green dress, and her red hair fucking glowing in the moonlight and I… I just lost control."

"I don't see what the problem is," Duncan said. "Rowan's an attractive woman, and before you stopped going to Gaston's, I smelled her lust for you more than once."

"She's fifteen years younger than me," Rafe snapped.

"So?"

"What do you mean so?" Rafe said. "I'm a dirty old man for wanting her."

"No, you're not," Bennett said. "Fifteen years isn't that big of an age difference."

"It is," Rafe insisted. "Plus, she's human, and I can't be

with a human. I thought it would be fine if I just avoided her and kept my distance from her. Except now I know what she tastes like, how soft her skin is, and my wolf is going insane over it."

He stared at Bennett. "Tell me how to resist her."

"You're asking the wrong guy," Bennett said. "I didn't exactly do a stellar job at resisting Belle."

"Does she know you're a shifter?" Rafe asked in a low voice.

Bennett nodded. "I couldn't keep something like that from her."

"How did she react?"

"Fine. She had seen me shift when we were kids, remember? Also, her mother was a tiger shifter."

Rafe blinked at him. "I had no idea."

"No one did. Belle didn't even know. Maurice told her before he went to rehab," Bennett said. He glanced at Duncan, who nodded. "Duncan told Ella he was a shifter, and it didn't go over quite as well, but it only took a few days for Ella to come around."

"Have you told them about the other shifters?" Rafe asked.

"No, of course not," Bennett said.

"What if they tell others about you?" Rafe asked.

"They won't," Duncan said. "They haven't even told Rowan, and she's their best friend."

"Are you certain of that?"

"Yes," Duncan said. "What's the big deal anyway? I've slept with human women who had no idea I was a shifter. Unless," he gave Rafe a small grin, "with your advanced age, you can't stop from shifting when you're banging a woman?"

Rafe growled at him, and Duncan laughed before

finishing his beer and grabbing another. "I'm just saying, Rafe, it probably happens to a lot of shifters."

"I can control the shift just fine," Rafe said.

"Then you being a shifter shouldn't be a barrier to sleeping with Rowan," Duncan said.

"It's more complicated than that, lion shifter," Rafe said.

"Your father," Bennett said.

Rafe gave him a startled look. "What do you know of my father?"

"I know he's seriously against shifters and humans being together," Bennett said. "My father and I spoke of it a few years before he died. Is that why you left the pack?"

"I don't wish to discuss it," Rafe said stiffly.

"Listen, don't take this the wrong way," Bennett said, "but why are you really here? Neither Duncan nor I can give you any advice on how to stay away from a human you're obsessed with, and you know that."

Rafe sighed and stared at his hands. "I don't have many friends, and I thought if I talked about what was happening, it would help. But I shouldn't have bothered you with this."

He stood to leave, and Bennett shook his head. "Sit down, Rafe. I consider you a friend and frankly, it's probably good for you to spend some time with others. Shifters who spend too much time alone tend to lose their human side. You know that."

"Especially wolf shifters," Duncan said. "Hell, I'm surprised you haven't gone insane without your pack."

Bennett rolled his eyes. "Not helping, Duncan."

"Sorry, Rafe. That didn't come out the way I meant," Duncan said.

"It's fine," Rafe said. "I just need to stay away from town. I won't be tempted if I don't see her, right?"

"If your wolf wants Rowan as much as my lion wanted

Ella," Duncan said solemnly, "you're up shit creek without a paddle, my friend."

"I can control my wolf, and I can stay away from her," Rafe said softly as he stared at his beer bottle.

"Oh, sure you can," Duncan said. "I have no doubt of that."

Bennett suppressed his grin when Duncan turned to him and mouthed, "Not a chance in hell."

"Do you want to stay for dinner, Rafe?" Bennett asked. "We're grilling some steaks."

Rafe shook his head before finishing his beer. "Thank you, but no. I should head home. The full moon isn't until tomorrow night, but I am already starting to feel its effects. With the way my wolf is obsessed with Rowan, it's best if I'm not anywhere near town this weekend."

He stood and placed his beer bottle on the table. "Thank you, Bennett."

"Anytime," Bennett said. "And I meant what I said earlier, Rafe. We're friends."

"Thanks," Rafe said. "Goodnight."

***

"You have got to be kidding me!" Rowan slammed her hands on the steering wheel as the car lurched, the engine light flashed rapidly, and her car died with a soft sputtering noise. She steered to the side of the road and shut off the car before turning the key and pumping the gas. Nothing happened, and she cursed again before popping the hood and climbing out of the car.

She lifted the hood and stared at the engine. She knew precisely jackshit about cars, and she poked and prodded at a few of the parts before giving up and slamming the hood shut. She pulled her cell from her pocket and wasn't surprised to see she had no reception. The woods were too thick for cell phone service to be reliable.

The sun was setting, and she looked up and down the road. How many times had she driven to Nana's and never once seen another car? Too many to hope that someone would come along and give her a ride, that was for sure. She was at least six miles from Nana's house, and she studied the woods to her left. It would be faster if she hiked through the woods to her grandmother's house, but the sun would set before she made it. Did she really want to be wandering through the woods in the dark? The chances of being eaten by a bear or cougar were disturbingly high.

And wolves. Don't forget the wolves.

Right. The wolves.

"The road it is," Rowan muttered before grabbing her backpack from the backseat and slinging it over her shoulder. She spared another glance at her cell phone, hoping that maybe the cell phone service gods were smiling upon her, before snorting and shoving it into her pocket.

She started down the road, walking briskly and trying not to think about how this was the exact way every horror movie in history began. A woman walking alone on a remote road in the middle of the woods. God, she was just asking for an axe murderer to keep her prisoner in his basement. Maybe he wouldn't make a lampshade from her skin if she was lucky. She should never have let Belle convince her to watch that horror movie marathon last month. Her imagination was way too active for –

Miracle of miracles – there the noise of a vehicle behind her. Her heart thumping in her chest, she swung around and squinted at the dark red truck driving behind her.

She recognized the truck immediately, and her heart began to pound for an entirely different reason.

"Goodbye horror movie, hello porno," she muttered under her breath before sticking out her thumb.

The truck stopped beside her, and she pulled open the passenger door. "Hello, Rafe."

"Hello, Ms. Jameson. Your car broke down."

It was a statement, not a question, but she nodded anyway. "Yes, can you give me a lift to my grandmother's?"

Without waiting for his reply, she climbed into his truck and dropped her backpack on the floor between her feet. Rafe inhaled deeply before grimacing and moving until he was pressed against the driver's door.

Rowan felt a flush rising from her chest. In the pretense of wiping sweat from her forehead, she quickly sniffed her armpit. She had showered after the gym and washed her hair, but Rafe's reaction suggested she smelled as appealing as a dead and decomposing skunk.

"Maybe I could look at your car," he suggested.

"Do you know anything about cars?"

"Not really," he admitted.

She grinned at him. "Well, thanks, but I think it will require an actual mechanic."

He drummed his fingers against the steering wheel. Obviously, he didn't want her in his truck, and she sighed before opening the passenger door, grabbing her backpack, and hopping to the ground. "See you around, Rafe."

She slammed the door shut and trudged down the road. She was surprised to realize that she was close to tears and berated herself fiercely. What did she care if Rafe Taggert didn't want anything to do with her?

He wanted something to do with you the night of the Centennial Celebration.

She ignored her inner voice. Thinking about that night would do nothing but get her all worked up, and there was no way she was masturbating with her grandmother sleeping in the room next to hers. That was just all kinds of ick.

"Ms. Jameson, wait."

She walked faster as Rafe's footsteps crunched in the gravel behind her. When his hand closed around her arm, a lightning bolt of lust lit up her insides, and she turned to face him. He inhaled again and immediately dropped her arm before backing up a few steps.

"Where are you going?" he asked.

"I told you - to my grandmother's house," she said.

"I'll give you a ride," he said.

She studied the pained expression on his face before shaking her head. "No thanks, I'd rather walk."

"It's at least five miles, and it'll be dark soon."

She shrugged. "I'll be fine."

"You're not walking down an isolated road in the dark, Ms. Jameson."

"I can take care of myself, Mr. Taggert," she said. "Have a nice evening."

"Get in the truck, Ms. Jameson," he said with a hint of annoyance.

"And if I don't?"

"I'll carry you to the damn truck," he said through gritted teeth.

"How will you carry me?" she asked.

"What?"

"How will you carry me? Will it be all romance novel-like where you gently cradle me in your arms, or will I be thrown over your shoulder like a sack of potatoes?"

"Sack of potatoes," he snapped.

"In that case, I'll save my dignity and your back and get

in the truck." She turned and marched back to the truck, climbing in and buckling her seatbelt as he slid behind the wheel and started the truck. She stared silently out the window as he drove. It didn't take him long to lower his window, and she risked a glance at him. He practically had his head out the window, and she felt another flush of embarrassment. Jesus, how bad did she smell?

He drove an older truck, and the front seat was a bench seat. Despite her embarrassment, an image of her sliding to the middle and unbuttoning his jeans flooded through her.

Road head! Her inner voice said delightedly. *Oh, hell yes, girl. Give the man road head!*

Shut up! He thinks I smell. He'll probably barf if I get any closer to him.

She folded her arms across her torso and grimly ignored her inner voice's insistent clamouring to suck Rafe Taggert's dick.

Rafe tried to take shallow breaths. Rowan's scent was driving his wolf mad. He was nearly sticking his entire head out the window, and he forced his head back into the truck as Rowan sighed softly and folded her arms across her torso. She wore a plain white t-shirt with a V-neck, and the movement pushed her small breasts upward into delightful little mounds. He stared at her cleavage as his wolf howled.

He gripped the steering wheel when an image of Rowan sliding across the seat and unbuttoning his jeans flickered through his head. She would pull out his cock and stroke it with her warm hands, and when the head was slick with precum, he would wrap his hand in that glorious red hair and guide her mouth down. She would lick him clean with her soft little tongue before sucking him and –

Focus!

His wolf snarled when he snapped out of his little fantasy, and Rafe growled at it in return. Rowan gave him a startled look, and he flushed as he realized he had growled out loud.

He cleared his throat as she returned her gaze to the window. He needed to speak to Rowan about what had happened between them, and this was a perfect time. He pushed the image of her mouth on his dick out of his head and tried to smile at her. "Ms. Jameson, we need to talk."

"Do we?" she said without looking at him.

"Yes. I need to apologize for the other night."

"What night would that be, Mr. Taggert?"

He scowled at her. "You know what night."

She shrugged. "You mean the night of the Centennial Celebration when we nearly had sex on the front lawn before you ran away like a scared little boy?"

"We didn't nearly have sex, and I didn't run away," he said.

She turned to face him, arching one perfect brow. "Really? Because I distinctly remember you telling me that you just had to fuck me before you ran away, leaving me extremely hot and bothered."

"I apologize. It was incredibly inappropriate of me to say that," he said.

"Why?"

"What?"

"Why was it inappropriate? We're both adults. I want you, and you want me. Why shouldn't we sleep together?"

"I'm too old for you, Ms. Jameson."

She scoffed. "Hardly."

"I am," he insisted. "I could be your damn father."

"My father is fifty-eight years old, Rafe," she said.

"I was drunk that night and -"

"Bullshit," she said. "Don't insult me by pretending you were drunk. At least be man enough to admit that you want to have sex with me."

"Fine," he snapped. "I want to have sex with you. It doesn't mean I should."

"I don't see why not."

"Because I'm too old for you," he repeated. "What part of that isn't clear?"

"You're forty, not ninety," she said.

"And you're twenty-five," he said.

"What if I was thirty and you were forty-five? Would that make it better?" she asked.

He shook his head. "No."

"Age is just a number," she said.

"I'm sorry, but I'm not comfortable with the age difference," he said. "I'm attracted to you, but I made a mistake that night, and I would like to apologize and tell you it won't happen again."

"What if I want it to happen again?" she asked.

God, the girl was relentless. He rubbed at his forehead. "Are you listening to anything I say, Ms. Jameson?"

"Yes, but what you're saying is ridiculous."

"It isn't. I'm too old for you. End of discussion," he retorted.

She rolled her eyes, and he couldn't decide if he wanted to spank her or kiss her when she muttered, "Yes, sir."

They were at her grandmother's cabin, and he said a silent prayer of thanks as he turned into the driveway. Lydia sat on the front porch and walked over to the truck as Rowan gave him a brittle smile.

"Thank you for the ride, Mr. Taggert."

"You're welcome, Ms. Jameson."

Lydia leaned against his door and smiled at him through the open window. "Hello, Rafe."

"Hi, Lydia. How are you?"

"Good, thanks. Rowan – did your car break down?"

Rowan nodded before grabbing her backpack. "Yeah, a few miles back. Mr. Taggert was driving by and gave me a ride here."

"How nice." Lydia smiled at him. "Come in for a piece of pie, Rafe."

"Oh, no thank you. I really should get going and -"

"Nonsense," she said. "I just baked a fresh one, and it's apple – your favourite."

"I really can't. I -"

"I won't take no for an answer," Lydia said as Rowan slid out of the truck and slammed the door shut.

Lydia held out her hand to Rowan and squeezed it gently as Rowan kissed her cheek. "I'm so glad you're here, honey."

"I am too, Nana."

Lydia looked over her shoulder. "Rafe? Come in, please."

Sighing softly, his wolf growling happily at the prospect of spending more time with Rowan, Rafe shut off his truck and followed the two women into the cabin.

CHAPTER 2

"Have a seat, Rafe," Lydia said over the loud barking of her two miniature schnauzers. He dropped into one of the kitchen chairs as Lydia pulled some plates from the cupboard. Usually, the dogs were all over him when he dropped by, but at this moment, Scrappy and Scruffy only had eyes for Rowan. They danced at her feet, jumping and yapping and licking eagerly at her hands when she reached down to pet them.

You are not jealous of a couple of damn dogs, Rafe snapped inwardly when his wolf growled possessively.

"I'm just going to put my stuff in the bedroom," Rowan said to her grandmother.

Panic flooded through him, and he couldn't stop from blurting out, "You're staying overnight?"

Rowan gave him an odd look as Lydia said, "I've got my girl for the weekend. It's been forever since we've had a sleepover, hasn't it, Rowan?"

Rowan nodded before disappearing into the bedroom. The dogs followed her, and he could hear her murmuring to them. He told himself not to look at her when she returned, but he couldn't stop tracking her across the cabin. She bent and rummaged through the fridge, and he studied the curve of her tiny ass. He knew exactly how firm that ass was, and his wolf made a hungry little growl of need. He jumped in his chair when Lydia's hand touched his arm, tearing his gaze from Rowan's ass.

Lydia stared at him with a small, shrewd smile on her face, and he blushed furiously as she placed a slice of pie in front of him. "Eat up, Rafe."

He ate a forkful of pie, barely tasting the sweet apples and flaky crust. His lust and sudden panic that Rowan would only be a mile away on the night of the full moon had taken away his appetite, but he ate another forkful and smiled at Lydia. "It's delicious."

"Thanks." She set a glass of water in front of him, and he drank half of it to try to force the down the pie stuck in his throat.

Scrappy and Scruffy had finally decided to say hello. They stood on their hind legs and pressed their front paws against his knee, but Rowan sat down in the chair across from him before he could pet them. They abandoned him immediately and raced each other under the table to get to her first. Barking excitedly, they bounced and jumped until they were both sitting on her lap. She put her arms around them and petted their chests as Lydia laughed.

"Don't take it personal, Rafe. As soon as they see Rowan, everyone else ceases to exist."

He smiled politely as Lydia gave Rowan an affectionate look. "My girl always did have a way with animals. Ever since she was a baby. When she was born, I had an old German shepherd who took to her right away. He wouldn't let anyone near that cradle when she was sleeping. Laid at the foot of it and kept her safe, he did. I always told her she should have worked in a vet's office. She's got the touch when it comes to dogs."

Lydia paused and drank a sip of tea. "Wolves too."

Rafe dropped his fork, wincing when it clattered on the table. "I'm sorry?"

"Wolves, Rafe," Lydia said. "My girl has a way with wolves. Did I never tell you about the time she was three and wandered off into the woods?"

"Nana," Rowan said. "I'm sure Mr. Taggert isn't interested in this story."

"I am," Rafe said. "Go on, Lydia."

He knew the story, hell, he'd been there, but he wanted to hear it from Lydia's perspective.

"Well, I told Rowan to stay in the yard while I answered the phone, but my girl's stubborn. I was only gone maybe five minutes, but sure enough, I came out into the yard, and she was gone. God, did I panic. I grabbed my shotgun and high-tailed it into the woods, screaming her name like a banshee. Didn't take me too long to find her. She was by the river."

She grinned at Rafe. "Only she wasn't alone. A wolf, biggest one I've ever seen, with dark grey fur and a white patch on his chest, stood there with her but not *just* standing there. He hovered over Rowan like he was keeping her safe, and Rowan," Lydia patted Rowan's hand, "why she had her arms around him like he was a big old teddy bear."

Rafe risked a glance at Rowan. She stroked Scruffy's ear - or maybe it was Scrappy's, he never could tell the damn dogs apart - and stared at the table.

"What happened then?" he asked.

"Well, you can imagine how afraid I was. Rowan was giggling and hollering about the doggie, and I was standing there trying not to wet my pants. I told Rowan to come to me, and she did, thank God, but not before she grabbed that wolf's head, yanked him down and kissed his nose. Twice, Rafe. Twice."

She sighed and took a bite of pie. "Truth be told, I did wet my pants a little when she kissed that wolf. But it never moved. It stood there, still as can be, while she squeezed its face and kissed its nose. I've never seen anything like it."

"It's impressive," he said quietly.

"It was probably someone's husky or wolf cross," Rowan said. "I doubt it was an actual wolf."

"You think I can't tell the difference, Rowan?" Lydia said crossly.

"I think you were terrified, and the mind can play tricks on a person when they're that frightened," Rowan said.

"It was a wolf, sweet girl. You don't remember, but - "

"You don't remember?" Rafe said.

Rowan shook her head, and a tingle of disappointment went through him.

Idiot! It's good that she doesn't remember.

"Didn't you say you saw a wolf at the Woodsmen Pub?" Rafe said.

Shut up!

"What?" Lydia turned to Rowan. "You saw a wolf at the Woodsmen?"

Rowan nodded. "Yeah. I was in the back parking lot having a," she paused, and a tinge of red coloured her cheeks, "getting some fresh air, and there was a wolf at the edge of the forest."

"What happened?"

"Nothing," Rowan said. "Well, it sniffed me, and I touched it, but then it left."

"What did it look like?" Lydia asked.

"Grey with a white patch on its chest," Rowan said.

Lydia blinked at her. "Maybe it was the same wolf as when you were a baby."

Rowan laughed. "Nana, even if that was a wolf, this wasn't the same one. That was twenty-two years ago, and this wolf didn't look old. It looked young and very healthy."

His wolf made a low growl of pride, and Rafe could barely stop from rolling his eyes. He glanced up and clamped his hand around his fork. Rowan stared at him, and he could smell her lust's sweet scent. With an inward groan, he shovelled the rest of the pie into his mouth and stood.

"I should be going. Thank you for the pie, Lydia."

"You're welcome, Rafe. Thanks for stopping and picking up my girl. The woods are no place for a young girl to be alone."

"My pleasure," he mumbled. He nodded to Rowan, "Nice to see you again, Ms. Jameson."

"You as well, Mr. Taggert," she said.

He walked across the cabin, acutely aware of Rowan's gaze, and waved half-heartedly before leaving. He climbed into his truck and backed out of the driveway.

What are you going to do about tomorrow night?

Nothing. So Rowan will be close by during the full moon – it's not a big deal. I can avoid her. I'll go deeper into the woods than I usually do.

What if you run into your pack?

Not my pack anymore, and I won't run into them. They'll be on the other side of the river.

His stomach churning with lust and panic, he drove home.

———

"That was nice of Rafe to give you a ride," Lydia said as she cleared the table.

"Mmm," Rowan said. Staring at Rafe's tight ass as he left had thrown her deep into a fantasy that involved her riding him in a distinctly unladylike way.

"He's a handsome man, isn't he?"

"What?" She stared at her nana as Lydia ran water into the sink.

"Rafe Taggert. He's quite handsome."

"I hadn't noticed."

"No? The way you were checking out his ass as he was leaving suggests otherwise."

"Nana!"

Lydia laughed. "What? I may be old, Rowan, but I'm not blind."

Rowan sighed and rubbed the top of Scrappy's head. "Fine, maybe I've noticed how attractive he is."

"He is a looker, that one," Lydia said. "And he seems to be fond of you, as well."

"He isn't," Rowan said shortly.

"Old, not blind," Lydia repeated.

"He says he's too old for me," Rowan said.

"Age ain't nothin' but a number, sweet girl."

"That's what I told him, but he disagrees," Rowan said. "He is attracted to me, Nana. We sort of made out a little the night of the Centennial Celebration, but he's avoided me since that night, and today he made it clear that it was a mistake."

She stood and dried the dishes that Lydia placed on the drying rack. "I can't get him to change his mind."

"You will," Lydia said.

"What do you know about him?" Rowan asked.

"Not much, to be honest. He's a quiet one and doesn't like to share. He's been a real help to me as of late, though. He drops in at least once a week to make sure I'm doing okay, and he's been helping me with some of the repairs around here. Fixed the leaking faucet and helped dig up my vegetable garden this spring."

"Has he always lived alone?" Rowan asked.

"If you're asking me if he's ever been married, no, he hasn't," Lydia said, "but he hasn't always lived alone. His family lives in the woods on the south side of the river."

"His family are those weirdos across the river?" Rowan said in surprise.

Lydia gave her a disapproving look. "Just because a person doesn't want to live in town surrounded by people who can't stop stickin' their noses in other people's business doesn't make them weird, Rowan. Don't be judgmental – your momma and I raised you better than that."

"Sorry, Nana," Rowan said. "I didn't mean it the way it sounded. It's just – no one knows anything about them. They come into town maybe every six months, homeschool their kids, and God knows how they even get money. They don't work in town, that's for sure. I know Rafe's a loner, but he doesn't completely cut himself off from the rest of the world like they do."

"Maybe that's why he left," Lydia said.

"What do you mean he left?"

"Well, about fifteen years ago, Rafe and his mother left. They moved away for a year or so, nobody knows where, and then Rafe returned by himself. He rented a place in town, started his landscaping company, and eventually bought the cabin just down the road."

"So, where's his mother?" Rowan asked.

Lydia shrugged. "No one knows, and Rafe refuses to talk about it. Most folks thought he would return to his father, but whatever happened between them wasn't solved with a year's absence. No one knows what happened between Rafe and his father, but they have nothing to do with each other."

"He's never said anything to you?" Rowan asked.

"No. Like I told you, he's a quiet one."

"He must be lonely," Rowan said.

"He is."

Rowan stared at her grandmother, and Lydia shrugged. "He won't admit it, but he's lonely. Some people are meant to live alone, but he ain't one of them. Sooner or later, he'll realize it and find himself a woman to settle down with."

A surge of jealousy went through Rowan, and Lydia grinned before tugging the glass from her hand. "You're going to break that, sweet girl. You thinking you'd like to be that woman he settles down with?"

"I hardly know the guy. And maybe he's right – there is a big age difference. That has the potential to cause all sorts of problems."

Lydia cupped her face with her warm hand. "Is it the age difference that's making you hesitate or that you just might be finally wanting something more than a roll in the hay?"

"Nana!" Rowan's face turned bright red, and Lydia laughed.

"You think I didn't have my fair share of boys back in the day?"

"And this conversation is over," Rowan said with a grin.

"Seriously, sweet girl," Lydia said, "that man's going to do everything in his power to push you away. Don't let him. There's something special between the two of you – anyone with half a brain can see that."

"Nana, what's this?" Rowan held out the tissue-wrapped folded piece of white fabric.

It was Saturday night, and she'd spent a pleasant day with her grandmother. She had spent most of the morning weeding Lydia's vegetable garden and the afternoon sunbathing in the backyard. After a light dinner, she showered, and they played cards for a couple of hours. Now, feeling restless and bored, she was digging through her grandmother's hope chest.

Lydia glanced up from the computer, and a smile crossed her face. "I forgot I had that."

"What is it?" Rowan ran her hand over the soft material.

"It's the night dress your grandfather bought me for our tenth anniversary," Lydia said.

Rowan unfolded the tissue paper and draped the night-gown across the hope chest. "Oh, Nana. It's beautiful."

"Ayuh, your grandfather had good taste," Lydia said. "Why don't you try it on? I was about your size when I was a young thing."

"I don't want to wreck it or get it dirty," Rowan said.

"Nonsense," Lydia said briskly. "It's meant to be worn, not sit in a hope chest. Try it on, sweet girl."

Holding the nightgown, Rowan disappeared into her bedroom. She returned a few minutes later. "What do you think?"

"Oh, Rowan," Lydia said softly. "You look beautiful."

The nightgown was made of soft cotton and was off the shoulder with an empire-style waist. The bodice laced up the front, and Rowan adjusted the bow she had tied before touching the soft material of the sleeves. The sleeves were wide and feminine, and lace edged the sleeves. Matching lace edged the nightgown's hem, and Lydia smiled at Rowan's toes peeking out from under the hem.

"It's a bit too long, but the dress fits perfectly across your bust." She grinned at Rowan. "None of the women in our family were blessed with much in the chest department, unfortunately."

Rowan laughed and twirled so the long skirt billowed around her hips and legs. "I love it, Nana. It makes me feel like a princess."

Lydia touched the soft cotton before smiling at her. "More like a pretty little wood fairy."

She stroked Rowan's long hair and kissed her cheek. "It looks beautiful on you, sweet girl."

"Thanks, Nana. I'd better take it off before I get it dirty."

Lydia shook her head. "No, don't. It'll wash, and it makes me happy to see you wearing it. Besides, we're going to bed soon, and you're not going to be getting it dirty in bed."

She glanced at the dogs before rubbing her lower back. "Would you mind taking the kids outside for me, Rowan?"

"Not at all." Rowan whistled, and the schnauzers jumped off the couch and followed her to the back door. She stepped outside and waited patiently as the dogs sniffed around the grass. It was warm and quiet, and she breathed deeply before staring at the sky. Stars shone brightly in the night sky. Living in town, she had forgotten how bright the stars were and how much she had loved to lay on her back in the soft grass and admire them.

The moon was huge and full and so low in the sky that she felt like she could touch it. She reached up, smiling a little at how silly she was, as both dogs growled low in their throats. They were staring into the woods that bordered the backyard, and she took a few steps forward, scanning the trees. She saw no gleam of eyes shining in the moonlight, heard no rustle of movement in the trees, and made a soothing noise when the dogs growled again.

"Hush, you two, it's probably just a squirrel," she said. "Come on. Time for bed."

She whistled, and the dogs followed her obediently into the house.

THE WOLF STEPPED OUT FROM THE TREES AND STARED unblinkingly at the cabin before lifting his head to the moon. He made a low, soft howl, staring with rapturous delight at the golden orb. The lights in the house blinked out one by one, and he trotted into the yard and sniffed at the two faint indents in the grass where Rowan had stood. He dropped to the ground and rolled in ecstasy over the indents before sitting on his haunches and staring at the moon again. Half an hour passed as he stared silently at the moon before he whined softly and stretched. Growling with excitement, he sniffed the air and trotted around the side of the house.

ROWAN MOVED RESTLESSLY IN THE BED. THEY HAD GONE TO bed nearly forty minutes ago, and she could hear her grandmother's snoring through the thin wall that separated their bedrooms. She sighed and shifted to her side, staring out the window at the moon. She wasn't the least bit tired, despite how much time she had spent in the sun today, and she had the ridiculous urge to slip out of the house and hike through the woods to Rafe's cabin.

And then what? Stand outside his house with your phone held over your head and play him some Peter Gabriel? Try to peer into his bedroom window like some crazed stalker? That's not at all creepy.

She stiffened when she heard the scratching. She sat up in bed and cocked her head, listening intently as there was more scratching. She gasped when the wolf's dark head appeared in the window. It blotted out the moon, and she leaned back against the headboard, clutching the quilt to her chest. The wolf stared silently at her before dropping out of sight, and she hesitated only briefly before scrambling out of bed and running to the window.

The wolf sat on his haunches just a few feet from the house. She studied the familiar white patch on its chest as he grinned at her. He glanced at the moon before staring at her, and she heard his faint whine through the glass. He stood and backed up a few steps before sitting and whining again. He panted, his tongue lolling out of his mouth, and she studied his green eyes before backing away from the window.

She crept from the bedroom, walking silently past her grandmother's bedroom and waiting for the dogs to start up a symphony of barking. To her surprise, there were no sounds from Lydia's bedroom other than her snoring. Rowan unlocked the back door and stepped into the warm night. She closed the door quietly and took a few steps into the yard, staring nervously around her.

Rowan, what are you doing? That wolf is a wild animal, not a damn dog and –

She gasped when she felt the wet nose touch her hand and staggered back. The wolf made a low whine, and, her heart pounding in her chest and adrenaline singing in her veins, she reached out with a trembling hand and touched his broad head. He nudged her hip with his face, and she stroked his thick fur as he leaned against her.

"Hello, boy," she said softly.

He woofed in reply, and she bit back her disappointment when he bounded across the yard and into the woods. She turned back to the house, but the wolf barked softly. He stood at the edge of the woods and stared briefly at the moon before barking at her again. It was obvious what he wanted, and without hesitating, she crossed the backyard and followed him into the woods.

She wasn't wearing shoes, and she held up the hem of her grandmother's nightdress as she walked carefully, watching for thorns and sharp rocks. The wolf trotted ahead of her, giving an impatient bark every few minutes or so.

"Just hold your damn horses," she muttered. "Not all of us have thick fur to protect our feet."

He chuffed at her, and it almost sounded like a laugh. She stuck her tongue out at him before skirting around a rock.

"I've lost my mind," she said. "I'm following a damn wolf into the woods in the middle of the night."

You're dreaming.

She stopped for a moment and stared up at the glimpses of the moon through the trees. She was dreaming. Of course. The wolf barked again, and she muttered, "yeah, yeah, I'm coming," before walking a little faster.

She could hear the low murmur of the river now, and she wasn't surprised when she rounded a particular thick grove of trees and saw the water. It looked black in the moonlight, and she crouched beside the river and dipped her hand in as the wolf bent his shaggy head and drank deeply. The water was cool but not cold, and she wiped her hand on the soft grass that lined the riverbank before staring up at the moon again.

She wasn't sure how long she studied it, but the wolf was gone when she finally lowered her gaze. She frowned and scanned the riverbank and the trees. This dream was turning out to be a bust.

She stood as the large clump of bushes to her right shivered. Her smile faded, and her breath caught in her throat when a naked Rafe stepped into the moonlight. She studied his broad shoulders and wide chest. A light layer of dark hair covered his chest and abdomen, and - *good night, Irene* - he had a six pack.

She swallowed thickly and followed the thin trail of hair below his navel to his cock. It stood out proudly from his body, hard and delightfully thick, and she licked her lips as she studied it. She wanted to walk toward him, wanted to take his cock in her hand and feel the hard steel of it surrounded by velvet-soft skin, but she remained frozen in her spot. This was the most fantastic dream of her life, and she was afraid to move a single muscle in case it ended.

Rafe apparently had no such fear, and she watched in breathless anticipation as he walked toward her. He stopped when only a few inches remained between them, and Rowan stared solemnly at him. "Am I dreaming, Rafe?"

He didn't reply. Instead, his strong hand gripped the back of her neck and tugged her closer so he could bend and press his mouth against hers. She moaned, lightning coursing through her veins, and parted her lips for him. His tongue slid between them and stroked hers in a light caress. She sighed and shuddered, her hands gripping his naked waist, as he sucked on the tip of her tongue before nibbling her bottom lip.

He took a step back, and she made a whine of need that brought a smile to his lips. He traced her bare shoulders before pulling on the strings that laced her nightgown together. He unlaced it slowly and, when it was loose, tugged her nightdress down her body. It pooled at her feet, and he stared at her naked body in the moonlight, his gaze lingering on the patch of red hair between her thighs.

"Rafe, please," Rowan said.

This was a dream, it had to be, but she was desperate to

find relief before it ended, and she woke up alone in her bed. If she couldn't have Rafe in real life, she was determined to have him in her dreams.

He bent his dark head, and she cried out and arched her back when his lips closed around one taut nipple. He pulled it lightly before circling his tongue around it, and she sank her fingers into his silky hair before guiding him to her other breast. He took his time, licking the soft hollow between her breasts and nibbling on the smooth curve of her left one. She moaned with pleasure when he scraped his teeth across her sensitive nipple.

He straightened and cupped her breast before kissing her again. He took her mouth with hard licks and nips, sucking on her bottom lip before biting it. When his hand trailed down her flat belly, she immediately parted her thighs. His other hand threaded through her long hair and gripped it tightly, pulling her head back as he ran his fingers through the soft curls between her legs.

She was desperate for him to touch her, but he continued to tease her, stroking the curls at the apex of her thighs as he kissed her throat and licked the curve of her jaw. She made a cry of impatience and grabbed his hand, pushing it between her legs and trying to make him touch her clit.

He kissed her deeply, her head held immobile in his strong hand as he tasted her. The tip of one rough finger brushed against her clit, and she shrieked into his mouth, her knees buckling. He released her hair and slipped his arm around her waist, holding her against him as he explored her wet pussy with his fingers. His middle finger slid deep into her hot core, and he groaned when she clenched around him. His thumb rubbed circles against her clit, and she gasped soundlessly as she clutched at his broad shoulders and dug her nails into his smooth skin.

"Rafe, oh God, I can't...."

She trailed off in a hoarse cry as her orgasm exploded within her. She shook violently, and when her knees buckled a second time, he scooped her up and carried her to the soft grass next to the river. He placed her on her back in the grass and knelt between her legs, pushing her thighs wide with his big, warm hands. He paused, and she followed his gaze to the moon.

"It's so beautiful," she said.

She couldn't tear her gaze from it as Rafe placed his hands on either side of her head. His cock nudged her opening, and she made a hoarse cry of pleasure when he pushed his way into her warmth. He filled her completely, and she clamped her thighs around his narrow hips at the twinge of pain as she stretched around him.

"No," he rasped into her ear. "Open for me. Always open for me."

His low voice made her insides tremble, and she immediately let her legs fall open. He was so big – so damn thick – she tried to tighten around him and failed miserably. Her effort made him moan, though, and she tried again.

"Stop," he said.

She gave him a naughty grin, but he thrust roughly inside her on her next attempt to squeeze him. She cried out, her pelvis bucking against his, and he began a slow and steady rhythm that made her toes curl into the grass. She gripped his tight ass, meeting each thrust as she kept her legs wide for him.

Tension coiled in her lower belly, and she urged him on with soft cries and moans. He ignored her pleas to move faster and kept the same even rhythm that drove her crazy.

"Please, Rafe," she cried. "Harder!"

When he didn't do as she begged, she raked her nails down his back and writhed beneath him frantically.

"Rafe, I need it!" she cried.

"The moon, my love. Look at the moon." He bent his head and kissed her mouth, swallowing her frantic cries before licking her lower lip.

She raised her gaze obediently to the glowing orb as Rafe sucked on one hard nipple.

"So pretty," she whispered as her hands tugged and pulled at Rafe's dark hair. He lifted his head and stared at the moon with her, and she made a cry of delight when his hips thrust harder and faster.

"Yes," she moaned. "Oh, yes."

She was awash with sensation, the warm wind, the soft grass beneath her body, and Rafe's hard nakedness on top of her. He was so warm, so solid, and she touched his face with a trembling hand.

"Am I dreaming?" she asked.

He dropped his gaze to her, and she made a low gasp. His eyes, usually the colour of hazel, were a bright glowing jade and she stared mesmerized at them as he made a low howl and thrust rapidly in and out of her tight pussy. She was so wet that her juices dripped down her thighs and her pussy sucked greedily at his cock as he groaned and fangs protruded from his mouth.

"Rafe?" She touched his jaw and made a startled shriek when he bent and pressed his mouth against hers. His tongue pressed against the seam of her lips, and she opened them before hesitantly running her tongue over the tips of his fangs. He moaned into her mouth, his hands digging into the soft ground, and then he was pounding into her.

He drove into her deeply, sending shockwaves of pleasure

throughout her body, and he kissed her again before growling, "Legs around my waist. Now."

She wrapped her legs around him, hooking her feet in the small of his back as he made another low growl and fucked her hard. Her orgasm was starting, and she had a moment of surprise that it was happening without touching her clit. Pleasure washed over her, and she screamed Rafe's name as her body bucked and throbbed beneath his.

He stared up at the moon, his hips thrusting wildly back and forth, and then his hand was between them, rubbing her clit, and she screamed again as another more powerful orgasm roared through her. Her back arched as wave after wave of pleasure washed over her, each more intense than the last. Vaguely she was aware of his warm seed soaking her insides as he howled, his fangs unbelievably long and a thick dark beard covering his lower jaw.

"Rafe!" She couldn't breathe, her head was spinning, and as one last wave of pleasure spiked through her, she screamed again and collapsed against the grass. Breathing harshly, Rafe hovered over her and pressed a kiss against her throat before rolling off her. He pulled her into his embrace, pressing her head against his chest and stroking her back as he stared dreamily at the moon above them.

Rowan's body was as pliant as a wet noodle, and she was suddenly incredibly sleepy. Could a person fall asleep in a dream, she wondered tiredly. She yawned, her eyelids just couldn't stay open, and she made a soft, snoring noise as she fell asleep.

CHAPTER 3

"Rafe!"

Rowan sat up with a gasp, blinking in the bright sunlight flooding through the window, before staring wildly around the room. She was in her bedroom at her Nana's cabin, and she slumped against the bed before touching her mouth.

"What the hell?" she said.

She threw back the covers, staring at her nightgown as she sat up in bed. She thought for a moment before studying the bottom of her right foot. It was clean, no pine sap or dirt clung to it, and she groaned and fell back on the bed.

"Just a dream," she muttered as disappointment coursed through her. It had felt so real, and she couldn't quite wrap her mind around the fact that it had been a dream. She sat up and slid out of bed, wincing a little before touching herself.

Her crotch was sore, it ached pleasantly, in fact, and she began to haul up her nightgown. Before she could examine herself, there was a knock on the door, and her grandmother stuck her head into the room.

"Are you going to sleep all day? It's almost -"

Lydia stopped and eyed the nightgown bunched around Rowan's upper thighs. "Rowan? What's wrong?"

"Nothing, Nana," Rowan said guiltily before dropping the nightgown. "Sorry I slept so late."

"Get dressed and come have some lunch with me, sweet girl," Lydia said.

Twenty minutes later, freshly showered and dressed, Rowan sat at the table as Lydia piled pancakes on a plate and handed them to her.

"Thanks, Nana," she said before pouring a healthy dose of syrup over the stack of pancakes. She ate a mouthful and made a low moan of pleasure. "These are delicious."

"Eat up. There's plenty," Lydia said before checking her watch.

RAFE PULLED INTO LYDIA'S DRIVEWAY AND SHUT OFF THE truck. He drummed his fingers on the steering wheel. When Lydia called him this morning and asked if he would mind driving Rowan into town, he should have said no. He should have made some excuse, but he hesitated only briefly before agreeing.

After last night, he needed to see her again. He had damage control to do in a serious way.

You're lucky she's a deep sleeper. You know that, right?

Yeah, he did know. He had cleaned Rowan's feet with water from the river, dressed her in her nightgown and carried her back to her grandmother's, sneaking through the back door and tucking her into her bed without Rowan even stirring. She slept like the dead, and he would use that in his favour. She had thought it was a dream last night, and if she brought it up, he would simply use her confusion against her and convince her that, yes, she had been dreaming.

Coward.

Maybe, but for the first time since he had danced with Rowan at the Centennial Celebration, his wolf was sated, and he could think clearly again. He didn't even remember coaxing Rowan out of her grandmother's house, didn't remember leading her into the woods. His wolf had taken over when he caught his first glimpse of the full moon. Rafe hadn't resumed control until they were by the river. He had shifted to his human form, and when he saw Rowan in the moonlight, her red hair flowing down her back and her bare shoulders glowing in the soft light, he was lost.

He shouldn't have slept with her, but there was an odd feeling of relief at finally doing so. His wolf had been obsessed with Rowan for the last three years – since the first night she started working at Gaston's. He had caught the occasional glimpse of her in town, shopping or eating at one of the restaurants, but, truthfully, he hadn't paid much attention to her. He had noticed her red hair, of course, but that was the extent of it. Until he had walked into Gaston's one night for a beer, and she had been waitressing. She had stopped at his table, smiling politely at him, and his wolf had caught one whiff of her scent and gone insane. He had stopped going to Gaston's when he began to smell her lust for him. She hadn't flirted, she hadn't touched him or made any indication that she wanted him – in fact, she was always slightly flustered and nervous around him – but he could smell her need for him. It had sent his wolf into a frenzy of desire.

Just the wolf?

He closed his eyes for a brief moment. Fuck, no, not just his wolf. But that didn't matter. What mattered was that his wolf had finally gotten what it wanted, and his obsession with Rowan was finished. His human side might still want her, but that was at least capable of rational thought, and it would be simple enough to ignore his lust.

He slid out of the truck, took a deep breath, and trudged toward the cabin. He could do this.

"Nana, why do you keep looking at your watch?" Rowan asked as she spread butter on her second helping of pancakes.

"No reason," Lydia said.

There was a knock at the door, and Scrappy and Scruffy barked shrilly as Lydia hollered, "It's open."

Rowan's heart knocked against her ribs when the door opened, and Rafe walked into the cabin. He petted the dogs roughly before joining them in the kitchen.

"Hi, Rafe. You're just in time for some pancakes," Lydia said.

"I ate already, but thank you," Rafe said. "Hello, Ms. Jameson."

"What are you doing here?" Rowan asked.

"I asked Rafe if he would mind driving you home since your car crapped out on you," Lydia said. "And he was sweet enough to say yes. Now, finish up your pancakes, Rowan."

Her cheeks flushed, Rowan poured syrup on her pancakes and ate a mouthful, licking away the drop of syrup on her lips, as Rafe stiffened and took a step backward. His tanned face was pale, and Lydia stared at him in concern.

"Rafe, what's wrong?"

"Nothing," he said hoarsely.

Lydia frowned and pointed to one of the chairs. "Sit

down, Rafe, and I'll get you a glass of water. You look like you're going to pass out."

RAFE SAT DOWN AND STARED AT THE FLOOR. WHAT THE HELL was happening? His wolf, which had been quiet and subdued all morning, had gone crazy the moment he smelled Rowan. Rafe tried desperately to calm the beast as Lydia set the glass of water on the table in front of him and pressed her hand against his forehead.

"You don't feel warm."

"I'm fine," he said.

He wasn't fine. He was about as far from fine as he could get, but how was he supposed to explain that to Lydia?

Hey, Lydia. So, I lured your granddaughter out of your house and fucked her in the forest last night even though I'm fifteen years older than her, and that makes me a dirty old man. But my wolf was driving me insane, and I had to do something. Only now the goddamn thing thinks she's his mate, and, uh, how do you feel about having wolf shifters as great-grandbabies?

He groaned inwardly and drank the glass of water in three large gulps. Oh yeah, that conversation would go over really well with the old woman. If he were lucky, she'd just cut off his balls and not straight up murder him.

Rowan pushed away her half-eaten pancakes and stood up. "Sorry, Nana. I'm really full. I'm going to pack up my stuff."

She disappeared into the bedroom, and Rafe clenched his hands into tight fists as his eyes turned jade. She wore a thin tank top and a pair of jeans shorts, and he was beyond tempted to follow her to her room, tear those ridiculously tiny shorts from her slender body and fuck her until she screamed his name. Scrappy and Scruffy, who were sniffing around at his feet, froze and stared up at him before making twin growls. His wolf snarled at them, and Rafe pushed down his need to shift with superhuman strength.

Give me my mate!

Enough! He snapped at his wolf. *Enough! You can have her later.*

A bald-faced lie, but it calmed his wolf down and allowed him to relax just a fraction. He was wondering if he could somehow get out of giving Rowan a ride home when Lydia said, "Thank you again for giving my girl a ride home, Rafe. I sure appreciate it."

"Uh, no problem," he mumbled. "I was heading into town anyway."

"Oh good," Lydia said. She cleared away the dishes, smiling when Rowan reappeared with her backpack. "All ready to go, sweet girl?"

"Yes. I'll call you tomorrow, okay?"

"Sounds good. Love you!" Lydia kissed her cheek, and Rowan hugged her before smiling nervously at Rafe.

He stood and followed her out of the cabin. She climbed into his truck, and they waved at Lydia, who stood in the doorway, and he backed out of the driveway and rolled down his window before driving down the road.

There were a few minutes of awkward silence before Rowan said, "So are we going to talk about last night?"

Rafe took a deep breath and pasted what he hoped was a curious look on his face. "I'm sorry?"

"Last night. Are we going to talk about it?"

"I'm afraid I don't know what you're talking about, Ms. Jameson."

She gave him a look of exasperation. "We were in the forest last night, and we…."

He arched one eyebrow at her. "We what?"

"We fucked," she said bluntly.

OKAY, SO MAYBE DECIDING TO BE PERFECTLY BLUNT WASN'T Rowan's hottest idea. Especially at the look of utter shock on Rafe's face.

"I'm sorry?" he said.

"We had sex in the forest last night," she repeated. She clutched her hands together and stared at her knees.

"No, we didn't," Rafe said. "I was at home all night."

"Bullshit," she said. "The wolf lured me out into the forest and disappeared. Then you showed up, and you were naked, and we had sex."

She groaned inwardly. Now that she was saying it aloud, it sounded idiotic.

"I can assure you I was not naked in the forest last night, Ms. Jameson. Nor did we have sex. You must have been dreaming."

She glared at him. "I know it wasn't a dream, Rafe."

"How do you know? Did you wake up in the forest this morning?" he asked.

"No," she admitted. "I was in my bed, but my…."

"What?"

"I was sore this morning," she muttered.

He stared blankly at her, and she groaned and covered her face. "Oh my God, it was a dream. I am unbelievably embarrassed right now."

He cleared his throat. "There's nothing to be embarrassed about."

Rowan stared out the window as her cheeks burned dully. While showering this morning, she had convinced herself that it wasn't a dream. She had been tender and sore, and while she supposed there was the off-chance that she had been finger-banging herself during her dream, it seemed more plausible that Rafe had been wandering naked in the forest last night, and they'd had sex. But that was before she had seen the look on Rafe's face.

"Ms. Jameson, I -"

"No." She shook her head and continued to look out the window. "I'm sorry, but I really don't want to talk. In fact, you should probably know that I'll never be able to look you in the eye again, but, uh, don't take it personally."

"You don't have to -"

"Please," she said, horrified at how obvious it was that she was close to tears, "can you just drive me home, Mr. Taggert?"

"Yes," he said, and she blinked back the hot tears as they drove silently through the forest.

"Ro, sweetie, please tell us what's wrong," Belle said gently.

"Nothing's wrong," Rowan said.

Ella leaned forward and rubbed Rowan's back. "There is. Let us help you."

Rowan took a drink of lemonade before staring at the backyard. "Bennett's doing a great job on the backyard."

"He is," Belle said before waiting patiently.

"Is he, uh, home right now?"

"No. He drove with Duncan to Newport. Duncan was

meeting with his agent, and they were going to pick up some supplies to fix the greenhouse."

"Crazy that Duncan is Samuel," Rowan said to Ella. "I still can't quite believe it."

Ella squeezed her hand. "It's still a little weird for me too. Don't change the subject, honey."

"I humiliated myself in front of Rafe Taggert again. Really, badly. Like, 'I can never look him in the eye again' badly," Rowan said.

"What happened?" Belle asked.

"It's a long story," Rowan said, "and I might need something a little stronger than lemonade to tell it."

Belle smiled at her and stood. "I think Bennett's got some whiskey."

Rowan grabbed her hand. "No, it's okay. I'm just kidding. I think. God, I don't even know where to begin."

"Start from the beginning," Ella said. "Tell us everything."

"I was so convinced it was real," Rowan said quietly. "But in the truck, the look on his face…."

She finished the last of her lemonade in two swallows. "God, I'm such an idiot."

There was no reply, and she looked up to see Ella and Belle staring at each other.

"What?" she asked.

"Nothing," Belle said quickly. "I don't think you need to be embarrassed. Everyone has sex dreams."

"It just felt so real," Rowan repeated.

"I think it was," Ella said. She ignored the pointed look

that Belle gave her and leaned forward. "It doesn't sound like a dream to me, Ro."

"So, the part where his eyes glowed, and he grew fangs was real?" Rowan said before snorting.

"Well," Ella gave Belle a look that Rowan didn't understand, "that part probably wasn't real. I mean, people don't just grow fangs, but I think you did have sex with Rafe in the forest. The fangs thing was probably because you had seen the wolf before running into Rafe. And if the sex was as good as you said it was, you probably had some kind of hot-sex hallucination. Hell, the other night Duncan made me come so hard, I swear I blacked out for a minute or two."

"Or maybe," Belle said brightly, "you have a furry fetish and are just starting to realize it. You imagined the fangs and fur."

Rowan frowned at her. "He didn't have fur, Belle."

Belle made a nervous little laugh as Rowan stood and walked to the end of the deck, staring out at the lush backyard. She glanced over her shoulder to see Belle punching Ella in the arm before muttering, "what are you doing?" under her breath.

Ella flapped her hands at her, and Rowan quickly turned to face the backyard again when Ella glanced her way. When she turned around, Ella's face was composed, and Belle was sitting on her hands like she was trying not to punch Ella again.

"Okay, so what if you're right? What if Rafe is, like, I don't know, some hippie who likes to run around naked in the forest, and we just happened to stumble onto each other and have sex? Why would he lie about it?" Rowan asked.

"Because he thinks he's too old for you," Ella said. "We've already established that."

"Yeah, but why go to all that trouble to convince me it

was just a dream? He would have had to dress me, clean my feet, and carry me back to Nana's. All without waking me."

Belle snorted. "Not waking you is the easy part. A tornado wouldn't wake you once you were asleep, Ro."

She nudged Ella. "Remember that time at summer camp when we had that terrible thunderstorm? Lightning struck the tree right outside our cabin and split it in two. Half the girls in the cabin were screaming in terror, and Rowan slept through the whole damn thing."

"Fine, I'm a heavy sleeper," Rowan said. "But, God, it would have just been a whole lot easier to tell me he made a mistake and that it was, I don't know, Mother Nature or the Moon Goddess that made him have sex with me."

"The Moon Goddess?" Ella said with a laugh.

"He kept telling me to look at the moon," Rowan said. "Shit, is there some kind of cult that worships the moon? It would be just my luck that Rafe is in some weird satanic cult."

Ella laughed again. "I highly doubt that, Ro. Now, tell the truth – do you think you were dreaming?"

Rowan hesitated before shaking her head. "No, I don't. It was the best goddamn sex of my life, and I refuse to believe it was a dream. I can still hear his voice in my head, feel his hands on my body and his…."

"Yeah, we get the picture," Belle said.

"I wouldn't mind a few more details," Ella said and then laughed when Belle smacked her on the leg.

"So, what are you going to do?" Ella said.

"What do you mean?" Rowan frowned at her.

"What are you going to do?" Ella repeated. "You like Rafe, it's obvious, and sex with him was amazing. Will you just let that go, or will you go after what you want?"

"He's not interested, Ella. He didn't -"

"Obviously, he is if he banged you in the middle of the forest," Ella said impatiently. "So he thinks he's too old for you, so what? Change his mind."

"How?" Rowan said. "He avoids me. He never goes to Gaston's anymore, and I didn't even know he was helping my grandmother at her place. He's never there when I am."

"Don't you normally go to your grandmother's on Sundays?" Ella asked.

Rowan nodded. "Yes."

"Maybe you need to start dropping in at your grandmother's during the week?" Ella suggested. "If that is, you're certain that Rafe Taggert is the one for you."

"He is," Rowan said. "I don't care what he or anyone else in this town thinks. I want him."

"Then take him," Ella said softly.

Rowan suddenly grinned at her before grabbing her empty glass. "I'm going to get some more lemonade. Anyone else want more?"

They shook their heads, and Rowan disappeared into the house, her mind buzzing with thoughts of Rafe.

As Rowan walked into the house, Belle gave Ella a look of panic. "What the hell, Ella!"

"What?" Ella said.

"What do you mean, what? You can't tell me that you aren't thinking the same thing I am."

"That Rafe Taggert is a wolf shifter," Ella said.

"Did Duncan tell you he was?" Belle asked.

"Of course not. You know how they are – they won't say a damn word about other shifters. But c'mon, Belle. It's obvious."

"Yeah, to us, but Rowan has no idea that shifters exist."

"Not yet she doesn't. But I think that's about to change," Ella said.

"You want her to find out," Belle said suddenly. "It's why you're pushing her to go after Rafe."

"No," Ella said. "I want her to go after Rafe because it's obvious that she wants to be with him. I know we've teased her for years about her crush on him, but I think it's become more than just a crush in the last few months. I want Rowan to be happy, and I think Rafe will make her happy."

She squeezed Belle's hand. "It is a bonus that he's probably a wolf shifter. Just think how much easier it would be if we didn't have to hide that our boyfriends are shifters from Rowan."

"It would be nice," Belle said. "But what if Rafe doesn't want her? It'll break her heart."

"Are you kidding me?" Ella said. "He lured her out of the house and then fucked her brains out. He wants her."

"Maybe it was because of the full moon," Belle said. "Did you ever think of that, Ella? Maybe Rafe goes around every full moon and seduces a different woman."

Ella burst into laughter. "You can't possibly believe that, Belle."

"Fine, I don't," Belle said. "But I'm worried Rafe won't get over this age difference."

"He will," Ella said. "Rowan will change his mind. You'll see."

Rowan came out of the house and smiled at them. "What are you two whispering about?"

"Just concocting plans for how you're going to seduce Rafe Taggert," Ella said. "Is your car still in the shop?"

Rowan made a sour face. "Yes. And it will be until next

week. If I'm planning on dropping in at Nana's house out of the blue, it'll have to wait until then."

"Well, lucky girl," Ella said, "you have a best friend who is more than happy to give you a lift to your grandmother's house any time you want."

CHAPTER 4

"Are you sure Rafe will be at your nana's today?" Ella asked as she pulled into Lydia's driveway.

Rowan nodded and grabbed her bag from the back seat. "Yep. I talked to Nana yesterday, and she casually mentioned that Rafe would be dropping by to fix the fence."

Ella laughed. "Go, Lydia."

Rowan grinned at her. "Nana thinks a lot like you, Miss Ella."

Ella leaned over and kissed her on the cheek. "Have fun seducing Rafe, honey. I'll be back at three to pick you up and drive you to work."

Rowan grabbed her hand. "Thanks, Ella. I appreciate this."

"Anytime. Now go…seduce your little heart out."

RAFE PARKED HIS TRUCK NEXT TO LYDIA'S CAR AND GRABBED his toolbox before heading to the backyard. Lydia stepped out on the front porch and waved at him. "Hello, Rafe!"

341

"Hi, Lydia. I'm just going to get started on the fence."

"Thanks so much. I can't tell you how much I appreciate this." She stared up at the sun for a moment. "It's such a hot day. I'll bring you some lemonade in a bit, okay?"

"Sounds good," he said.

She disappeared into the house, and he grabbed the new boards that leaned against the shed. Twenty minutes later, he had the rotting boards ripped away, and he stopped and stripped off his shirt, using it to wipe the sweat from his face before placing a new board against the fence. He heard the back door open and set his hammer down. He was hot and thirsty and –

He froze as Rowan's scent drifted to him. He turned around. His wolf made a mad howl of need, and he inhaled sharply. Wearing nothing but a ridiculously tiny green bikini, Rowan smiled and waved at him. "Hello, Mr. Taggert."

"What are you doing here?" He took a stumbling step back as she moved toward him.

"Visiting my grandmother," she said, "and sunbathing. It's the perfect day for sunbathing, don't you think?"

His gaze drifted to her small breasts. Fuck, his goddamn mouth watered at the thought of sucking on her perfect, pink nipples. His eyes moved to her crotch, and he clenched his hands into tight fists, remembering the feel of her smooth, soft skin, the way her pussy had clung so tightly to his cock.

"Mr. Taggert? Is everything okay? You look kind of tense," Rowan said.

"I'm fine," he snapped before turning away.

He told himself not to look, then looked anyway when he heard her move away. She was bent over, spreading a blanket out on the ground, and he made a low growl of need at the sight of her ass. For how slender she was, she had a great ass

- a fucking amazing ass, actually – and he growled again as his cock hardened.

She looked over her shoulder at him. "Did you say something?"

"No." He swung around again, embarrassed that she had caught him ogling her ass like the dirty old pervert he was and picked up the hammer. He would finish the fucking fence and get the hell out of here before he did something he'd regret.

He had only hammered a single nail when she tapped him on the back.

"Would you mind putting some sunscreen on my back, Mr. Taggert?"

Rafe set the hammer down and turned. Rowan held out a bottle of sunscreen, and he deliberately kept his eyes on her face as he shook his head. "Your grandmother is inside. Ask her."

"But then I'd have to walk all the way back inside. Why do that when you're standing right here?" she said sweetly.

She took a step toward him, and, like a coward, he scooted to the left and backed away. A grin crossed her face, and she moved forward again. Feeling more like prey than predator, he continued to retreat until he felt the cool wood of the cabin against his naked back.

"Something wrong?" she asked as she stopped before him.

"No," he muttered.

"Good. Are you sure you can't help me? I burn really easily."

He made the mistake of dropping his gaze to her breasts when she ran her hand over her chest. Her nipples were hard and poking against her bikini top's thin material, and he groaned. Her grin widened at the sound, and she moved forward until her small breasts almost brushed his chest.

"Be a sweet man and help me, won't you?" She placed her hand on his chest and rubbed lightly.

He growled, and she gasped and dropped the sunscreen when he grabbed her by her upper arms and turned her before pushing her up against the cabin wall.

"You are playing a very dangerous game, Ms. Jameson," he snarled at her.

"Am I?" she asked. "Would you like to play with me, Mr. Taggert?"

"Your grandmother is in the cabin," he reminded her through gritted teeth.

"I know. So, we'll have to be very quiet and fast," Rowan said, leaning forward and pressing her soft mouth against his chest.

With a herculean effort of self-control, he said, "I can't."

"Really?" She wiggled her hand between them and squeezed his stiff and throbbing cock. "Because it certainly feels like you can, Mr. Taggert."

At her touch, his tightly coiled control snapped, and he lifted her until her pussy was at his crotch and her breasts were at his mouth. He pinned her to the wall with his lower body as she wrapped her slender thighs around his waist. He yanked the cups of her bikini top to the sides, baring her small breasts.

He growled and sucked greedily at one pink nipple, biting and licking with barely controlled hunger as her hands tangled in his hair, and she gasped quietly. He switched to her other nipple, teasing it until it was hard, and the light pink colour became a deep rose.

She yanked on his hair, and he lifted his head and kissed her hungrily. She thrust her tongue into his mouth, and he sucked hard on it as her nails dug into his back. He cupped her breasts, pulling on her nipples until she moaned and her back arched helplessly.

His control was gone entirely now. He had forgotten about Lydia in the cabin, had forgotten about being too old for Rowan, and he tore at his belt before unbuttoning and unzipping his jeans. He pulled out his cock and used his other hand to guide Rowan's hand to it.

"Touch it," he half-growled, half-moaned into her ear and then had to bite back his howl of pleasure when she curled her fingers around his thick length and stroked him.

He yanked the crotch of her bikini bottoms to the side and cupped her naked pussy. She jerked against him, and he snarled in satisfaction when he sank two fingers into her without any resistance. He pulled his fingers free, knocked her hand from his cock and shifted her a little higher before guiding his cock to her wet entrance. He slammed into her, swallowing her cry of pleasure with his mouth as her greedy little pussy took all of him in one hard push.

She was tight, so fucking tight, and he threaded his fingers in her hair and held her firmly as he forced her gaze to his.

"Rowan," he whispered.

"Rafe." She touched his face with a trembling hand, and he kissed the palm of her hand before burying his face in her neck. His hands gripped her smooth thighs and held her up and open as he pounded into her.

Despite taking her only a few days ago, he could barely control himself and groaned harshly when she gripped his ass through his jeans and whispered, "Harder, Rafe."

He pumped harder and faster, her pussy a tight, wet glove around his cock as she made little gasps of pleasure. He couldn't stop. He couldn't think past the need to come, and his fingers dug into her pale thighs as she moaned his name.

"Rowan, fuck! You feel so fucking good," he panted into her ear, and she shuddered before clawing her nails down his back and coming all over his cock. Her climax, the hard rhythmic squeezing of her pussy, sent him over the edge, and his fangs descended with a light pop. He pressed them against her throat, sucking and biting compulsively before howling. Her soft skin muffled the sound, and he howled again as his balls tightened, and he came deep inside her warm pussy. He twitched and convulsed against her as his hips made a few more jerky thrusts before he lifted his head from her throat.

She was panting, and her hair was a tangled mess around her scalp, but she gave him a weak smile. "Rafe, that was -"

"Shit," he muttered. He stared at her breasts. They were covered in bright-red bite marks, and feeling sick to his stomach, he hurriedly tugged her bikini top back into place. "I'm so sorry, Rowan."

She shrugged. "It's fine."

He eased out of her and set her on her feet before tucking away his cock and quickly buttoning his jeans as she straightened her bikini bottom. He groaned again when he saw the marks on her thighs - fuck, she would have bruises - and she placed her hand on his chest.

"Don't look like that, Rafe. I'm fine."

She suddenly brushed her long hair over her neck but not before he caught sight of the already bruising mark on her smooth skin.

"Oh my God." He gave her a sick look, and she rubbed his chest soothingly.

"Rafe, don't. It's no big deal. Listen, why don't you come to my place tonight and -"

He cocked his head, a look of panic crossing his face. "Your grandmother is coming outside."

He turned and jogged to the fence, picking up the hammer and staring fixedly at the wooden board in front of him. Vaguely he was aware of Rowan sprinting to the blanket she'd spread out on the grass and folding it.

The screen door banged open, and Lydia emerged with a tray of lemonade. "Who's thirsty?"

Rowan smiled at her. "I'd love some, Nana, thank you. I'm just going to use the washroom and change first."

"Finished sunbathing so soon?" Her grandmother said as Rowan hurried past her.

"Um, yes. It's too hot today."

"You are rather flushed," her grandmother said. The tone of her voice made Rowan stumble to a stop, and she glanced over her shoulder at her nana. Rafe groaned inwardly at Lydia's cheeky grin, and Rowan, blushing furiously, escaped into the cabin.

Shit, he needed to get the fuck out of here right now.

"Rafe, where are you going?" Lydia called as he shrugged into his shirt and hurried past her. "I've made fresh lemonade."

"I'm sorry, Lydia, I just remembered that I have an appointment. I'll finish fixing the fence later." He waved his arm and climbed into his truck, tearing out of the driveway and down the gravel road toward his cabin.

RAFE SCANNED GASTON'S. HE HAD COME TO THE BAR because he needed to talk to Rowan about what happened yesterday at her grandmother's cabin, and he needed it to be in a public place. He didn't trust himself not to try to fuck her again if they were alone. He had lost all control when it came to her, and it both excited and frustrated him.

He spotted her red hair and weaved through the people until he was standing behind her. He touched her arm, and she turned. His pulse quickened, and his wolf growled happily when she smiled at him. "Hello, Rafe."

"Hello, Ms. Jameson."

She rolled her eyes before leaning against the bar. Her tight blue t-shirt and short jean skirt were driving his wolf insane, and he tried to block out the scent of her desire as she looked him up and down. "You left my grandmother's rather quickly yesterday, Mr. Taggert."

He cleared his throat, dragging his gaze from her breasts, and gave her a half-smile. "It's why I'm here now. I was hoping to speak to you about yesterday."

"Are you going to try to convince me it was a dream?" she asked.

He flushed before shaking his head. "No."

"In that case, yes, we can talk." She glanced at her watch. "My first break is at eight. We can talk then if you don't mind waiting."

"That's fine," he said.

She grinned at him. "Grab a seat on the left side – that's my section tonight – and I'll bring you a beer, okay?"

He nodded and stared hungrily at her tight ass as she walked away.

"MR. TAGGERT? I'M ON MY BREAK NOW." ROWAN APPEARED at his table, and he indicated for her to sit across from him.

She shook her head. "No, not here. It's way too noisy, and there are too many gossips. Follow me."

He frowned but slid out of the booth and followed her across the bar and down the hallway toward the bathrooms. She opened a door marked 'employees only' and disappeared inside. He followed her in and grunted in surprise when she slammed the door shut, and they were plunged into darkness. When she squeezed by him and flipped the light switch, his eyes had already adjusted to the dark.

"A broom closet?" He backed up against the door as she looked around the tiny space.

"It's private," she said.

"Right," he muttered. It was private, but there was not nearly enough room for them. The mop and bucket took up most of the floor space, and shelves filled with cleaning supplies, extra toilet paper, and paper towels lined the walls. She almost touched him despite his pressing against the door, and her smile was too wicked for her own good.

"Ms. Jameson," he said, jerking when her tiny hands popped the button on his jeans. "What are you doing?"

"What does it look like I'm doing?" she said innocently as she yanked down his zipper with a hard tug.

He tried to push her hands away, but she was powerful for her size, not to mention nimble, and she dodged his hands and slipped hers into his underwear. Her hand curled around his dick, and she smiled happily when he immediately hardened.

"I came here to talk to you," he gritted out.

"So talk," she said. He groaned loudly when she dropped to her knees and pulled down the front of his briefs. His cock popped out, and she made a soft noise of appreciation before sliding her mouth over it.

"Fuck!" he groaned as his hips jerked forward.

She sucked him lightly before lifting her head and grinning at him. Her soft hand stroked the base of his cock. "Go ahead and talk, Rafe. I'm listening."

"I – oh Jesus – what happened yesterday shouldn't have – oh fuck!"

Her hot, wet mouth worked overtime on his cock, sliding back and forth as she sucked firmly while rubbing the base with her hand. He watched her lips stretch around his width before she released him with a soft pop.

"What were you saying, Rafe?" she asked.

"Rowan, I…"

"Yes?" She raised her eyebrows at him, and with a harsh groan, he wrapped his fingers into her hair and nearly shoved her mouth toward his dick.

"Suck," he growled.

She immediately sucked him back into her mouth, and he thrust wildly, his hands holding her head as he fucked her mouth. She tightened her lips around him and slid her tongue along his slit. He moaned as his balls tightened, and he released her hair and flattened his hands against the door.

She sucked, licked, and squeezed for ten long, torturous minutes as he moaned softly and pumped his hips back and forth. "Rowan, oh God, Rowan, I'm going to come. Stop, baby, please stop."

She sucked harder and faster, and he groaned again. She hummed softly and squeezed the base of his cock before swirling her tongue over the sensitive ridge. He howled hoarsely as his back arched, and he came with a roaring rush that made his fangs pop out. He couldn't stop watching Rowan as she swallowed all of his seed before releasing his cock and licking her lips.

"Oh, Jesus," he moaned as he collapsed against the door and forced his fangs to retract.

She popped up and wiped her thumb across her bottom lip before grinning at him. "Well, that was kind of hot, yeah?"

"Rowan," he said hoarsely, "that was the best fucking blowjob of my goddamn life."

She gave him a pleased look. "Good."

She pulled a package of mints from the back pocket of her jean skirt and popped two into her mouth.

"We still need to talk," he said.

She glanced at her watch before smiling sweetly at him. "Sorry, Rafe. My break's over. If you want to stick around, I've got another one at ten."

He shuddered with pleasure when she tucked his cock into his jeans and buttoned them before planting a kiss on his cheek. "Are you going to wait, Mr. Taggert?"

He nodded, and she gave him another pleased look before opening the door and checking the hallway. "All clear. Go back to your table, and I'll bring you a burger and fries in a bit."

RAFE COULD BARELY HOLD IN HIS GROWL OF ANGER WHEN the human let his hand brush against Rowan's ass. He half-stood from his chair, and Rowan glanced at him. She shook her head, and he glared at her before returning to his seat. She smiled at the human, blocked his hand when he tried to grab her ass and said something that made his cheeks flush with embarrassment. He mouthed an apology, and she nodded before sauntering toward Rafe.

"How was your food?" She glanced at the half-eaten burger and untouched fries before popping a fry into her mouth. "Not hungry?"

Rafe still stared at the guy who'd touched her ass, and he jerked his gaze to her when she brushed her soft hand across his chest. "Rafe?"

"If he touches your ass again, he'll have my boot up *his* ass," he snapped.

She laughed and ate another of his fries. "Sweet but not necessary. I can take care of myself, Rafe."

"I mean it, Rowan," he snarled. "He's not allowed to touch you. Do you hear me?"

"I hear you," she said with a grin. "I'll let him know that you're the only one allowed to touch me."

He blinked at her, "Rowan, you can't say that. We're not, I mean -"

She grabbed his empty beer glass and walked away before he could finish. He muttered a curse and glanced at his watch. Half an hour until her next break. He would talk to her, explain that they couldn't let anything sexual happen between them again, and then get the hell out of the bar before he tried to kill the next human who touched her.

"No," he said half an hour later. "Not the broom closet again."

"There's no place else private enough to talk," she said before opening the door and disappearing inside. He hesitated and hurried into the closet and shut the door when the men's bathroom door opened.

"Listen to me, Ms. Jameson, we can't keep… what the hell are you doing?"

She paused in sliding her panties down her legs. "Taking off my panties."

"Why – why would you do that?" he said as his wolf howled happily, and his cock stiffened in his pants.

"Because you're going to eat my pussy," she said. "Why else would I take them off?"

"Ms. Jameson, I can't eat your pussy," he said.

"Can't or won't?"

He didn't reply, and she stepped out of her panties and folded them neatly before placing them on a shelf. He pressed against the door and shook his head. "We can't do this."

She folded her arms across her chest. "You know, I never took you for a guy who would take and not give. I assumed that since I sucked your cock, you'd return the favour and eat my pussy."

Her disappointed look killed him. "I guess that's what I get for assuming. Unless you're just not very good at eating pussy? Is that it, Rafe? Are you lacking in pussy eating skills? It's okay if you are. Not every guy is good at -"

She squeaked with surprise when he growled at her and yanked her body against his before cupping her ass through her skirt and squeezing. "I am very fucking good at eating pussy, Ms. Jameson. I guarantee you'll scream and scream loudly."

"That's pretty big talk from a guy who keeps saying he can't eat my pussy," she said breathlessly. "Sorry, but I'm not just going to take your word for it that you'll make me scream."

He growled again, his eyes flashing angrily before he dropped to his knees in front of her. "Lift your skirt," he snapped.

She grinned and hiked her skirt up around her waist. He stared at the flame-coloured patch of hair at the top of her pussy before nuzzling it with his mouth. She sighed happily and wound her fingers in his hair. "Go on, Rafe. Make me scream."

He cupped her smooth thighs before placing his fingers lightly on the bruises visible on her pale skin. They matched perfectly, and shame washed over him. "I'm so sorry, baby."

She petted his hair and smiled at him. "It's fine."

He leaned forward and pressed a gentle kiss against each bruise. Her legs trembled, and she spread her thighs before tugging on his hair. "Do it, Rafe. I need your mouth."

He pressed his nose against her pubic hair and inhaled deeply before kissing his way down to the lips of her pussy. They were already wet, and he made a murmur of approval before licking her clean.

"Ohh," she sighed and tilted her pelvis forward as he hooked her right leg over his shoulder. He spread her lips with his thumbs and growled when it exposed her swollen, glistening clit. He sucked on it and cupped her ass, pulling her against his mouth as he rapidly flicked his tongue over her clit before sucking again.

"Oh Jesus," she said in a soft mutter. "That feels so damn good, Rafe." Her hands pulled his hair as he nibbled lightly on her clit. He massaged her clit with his fingers before licking it gently. When his finger slid into her pussy, she ground her face against his finger and mouth. He pushed another finger inside of her and thrust them back and forth. Her soft gasps of pleasure drove him insane, and he sucked at her clit as she moaned loudly.

"Quiet, Rowan," he said.

She clapped one hand over her mouth as her head fell back, and she circled her hips against his mouth.

He growled, his lips vibrating against her clit, and she squealed against her hand as he pulled her even closer. She tasted so damn good, like sweet, warm honey, and he made another growl of approval when fresh wetness coated his lips. He licked her clean, his fingers still thrusting in and out, and when her legs began to shake uncontrollably, he released his fangs with a soft pop. He dragged the tip of one against her clit and grinned with hard satisfaction when she screamed into her hand, and her entire body shuddered against his mouth. As she came, her pussy squeezed his fingers in a tight grip, and he licked away her sweet cream. When her knees buckled, he retracted his fangs, released her leg and stood, catching her before she could collapse on the floor.

He pulled down her skirt as she leaned against him and panted harshly. "Holy shit, Rafe, I take back everything I said about you not being good at eating pussy. I may never be the same."

She stared up at him, her cheeks flushed and her eyes wide and warm with pleasure. She studied his mouth, and he groaned when she stood on her tiptoes and licked his lips clean with her warm, wet tongue.

"I taste good," she whispered.

"You taste fucking delicious," he said in a harsh growl.

She reached into her back pocket and pulled out the tin of mints. "Open," she said. He did what she asked, and she placed a mint on his tongue.

"Ms. Jameson," he said as peppermint replaced her taste in his mouth. "We really need to -"

She pressed her fingers against his mouth. "I have a personal rule, Rafe. Once a man's tongue has been in my pussy, he's only allowed to call me by my first name."

He flushed, and she made a low laugh. "Aww, you're blushing. That's cute."

"Rowan," he tried again, "please talk to me about -"

"I can't," she said with fake disappointment, "my break is done."

She pushed out of his arms and picked up her panties. She started to unfold them before giving him a small grin and shoving them into the pocket of his jeans. "Why don't you keep them?"

"You're not going out there without panties," he said.

She just smiled, and he caught her arm as she slipped by him. "What time are you done work?"

"Not until one," she said. "Sorry."

"I'll wait," he said before pulling her panties out of his pocket. "Put these on, Rowan."

"No, thank you," she said.

He growled, and she kissed him on the cheek. "You don't have to wait for me, Rafe. We can talk another time."

"Like hell I don't," he said. "If you think I'm leaving you alone while you're parading around without panties, you're wrong."

"Oh, for God's sake, I'm not going to hike up my skirt for the bar patrons," she said. "I'm not interested in anyone but you."

A stupid little thrill of happiness went through him, and he had to clamp his mouth shut against his wolf's pleased howl. He forced a scowl at her. "I'll wait for you, and we'll talk after your shift."

"Sure," she said before smoothing her shirt. "Actually, that would be helpful. My car is still in the shop, and I could use a ride home."

"I'm not going into your apartment," he said quickly.

"I know." She opened the door and slipped out into the hallway.

"I'M SORRY." ROWAN GAVE HIM AN APOLOGETIC LOOK AS HE parked in front of her apartment building, and she continued to text. "I know this is rude, but my cousin is having a bit of a crisis. Two more minutes, okay?"

He nodded and shut off his truck, staring moodily at her apartment building. If she had found it odd that he hadn't needed directions to her place, she hadn't mentioned it. He had driven by her home more times than he cared to admit, always at night and always when he felt particularly lonely. He'd even occasionally parked and watched her window. He would berate himself the entire time, calling himself a stalker and a dirty old man, but about once a month, he would find himself back at her place, hoping to catch a glimpse of her sweet face through the window.

"Okay," she shoved her phone into her purse and dropped it on the floor before smiling at him, "I'm sorry, Rafe."

"That's fine." He cleared his throat as she studied the empty street. It was almost one-thirty, and her street was quiet and dark. He gave her an alarmed look when she slid across the front seat of his truck toward him.

"Rowan, don't -" His breath hissed out between his teeth when she straddled him, wedging her slender body between the steering wheel and his body. "Don't -"

"Shh," she said and pulled her shirt over her head. He stared at her breasts, and she pressed a soft kiss against his mouth as lust roared to life within him.

"I want you so much, Rafe," she said. "It's all I can think about."

"Me too," he admitted in a harsh groan, and she smiled at him before unclipping her bra and dropping it to the seat beside them.

"Rowan," he looked out the windshield behind her, "we can't do this right here. Someone could walk by."

"No one will walk by," she said. "And really, you're leaving me no choice since you won't come into my apartment."

She cupped her breasts and pulled lightly on her nipples as his hands gripped her hips and tugged up her skirt.

She leaned forward, and he pressed a soft kiss on the bite mark on her breast. "Jesus, Rowan, this is really bruised."

"It was a little intense yesterday. I don't mind, honey."

"I mind," he said. "I should have been gentler. I lost control."

"I like it when you lose control," she said before brushing her nipple against his lips. He kissed it lightly and traced a circle around it with the tip of his tongue. Her skirt was around her waist now, and he kneaded her naked ass as he sucked on her nipple before kissing his way up her chest.

"Move your hair," he whispered.

She hesitated, and he growled, "Move your hair."

She pushed that gorgeous red curtain of hair back, and he inhaled sharply at the hickey on her neck. "Fuck!"

"I find it hilarious that you gave me a hickey," she said with a grin.

"I'll never hurt you again, Rowan, I promise." He licked the dark mark on her neck.

"I know," she said. "Take off your shirt."

She helped him tug it over his head, and he moaned and cupped the back of her head when she pressed kisses across his chest.

"I love your body," she said.

He jerked when she nipped the base of his throat. "I'm going to fuck you, Rafe Taggert, and you're going to let me."

"Yes," he muttered. "God, yes."

"Before we do," she said, "it's a little late for this talk, but my tests are negative, and I'm on the pill."

"My tests are negative, too," he said. "I'm sorry. I should have been using a condom."

She gave him an embarrassed look. "Until you, I've never once let a man fuck me without a condom. I seem to lose my goddamn mind when I'm around you."

He cupped her face. "After tonight, we can't do this again. You know that, right?"

She sighed. "I know you believe that."

"Rowan, I -"

She shook her head and rubbed her breasts against his chest. "We don't need to talk about this, Rafe. I know all your reasons."

She reached down and unbuttoned his jeans. He watched, lust flooding through him as she unzipped his jeans and tugged out his cock. She stroked it lightly for a few minutes until he was moaning under his breath and his hips were rising and falling, and then ran her thumb through the bead of precum at the tip.

"I love the way you taste, Rafe," she said before licking her thumb.

"Fuck," he muttered.

He lifted her, and she guided his cock into her wet core. She sank onto him with a hoarse moan. She braced her hands against the window and the headrest as he teased her nipple with his tongue and teeth. His hands clamped down on her hips, and he thrust rapidly as she bit at her bottom lip.

"Touch yourself," he demanded.

"So bossy," she said but slipped her hand between their bodies and rubbed obediently at her clit.

"Are you sure you can't come up to my apartment, Rafe?" She panted as she circled her clit. "I have a really comfortable bed."

"I can't," he groaned. "Please, Rowan."

She clenched around him, and he grunted a curse before thrusting even harder. She gasped and met each of his strokes eagerly as she rubbed her clit. She leaned forward and nibbled at his ear as he threaded his fingers through her hair.

"I love your hair," he rasped. "I love your body and your hot little pussy."

She moaned into his ear, her fingers digging into his broad shoulders. "I love fucking you."

He groaned harshly and twitched when she bit him on the base of the throat. She started to suck, and he tried to pull her away. "Rowan, stop that."

"It's only fair," she said. "You've marked me, and now I'm marking you."

"I am way too fucking old for hickeys," he said desperately as she sucked harder. "Stop."

"Make me." She laughed and squeezed him with her inner muscles.

"Fuck!" He arched his back, and she bit him again before making a soft noise of satisfaction.

"There," she said happily.

He wound her hair around his hand and pulled until her throat was bared to him. He placed kisses across her neck as she rubbed her clit.

"Going to mark me again, Rafe?" she asked. "Show all the other boys that I'm yours?"

She was way closer to the truth than she knew. Wolves marked their mates, and his wolf was howling at him to mark the soft, warm female riding him. He tore his mouth from her throat, keeping his fangs from popping out by sheer willpower alone, and shook his head.

"No," he rasped. "You're not mine."

She cupped his face and sucked on his lower lip. "I am."

His cock swelled inside of her at her words, and he could barely stop from coming.

"Don't say that," he said.

"Don't say what?" she asked. "Don't say that I'm yours?

360

That from this moment on, I'll never let anyone but you fuck me?"

His wolf howled happily, and he dragged her closer, fucking her rapidly as she kissed him. He thrust his tongue into her mouth, and she sucked at it as he continued to plunge in and out of her. Her scent filled his truck, driving him mad with the need to claim her, and she nipped his bottom lip before smiling at him.

"I'm yours, Rafe, and you're mine. Tell me you won't fuck anyone else but me."

"I won't fuck anyone else but you," he said. "I can't."

"Because I'm the only one you want."

"Yes," he moaned.

"You're the only one I want too," she said. "Always, Rafe."

He made a short howl at her words, his hips thrusting up, and she rubbed her clit as his hot seed soaked into her. He shuddered and gasped beneath her, and she kissed him before tugging at her clit. Her climax rolled through her, and he howled again as she clenched around him and milked the last of his seed from him.

She collapsed against him, and he rubbed her back as their breathing slowed and returned to normal. Too soon for him, she straightened and tugged her shirt over her head before stuffing her bra into her purse. She wiggled off his lap and straightened her skirt. He waited for her to invite him in – God help him, he would say yes when she did – but she only smiled at him and pressed a soft kiss against his mouth.

"Thanks for the ride home, Mr. Taggert."

She opened the door and slid out of the truck, slamming it shut behind her before walking quickly to her apartment building. She paused at the door and waved at him, and he waited until the light came on in her apartment before starting the truck and driving away. His wolf made small, pleased growls, but his mind reeled with what he had said to her. He touched the mark on his neck. Why the hell had he let her do that?

Because you wanted her to mark you. You wanted to feel like you were a part of a pack again.

He jerked, the truck weaving on the road and gripped the steering wheel tightly. He didn't need a pack. He was doing fine on his own and definitely didn't need to make Rowan a part of his pack. She was human, and she would never understand his wolf side. His mother had tried for years, and look how that turned out. Fear trickled down his spine. He couldn't let Rowan any closer.

CHAPTER 5

"How's avoiding old Red over there going?" Duncan sat down next to him, and Rafe scowled before his gaze drifted back to Rowan.

Bennett joined them, setting three beers down on the table, and grinned at Rafe. "Why does Rowan reek of you?"

"You know why," Rafe growled. It had been two days since he'd had sex with Rowan in his truck, but his scent would linger on her for a few more days. The thought made him ridiculously happy. Not that his former packmates ever frequented Gaston's, but on the off-chance they did, they would know immediately that Rowan belonged to him.

"Can't say I blame you, wolf boy," Duncan said. "Rowan's a hottie."

Jealousy tore through him, and he growled at Duncan as his eyes turned jade.

"Knock it off, Duncan," Bennet said. "He's just trying to get a rise out of you, Rafe."

"I am," Duncan agreed cheerfully. "Is that a hickey on your neck?"

"No!" Rafe touched the hickey that Rowan had given him before yanking his collar over it.

"You let her give you a hickey?" Duncan grinned at him. "That's delightful."

"Shut up, Duncan," Rafe said through gritted teeth.

Duncan laughed. "You know what I find weird? Human women bite way more than shifter women during sex. What's up with that?"

Bennett grinned at him as Rafe sighed.

"It's not that I mind," Duncan said. "Ella can do whatever she wants to me in bed, and you won't hear me complaining, and obviously, Rafe doesn't mind, but -"

"Sex with Rowan was a mistake, and it's not going to happen again," Rafe said.

"No? Then why are you sitting here at Gaston's, watching her like you want to gobble her up?" Duncan asked.

Rafe didn't reply. He had tried to stay away and had succeeded last night, but tonight, after pacing his house restlessly and his wolf howling incessantly at him, he had driven to Gaston's. Just seeing Rowan soothed his wolf enough for the damn thing to finally shut the fuck up and give Rafe a moment's peace.

He stiffened when Rowan approached their table. His wolf growled when she squeezed Duncan's shoulder and kissed Bennett on the cheek. "Hey, guys. Your lovely ladies joining you tonight?"

Bennett nodded. "Yes, they should be here any minute."

"Good," Rowan said. "Hello, Rafe. How are you?"

"Hello, Rowan," he replied. "Good. You?"

"Can't complain," she said. She gave Rafe a flirty little smile but didn't touch him before walking away, and he rolled his eyes at the petulant little whimper his wolf made.

"Now that's some sexual tension," Duncan said before taking a drink.

"Shut up, Duncan," Rafe said.

Before Duncan could reply, Belle and Ella joined them.

"Hello, beautiful," Duncan said with a grin as Ella sat beside him.

Ella leaned forward and pressed a kiss against his mouth before making a face. "Ugh, beer."

Belle took Bennett's hand. "Dad's doing well. He said to say hello."

"Good." Bennett squeezed Belle's thigh gently.

"Hi, Rafe," Belle said. "How are you?"

"I'm good. It's nice to see you."

"Nice to see you too. It's been a while since you've been to Gaston's," she said.

Rafe cleared his throat before grabbing his half-empty beer and drinking the rest of it. "I've been busy lately."

"Doing what?" Ella asked sweetly as Duncan snickered.

Rowan stopped at their table again. "How are my favourite girls?"

Belle grinned at her. "We're good."

Rowan placed a glass of wine in front of each of them. "I assumed you wanted your usual?"

"Thank you, Ro," Ella said.

"You bet." Rowan stood next to Rafe and picked up his empty beer bottle. "Another beer, Rafe?"

"Here," Bennett slid the third beer across the table, "I got this for you, Rafe."

"Thanks." Rafe tore his gaze from Rowan's chest and took another drink of beer as Rowan winked at Belle and Ella and walked away.

Jesus, he needed to get control of himself. His face reddened when Ella and Belle gave him matching grins. They wouldn't be able to smell his wolf on Rowan but no doubt she had told them what happened between them.

Don't be a dirty old man, he told himself fiercely. *Have some goddamn self-control.*

"YOU ARE NOT GIVING THAT ASSHOLE MARTY A MASSAGE," Duncan said as his eyes glowed yellow.

Ella rolled her eyes and squeezed Duncan's arm. "Calm down, honey."

"I mean it, Ella. I don't want you going anywhere near him," Duncan said.

"One – I told him no and two – stop with the caveman attitude," she said.

Duncan growled at her, and she squeezed his arm again. "Growling at me will not get you what you want."

"That guy is such a dick," Duncan said.

"He is," Ella said. "Which is why I said no when he tried to book a massage appointment."

She glanced at Bennett. "Speaking of massage – do you mind if I bump up our appointment tomorrow by half an hour? Marjorie Wilkins phoned earlier and insisted on a two o'clock appointment."

"Sure," Bennett said.

"Thanks so much," Ella said. "I appreciate it, and if it were anyone else but Mrs. Wilkins, I wouldn't ask, but it's challenging to communicate with her over the phone. I swear she deliberately doesn't wear her hearing aids when she -"

Rafe growled loudly, and Ella and the others stared at him. A rush of adrenaline went through Ella. Rafe's eyes were bright green, and the usual scruff on his jaw was now a thick layer of hair. She followed his gaze, staring at Rowen and the man who flirted with her.

"Uh oh," Belle said.

"Who is that?" Duncan asked.

"Bruno Morris," Belle said. "We went to school with him. He and Marla Finton started dating just after high school and got engaged last year. Then he caught Marla sleeping with some guy from Newport. They broke up three months ago, and he's been hitting on every woman in town since. I'm surprised it took him so long to get to Rowan. He used to flirt with her like crazy in high school."

"You know," Ella said with an impish grin, "I didn't realize your eyes were green, Rafe. I always thought they were hazel."

Duncan cleared his throat before giving Rafe a pointed look. "Rafe, how's the landscaping business going?"

Rafe continued to ignore Duncan and the alarmed look he gave Bennett.

"Rafe!" Bennett said. "Maybe you should head out."

"No," Rafe snarled.

"She can take care of herself," Ella said quickly, her humour disappearing when Bruno reached out and tugged on Rowan's long hair, and Rafe made another terrifying growl. "She's an excellent boxer, Rafe."

"Oh, fuck," Bennett said in a low voice as Bruno moved closer to Rowan, trapping her against the bar. He leaned down and whispered something into her ear. She smiled politely and shook her head no before tapping him on the chest. He didn't move, and Rafe abruptly stood and stalked toward them with another growl.

"That dude is totally going to wolf out," Belle said.

Duncan jerked and stared at her in surprise. "How do you

know Rafe is a wolf shifter?" He stared accusingly at Bennett. "You can't just be telling -"

"I didn't," Bennett said. "I didn't say anything."

"Oh please," Ella said, "it's more than obvious. His eyes are glowing, and he's growling non-stop. Rowan gave us details that made it pretty clear to both Belle and me that he's a wolf."

"Sweetheart, you can't say anything to Rafe. He'll freak out if he finds out that you know he's a wolf. Okay?" Duncan said.

"I won't say anything," Ella said.

"Shit." Bennett stood up. "She won't have to say anything. Rafe's about to lose it, and everyone in the goddamn bar will know he's a wolf shifter. C'mon, Duncan. We need to stop him."

ROWAN SIGHED IRRITABLY WHEN BRUNO DIDN'T MOVE.

"C'mon, Ro, just one date," he wheedled as he tugged on her hair again.

"I said no, Bruno. And stop touching my hair before I punch you," she said with a sweet smile.

"I like it rough." Bruno grinned.

"I'm not interested in you. Now move so I can get back to work," she said.

He grabbed her arm lightly when she tried to move past him. "Just one date, Ro. Hell, you've fucked half the guys in this town. I don't get why you won't give me a chance. Everyone knows you're a slut."

"Oh my God, why do guys always try the slut shaming card?" Rowan laughed. "Just because a girl likes fucking doesn't make her a slut, you shithead."

Bruno turned red. "I'm not slut shaming. I want to fuck you. Jesus. Get that through your stupid little -"

"Let her go."

He turned his head and stared in surprise at Rafe before scowling. "Get lost, Taggert. This doesn't concern you."

"She's mine. Now let her go before I break your goddamn arm," Rafe snarled.

Bruno stared at Rowan. "You're fucking him? So, what, you go through all the guys your own age in town and decide to start fucking old men?"

———

His wolf's rage made Rafe lose his tenuous control. He reached for the man, but Bruno's head snapped back before he could grab him. Blood poured from Bruno's nose, and he cupped his hand over it before staring at Rowan.

"You broke my fucking nose," he choked out.

Rowan shrugged before uncurling her fist and shaking out her hand. "Stop talking shit about Rafe."

"Bitch!" Bruno snapped and lunged for her.

He squealed in surprise when Rafe's hands landed on his shoulders, and he was lifted off his feet. He made another girlish squeal when he was thrown across the room and landed on an empty table with a crash. The table collapsed under his weight, and he moaned in pain as Rafe started toward him.

His blood pounding in his ears and his wolf snarling and snapping at the man who dared to touch his mate, Rafe made a harsh growl before grabbing Bruno by the legs. He dragged the man forward and snarled when Bennett and Duncan appeared, tearing him away from the frightened man.

"Rafe, enough!" Bennett snapped. He and Duncan struggled to hold him back as Rafe made a low howl and fought to tear his way free of them.

"Fuck, we need to get him out of here," Duncan said.

Rafe could feel his body swelling, and Bennett quickly stepped in front of him, blocking Bruno's view when Rafe bared his fangs.

"Jesus, Rafe. Control it!" Bennett said.

"Let me go, bear shifter, or I'll tear you apart," Rafe snarled in a low voice.

"Have you gone fucking insane?" Duncan said quietly. "You're about to fucking shift."

Rafe ignored him. His wolf was very close to the surface now, and he wanted – *needed* – to let it free. He needed to show that asshole and everyone else in the bar what happened to men who touched his mate.

"Rafe, stop." Rowan stepped between him and Bennett and cupped his face. His wolf made a pleased whine at her touch, his anger starting to fade. "Stop, honey. I can take care of myself."

"If he touches you again," Rafe said, "I'll kill him."

Rowan smiled and stroked his cheek with her thumb. "That's awfully sweet, Rafe Taggert, but going to prison for murder isn't a smart life goal."

"This isn't a joke!" Rafe barked. "I don't want him touching you."

"He won't," she said.

He stared at her, lust and anger warring within him. He wanted to kill Bruno. He wanted to throw Rowan over his shoulder and take her to his den. He wanted to push her up against the wall and fuck her in front of everyone so they would know she was his.

"You belong to me," he said loud enough for everyone in the bar to hear.

"Yes," she said.

"Only me."

"Yes," she repeated. "Only you, Rafe."

He continued to stare at her, and she stood on her tiptoes and pressed her mouth against his ear. "I'm yours, Rafe. I won't let anyone else touch me but you."

He shuddered with pleasure at the feel of her warm breath, and she placed a quick kiss below his ear before stepping back.

"Let go of him, guys," she said.

"Not a good idea," Duncan said.

"It's fine," she said. "Rafe isn't going to do anything."

Duncan glanced at Bennett, who shrugged and released Rafe's arm. Duncan also let go and gave Rafe a cautious look as he stared at Rowan.

"Rafe? How are you feeling?" Bennett said in a low voice.

Rafe blinked rapidly as his wolf retreated with a growl. He looked around the bar. Every person in the bar stared at him, and he closed his eyes. Jesus, he had been about thirty seconds from shifting. If Rowan hadn't touched him when she did…

He blew his breath out in a shuddering rush. "I'm sorry," he said hoarsely.

"It's fine," Rowan said. "Why don't you sit down and -"

"No," he said. "It was a mistake for me to come here tonight."

He turned and walked out of the bar, sucking in a breath of cool air before climbing into his truck. He started it and drove away from the bar, staring grimly at the road ahead and trying to ignore the realization that he'd nearly shifted in front of a bar full of humans.

"I'M FUCKING SUING YOU, ROWAN," BRUNO SAID PETULANTLY as Gaston, the bar owner, came striding out of the back office.

"Like fuck you are," he snapped as he grabbed Bruno's arm and hauled him to his feet. "Get the fuck out of here, ya little asshole, and don't come back."

He shoved Bruno toward the door, and with blood dripping down his face, Bruno slunk from the bar.

"You okay?" Gaston grunted to Rowan.

"Yes, thanks," Rowan said.

Gaston scowled at the tall blond man standing silently with everyone else. "Jesus Christ, Mickey, I hired you to be a goddamn bouncer. The next time a customer grabs one of the waitresses, fucking do something about it."

"Yes, boss," Mickey said. "Sorry, Rowan."

"Don't worry about it, Mickey," Rowan said.

She was acutely aware of the way the people in the bar stared at her, and she touched Gaston's arm. "Can I take a ten-minute break?"

He nodded, and she headed toward the back door. She stepped out into the cool night air, pulled the worn and battered pack of cigarettes from her pocket, and lit one.

The door opened behind her, and she gave Belle and Ella a guilty look before waving away the cigarette smoke. "I need this."

Belle frowned but didn't scold her as Rowan took another puff. They stood silently for a moment before Ella said, "I thought Duncan was over the top with his 'this is my woman, don't touch her' attitude, but Rafe Taggert takes it to a whole other level."

"I'll say," Belle said. "Hey, is it just me, or did you find it hot as hell when Rafe tried to kill Bruno?"

Ella laughed. "Homicide isn't exactly sexy, Belle."

"I suppose not, but holy shit, the way Rafe eye-fucked Rowan all night was almost enough to make *my* panties catch on fire. That guy has it bad for you, Ro."

Rowan didn't reply, and Ella took her hand. "Did you hurt your hand when you punched Bruno, honey?"

"No," Rowan said.

"What's wrong?" Belle asked.

"Nothing," Rowan said. "It's just – every time Rafe and I are in the same room, it always ends with him saying it was a mistake."

"He said you belonged to him," Ella said. "Everyone heard it."

"Yeah, but I guarantee you the next time I see him – if he even comes near me again - he'll tell me he didn't mean to say it and that we can't be together."

She took an angry drag of her cigarette. "Fucking Bruno. He called Rafe an old man, and I know that will fuck with Rafe's head. I'll have to hear him tell me repeatedly that he's too old for me."

"So, the next time you see him, don't let him talk," Ella said. "Just fuck him into admitting he wants to be with you."

Belle blinked at her. "Shit, Ella. Being with Duncan has turned you into a sex maniac."

"Yep, probably," Ella said. "Rafe might insist that he's too old for you, but I have faith you can change his mind, honey."

"I just want to get to know him better, you know?" Rowan said. "I mean, the sex between us is incredible, but for the first time in my life, I want…."

Belle smiled at her. "You want the boyfriend experience."

"Yeah, I guess I do," Rowan said. "How ironic is it that I want something more than just sex with a guy for the first time in my life, and he's not interested."

"He's interested," Belle said. "He tried to beat the crap out of Bruno for touching you. He wants more than sex, even if he won't admit it. You just need to get him to realize that he wants more."

"Super," Rowan sighed before dropping her cigarette and crushing it under her shoe. "That shouldn't be too horrifyingly difficult."

Ella grinned. "If anyone can do it, you can, Ro."

RAFE LEANED AGAINST THE GIANT OAK TREE AND STARED AT Rowan's window. He stiffened at the noise behind him and scanned the darkness. A cat, its grey tail twitching, hissed before strutting past him. He took a deep breath as the light in Rowan's apartment switched on. She hadn't seen him when she'd parked and walked into her apartment building, he was sure of it, but there was a part of him that wished she had caught him. It would have given him an excuse to talk to her again, to stand next to her and inhale her sweet scent. It was covered heavily by his at the moment, but he could sniff out his mate's scent no matter what.

You know how pathetic you are, right? Standing outside staring at a woman's apartment like a love-sick fool? Or better yet – a love-sick stalker?

Yeah, he knew. He had berated himself fiercely the entire time he was parking his truck on the street next to hers, the entire time he was slinking through the dark to stand under this goddamn tree and wait for Rowan to come home. He shouldn't be with her but just standing here calmed his wolf a little. In a little while, he'd go home and –

His wolf made a low snarl of anger at the thought of leaving, and he closed his eyes briefly. Jesus, if he had to listen to his wolf snarl and whine and plead for Rowan for the rest of his life, he really would go insane.

His phone buzzed in his pocket, making him jump like a startled deer, and he fished it out of his pocket. Who the hell was calling him at one-thirty in the morning?

"Hello?"

"Hello, Rafe."

His wolf whined happily, and he quickly checked her apartment window. "Uh, hi, Rowan. How did you get my number?"

"It's your business number," she said with a soft laugh. "You have it on your website, remember?"

"Right," he said as his cheeks heated.

"What are you doing?" she asked

"Just heading to bed," he said.

"Whose bed?"

"I – what?"

"You're standing outside my apartment, so I'm wondering if it's my bed you're planning on heading to."

"I'm not outside your apartment," he said.

She laughed again, and her low laughter made his dick harden in his jeans. "Liar, liar, pants on fire, Mr. Taggert."

He cleared his throat and decided to make the best of the situation. "I came by because I wanted to apologize for what happened earlier. Rowan, I -"

"Yes, I know what you're going to say," she said with a touch of impatience. "What's happening between us is a mistake, you're too old for me, we really can't do this, blah, blah, blah. No offense, Rafe, but you're starting to sound like a broken record."

"Actually, I wanted to say sorry for making you say that you belonged to me in front of everyone in your place of employment."

"That's kind of a weak-ass apology," she said.

His hand clenched around his phone when she appeared in her apartment window. She shimmied out of her skirt, leaving her in just her shirt and a pair of red panties, and he made a low growl.

"Put your skirt on, Rowan."

"I'm going to bed."

"Stop undressing in front of the window."

"You don't like the show?" she asked sweetly as she switched her phone to her other hand and unbuttoned the first two buttons of her shirt.

"I don't want anyone else seeing the show," he said heatedly.

Her hand lingered on the third button, and he made another low growl. "I'm leaving. I'm sorry that I -"

"I don't accept your apology." She unbuttoned the third button.

"What?"

"It's not good enough," she said with a wicked grin. She rested her hand on the window and traced slow circles with her fingertips. "You've seriously limited my dating options," she ignored his angry snarl, "by making me say I belonged to you in front of a bar full of people, and it's going to take more than a verbal apology to make up for it."

"What did you have in mind?" he asked hoarsely.

This was wrong - *so very fucking wrong* - but he was dying to touch her again.

"Did you like eating my pussy, Rafe?"

"Yes."

"I liked it too. Eat my pussy again, and I'll accept your apology."

"Rowan -"

"The building code is 1162, and my apartment's

unlocked." She dropped her shirt, and he stared hungrily at her in her matching red bra and panties.

"See you soon," she said and ended the call. She walked away, and his wolf howled longingly at him.

Rafe pocketed his phone and started toward her apartment building.

SHE SAT NAKED ON HER BED, HER BACK RESTING AGAINST THE headboard and her red hair curling around her shoulders when he entered her bedroom.

"Hello, Mr. Taggert," she said and opened her legs.

He groaned and stripped off his clothes before climbing onto the bed and wedging his body between her legs. She stroked his hair and smiled sweetly at him as he nuzzled the patch of red flame between her legs. He slid his hands underneath her and cupped her ass, pulling her up against his mouth as he licked a slow path across the wet lips of her pussy. She moaned happily, and her hands tightened in his hair when he let his fangs descend and brushed them across her damp skin.

"Oh God," she muttered as her hips arched into his mouth.

He lapped at her clit, flicking it with his tongue before sucking on it. She pulled on his hair and made a low cry of pleasure. He took his time, concentrating solely on her clit as she moaned and pressed her pelvis into his face. Moisture was soaking into his face, and he licked her clean before sucking on her clit again. After nearly ten minutes, he slid one finger deep into her hot core, groaning when her pussy tightened around his finger.

He wanted to fuck her so badly it hurt, but he continued to

tug firmly on her clit with his lips. He traced his tongue across it, and she shrieked with pleasure before her body arched, and she came against his mouth. Her body shuddered, and he pulled his finger free and rubbed her firm thighs as she panted and moaned. He gave her clit one last slow lick, and she jerked against his mouth before pulling on his hair. He sat up, and she reached eagerly for him as she slid her body down until she was lying on her back.

"Fuck me, Rafe," she demanded.

Helpless to deny her, he positioned himself between her legs and thrust his throbbing cock into her tight pussy. She clamped her thighs around his hips, and he gave her a look of disapproval as he propped himself up on his hands above her.

"Rowan."

She flushed and let her legs fall open. "Always open for you."

"That's right. Always," he said.

She clutched at his arms as he thrust in a rough and hurried rhythm. He didn't want to rush, but Rowan's small cries of pleasure, her tight pussy, and the feel of her under him destroyed his self-control. He plunged in and out, his fangs descending and a hoarse and continuous growl erupting from his throat.

Her eyes were squeezed shut, and she pushed her hand between their bodies and rubbed at her clit as she rocked her hips against his. Her cries of pleasure turned frantic, needier, and he bent his head and sucked on one hard nipple. She arched her back, and her pussy tightened around him as she climaxed hard for a second time.

He growled his approval and rested his mouth against the soft curve of her shoulder. As his balls tightened and his orgasm began, he held her arms down and thrust deeply, pinning her to the bed as he filled her smooth pussy with his seed. He wanted to bite her, hell, he needed to bite her, and he pressed the tips of his fangs against her smooth flesh.

Have you lost your mind? You can't claim her!

His wolf howled angrily. He wanted to claim their mate, and he snarled and howled again when Rafe retracted his fangs and licked the faint indents in Rowan's skin. He buried his face in the curve of her neck and inhaled deeply as she rubbed his back in slow, smooth strokes.

"Too heavy?" he mumbled.

"No, don't move."

He tried to soothe his wolf as Rowan continued to rub his back. After a while, his wolf retreated, growling softly, and he rolled off her. She curled next to him and wrapped her body around his, squeezing him tightly before resting her head on his shoulder. He needed to leave. Staying in her bed all night wasn't a good idea. But he was tired of fighting with his goddamn wolf, and if he left, it would start up its incessant clamouring for Rowan again.

Just the wolf?

He stared blankly at the ceiling. No, not just his wolf. He didn't want to leave her bed tonight – ever if he was honest with himself – and decided he'd allow himself to stay with her tonight. Tomorrow, he would end it. He had to, for both their sakes.

And when your wolf demands to see his mate?

He sighed inwardly. Rowan wasn't his mate, and just because his wolf thought she was, didn't make it true. He just had to be strong, ignore his wolf, and eventually, the damn thing would forget about the redhead.

"Rafe? Will you stay with me tonight?" Rowan asked sleepily.

"Yes." He pulled her even closer before reaching down and tugging the quilt over their naked bodies.

"Good," she mumbled. She kissed the hickey on his neck before squeezing his waist. She was asleep within minutes, and when her breathing was deep and even, he kissed her affectionately on the forehead and stroked her soft red hair. He was growing tired, and as he drifted toward sleep, he didn't argue when his wolf growled softly at him.

Bring our mate to our den. We need to keep her safe.

"My mate," he murmured, his arm tightening around Rowan as he began to snore softly.

ROWAN SQUIRMED AGAINST THE SHARP PRESSURE ON HER RIBS before opening her eyes and squinting blearily at Rafe. "Too tight, honey."

He didn't reply, and she poked him in the ribs. "Rafe, stop squeezing me so hard."

A frown flickered across his face before he relaxed his grip on her. Without opening his eyes, he muttered, "I'm sorry, my mate."

Rowan's eyes widened, and she half-sat up. Rafe immediately pulled her back down, flipping her to her back and slinging one heavily muscled thigh across hers before cupping her breast.

"You're mine. Sleep, my mate," he sighed into her hair before lapsing into snoring again.

Rowan stared at the ceiling, her heart pounding too fast and her limbs vibrating. Rafe wanted her for more than just fucking. He wanted a relationship with her. Calling her his mate was a bit – okay, a lot – weird, but she didn't care what the fuck he called her. She had fallen head over heels for Rafe Taggert, and while she wasn't entirely certain it was love, she knew she wanted to be with him and only him.

He would try to push her away in the morning, she had no doubt of it, and she wouldn't fight him on it. A small grin crossed her face. She didn't need to fight him on it – he'd come back to her. He couldn't resist her any more than she could resist him, and after what happened at the bar tonight, he wouldn't stay away from her for more than a day or two.

Hey, Ro? You wanna think this through for a minute? The guy is fifteen years older than you, and you know nothing about him. Just because you're good at fucking each other doesn't mean you're destined to be together forever. He could kick puppies or love those wretched rom-coms for all you know. Plus, he growls when you're having sex. Oh, and the fangs? Did you forget about the fangs?

She rubbed his arm again before closing her eyes. Rafe didn't have fangs. She had just imagined them the night they had sex in the woods. And the growling – was it real growling? Guys made lots of weird noises during sex. Hell, she probably did too.

Rowan, you're being deliberately obtuse about –

She shut down her inner voice and shifted closer to Rafe's warm body. She was tired and wanted to enjoy having Rafe in her bed. She didn't need to worry about that other shit right now.

CHAPTER 6

"Morning, Rafe," Rowan said when he joined her in her tiny kitchen early the next morning.

He was fully dressed, and she studied his jean-covered ass. "I guess morning sex is off the table, huh?"

He flushed and edged for the door. "I need to go, Rowan."

"I know," she said before turning back to the stove. She opened the oven door and bent, and his wolf growled happily. Unlike him, she hadn't dressed, and he studied the curve of her ass in her tiny sleep shorts. Jesus, her ass was practically hanging out of them, and he had to stop from stalking over, yanking down her shorts, and fucking her doggy style against the counter.

His wolf made another growl of happiness both at the thought of fucking his mate and at the delicious smell that permeated the kitchen. Rafe lifted his head and inhaled deeply as Rowan straightened. Her face was flushed, and she shut off the oven before moving to the fridge.

"What's that smell?" he asked.

His stomach growled loudly, and Rowan laughed as she

pulled some eggs from the fridge and set them on the counter. "Breakfast. Steak and eggs today."

His jaw dropped. "You eat steak and eggs for breakfast?"

"I am this morning. I'm always starving after sex, and it sounds like you are, too," she said.

His mouth watered as she cracked the eggs into the pan on the stove. "Can you make yourself useful and set the table? Plates are to the right of the stove, and the silverware is in the farthest drawer. There's juice or water in the fridge and coffee. I'll have water and a coffee, please."

His stomach growled again as Rowan took the two steaks from the oven and set them on a hot pad on the counter.

"Rafe," she prompted, and he moved into the kitchen and set the table as his wolf howled with delight.

Fifteen minutes later, he sat across from her and ate the most delicious steak he'd ever tasted. She had cooked them rare, and he cocked his head at her as she ate a bite of steak before taking a sip of coffee.

"How did you know I liked it rare?" he asked.

"Lucky guess." She finished off her egg before cutting another piece of steak. "Enjoying it?"

"It's delicious," he said.

"Good," she replied before cutting one more piece and then placing the remainder of her steak on his plate. "Eat more."

He frowned at her. "You only ate a few bites."

"I'm getting pretty full," she said before grabbing an apple from the bowl on the table and biting into it. "Stop looking at me like I'm about to starve. I eat smaller and more frequent meals."

He studied her as he chewed. His mate was on the small side - female wolf shifters tended to be larger - but he loved everything about her body, from her small, pert breasts to her tiny, firm ass.

"Did I hurt you last night?" he asked.

"Of course not," she said. "Why would you think that?"

"I'm a lot bigger than you."

She laughed. "I'm tough, Rafe. Don't worry about it."

Yes, for how small she was, his mate was rather tough. It was part of his attraction to her. Watching her take on the three assholes in the parking lot of the Woodsmen Pub had made him so horny that he'd had to deliberately stop from shifting to his human form, or he would have fucked her in the parking lot. He had scared her by approaching her in his wolf form, but he needed to touch her and reassure himself that she was okay. Surprisingly, she had not freaked out nearly as much as she should have.

He finished his steak and helped her clear the table, placing the dishes in the dishwasher as she scrubbed the pan. It was surprising how much he enjoyed the domesticity of the moment, and he ignored his wolf when it growled at him to take Rowan to their den.

He couldn't take Rowan to his cabin. If he did, there was a strong possibility that he'd never let her leave. Although he thought with a slight grin, he was pretty sure if she wanted to go, he wouldn't be able to stop her. He had a feeling that what Rowan wanted, Rowan got.

"What's funny?" She dried her hands with the dishtowel and leaned against the counter.

He studied how her thin tank top clung to her breasts and licked his lips as his fangs threatened to pop out.

"Rafe?"

He tore his gaze from her chest and blushed slightly at the look on her face.

"Uh, nothing. Listen, I'd better go. I'm cutting Marjorie

Wilkins' lawn this morning, and if I'm late, she'll give me hell."

She nodded, and he shuddered with pleasure when she pressed her slender body against his and kissed him lightly on the mouth. "Bye, Rafe. Thanks for last night – it was fun."

His wolf made an indignant whine, and he tried not to scowl at his mate's flippant remark. He was about to tell her they couldn't do this again - it was better if she wasn't attached to him.

"Um, yes, it was," he said before plunging forward. "But, Rowan, we can't keep doing this, okay? It's all kinds of wrong, and if people found out that we were sleeping together…."

He stared anxiously at her. "Listen, I get that I'm being an asshole and giving you all sorts of mixed messages, but I mean it this time. We can't have sex again. Okay?"

"Okay," Rowan said. "I'll see you around, Rafe."

He gaped at her as his wolf snarled in horror. "I – what?"

"I said okay," she said. "I want you, but I'm not going to keep begging. I'm not that pathetic. Besides, there are plenty of other guys in this town."

He growled and pushed her up against the counter, one hand cupping the back of her neck and the other squeezing her narrow hip. "You are not to go near another male. No one touches you but me. Say it, Rowan."

She shook her head. "No. You won't sleep with me, but I'm not allowed to sleep with other men? That isn't how it works, Mr. Taggert. You don't get to tell me who I can and can't have sex with."

He growled again and twitched wildly when she stood on her tiptoes and kissed his chin. "Let me go, please. I need to have a shower and run some errands."

He released her and said, "You told me you didn't want

anyone else but me. You said that I belonged to you and that you wouldn't fuck anyone but me, remember?"

She cocked her head before nodding. "I did say that, didn't I?"

"Yes," he said anxiously. "You did."

She grinned at him before patting his broad chest. "Thanks again, Rafe. Lock the door on your way out, would you?"

"Rowan," he said as she left the kitchen, "are you going to fuck someone else?"

"Not today," she called out cheerfully. "Bye, Rafe."

"So, you let Rafe believe you're going to sleep with other men?" Ella asked as she sank onto the couch next to Belle.

Rowan grinned at her from the armchair. "Sort of, but in my defense, I told him I wouldn't sleep with anyone yesterday."

Belle laughed and sipped at her glass of wine. "Did he show up at Gaston's last night?"

"No," Rowan said. "I thought maybe he would be waiting for me here when I was finished work, but he wasn't."

"Are you worried that he will stay away from now on?" Belle asked.

"I'm not," Rowan said. "He can't resist me any more than I can resist him. You saw how he reacted at Gaston's on Friday and heard what he said. He wants more than just sex. I know it. He called me his mate, for God's sake."

She gave her friends a hesitant look. "Calling me his mate is weird, right?"

"I've heard weirder," Ella said. It wasn't that she wanted

to tell Rowan about Rafe, but if Rowan figured it out on her own, that wouldn't be her or Belle's fault, right?

"It's not that I mind, but who calls someone their mate?" Rowan stared at the beer in her hand before taking a swig from the bottle. "I like Rafe, hell, I like him way more than I should, but there's some weird shit about him."

"What do you mean?" Belle asked. Her voice was so high-pitched with obvious anxiety that Ella gave her a soft kick to the calf.

"He growls in bed, like an honest-to-God growl, and I swear sometimes his eyes change colour. Then there's the whole mate thing and the strolling through the forest nude, and I think his stubble thickens when we're having sex."

"How strange," Ella said.

"Are you sure you're not just imagining it?" Belle asked. "Like, maybe he's so good at sex that you hallucinate."

"Those are weird things to hallucinate, Belle," Ella said.

Belle gave her a pointed look. "No, they're not, Ella."

"I think they are," Ella said.

Rowan finished her beer and stood as Ella ignored Belle's death stare. "So, Rafe growls, his eyes change colour, and he grows a beard... what could that mean?"

"Ella," Belle hissed as Rowan started toward the kitchen.

"I don't know," Rowan said. "As I said – it's weird. I'm going to grab another beer. Do you want more wine?"

"No, thanks," Belle said. She waited until Rowan left the room before grabbing Ella's arm. "What are you doing? Duncan and Bennett will kill you if you say anything."

"I haven't said anything," Ella said. "I'm just trying to help my friend figure out the mystery that is her new boyfriend."

Belle snorted soft laughter as Ella grinned at her. "C'mon,

Belle, it would be much easier if Rowan knew about our men."

"It would," Belle admitted. "But we promised them we wouldn't say anything."

"And we're not," Ella said. She checked the doorway before saying in a low voice, "Neither of us has told Rowan that Rafe is a wolf shifter. And it's not our fault that he can't keep his wolf side under control when they're having sex."

"True," Belle said.

Ella grinned at her. "So, are you going to help me to help Rowan figure out what's going on with Rafe?"

Belle hesitated before nodding. "Yup."

"That's my girl!" Ella said.

RAFE STOOD OUTSIDE THE DOOR OF HIS MATE'S APARTMENT. It was Sunday night, and he could no longer stand the ceaseless whining of his wolf. He hadn't slept at all Saturday night, and he had spent most of today pacing restlessly back and forth in his cabin as his wolf growled and whimpered incessantly for his mate. He didn't think she would sleep with another, and he *hoped* she wouldn't, but she wasn't a shifter, and she wouldn't feel the same pull for him as he felt for her.

Bite her, claim her, and we won't need to worry about other males taking our mate, his wolf demanded.

He cocked his head, his eyes glowing bright green as he heard his mate's soft footsteps. He could smell her scent and sniffed the air, growling under his breath before knocking on the door. His cock was a stiff spike in his jeans, and his heart pounded. His wolf whined in delight when the door opened.

"Rafe?" his mate said in surprise. "I didn't expect to see you -"

He growled and reached for her. He kissed her hard, shoving his tongue into her mouth as he propelled her backward into the kitchen. She made a muffled noise, and he boosted her up on the counter, wrapping one hand in her thick red hair to hold her steady and sliding his other hand under her shirt. He grunted impatiently at the feel of her bra and lengthened one nail into a razor-sharp point, slicing through the shoulder strap before yanking the cup down. He squeezed her breast, pinching the nipple and kissing her more deeply when she tried to pull her mouth from his.

His mate was saying something, her small hands were pushing at his chest, but he was frantic with need for her. He pushed his body between her narrow thighs, grinding his erection against her pussy.

"Rafe, stop!"

"Please, my mate," he muttered against her mouth. "I need you. Don't push me away."

He tried to yank her shirt over her head, and she punched him firmly in the side. He winced, the pain cutting through his haze of desire, and stared at her in surprise and hurt.

"I'm sorry," she said, "but you need to listen to me."

"I need you, my mate," he said. "I need you so badly, and I can't -"

He stopped, his body stiffening as he tasted two new scents in the air. He began to growl, and his mate tightened her thighs around his waist as he bared his teeth in an angry snarl and looked over his shoulder.

"Hello, Rafe," Belle said as Ella grinned like a maniac.

He stared silently at her, embarrassment rushing through him when Belle's gaze dropped to his hand still cupping Rowan's breast. He yanked it out from under her shirt but stayed where he was between Rowan's thighs. He was horrified by his actions, but his cock was still erect and extremely noticeable against his jeans.

"I'm sorry," he said, "I didn't realize that my ma – that Rowan had company."

"She doesn't," Ella said. "We were just leaving."

She grabbed Belle's hand and dragged her toward the front door. "Nice seeing you, Rafe. Rowan, we'll talk to you later this week."

They walked out of the apartment, slamming the front door behind them, and Rafe stepped away from Rowan. He gave her a shameful look as she hopped down from the counter.

"I'm so sorry."

"You need to listen to me when I tell you to stop, Rafe."

"I know," he said hoarsely. "It won't happen again, I promise."

"It will," she said. "Especially if you keep waiting until you're so damn horny for me that you can't control yourself. Not that I mind how hot you are for me, but I'll feel horrible if I have to beat the crap out of you because you aren't listening to me."

A small grin crossed his face, and she scowled at him. "I can take you, Rafe."

"I know," he said. She probably could. Not because she was stronger or faster than him – his mate was tough, but she was no match for him – but because he would never do anything to hurt her, nor could he deny her what she wanted. If that meant allowing her to beat the shit out of him, so be it.

"I'm sorry," he said again.

His wolf howled in delight when Rowan stripped off her shirt. She studied the slice through her bra strap and gave him a thoughtful look that made him extremely nervous.

"I'll buy you a new one," he said. "Do you want me to go? I can leave."

He hoped she wouldn't say yes. Truthfully, he wasn't entirely sure he could leave. He needed to be with his mate and not just for sex. Being away from her was a physical ache, and he was almost frantic to be with her.

"Of course, I don't," she said. "I want to fuck you just as much as you want to fuck me. Why didn't you come by last night?"

"I – well, I shouldn't …."

She sighed before walking toward the bedroom. "Come with me, Mr. Taggert."

He followed her like an eager puppy, a little surprised his tongue wasn't hanging out of his mouth. He groaned harshly when she flicked open her bra and dropped it to the floor before wiggling out of her jean shorts and panties.

"Take off your clothes, Rafe," she said.

He shed his clothes, and she admired the way his cock stood out from his body before patting the bed. "Lie down on your side."

He did what she asked, and she curled onto her side next to him, her head next to his crotch and her pussy only inches from his face. He inhaled, then cried out hoarsely when her warm, wet mouth slid down his cock. Her hand squeezed the base of his cock as she licked around the ridge before sucking firmly.

He moaned and panted and growled loudly when she stopped sucking. She sat up and gave him a pointed look before raising her top leg slightly. "Eat my pussy, Rafe."

"Yes, my mate," he rasped before holding up her leg and leaning forward. He buried his face in her pussy, licking and sucking at her clit as she cried out with pleasure. Her mouth surrounded his cock again, and he intensified his efforts,

392

sucking at her clit as she sucked at his cock, before sliding two fingers deep into her wet core.

She made a muffled sound of pleasure around his cock before sucking aggressively and pumping the base of him with her hand. He let his fangs pop out and brushed them against the wet lips of her pussy before using his fingers to part her lips. He licked her clit with soft, wet tongue strokes before swiping the tips of his fangs against it. He growled with satisfaction when she shrieked around his cock, her entire body shuddering, and warm wetness covered his face and mouth. He licked her clean as she trembled against him before collapsing on her back. One hand still held his dick, and she stroked him lazily as she panted and stared up at the ceiling.

"Jesus, I think I just came in less than a minute," she said. "You do this thing where… fuck, I don't even know what it is, but it feels incredible."

He retracted his fangs before kissing the top of her pussy and smiling at her. "I want to make you feel good."

"Oh, you do," she said with a small grin. "Lie on your back. I want to be on top, okay?"

"Whatever you want, my mate," he said as he rolled to his back.

An odd look crossed her face, and he cursed inwardly. He hadn't meant to do that, it had just popped out before he could stop it, but he couldn't keep calling her his mate. Normal people didn't do that, and sooner or later, she would ask him about it and then what the fuck would he say? What human used the term 'mate' as an endearment?

Besides, he told himself as she climbed onto him and straddled his hips, she wasn't his mate, no matter what his wolf thought. He couldn't take her as his mate, not when he was old enough to be her father and not with…

"Fuck!" he shouted with pleasure, his hands digging into her hips as she lowered her tiny pussy down his cock. He watched his dick slide into her, watched the way her wet pussy lips stretched around him and nearly climaxed right there.

He looked up at the ceiling, trying to ignore his mate's wet, tight feel as she braced her hands on his chest and moved slowly up and down.

"Look at me, honey," she murmured.

He stared at her, knowing his eyes were now green and the stubble on his face thickened to a beard, but he couldn't resist anything she asked him.

She smiled sweetly. "I love how thick you are, Rafe."

He bit his bottom lip and willed his fangs to stay hidden as he moved his hips in slow thrusts. She moaned and rode his gentle movements, her fingers digging into his chest as he cupped her breasts and tugged her nipples.

"Oh God," she muttered before bracing her hands on either side of his head and leaning over him. She kissed him deeply, sliding her tongue into his mouth to taste and tease, and he moved a little harder and faster, holding her around the waist as he thrust.

She released his mouth, her head falling back to expose her throat, and he licked his lips before looking away. He wouldn't mark her. He *couldn't* mark her.

"It feels so good," she murmured again as she reached down and rubbed her clit.

The sight of her small hand rubbing at her pussy sent a surge of lust through him, and he licked her collarbone. "I like pleasing my mate."

She smiled at him as he pushed and retreated. "Oh, believe me, handsome, your mate is very pleased."

He growled happily before threading one hand through her red hair. "You are my mate. Say it."

"I'm your mate," she said obediently.

Hearing her say she was his mate destroyed the tenuous grasp of his control, and he fucked her roughly, driving in and out of her as she clung to him with one hand and rubbed at her clit with the other. He growled and roared and made a long, drawn-out howl as her pussy squeezed around him and his climax rushed through him. He held her tightly, pumping in and out of her as she came with a soft little cry before he collapsed in a panting, sweating heap on the bed. She crumpled against him, resting her face on his chest. He stroked her hair, repeatedly running his fingers through it as he waited for his pulse to subside to a regular rate.

She sat up a little, resting her elbows on his chest, before saying in a demanding voice, "You're staying the night."

"Yes, my ma -"

He stopped, clearing his throat as she grinned at him. "What's with the 'my mate' thing, Rafe?"

"I don't know what you mean."

She arched her eyebrow at him, and he cursed his stupidity before saying, "It's just a weird endearment that I use."

"So, you call every woman you sleep with your mate?" she asked.

He shook his head, and she tapped him on the chest. "How many women have you called your mate, Rafe?"

"Rowan, what does it matter? I don't -"

"Tell me," she insisted.

"Only you."

A grin crossed her face, and she rolled off of him, curling up next to him and running her fingers through the hair on his chest. "You are so smitten with me, Rafe Taggert."

He should have argued, but instead, he pulled her closer and kissed her forehead. "Rest, Rowan."

"Not tired," she said.

He laughed and stroked her smooth back. "How did you learn to fight?"

"Nana taught me the basics of boxing when I was about fourteen. I practiced with her until I turned eighteen, and then she introduced me to Joey Miller."

"From Miller's Gym?" he asked.

She nodded. "Yes. He's been training me ever since."

"Are you trying to go pro?"

"No. It's just perfect for getting the aggression out, and I like knowing I can protect myself."

"How did your grandmother learn to box?"

She grinned at him. "I don't know. I never asked. But she taught my mom and my aunt to box when they were kids, and Joey says that in her youth, Nana was the best female boxer he had ever met. Said she could have made a career from it, but then she met my grandpa and walked away from it."

"Do you think she regrets it?"

"No. She loved Grandpa very much. He was twelve years older than her, and -"

Rafe jerked against her. "He was that much older than her?"

Rowan grinned at him. "Yes. He was anxious to start a family right after they were married, and Nana decided he was more important than her boxing career."

He stared silently at the ceiling as Rowan traced circles on his flat stomach. "Apparently, going after older men is in my genes."

He rolled his eyes, and she laughed and kissed his chest as he squeezed her firm ass. "You're close to your entire family?"

She nodded. "We're pretty close. Mom and Dad moved to Newport almost a year ago, so I only see them a few times a month now, but I text a lot with them."

"Why did they move?" he asked.

"Dad's firm asked him to head their new division in Newport. It's not permanent – only for about three years – and then they'll probably move back here. They didn't sell their house, just rented it out."

"How come you didn't move into the house?"

She shrugged. "I like my little apartment. The house is way too big for one person."

He stared at the ceiling again. His den was small, the cabin only a two bedroom with a tiny living room and kitchen by today's standards, and he wondered if his mate would be happy there or demand something larger.

He sighed inwardly. It didn't matter what Rowan wanted – she would never see his den. He had to stop living in a stupid fantasy world where Rowan belonged to him. She might be saying she wanted only him now, but when he was an old man, and she was still young, she would leave him, and he'd turn into his father – bitter and hateful toward his mate. Hell, toward humans in general.

Forget the age difference. Do you think you can hide your wolf side from her forever? You act like she won't freak out when she finds out you're not human. Jesus, man, get your fucking head out of the clouds. There is no future for the two of you.

"What about you?"

He shook his head briefly, and Rowan cupped his face and pressed her mouth against his when he didn't say anything. "Tell me," she said.

"There is nothing to tell," he lied.

She cupped his face again and stroked his jawline with

her thumb. "Tell me about your family," she said. "I want to know more about my mate."

His wolf growled happily, and Rafe wrapped his arms around her waist. "You think of me as your mate?"

She smiled at him and affectionately rubbed the tip of her nose against his. "Yes. Although I usually say boyfriend, I can work with mate."

"I imagine you already know about my family," he said. "Small-town secrets never stay secrets for long."

"I know you left with your mother for a year and then returned alone. Your family lives across the river, but you don't speak with them. Why not?"

"My father is angry with me for leaving with my mother," Rafe said.

"Even after all these years?" she asked.

He nodded, and she squeezed him tightly. "I'm sorry, honey. Where is your mother now?"

"She remarried and lives in California with her new husband."

"You didn't want to stay with them?"

"She married him about ten years ago. I was already living here again."

"Why did you return?"

He stared at the ceiling, deciding how much to tell her. He wanted to tell her everything, but that was impossible.

"When my mother first left my father, she was eager to experiment. We moved around that first year, and she had many," he paused and said dryly, "boyfriends. After a year, I told her I wanted to settle in one place. She refused, we argued, and she kicked me out. I returned here."

Rowan frowned at him. "Your father wouldn't take you back?"

"He was still very angry with me for abandoning the pa – our family – and refused to speak to me."

"He sounds like an asshole," Rowan said indignantly. "You're still his son."

Rafe shrugged. "He believes that I betrayed him."

"Why did your mother leave him?" she asked.

"They were very different, and eventually, that difference drove them apart."

"Was he older than her?"

He shook his head. "No, they were close in age."

"Do you have siblings?"

He nodded. "I have two younger brothers."

"Do you see them?"

"No," he said as a pang of loss, one he thought was long buried, went through him. "I do not."

"Are you telling me you never run into them in town?" Rowan said.

"Occasionally," he said, "but they refuse to speak to me."

She studied him carefully. "That hurts you."

"I'm used to it," he said.

She squeezed his face. "You don't have to lie to me, Rafe."

He sighed. "I miss my brothers very much. Do I wish they would speak to me? Yes. But they will not do what I did and break my father's rules."

"Rules? What rules?" Rowan asked.

"It doesn't matter. Can we stop talking about this? It is," he paused, "painful."

She hugged him and kissed his mouth. "Of course, we can. I'm sorry, honey."

He buried his face in her throat and inhaled her scent. "Are you sleepy yet?"

"No. Maybe you should give me another orgasm," she said with a grin. "That will help me sleep."

He laughed and nuzzled her throat. "Whatever you say, my mate."

"WAIT, WHAT'S THE OPERATION CODE NAME AGAIN?" BELLE asked as Rowan grabbed the plastic bag from the diner counter.

"I told you, Belle-baby, it's 'Operation show Rafe that no one cares about the age difference between us by forcing him to be seen with me in public'."

"Hmm, despite its cumbersome name, I feel like it might work," Belle said.

Rowan grinned at her as they headed toward the door of Snow's diner. "Of course, it will. In fact, I'm putting it into effect right now. I learned before he left this morning that he's starting a big landscaping job at the Farthen place today."

Belle grinned at her. "The Farthen's live right on Main Street."

"I know," Rowan said. "Lots of foot traffic, and people will see us together."

"If he doesn't run away," Belle said. They stepped out into the warm sunshine, and she waved at Bennett, who was coming out of the hardware store.

"He won't. He can't resist me," Rowan said. "Besides, why wouldn't he like a visit and a nice lunch from his mate?"

Bennett, who had joined them, gave her a startled look. "You're Rafe's mate?"

He studied her throat so intently that Rowan frowned at him. "What? Why are you looking at my neck like that?"

"Uh, no reason," he said. "So, you're Rafe's mate?"

She shrugged. "He keeps calling me that. It's just a weird endearment."

"You're dating Rafe?" Bennett said.

"Yes," Rowan said defensively. "Why is that so odd?"

"It isn't," Bennett said as Belle elbowed him lightly in the side. "But Rafe has been alone for a long time, and I didn't think he was the boyfriend type."

Rowan paused, "Well, he hasn't exactly said we were dating, but it won't be long until we are."

Belle laughed as Bennett grinned at her. "Rafe doesn't stand a chance, does he?"

"No," Rowan said happily. "We're meant to be together. I'd better run. It's almost lunch, and I want to get this to Rafe."

She kissed Belle on the cheek before walking to her car.

BENNETT WAITED UNTIL ROWAN DROVE AWAY BEFORE SAYING in a low voice. "Does she know he's a wolf shifter?"

"No," Belle said.

Bennett frowned. "He needs to tell her. If he's calling her his mate, his wolf has already decided. If Rafe tries to go against his wolf's wishes…."

Belle stared at him. "What, Ben?"

"He'll go mad," Bennett said. "Frankly, it's already surprising that he's gone this long without a pack without going crazy. If his wolf wants Rowan as their mate and Rafe denies him repeatedly, his human side will go insane."

"Seriously?" Belle said.

Bennett nodded. "Have you seen any bite marks on Rowan's shoulders?"

"No." Belle gave Bennett an alarmed look. "Is Rafe going to bite her? Is he trying to turn her into a werewolf?"

Bennett shook his head. "He's not a werewolf, Mirabelle. He's a shifter. And he can't turn Rowan by biting her. But wolf shifters do claim or mark their mates with a bite."

"Why do you look so worried?" Belle asked.

"Shifters, especially wolf shifters, aren't like humans. When they find their mate, it really is for life. They don't have affairs and will never leave their mate for another. Rafe and Rowan aren't even dating yet, and I know Rowan likes him, but...."

"But what?" Belle asked.

"Duncan says Rowan's never really been into dating anyone. If she isn't serious about Rafe, and he bites her, and then she moves on to someone else, it won't be good, Mirabelle."

"Would he hurt her?" Belle asked.

Bennett shook his head. "Of course not. Shifters would never hurt their mates. But he might go after the next guy she dates."

"She's not going to move on to someone else," Belle said.

"How can you be so sure?"

"I've known Rowan forever and never seen her act like this over a guy. She's usually, well, aloof with the guys she sleeps with. They're always chasing after her, and she keeps them at arm's length. She's not like that with Rafe. Plus, she's had a crush on him since she was fourteen."

A look of relief crossed Bennett's face, and Belle squeezed his arm. "I think we need to be worried that Rafe will break her heart. He's adamant about the age difference being a problem."

Bennett shrugged. "If he's already calling her his mate, it

won't be long until he claims her. I'm surprised he hasn't already."

"Ben, maybe we should," Belle hesitated, "tell Rowan about Rafe. She already suspects something weird, and she'll freak out if he bites her without telling her what he is."

"We can't," Bennett said. "I'm sorry, Mirabelle, I know that Rowan is your friend, but you cannot tell her about Rafe. Promise me."

"But if he bites her…"

"I will speak to him about telling Rowan," Bennett said. "But you have to promise me you won't say a word to her. Please, Mirabelle."

"Ella thinks we can nudge her into figuring it out on her own," Belle said. "Technically, that's not telling her, right?"

Bennett gave her an anxious look and she sighed. "Okay, fine. I promise, Ben."

CHAPTER 7

R owan slowed to a stop, her hand tightening around the plastic bag she held and a very odd sensation coursing through her belly. After a moment, she recognized it as jealousy, and she grinned to herself. For the first time in her life, she was jealous because there were other women around her man.

Not that she blamed them, she thought as she hurried down the sidewalk toward the Farthen's front yard. Rafe looked unbelievably sexy. He wore jeans and a plain white tank top. It clung to his lean abdomen and broad chest, and the dirt smeared across his arms and the sweat trickling down his neck made him look even more fuckable, in her opinion. He was sweaty and dirty and so goddamn manly that she wanted to ride him right there in the Farthen's front yard. She wondered briefly if Rafe had any damn clue how many women in this town lusted after him.

She slowed to a stop again, standing unnoticed behind the group of five women – no, not women but girls, she realized - who were clustered together in front of the Farthen's home. Leaning against his shovel, Rafe gave them a polite but puzzled smile, and Rowan swallowed her laughter as the group leader stepped forward.

"Mr. Taggert, Andy Tonks said that you were looking for some part-time employees for the summer. We wanted to give you our resumes."

"All of you?" Rafe asked in surprise.

"Well, not Jenna or Tillie, they're only fifteen, but the rest of us are all eighteen," the young girl said.

"Unless you'll hire us before we turn sixteen?" A chubby dark-haired girl asked. She smiled brightly at Rafe, her braces gleaming in the sunlight, and he gave her a confused smile in return as the leader took another step into the yard.

"What do you think, Mr. Taggert? Can we give you our resumes?"

"Oh, well, the thing is, Erin, I only need a couple of employees, and it'll only be a month of work. You're probably better off trying to get a job where you can keep working part-time while in high school."

The girl, who wore a tiny little sundress that revealed a healthy amount of cleavage, thrust her chest out the slightest bit. Rafe's gaze remained on her face, and her smile faltered before she cleared her throat.

"I'm finished school, Mr. Taggert. I graduated in May, and I'm all grown up now."

She reached out and touched his arm, letting her fingers linger on the curve of his bicep and Rafe stared at her hand with an odd look. Rowan could barely keep the laughter from spilling out as understanding dawned in his eyes, and he immediately took a nervous step backward, shaking free of Erin's touch. Taking pity on him, she ducked around the group of girls and looped her arm around Rafe's waist before standing on her tiptoes and kissing his jaw.

"Hi, honey. I brought you lunch."

Rafe gave her a clear look of relief before dipping his head and kissing her on the mouth. "Thanks, Rowan. That's nice of you."

She reached down and squeezed his ass briefly before smiling at Erin. "Hi, Erin. How are you? I heard you graduated this year."

"I did," Erin said. "Uh, me, Christy, and Tammy all graduated."

"Congratulations," Rowan said.

"Right, thanks. Um, so you and Mr. Taggert are dating?" Erin asked with a quick look at her friends.

"We are," Rowan said. "I just brought him lunch, so if you'll excuse us…."

Christy grabbed Erin's arm. "C'mon, Erin. Let's go."

Erin hesitated a moment longer, and the blonde rolled her eyes. "Erin, c'mon, I wanna hit the mall before my mom picks me up at three."

"Bye, girls!" Rowan called as the group trudged down the sidewalk.

She waited until they had turned the corner before grinning up at Rafe. He gave her an uncertain look and said, "Were they – did they want a job, or were they kind of hitting on me?"

She burst into laughter and squeezed his waist. "They were hitting on you, honey."

"I'm old enough to be their father!" He gave her an aghast look, and she laughed again.

"Those girls, yes. So maybe don't hire them."

He shook his head as she took his hand and led him toward his truck. "Definitely not. Thanks for rescuing me."

"You're welcome," she said as she pulled down the truck's tailgate. She sat the bag on the tailgate and boosted herself up before patting the spot beside her. "Sit down, Rafe."

He glanced down the street. "Rowan, there are people all over the place. Thank you for bringing me lunch, but I probably should work through lunch. I have a lot to get done."

"I brought my mate lunch, and now he won't even eat with me?" she said teasingly.

His eyes lit up when she called him her mate, and she watched the happiness flash across his face as he sat beside her. She squeezed his thigh before opening the bag and handing him the sandwich.

"Roast beef on whole wheat with extra pickles, no mayo and Dijon mustard," she said.

"How do you know my favourite sandwich from Snow's Diner?"

"Well," she said as she unwrapped her sandwich and took a bite of it, "don't judge me for this, but I've had a crush on you since I was fourteen years old, and I may or may not have done some slight stalking of you from time to time."

"Fourteen," he said. His sandwich was forgotten in his hand, and she nudged him lightly.

"Eat, honey. And yes, fourteen."

"Why?" he asked before taking a bite.

She laughed and held out a bottle of water. "Can you open this for me? Also - do you even have a mirror in your cabin, Rafe Taggert?"

He opened the water bottle, and she took a drink and then handed it back to him. He drank before saying, "Of course I have a mirror. What does that have to do with your crush on me?"

"You have no idea how hot you are and it's quite charming," Rowan said. "You just had a group of teenagers hitting on you, and you didn't have a clue."

"Does every teenage girl in this town have daddy issues?" He grumbled under his breath before taking a huge bite of his sandwich.

She scowled at him. "Do you think I'm with you because I have daddy issues?"

"Don't you?"

"Of course not," she said. "I have a perfectly normal, perfectly healthy relationship with my dad, and I'm not looking for a father figure. I had a crush on you - I wanted to be with you - for the same reason that a good seventy percent of the women in this town masturbate to fantasies starring you. Because you're damn fucking hot, Rafe Taggert."

His mouth dropped open, and she grinned at him before taking another drink of water. "It's true, Rafe."

"Women don't – don't masturbate to fantasies of me," he said.

"They do," she said. "The point is, I'm with you because you're kind, because I think you could be a lot of fun to hang out with when you're not freaking out over our age difference, and because you have a huge dick and your pussy eating skills are fucking incredible."

He blushed furiously, and she leaned in and kissed him before taking another bite of her sandwich. "Also," she said when she had finished chewing, "you're irresistible when you blush."

"I don't blush."

"Of course you don't," she said before throwing her leg over his and placing his hand on her thigh. He rubbed her thigh as she leaned against him and finished her sandwich. "How is work going?"

"Good," he said. "I'll be here for the next couple of weeks which is why I'm looking to hire some part-time help. Are you working tonight?"

She nodded and produced an orange from the plastic bag. She peeled it and gave him half before eating the other half. "I'm working tonight, but I'm off Tuesday and Wednesday."

"I could come by your place after you're finished work tonight," he said.

"I'd like that," she said. "It'll be pretty late, though."

"It's fine."

"I could come by your place after work," she said. "Then you don't have to drive all -"

"No," he said quickly. "I'll come into town."

"I don't mind driving out to your cabin," she said. "You could sleep if you're tired. Just leave your door open, and I'll let myself in."

He shook his head again. "No, it's okay. I don't need that much sleep."

She studied him, ignoring the small trickle of hurt that he didn't want her at his place, before smiling at him. "That's good because I plan on fucking your brains out."

"Rowan?"

She glanced up, moving Rafe's hand back to her thigh when he automatically yanked it away and covered it with her hand, forcing him to leave it where it was.

"Hello, Mrs. Staples. How are you?"

The older woman leaned against the truck as her dog, a beagle named Betsy, barked excitedly before standing on her hind legs and leaning her front paws against Rafe's lower legs. He petted her roughly with one hand and avoided looking at Mrs. Staples as the woman gave them both a long look.

"I'm good. Just taking Betsy for a walk. I do love the summer holidays. Not that I don't love teaching, but it's so nice to take her for a walk in the middle of the day."

Rowan smiled. "I bet. Not teaching summer school this year?"

"No, took the summer off for a change." Mrs. Staples shifted against the truck. "Are you and Mr. Taggert dating?"

"We are," Rowan said.

"About time," Mrs. Staples said. "Why, you had a crush on Rafe back when I taught you grade twelve biology."

Rowan laughed. "I did."

Rafe looked up from Betsy's madly wagging tail when Mrs. Staples poked him in the shoulder. "You treat her well, Rafe. Rowan was always one of my favourite students."

"You were my favourite teacher, Mrs. Staples," Rowan said.

Mrs. Staples poked Rafe again. "Did you hear me, Rafe Taggert?"

"Yes, ma'am," he said. "I'll treat her well."

"Good. Come, Betsy." Mrs. Staples tugged lightly on Betsy's leash, and the dog dropped to all fours and trotted happily after her, her nose to the ground and her tail still wagging madly.

"You okay?" Rowan asked before rubbing Rafe's back. He stared at his hand still resting on her thigh and nodded.

"Yes, I -"

"Hey, Rafe."

He looked up and forced a smile onto his face. "Hey, Clark."

"Working on the Farthen yard?"

Rafe nodded as Rowan studied the short, balding man who stopped beside the truck. His face was red, and he puffed loudly and marched in place as he held two fingers to his pulse. He was one of two barbers in their small town, and she grinned at the bright green, fluorescent striping that ran down his track pants.

"You haven't been in for a haircut in a while." Clark studied Rafe's head before turning his gaze to Rowan. "How are your parents enjoying Newport, Rowan?"

"They like it," Rowan said.

"They aren't thinking of staying there, are they?"

"No, sir," she said. "They'll be back in another year or so."

"Good," Clark said. "Beautiful weather we're having for this early in the summer, don't you think?"

"It is quite nice," Rowan said.

"Last year at this time, it was pouring rain every day. I didn't get my daily lunch run for nearly two weeks," Clark said.

He glanced at the sky before giving them both a small smile. "I'd better go. Rowan, get your man into my shop for a haircut. He's looking raggedy."

"I will," Rowan said with a small grin. "Have a good day, Clark."

The barber nodded and jogged away as Rowan squeezed Rafe's hand. "That's two. Now how are you doing?"

"Rowan, just because a couple of people aren't shocked doesn't mean -"

"No one cares," Rowan said. "And if they do – fuck them. It's our life. We can live it the way we want."

"What happens in twenty years when -"

"Hello, Rafe!" A blonde woman waved as she pulled into the Farthen's driveway. Her thin body was clad in a sweatshirt and a pair of yoga pants, and she wandered down to the truck with a look of shock.

"Wow, I can't believe how much you've done already," she said before staring delightedly at the yard. "Boyce is going to be so happy."

"It's going well," Rafe said. "Not as much rock as I

thought, and I should have the new flowerbeds dug out by the end of the day. I'm just taking my lunch, but I -"

"Take your time," the woman said with a careless hand wave. "You don't need to explain your lunch break to me."

She glanced at Rowan. "Hello, Rowan."

"Hi, Bonnie," Rowan said.

Bonnie studied Rafe's hand on Rowan's thigh. "Are you working with Rafe this summer?"

Rowan shook her head. "No, we're dating now. I brought him lunch."

"Isn't that nice," Bonnie said distractedly as she pulled her buzzing cell phone from her purse. "Oh, for the…"

She sighed and gave the two of them a look of annoyance. "I'm on the committee for the town-wide yard sale this year, and I swear to you, it's going to be my death. The women on that committee are petty little assholes."

Rowan laughed as Bonnie shoved her phone into her purse. "I've got to go. Apparently, there's some crisis over who is getting the prime spot next to the bathrooms in city park. Daphne texted that Mrs. Tutt and Mrs. Wickenbock are about to exchange blows."

She hurried off, waving and calling over her shoulder, "Rafe, just text me if there are any problems."

As she pulled out of the driveway, Rowan leaned over and kissed Rafe again. "No one cares, Rafe."

She slid off the truck, dusting off her ass with her hands before stuffing the garbage into the bag and taking one last swig of water before handing the bottle to him. "I'd better go. I'll be home around one-thirty, okay?"

He nodded. "I'll drop by Gaston's and walk you to your car when your shift is over."

"Aren't you the sweetest?" She stepped between his legs and draped her arms over his shoulders before tugging him down. She pressed her mouth against his, and he kissed her thoroughly as he held her hips.

She pulled away, her face slightly flushed and her eyes sparkling. "I'll see you tonight, all right?"

"Yes, my mate," he said, and she kissed him again before leaving.

"ROWAN, CALL IT A NIGHT."

Rowan looked up from the table she was wiping down. It was dead in the bar, with only two customers sitting in Jana's section. Gaston had come out of his office and stood in front of her.

"Are you sure?"

He nodded. "Jana went home early last week. It's your turn."

She blew him a kiss as she walked by him. "Thanks, Gaston, you're the best."

"Big plans?" he called.

She shrugged. "It's only ten, so, yeah, I might find something to do."

He laughed. "That something to do wouldn't be Rafe Taggert, would it?"

"Jealous?" she asked, and he laughed again before shaking his head at her.

"Get out of here, Ro. I'll see you Thursday."

RAFE'S CABIN WAS SILENT AND DARK, AND SHE PARKED NEXT to his truck and climbed out of her car. She wondered if he was having a nap. It made sense, especially if he was going to be up late tonight. She smiled to herself and walked quickly toward the front door. She couldn't wait to see the look on his face when he saw her.

She raised her hand to knock, stopping when she heard a screen door slamming. It came from the back of the cabin, and she tiptoed through the side yard. It was dark, but the moon was out, and she could easily navigate around the lush flower beds and ornamental trees that dotted the yard. She stared at the half-full moon before peeking around the side of the cabin.

Her breath caught in her throat. Gloriously naked, Rafe stood in the backyard staring up at the moon, and she studied his bare ass in the moonlight as he stretched. Fuck, he was gorgeous, and she took another step toward him. She had no idea why he stood naked in his yard, and frankly, she didn't care. She was struck with the sudden urge to strip off her clothes, drop to her hands and knees in the soft grass, and beg Rafe to fuck her under the light of the moon. Her hands reached for her shirt buttons when he made a low growl, and his body rippled.

She froze in place, staring wide-eyed at Rafe as fur sprouted on his body, and she heard his bones cracking. He threw his head back, staring at the moon as his body shifted and became something different. Something not human.

She stared at the large grey wolf. His back was to her, but she didn't need to see his front to know he would have a white patch on his chest. She staggered back on wooden legs, her ass hitting the rough wood of his cabin, and slid down until she sat on the ground. She watched in shocked silence as Rafe lifted his head to the moon and howled piercingly. The sound sent goosebumps chasing across her skin, and she shivered with an odd combination of fear and lust as the large wolf bounded into the forest and disappeared.

"Holy shit," she said. "Rafe's a wolf."

She said it again, hoping it would sound a little more natural, and to her relief, she didn't think she sounded completely crazy. She sat against his cabin for nearly an hour, her thoughts going in every direction, trying to comprehend what she had seen.

"Okay, Rowan," she said out loud as she finally stood. She stretched out the kinks and paced in front of his back door. "So, Rafe is a werewolf. That explains the growling and the changing eye colour, and the fangs. You're not crazy. But you are dating a – a werewolf."

She yanked her cell phone from her pocket and stared fixedly at it before putting it away. She wanted desperately to call Belle or Ella, but she couldn't. Not yet, anyway. They wouldn't believe her, and she wasn't sure that Rafe wouldn't deny what she had seen when she talked to him about it. He was obviously keeping it a secret.

"That makes sense," she said out loud again. "If you're a werewolf, you don't want people knowing you're one. That's pitchforks and burning territory."

She took a deep breath and stared at the moon. "Okay, your boyfriend changes into a wolf and howls at the moon. No big deal. You dated Alan Stint for three months, and he had an extra toe on his left foot, remember?"

She burst into wild and a little hysterical laughter. She bent over and laughed until her stomach hurt, her ribs ached, and tears spurted from her eyes.

"Get a hold of yourself!" she admonished sternly when her laughing jag dried up. "This is serious."

Totally serious. Rafe Taggert, the man she had loved since she was fourteen years old, was a goddamn werewolf, and instead of running away screaming, she was standing in his backyard and trying to convince herself it was no big deal.

It isn't. So, he's a little different. Who cares?

"A little different? What if he bites me? What if he turns me into a werewolf? What if I marry him and get pregnant and have little werewolf babies?" she nearly shouted into the cool air.

Don't you think he would have bitten you already if he wanted to turn you into a werewolf?

Okay, her inner voice had a point there. Besides, she had a feeling that Rafe would die before he did anything to hurt her. She had no basis for that feeling, but it was impossible to ignore. Rafe would never hurt her.

No, he really wouldn't. He was there when those guys tried to attack you in the parking lot at the Woodsmen Pub, remember? Also, what do you want to bet that he was the wolf you were mackin' on when you were lost in the woods as a baby?

A large shiver wracked her body, and she wrapped her arms around her torso and stared at the moon. Rafe had saved her life when she was a baby, he had protected her at the Woodsmen Pub, and he had gone to her grandmother's house and led her into the woods the night of the full moon so he could fuck her.

Another shiver went through her, this one pure lust, and she licked her lips and stared at the moon. Shit, her boyfriend was a goddamn werewolf, and she thought it was fucking hot. She was the freak, not him.

Maybe. Or maybe you know that you're meant to be with Rafe. He's your mate.

"My mate," she whispered to the moon. She tried the screen door. It was unlocked, and she slipped inside Rafe's cabin with one final look at the moon.

CHAPTER 8

R afe trotted into his yard. It was almost midnight, and he would need to have a quick shower before he drove to Gaston's. He had run longer than he should have, but it had been a few days since he had shifted to his wolf form, and he'd needed to shift. He loved being with Rowan, and it calmed and soothed his wolf, but it was also difficult. Not being able to shift on a regular basis would be extremely painful for both him and his wolf. He ignored the unease growing in his belly.

He would figure out a way to have Rowan in his life without revealing his true nature. He could maybe tell her he was a nature enthusiast and liked to take long walks in the woods every night. He could shift and run, and, on the night of the full moon, he'd think of something for why he would be out all night. He could make this work.

You need to tell her.

He couldn't. His father revealed his true nature to his mother, and look what happened. He couldn't risk losing Rowan. Losing his mate destroyed his father, and he knew without a doubt that the same thing would happen to him if Rowan left him.

His den door was ajar, and he nosed it open without shifting into his human form and trotted inside. He would eat the rest of the raw meat in the fridge before having a shower and –

He froze, his head lifting to sniff the air as he smelled Rowan's scent. His wolf howled with approval, and he turned to see his mate sitting on the couch in the living room. He stared silently at her, panic roaring through his belly as she returned his stare.

"Hello, Rafe," she said, and he chuffed in surprise.

She smiled and shook her head when he backed toward the door.

"Don't leave. I know it's you, Rafe. I watched you change in the moonlight."

Dismay swept through him, and he shifted to his human form. Rowan's gaze dropped to his dick, and he hardened immediately. He cursed inwardly, but he couldn't help it. His mate was finally in his den where she belonged, and the urge to take her, to sink himself into her soft warmth, was so strong it was almost undeniable.

"We need to talk," she said as she stood up from the couch.

He licked his lips and tried to keep his fangs from popping out. He could smell Rowan's lust, could smell her sweet cream, and he studied her crotch with a desperate need.

"Rowan," he said hoarsely. "I -"

"We need to talk," she repeated, "but considering that most of your blood is currently in your dick and I'm pretty sure you won't be able to concentrate, I think fucking first, talking second. What about you?"

His cock twitched wildly, and she grinned at him. "Do

you know what I've been doing since you changed and ran into the woods, Rafe?"

He shook his head, and she traced her fingers over her flat abdomen. "Touching myself."

He inhaled sharply, and she smiled at him. "It's true. Well, mostly true. I spent the first hour convincing myself that what I saw was real and the last half hour sitting on your couch and rubbing my pussy. You make me so fucking hot that I don't even care that you're a werewolf."

"I'm not -"

"I don't care," she said a bit crossly. "I need you, and I need you right now. You're going to fuck me, Rafe Taggert, and then we'll have a nice long talk about what exactly you are and what it means for us. Do you understand?"

"Rowan, we shouldn't -"

"Your mate needs you," she said. "Will you deny me what I want?"

"No," he rasped. "Never, my mate."

"Good. Now fuck me," she demanded.

He lunged across the living room, tearing at her shirt as she shoved her jeans and panties down her legs. She kicked her way out of them as he pulled her shirt over her head and then flicked open her bra. She shimmied out of it, and he stared hungrily at her naked body. He wanted to fuck her desperately, but he reined himself in. He didn't want to hurt her, and if he took her now before she was ready, he would. He cupped her breast and leaned down to kiss her, grunting in surprise when she pushed against his chest.

"No," she said. "I don't want kissing, and I don't want teasing. I want fucking."

Without replying, he turned her around and pushed her onto the couch on her hands and knees. He knelt behind her, shoving her thighs apart and wrapping his hand in her hair.

He yanked her head back as he pushed his cock in to the hilt. She was soaking wet, and he immediately forgot his worry about hurting her. He squeezed her hip as she cried out. Her pussy clenched around him, and he made a low growl before fucking her roughly. He was reaching beneath her to touch her clit when she tightened around him and climaxed with a loud cry of pleasure. Her back arched, and he held her shoulder as he drove in and out of her.

"Touch yourself, my mate," he demanded as her tiny body rocked beneath him.

She rubbed her clit obediently, gasping and making small whimpers of pleasure as he took what was his. Her body was starting to shake, her hand rubbing furiously between her thighs, and when she screamed his name and climaxed for a second time, he howled loudly and came deep inside her.

———

"Drink this, Rowan," Rafe said. He handed her the glass of juice, and she took a few small sips. She sat on the couch wrapped in a blanket, and he gave her an anxious look as he sat next to her.

She frowned at the space he left between them and wiggled over until she curled against his naked body.

"Are you okay?" he asked.

She nodded. "Yes. I needed it like that, honey. Stop worrying."

"I'm not worrying."

"You are," she said with a small smile before kissing his bare chest. "I told you – I'm tough. Besides, I liked it like that – all rough and kind of desperate. It would have been better if we had been outside under the moon, though. Don't you think?"

His cock twitched, and she grinned at him. "I'll take that as a yes."

"We could go outside right now," he said.

"We need to talk," she said. "Now that we've taken the edge off, we should talk about you being a werewolf."

"I'm not a werewolf," he said a bit indignantly. "I'm a shifter. A wolf shifter."

"I'm sorry. I didn't mean to hurt your feelings."

"You didn't," he said. "It's just – werewolves are a stupid myth about ugly creatures who can't control their urges during a full moon."

She cocked her head at him. "So, don't take this the wrong way because I don't think you're ugly or not in control, but you did lure me out of my grandmother's cabin the night of the full moon so you could fuck me."

He turned a dull red. "That was my wolf. He wanted you badly, and I lost control briefly. It can be a little more difficult to control the urge to mate during a full moon, and knowing you were so close to our den made my wolf a little crazy."

"Den?" she asked. "You call your home your den?"

He nodded, and she smiled. "That's awesome. So, you're not a werewolf, you're a wolf shifter, and you think of your wolf as separate from you, right?"

"Yes."

"And usually, you're in control except for full moons, and then the wolf takes over?"

He shook his head. "No, that's not – I mean, the last full moon, yes, my wolf took over, but that has never happened to me before. Even in my wolf form, I usually maintain control."

"But you and your wolf were so hot for me that you couldn't, huh?" Rowan said.

"Shamefully, yes," he said dryly.

She kissed his chest again. "Nothing to be ashamed of. I like that you want me that badly. I want you just as much."

"Rowan," he said, "not that I want you to be, but why aren't you freaking out over this?"

She thought silently for a moment. "I guess – I guess I knew there was something off about you. You growl, and your eyes turn green when we're having sex. I was sure I'd seen fangs when we had sex in the woods. I mean, I didn't know you were a wolf shifter, but once I saw you change, it all made sense."

She took another drink of juice before offering him the glass. "The thing is, Rafe, I *was* freaked out when I first saw it happen. I basically fell on my ass and stayed there for a good hour. But knowing that wolf shifters exist isn't - I don't know - all that surprising to me. I never really thought that humans were the only species on the planet. It seems arrogant to believe that."

He handed the juice back to her, and she finished it as he said, "Why aren't you at work?"

"It was slow, so Gaston sent me home early," she said. "I thought I would surprise you by coming by your place."

"I guess you were the one surprised."

She laughed. "You got that right. I do have some questions, okay?"

He nodded, and she squeezed his hand. "Relax, Rafe. I'm just curious about a few things."

He relaxed a little, and she leaned against him. "First question – if you bite me, will I turn into a shifter?"

He shook his head. "No. Shifters are born, not made."

"Okay. Good to know. Do I need to worry about you shifting when we're having sex?"

"Of course not," he said. "That's kind of gross, Rowan."

"Hey, you can't blame me for asking. You get a bit

hairier, and you grow fangs when we're having sex, remember?"

"That's as far as it will go," he said. "I have excellent control over my shifting."

"Does it hurt when you shift?"

"No. It mostly just…tingles."

"If we have babies together, will they be shifters?"

He jerked against her, and she raised her eyebrows at him. "Well, will they?"

"Uh, maybe. They have a fifty-fifty chance of being a shifter."

"Are there other wolf shifters living in town?"

"No. My pack lives across the river."

She studied him. "Do you miss your pack?"

"Sometimes," he said, "but I have been alone for a long time."

"Not anymore," she said, and his heart made an undignified leap in his chest.

"Rowan, you can't still want to be with me after -"

"Does anyone else know you're a shifter?"

"There are a few who know," he said.

"Were you the wolf in the forest when I was a baby?" she asked.

He grinned, his white teeth flashing in the dim light, and she laughed. "It was you."

"Yes. I was drinking at the river when you came toddling out of the trees. I shifted to my human form, and you told me your name and how old you were. I was going to take you back to my pack so I could take my father's truck and bring you into town, but then we heard your grandmother, and you started calling for her."

"Why didn't you just stay in your human form?" she asked.

"I was naked. I didn't think your grandmother would appreciate a naked teenager holding her granddaughter in the middle of the forest. I told you to stay where you were and wait for your grandmother, and you said you would, so I ducked into the bush and shifted to my wolf form. That's when you decided to try and take a dip in the river."

She laughed. "You're kidding me."

"I'm not," he said. "I had to grab you before you could fall in, and even though I was in my wolf form, you weren't afraid of me. You called me doggie and started hugging and kissing me, and that's when your grandmother showed up."

"I wish I could remember," she said.

"You were very young."

"And it was you at the Woodsmen Pub."

He nodded. "I'm sorry for scaring you."

"You didn't. Well, maybe a little, but I liked it," she said.

He laughed and kissed the top of her head as she said, "Are there different types of shifters."

He cleared his throat. "Yes."

"Is Bennett Saxby a bear shifter?"

His mouth dropped open, and he stared at her. "How did you…"

She laughed. "That's a definite yes. Belle said she saw him shift into a bear when she was a girl, remember? Does Belle know he's a shifter?"

He nodded, and she frowned a little. "She didn't tell me."

"Shifters are wary of humans knowing of their existence. It's why Bennett's father moved them away after he saved Belle as a child. Bennett told Belle when they started dating, but he would have asked her not to say anything to anyone."

"Does she know you're a wolf shifter?"

"I believe she does but not because Bennett told her. She

knows what to look for now, and that night in the bar, both she and Ella would have recognized -"

"Ella? Ella knows about shifters?" Rowan said. "So, Belle told her but not me?"

Rafe rubbed her back lightly. "Ella knows because Duncan is a shifter."

Rowan's mouth dropped open. "Are you serious?"

"Yes."

"What kind?" Rowan asked.

"He's a lion shifter."

She sat back on the couch and stared blankly at her lap.

"Rowan? Are you all right? I know this is a lot, and I'm sorry I didn't tell you, but I couldn't," Rafe said.

"Why not?" she asked.

"Well, because shifters don't tell humans -"

"That's not true," she said. "Maybe shifters don't tell the average human, but if they're dating them, having sex with them, they seem to tell them. Both Ella and Belle know their boyfriends are shifters. What's the real reason you kept it a secret, Rafe? You can't be worried that I would freak out, not when my two best friends are dating shifters, and I imagine they would have been happy to help you explain it, so why not tell me?"

He sighed deeply and set the empty glass on the coffee table. "Rowan, I didn't think I needed to tell you. I thought that we would have sex a few times and get it out of our system, and that would be it. The age difference -"

"Fuck the age difference," she snapped. "There's more between us than just sex, and I won't let you pretend it isn't. You call me your mate – do you mean it?"

He nodded. "Yes."

"Then why keep your shifter side hidden from me?"

"My mother left my father because he was a shifter," he said.

She blinked at him. "What? She had to know he was a shifter before they married and had babies."

"She did," he said. "My father told her very early in their courtship what he was. It made my grandfather angry because he didn't want humans in the pack, but my father refused to stop seeing my mother. He married her and left the pack for nearly three years. He and my mother lived in the woods on their own. When I was two, my grandfather died, and my father returned to the pack and became alpha. They had my brothers, and we lived with the pack for many years."

"Until your mother left," Rowan said, "and you went with her."

Rafe nodded. He tried to pull away from her, and Rowan moved closer, wrapping her arms around his waist and kissing his shoulder and chest until he relaxed.

"What happened, honey?" she asked.

He laughed bitterly. "Nothing really happened. My mother just grew tired of being the only human in a pack of wolves, of living in the middle of the woods away from civilization, of being my father's mate."

She kissed his shoulder again. "I'm sorry."

"My father tried to make her happy. I couldn't see that when I was younger, but I see it now. He wouldn't move into town because wolf shifters need to be near the woods. They can't live surrounded by humans. It's not in their nature. Do you understand?"

She nodded, and he studied her face before continuing. "He wouldn't move to town, but he tried to take her there as much as possible, even encouraged her to get a job and make new friends. She refused. I think even then she was preparing to leave."

He paused. "I should never have left the pack, but she was my mother, and I was worried for her. She told me my father was emotionally cruel to her for many years. She begged me to go with her, and I could not say no."

His chest tightened until breathing was painful. "I did not want to leave my pack, but she was my mother."

She hugged him hard, pushing his head to her chest and stroking his thick hair. "I'm sorry, Rafe."

When he raised his head, she stroked his jaw. "Do you believe your father was cruel to your mother?"

"No. My mother became very different when she was away from my father. She wasn't the person I thought she was, and I begged her many times to return to the pack. She refused, and we moved from place to place while she dated different men. Like I told you before, we fought when I asked her to settle in one place, and she kicked me out. I returned to my father, to my pack, but" he stopped and swallowed hard, "he refused to allow me to return. Artemis and Tagon – my brothers – tried to get him to change his mind, but he was so angry and bitter that we had left."

"I'm sorry, Rafe," Rowan repeated.

"Once I realized that my father would never allow me to return to my pack, I rented a place on the outskirts of town, started my landscaping business, and saved my money to buy this place out here in the woods."

"Why didn't you marry?" she asked. "Why didn't you start your own pack?"

"My father wouldn't allow the female shifters in our pack to even speak with me," he said.

"There have to be other wolf packs around," she said.

"There are," he said, "but no self-respecting female shifter would marry or even date a male without a pack."

She made a snort of anger, and he smiled at her. "It's fine, Rowan. I'm used to being alone."

"But do you like it?" she asked. "Are you like my grandmother, who prefers solitude or are you alone because you believe you have no other choice?"

"Does it matter?"

"Of course it does," she said. "Tell me the truth, Rafe."

He looked away. "I'm alone because I disobeyed my father's rules and abandoned my pack. Do I want to be alone? No, of course not. Wolf shifters need a pack, and it's been," he paused, "difficult at times to be without one."

She cupped his face and made him look at her. "I'm your pack now, Rafe. You and me – we're a pack. A small pack, but still a pack."

"Rowan," he said gently, "we are not meant to be. Don't pretend otherwise. I should never have let it go this far, and I shouldn't have called you my mate."

He waited for her anger, but she grinned at him. "So, you have two reasons why we can't be together – the age thing and the wolf thing, right?"

"A little simplistic, but yes," he said.

"The good news is that we already know that people in this town don't care if we're dating and," she held up her hand before he could speak, "for those who do think it's inappropriate because of the age difference – we don't care what they think. Do we?"

He paused before shaking his head slowly. "No, we don't."

She smiled happily at him. "No, we really don't. And as far as you being a wolf shifter – I'm fine with it. In fact, I think it's pretty cool."

"My mother was fine with it as well," he said shortly.

She scowled at him. "I am not your mother, and you are

not your father. Don't compare me to her just because we're both humans. That's not fair."

"Rowan, when a wolf takes a mate, it is for life," he said. "We don't find other mates, have affairs, or walk away when we're unhappy. Do you understand that? We mate for life. My father was destroyed when my mother left him. Even now, he has taken no other mate, and he never will."

"Why don't you believe I want to be with you for life?" Rowan asked. "I've been in love with you since I was fourteen years old, Rafe Taggert."

"You aren't in love with me."

She laughed. "You can't tell another person who they are and aren't in love with."

"You aren't – I mean, you can't be."

"I am," she said. "And you love me too. You've already made me your mate, Rafe."

"No," he said slowly, "I haven't."

She frowned at him. "You call me your mate all the time. You said you've never called another woman that before."

"Wolf shifters bite their mates to claim them. I haven't bitten you."

"But you want to, don't you?" she asked.

"No."

"Liar, liar, pants on fire," she said before dropping the blanket and climbing into his lap. She straddled him and reached between them, rubbing his cock with her soft hand until he was hard and throbbing.

"How many times have you thought about biting me, Rafe?" she asked before rising and pushing the head of his cock against her narrow entrance. He moaned and cupped her small breast as she rubbed his cock back and forth over her clit. When the head was slick with her cream, she pushed herself down, taking him deep inside her as he made a low growl of need.

"How many times?" she asked again.

"Many," he snarled before kissing her hard on the mouth. Their tongues twisted and tangled, and she gasped when he fisted his hands in her hair and pulled. She rode him slowly as his eyes turned to jade, and his fangs descended with a soft pop.

"Where would you bite me?" she asked breathlessly.

"The throat or the shoulder," he muttered.

He groaned when she shook free of his grip and climbed off of him.

"My mate," he said in a low voice, "fuck me right now."

"So impatient," she said before turning her back to him. She straddled his legs again, and he couldn't help but squeeze her firm ass as she lowered her pussy over his cock. She swept her hair out of the way, braced her hands on his knees, and fucked him.

"Make sure it's my right shoulder," she said. "I want to get a tattoo on the left."

"Rowan," he groaned, "I cannot bite you."

"You can," she said as she rode him harder, "I want you to."

He gripped the back of her neck, holding her steady as he thrust back and forth. "Please, Rowan."

"I'm your mate, Rafe," she said as he reached around and rubbed at her swollen clit. "You're supposed to claim me, remember?"

He made another hoarse groan before shaking his head. "I cannot, my mate. I'm sorry."

Disappointment flashed across her face before she shrugged. "All right."

He felt his own disappointment when she didn't force the

issue. If she demanded him to bite her, he would do it. He couldn't deny his mate anything.

Bite her, his wolf snarled. *She's ours. Bite her.*

With incredible willpower, he retracted his fangs before leaning forward and kissing Rowan's shoulder. "I'm sorry."

She squeezed his forearm before pressing his fingers more firmly against her clit. "It's all right, honey. I understand. Now, no more talking. Let's just make each other feel good, okay?"

"Yes, my mate."

CHAPTER 9

The loud knocking woke Rowan. She squinted in the bright light and fumbled for her cell phone, staring blearily at it. It was almost ten, and as she crawled out of Rafe's bed and stumbled naked to his shirt draped across the chair, she vaguely remembered Rafe whispering in her ear earlier that he was going for a run in the forest.

The knocking continued, loud and insistent, and she dragged Rafe's shirt over her head before staggering out of the bedroom. God, she hoped that Rafe wasn't an actual morning person. They hadn't gone to bed until almost six, and she thought it might have been nine when he had left for his run.

"Who only needs three hours of sleep?" she grumbled. "Fuck! Son of a bitch!"

She glared at the footstool she had tripped over and, holding her aching foot, hopped the rest of the way to the front door as the knocking began again.

"Jesus, what?" she snapped as she yanked open the door and glared at the dark-haired man standing before her.

He stared wide-eyed at her before taking a step back and

staring at the cabin. "Is this – I'm looking for Rafe Taggert. This is his cabin, isn't it?"

She nodded and rubbed her foot. "Yes. He's not here right now."

The man leaned forward and inhaled deeply, and she raised her eyebrow at him. "Stop sniffing me."

He flushed, and she smoothed her hair down when his gaze drifted to it. She could only imagine what it looked like. She and Rafe had fucked like bunnies for most of the night, and a healthy portion of it had been outside under the bright light of the moon.

"Can I take a message for him?" she asked.

He frowned. "I need to speak with him. When will he return?"

"I'm not sure," she said.

"Are you sleeping with him?" he asked.

"That's none of your business, sweetie," she said.

His scowl deepened. "Just tell Rafe that his brother -"

"Brother!" She gave him a look of delight. "Are you Artemis or Tagon?"

"Tagon," he said slowly.

"It's so nice to meet you!" She smiled at him. "I should have known you were Rafe's brother. You look like him."

"I'm sorry, but who are you?"

"I'm Rowan Jameson," she said, "I'm Rafe's mate."

His jaw dropped. "You – you are my brother's mate?"

"I am," she said. "Come inside. Rafe went for a run in the woods, but I'm sure he won't be long."

She took him by the arm and dragged him into the cabin before shutting the door. He stood awkwardly in the living room, and she urged him toward the kitchen. "I'll be right back. Don't leave, okay?"

"Um, okay," Tagon said.

She used the bathroom quickly before rinsing her mouth with mouthwash and wrangling her tangled hair into a braid. She tossed her panties into the clothes basket at the end of the bed before wiggling into the rest of her clothes. Tagon still waited patiently in the kitchen, and he watched silently as she padded barefoot to the coffee machine.

"Would you like a cup of coffee?" she asked.

"No, thank you," he said.

She popped a pod into the machine and smiled at Rafe's brother as the coffee poured into the cup. "Are you sure?"

He nodded, and she carried the steaming mug to the table before sitting across from him. She sipped the coffee as Tagon cocked his head and studied her face.

"How old are you?" he asked.

"How old are you?"

"Thirty."

"Do you have a mate?" she asked.

"Yes."

"What's her name?"

"Sophina."

"What a pretty name," Rowan said. "Is she a wolf shifter?"

Tagon frowned at her. "Of course, she is. I would never marry a human."

"Your mother was a human."

Tagon's eyes glowed a dark yellow, and he began to growl.

"Don't growl at me just because you have mommy issues," Rowan said.

His growling stopped abruptly, and he blinked at her as she stood and wandered to the counter. "I'm hungry. Are you hungry?"

"When will my brother return?" Tagon asked.

She shrugged as she opened the pantry and rummaged through it. "Soon, I would imagine. Ooh, bread – would you like some toast?"

"No," he snapped.

She rolled her eyes. "Jesus, are you always this testy in the morning? Chill out. It's been years since you've spoken with your brother. I think you can wait another few minutes."

"How much do you know about me?" Tagon asked.

"Enough," Rowan said as she put the bread into the toaster. She pulled some jam from the fridge and opened the drawers until she found the cutlery.

"How long have you and my brother been mates?"

"Not long."

"Aren't you a little young for him?"

Rowan grinned at him. "I'm very mature for my age."

"Why would my brother take a human for a mate?"

"He likes my hair."

Tagon studied her red hair before giving her a confused look. "My brother took you as his mate because of your hair?"

Rowan snickered as the toast popped up. She spread jam on it as she said, "Probably not just the hair. But I'm kind of pushy and know what I want, and I want your brother. And just between you and me - I always get what I want."

He blinked at her as she licked the jam from her fingers. "Maybe the four of us could get together one night. Have a double date, maybe play cards, and catch up on events of the last twenty years."

"I do not associate with humans," Tagon said with a low growl of disgust.

"Watch it, buster," she pointed the jam-covered knife at him before winking, "I don't like being discriminated against just because I can't grow fur or fangs."

She rinsed the knife and placed it in the sink. "You know, your brother – oh!"

Tagon had crossed the kitchen silently to stand directly behind her. She glared at him when he said, "Do you carry his pup? Is that why he is with you?"

"That's a rude question. Do you ask every woman you just met if they're knocked up?" She said irritably as he stepped closer. "Move back, please. You're in my bubble."

He sniffed at her. "Your scent doesn't indicate you're carrying a pup, but maybe it's different with humans?"

"Sweetie, you need to stop sniffing me and take a step back," she said. "You're in my personal space, and I don't appreciate it."

"Does Rafe still speak with our mother?" he asked. "Do you know her?"

"You can talk to your brother about that," she said before pushing lightly on his chest. "Step back."

"Don't touch me, human," he said with a growl.

"Then get out of my space and stop growling at me."

"I'm not going to listen to what a human says," Tagon said before grabbing her arm. "You're very small and not even -"

Before he could finish his sentence, the back door swung open, and there was an angry howl. Naked and moving so quickly he was a blur, Rafe shot across the kitchen and tore Tagon away from her. She stumbled back against the counter as Rafe slammed his brother into the wall and wrapped one large hand around his throat. He howled again as he squeezed tightly.

"You dare to touch my mate?" he shouted as his eyes turned green and his fangs popped out. "I will kill you, you insolent little pup."

"Rafe! Stop!" Rowan grabbed his arm. "Stop it right now. He's your brother."

Rafe stared at her before turning his gaze to the man in his grip. "Tagon?"

He released him and took a step back as Tagon, coughing and choking, rubbed at his throat.

Rowan poured a glass of water and handed it to Tagon. "Here, drink this."

He took the glass but didn't drink, staring sullenly at Rafe as he rubbed one shaking hand over his jaw.

"Tagon? What are you doing here?" Rafe asked hoarsely.

"Father sent me," Tagon said. "He wishes to speak with you."

"About what?"

Tagon glanced at Rowan, a look of disgust crossing his face. "I will not speak of it in front of the human."

"The human is my mate," Rafe growled. "And if you touch her or look at her in that manner again, I will break your arm, baby brother."

Tagon snarled at him, and Rafe snarled back, baring his fangs.

"Oh, for God's sake, you two haven't spoken in how many years, and you're going to get into a fight just because of a human? Both of you grow up," Rowan said.

Tagon looked startled as Rowan put her arm around Rafe's waist. "I'm going to go."

"You don't have to," Rafe said heatedly. "My brother is -"

"I know I don't," Rowan said. "But I think it's better if you speak with your brother alone. Drop by my place after you finish work today, okay?"

He nodded, and she stood on her tiptoes and pressed a kiss against his mouth. "Bye, honey. I love you."

Rafe jerked against her, and she laughed before patting

his naked ass and winking at Tagon. "Bye, Tagon. It was lovely to meet you."

She grabbed her purse and walked out of the cabin as the wolf brothers stared silently at her.

TAGON STOOD BY THE KITCHEN WINDOW WHEN RAFE returned from dressing. He picked up Rowan's coffee from the table and sipped at it as Tagon stared out the window.

"You look good, brother," Rafe said.

Tagon rubbed at the marks on his neck. "You look older."

Are you mated?" Rafe asked, ignoring the insult.

"Yes. Her name is Sophina. She is Alden's youngest daughter."

"I remember her," Rafe said. "Do you have pups?"

"She carries a pup in her belly now," Tagon said with a tinge of pride. "She is due in four months."

"Congratulations. How is Artemis? Is he mated as well?" After years of no contact with his pack, he was eager for whatever information he could get on his family.

"No, not yet," Tagon said. "Father has been hounding him for years to find a mate, but Artemis has shown no interest in the females in our pack or other packs."

His brother finally turned and faced him. "Have you gone insane without your pack, Rafe? Is that what's happening?"

"Of course not," Rafe said with a frown. "I'm perfectly fine."

"Perfectly fine?" His brother gave him a look of disbelief. "You are fucking a human. A human! If father found out, he would -"

"The human is my mate," Rafe said, "and I have long stopped caring what father thinks of me."

"You haven't bitten her," Tagon said. "You call her your mate, but I smell no claiming scent on her. She is not your mate. You could still do the right thing and find a more," he paused, "age appropriate shifter to be your mate."

Rafe flushed a dull red. "No female shifter will have anything to do with me. You know that, Tagon."

"So, you choose a human because you have no choice?"

"No," Rafe said. "Rowan is not my mate because I can't be with a shifter. She is my mate because I love her."

A little rush of excitement and pride went through him. It was the first time he had admitted out loud – hell, admitted at all – that he loved Rowan, and it made him and his wolf stupidly happy.

"In love with a human?" Tagon scoffed. "It is better for you to be alone forever then take a human as your mate. Consider it your punishment for abandoning your pack for our wretched excuse of a mother."

"Watch your tongue, Tagon," Rafe snarled. "She is still your mother. You will speak respectfully about her or feel my claws in your flesh."

Tagon bared his fangs at him before taking a step back. "You still defend her. Even after she revealed her true nature."

Rafe didn't reply, and Tagon sighed. "I am not here to speak about our mother, Rafe. I'm here because father wishes to speak with you. Will you meet with him?"

"Of course," Rafe said. "What does he want to talk about?"

"He can tell you himself," Tagon said bitterly. "I'll tell Father you'll come by at six tonight. Unless you would rather be fucking your human?"

"I'll see you at six," Rafe said. "It was good to see you again, brother."

Tagon shrugged. "I'm only here because Father asked me to come. Goodbye, Rafe."

He strode out the back door, slamming it shut behind him. Rafe sank into the kitchen chair. His heart thudded, and he felt sick to his stomach. The prospect of seeing his father, maybe even Artemis, filled him with excitement and dread. He took a deep breath and finished Rowan's coffee in three large gulps. He would have a quick shower, work at the Farthen's for a few hours, and then call Rowan.

"ELLA?" BELLE STARED AT THE CHUBBY BLONDE IN SURPRISE. "What are you doing here?"

"Rowan texted me and asked me to drop by your place," Ella said. "I thought you knew."

"She texted me and asked if she could come by, but that's all she said," Belle said. She stepped back and ushered Ella into the house.

"I was just working in the library," she said as Ella followed her into the kitchen. "Do you want some tea?"

"Yes. I can make it." Ella grinned at Belle and tugged on her ponytail. "You're covered in dust."

Belle laughed. "I was pulling books from shelves that haven't been dusted in twenty years. I'm surprised I'm not covered in cobwebs."

She sat down as Ella put the water on and dropped tea bags into the mugs. "What are you up to today?"

"I had a few massage appointments this morning – business has been really picking up the last few weeks – and then I'm going with Duncan to Newport later this afternoon. He has a meeting with his agent to go over the details of his show in London."

The doorbell rang, and Belle disappeared down the hall. She returned a few minutes later with Rowan trailing after her, and Ella smiled at the slender redhead. "Hey, Ro. You look tired."

"Do I? It's been an absolute *bear* of a day," Rowan said as she sat down. "I bet you know what that's like, huh, Belle-baby?"

Belle blinked at her. "Oh, um, my day's been good. Just working in the library."

"Is your man around?" Rowan asked.

"He's in the backyard," Belle said.

"Picking berries?"

Belle glanced at Ella before giving Rowan a curious look. "Honey, are you okay?"

"Just fine. Why?"

"You're acting weird," Ella said as she poured hot water into the mugs.

"Am I?" Rowan said. "Well, Miss Ella, I'd be *lyin'* if I said the last twenty-four hours haven't been weird. How's Duncan, by the way?"

"He's fine." Ella set the mugs of tea on the table before sitting next to Belle. "Painting this morning. Why have the last twenty-four hours been weird?"

"Maybe because I found out my boyfriend is a wolf shifter, and my two best friends are dating a bear shifter and a lion shifter?" Rowan said before sipping at her tea.

"Oh, thank fucking God – you know," Ella said as Belle's mouth dropped open.

"Rafe told you?" Belle said.

"Not exactly," Rowan said. "I went to his cabin to surprise him last night and watched him shift to his wolf form."

"Shit," Belle said. "Did you freak out?"

"A little at first. He didn't know I was there and went for a run in the woods, so that gave me some time to mull over what I'd seen. By the time he returned, I had mostly accepted that I wasn't crazy and that my boyfriend was a wolf."

"What did you do?" Belle asked.

"Fucked his brains out, of course," Rowan said.

Belle and Ella stared at each other in silence before simultaneously bursting into laughter. Rowan sipped at her tea and waited patiently until their laughter died off.

"So, after you fucked his brains out, what did you do then?" Ella asked.

"We talked about him being a shifter. I asked him if Bennett was a bear shifter, and he confirmed it, and he told me Duncan was a shifter too," Rowan said.

"Are you mad at us for not telling you?" Belle asked.

"I was a little at first, but not now. Rafe told me how important it is that humans aren't aware shifters exist."

"We wanted to tell you, Ro, I swear we did, but we really couldn't," Belle said.

"I know," Rowan said.

"So, you really are cool with the whole shifter thing?" Ella asked. "It took me a few days to stop freaking out."

Rowan grinned at her. "I really am. Rafe is my mate, and I love him."

Ella and Belle stared at her in shock before Ella said, "You love him?"

"Yes. Is that so hard to believe?"

"You haven't known him that long, and there is the age difference and the fact that you…."

Ella trailed off, and Rowan laughed. "Fucked a bunch of guys without ever falling in love?"

Ella just shrugged, and Rowan took a sip of her tea. "I love him, and I don't care about the age difference or that

445

he's a wolf shifter. We're meant to be together. It's that simple."

Belle leaned forward and squeezed her hand. "I'm happy for you, Rowan."

"Thanks, Belle. Now, I just need to convince Rafe to bite me, and we'll live happily ever after," Rowan replied.

"Bite you?" Ella gave her a look of horror. "Why the hell would he bite you?"

"Wolf shifters bite their mates to claim them. Rafe thinks of me as his mate but refuses to bite me because his mother is human. She eventually left his father because she grew tired of being with a wolf shifter. Rafe thinks the same thing will happen with me."

"So, what happens when he bites you?" Ella asked.

"We're mated for life."

"Whoa. Are you ready for that kind of commitment?" Ella said.

Rowan nodded. "Yes. I've spent what feels like my entire life searching for something – *someone* – that would make me feel complete. I've found him, and I'm not letting him go. This is the happiest and most content I've ever been."

She smiled happily. "I stopped at Nana's on the way home from Rafe's house and told her we were officially dating. She was thrilled. Not so sure that Mom and Dad will be, but I'll cross that bridge when I come to it."

"So, 'Operation make Rafe bite you', has officially begun?" Belle said with a small grin.

Rowan nodded. "Damn straight it has. I spent the night with him, and he's coming by my place after work tonight. His brother – who he hasn't seen in forever – came by the cabin this morning to tell him that his father wants to meet with him."

"I thought they were estranged," Belle said. "Ben said something about Rafe leaving his pack years ago."

"They are. It's a long story, but Rafe left with his mother. When he returned, his father refused to allow him back into the pack. He's been alone ever since."

"That's horrible," Ella said with a scowl. "What kind of father would abandon his child like that?"

"Well, maybe he's had a change of heart," Rowan said. "There has to be a reason why he wants to meet with Rafe. I'll let you know when I find out."

She took another sip of tea as Belle smiled at her. "Ro, honey, you have no idea how happy we are that you know about shifters. It was killing us to keep it a secret from you."

Rowan smiled at her. "I'm happy too, Belle. Now, feed me before I collapse from hunger. Sex with a wolf shifter works up an appetite."

RAFE CLIMBED OUT OF HIS TRUCK AND STARED apprehensively at the cabins scattered throughout the trees. No pack members were outside, and not a single curtain stirred. He started toward the largest cabin, stopping when he heard the noise behind him.

"Hello, brother."

He turned and studied the shifter standing behind him. "Hello, Artemis."

"You look good."

"Tagon says I look older," Rafe said.

A small smile crept across Artemis' face. "His sharp tongue has not dulled with age."

Rafe hesitated and then stepped toward his brother, holding out his hand. "It's good to see you again, Artemis."

Artemis stared at his hand, and Rafe's stomach churned. He hadn't been surprised by Tagon's reaction to him - even as boys they had never been close, and Tagon's disposition had never been a sunny one – but he and Artemis had been best friends. Out of everyone, he had missed Artemis the most and even now, his rejection wounded him to the core.

He grunted in surprise when Artemis ignored his hand and put his arms around him. He hugged him roughly, and Rafe returned his hug, feeling his throat burn as he inhaled the familiar scent of his sibling.

"I've missed you, brother," Artemis said in a low voice.

"I've missed you too," Rafe said. "More than I can say, Artemis."

He leaned back and studied his brother's face. "You look tired."

"There is much to discuss," Artemis said. "Father is -"

"Father wishes to speak to our lost brother himself. You know that, Artemis," Tagon said behind them.

Rafe stepped away from Artemis and smiled at Tagon. "Hello, Tagon."

"Father is waiting," Tagon said.

He walked toward the alpha's cabin, and Rafe fell into step beside Artemis. "It's quiet. Where are the other pack members?"

"Father asked them to remain in their cabins." Artemis glanced at Tagon before lowering his voice. "Rafe, do not be shocked by father's appearance. His healing powers have faded, and he is not doing well."

"What is wrong with him?"

Artemis sighed. "We do not know for certain, and father refuses to go to the shifter doctor in Newport."

"Why?"

"Because he is tired of living," Artemis said bluntly.

At the cabin, Rafe followed Tagon inside his childhood home. Very little had changed on the interior, and memories surged through him. He pushed them down – now was not the time for a trip down memory lane – and followed Tagon into the study. Artemis stood behind him, and when Rafe caught sight of his father for the first time, his brother placed a hand on Rafe's shoulder at his low whine.

"Steady, brother," Artemis whispered.

"Hello, Rafe," his father rasped. After hesitating, Rafe crossed the study and knelt at his father's feet.

"Hello, Father."

His father cupped his face as Rafe stared silently at him. The man he remembered was gone, replaced by a thin, ashen-skinned shifter with bloodshot eyes and pain etched into every corner of his face.

"You look good, son," his father said.

"So do you."

His father barked laughter that turned into a harsh coughing jag. Tagon hurried forward and held a cloth to his father's mouth as Rafe rubbed his leg. The cloth was stained with blood when his coughing fit eased, and Rafe gave Artemis a worried look as Tagon held a glass of water to their father's mouth.

"Drink, Father," Artemis said.

He drank a few swallows before pushing the glass away. "I wish to speak with you about something important, Rafe."

Rafe nodded his thanks when Artemis set a chair next to him. He sat, and when his father reached out his hand, Rafe took it and squeezed it lightly.

"I am dying," the old man said.

"Father, perhaps if you allowed us to take you to Newport, you could -"

His father shook his head. "I hear enough about Newport

from your brothers. Hold your tongue, Rafe." He cleared his throat roughly. "I should never have turned you away when you returned to the pack."

Rafe stared at him in surprise. It was the closest to an apology he would ever get. He squeezed his hand again as his father stared at him. "I am dying, and our pack will be without an alpha. You are to return to the pack immediately and become alpha."

"Father, I…" Rafe trailed off and glanced at his brothers. Tagon glared at him, but Artemis' face held no expression.

"You may return this evening if you wish," his father said.

"It has been years since I've been in the pack," Rafe said. "I am not fit to be the alpha. Artemis should be."

His father glanced at Artemis. "Artemis is a good boy, Rafe. He is smart and strong and has many qualities of a leader, but he is not the eldest. Tradition dictates that -"

"Fuck tradition," Rafe said. He released his father's hand and stood, ignoring Tagon's warning growl. "You refused to let me into the pack for years, and now that you're dying, you expect me just to return and take up the alpha position as though nothing happened? The pack members would not follow me, and you know it. Why should they? They know nothing of me. Make Artemis the alpha – he deserves it."

"It's not about who deserves it," his father snapped. "You are my eldest-born, and you must be the alpha. We cannot break tradition."

Rafe shook his head. "I already told you -"

"Father is right," Artemis said. "You should be alpha, Rafe."

"Have you gone mad, Artemis?" Rafe said. "You know that makes no sense."

"Listen to Rafe," Tagon said. "You have been father's right-hand man for years, Artemis. You know how to be alpha better than anyone else, and that includes Rafe. Our pack members trust you and think highly of you. Don't let -"

"Hold your tongue, Tagon! This does not concern you, so keep your mouth shut!" Their father shouted, his eyes glowing a dark yellow. Tagon made a low snarl before falling quiet.

"Father," Rafe said, "I cannot be alpha."

"Because you don't want to be or because you foolishly believe you are in love with a human?" His father asked.

Rafe didn't reply, and the old man said, "Your brother told me about your silly obsession with the red-haired human. And even if he hadn't, I can smell her all over you."

His nose wrinkled for a moment. "Why would you be so foolish, boy?"

"She is my mate," Rafe said.

"So, you've bitten her then?" his father asked. "She bears your claiming mark?"

Rafe glanced at Tagon, "You know I have not."

"Then she isn't your mate," his father said dismissively. "Forget the human and come join your pack. It's what you've wanted most for years – don't try to deny it."

Rafe stared at his father's grey face. Until a month ago, being a part of a pack again *was* what he wanted most, but that was before Rowan, before she kissed him, before she touched him…before she loved him.

"I will not join the pack without my mate," he said.

His father sighed. "After what your mother did to you, to this family, you would still take a human as your mate?"

"She is not like our mother," Rafe said.

"She will leave you, Rafe," his father said. "Humans can't live with shifters."

He coughed harshly before leaning forward. "Join your family again, Rafe. We need you. Is this silly little human girl more important to you than your family? When she leaves you, and she will, do you want to end up like me? Alone and in love with a woman who will never return your love?"

"She isn't like that," Rafe said.

His father snorted before leaning back. "Are you joining the pack again or not, Rafe? I want your answer."

Before Rafe could say no, Artemis said, "Father, give him a few days to consider it."

Their father nodded. "Very well. Go back to your lonely den and think strongly about my offer. You will be a part of a pack again. You can find your mate here and have pups. It isn't too late for that, son."

Rafe didn't reply, and the old man closed his eyes and said, "Tagon, help me to bed."

Artemis took Rafe's arm and led him out of the cabin. They stayed silent until they were at Rafe's truck, and then Artemis smiled hesitantly at him. "You should return to the pack, Rafe."

"What is wrong with you, Artemis?" Rafe said. "The pack would never follow me."

"They will," Artemis said. "If Father tells them to, they will follow you."

"What kind of alpha does that make me?" Rafe asked. "Besides, I have no wish to be alpha. I never did – not even when I was younger. It should be you, Artemis. Why do you fight against that?"

"Because father will never allow it," Artemis snapped. "He wants you as the alpha, and I want you to return to our pack. I've missed you, brother. You have no idea how much I've missed you."

Rafe squeezed his shoulder. "I've missed you as well."

"Are you really in love with a human?" Artemis asked.

Rafe nodded. "Yes. It's completely wrong on every level

– she's fifteen years younger than me, and she had no idea shifters existed until last night, but I love her."

"Then why haven't you bitten her?" Artemis asked.

Rafe hesitated, and Artemis said, "Perhaps deep down, you know you will forever lose your chance at being in the pack if you take the human as your mate."

"I could make my own pack with her," Rafe said.

"It is not the same, and you know it," Artemis said. "You can't tell me you haven't missed being part of a pack, Rafe."

"Of course I have," Rafe said. "Many times, I thought I'd go crazy from the loneliness."

"Then come back to us," Artemis said. "I'm tired of being separated from my brother. I know you love the human, but sometimes you must make sacrifices for the pack's good. It hurts, but you will get over it with time."

Rafe studied Artemis closely. "What is her name, brother?"

"What are you talking about?"

"The human you're in love with. What is her name?"

Artemis shook his head. "I'm not in love with a human, Rafe. I just -"

"You were never good at lying, Artemis," Rafe said. "Tell me her name."

"Cassia," Artemis said in a low voice. "She lives in Newport."

"Does father know about her?"

"No. I," he paused before shaking his head, "it doesn't matter. I ended it a moon ago. It was growing more and more difficult to conceal her scent on my skin, and it was not fair to her to ask her to keep our love a secret."

"Artemis," Rafe said, "you can't live your life trying to please Father. This should give you even more of an incentive to be the alpha. If you're alpha, you can bring humans into the pack. You can have Cassia's love."

"Father has spent years poisoning the pack against humans," Artemis said. "They would never accept humans."

"Are you certain? I have seen more than a few of them hitting on human females at the Woodsmen Pub," Rafe said.

"Fucking them is one thing," Artemis said, "but they would never mate with them and allow them to join the pack. It would destroy the pack if I tried to force them to do so."

"You don't know that," Rafe said.

"I do," Artemis said. "You don't know what the pack is like now."

He gripped Rafe's arm. "Think about it for a few days, will you? I know it isn't easy to give up your love for your human, believe me, I do, but promise me you'll at least consider Father's offer. I miss you, Rafe."

"I will consider it," Rafe said.

"Thank you, brother."

"TAGON?"

"Yes, father?" Tagon moved to the side of the bed and adjusted the covers. "What is it?"

"I need you to do something for me. I want you to find Rafe's human and bring her to me."

"What? Why?" Tagon asked.

His father gave him a grim smile. "So, I can convince her to leave my son alone."

"Father, I don't think this is a good idea. If you hurt Rafe's mate, he will -"

"She is not his mate," his father said. "Bring her to me."

"She won't come without Rafe," Tagon said. "He will tell her what you said, and -"

"Then you must convince her that I wish to meet with her because I want to find a way to make this work for all of us," the old man snarled. "Do as I ask, Tagon, and stop arguing with me."

"Yes, Father," Tagon said.

The old man patted Tagon's face. "You're a good boy, Tagon."

CHAPTER 10

"Hey, handsome," Rowan said happily when she opened her apartment door. "How did it go with your father?"

Rafe stepped inside and, without speaking, pulled her into his embrace and buried his face in her hair. He breathed deeply as she made a soft, comforting sound and rubbed his back. He felt completely at peace for the first time in hours, and he kissed Rowan's neck. He couldn't leave his mate. He missed Artemis and even surly Tagon, and he missed being in a pack, but he couldn't abandon his mate. He would go crazy without her.

"I take it that it didn't go well," Rowan said when he finally released her.

"It wasn't…." He gave her a helpless look. He had no idea where to even begin.

Rowan took his hand and led him toward the kitchen. "Come on, honey, I've got supper waiting for you. You can tell me everything while we eat."

"I AM SORRY, MY MATE," RAFE SAID AS ROWAN PUSHED THE uneaten food around her plate. Halfway through supper, she had abandoned eating, and he stared worriedly at her.

"It's not your fault your father gave you such a terrible choice."

"It isn't a choice," he said. "I'm not leaving my mate."

"I'm not your mate, though, am I?" she said. "You haven't bitten me."

"I'll bite you right now," he said. "Rowan, I love you and want to be with you."

He expected her to be happy, and when she continued to give him a grave look, his heart sank. "Do you not love me?"

"Of course I do," she said.

"Then let's go to the bedroom," he said. "I'll claim you as my mate, and we'll -"

"You promised Artemis you would take a few days to consider it," she said. "If you bite me tonight, the choice has been made."

"I told him that to ease his mind," Rafe said. "I love my brother, and I miss him, but it's you I need."

"You miss your pack," she said. "I know you do. If you take me as your mate, you'll never be a part of a pack again."

"We're a pack," he said. "Remember?"

"I know I don't know a lot about wolf shifters, but I'm pretty certain that a pack of two isn't how it works," she said softly. "It's one thing when we have no choice, but now your father has -"

"I don't care!" he said. "Listen to me, my mate. I will not leave you – I *cannot* leave you."

"I think you should honour your promise to your brother," Rowan said. "Biting me tonight would be a mistake."

"You're having second thoughts about being with an old

man," Rafe said, "and my father's offer is a convenient way for you to not -"

"Stop it." She pushed her chair back and stomped over to him before sitting on his lap and cupping his face. "I love you, Rafe Taggert, and I don't fucking care how old you are or that you're a goddamn wolf who howls at the moon. I am not having second thoughts. What I'm trying to do is not be selfish for once in my fucking life. I want you, I love you, and the thought of not being with you is killing me. But do you know what's worse?"

She squeezed his face, and he shook his head. She rested her forehead against his before saying, "What's worse is thinking that someday you'll regret your decision today. That you'll wish you had made a different choice, and you'll grow to hate me because of it. I couldn't stand that, Rafe. I couldn't."

"That won't happen, Rowan," Rafe said. "I love you, and I'll always love you. A shifter will never abandon his mate. Please, let me bite you."

She pressed her mouth against his in a brief, warm kiss. "Honour your promise to your brother, Rafe. Give it a few days. You can bite me if you still feel the same as you do now."

"Do you promise?" he asked hoarsely.

She gave him a small smile before making an 'x' over her heart. "Cross my heart, hope to die."

"I love you, Rowan."

"I love you too, Rafe."

They sat silently for a few minutes before she squeezed his shoulder and started to stand. He immediately pulled her back into his lap, holding her tightly around the waist.

"Let me up, honey," she said. "I want to clean up the supper dishes and go to bed. I'm tired."

He swallowed heavily. "Do you want me to leave?"

She shook her head. "No, absolutely not. Unless you want to go? I understand if you do."

"I want to stay with my mate," he said.

She nuzzled his throat affectionately, and he cupped her breast, kneading it gently before kissing her. She rubbed her ass against his growing erection. "Maybe I'm not that tired."

He grinned at her, and she cupped his face. "Honey, you can't bite me during sex. Promise me you won't."

He hesitated, and she poked him in the chest. "Promise you won't bite, or you're banished to the guest room."

"You wouldn't do that," he said with a small grin. "You're way too horny for that."

"I have a vibrator, Mr. Taggert," she said primly. "And a package of fresh batteries."

He growled at her, and she laughed before kissing him. "No biting. Promise me, honey."

"I promise," he said.

"Thank you. Now, Mr. Big Bad Wolf - take me to the bedroom and ravish me."

"So, you really wouldn't let Rafe bite you last night?" Belle panted into the phone.

"No. I– I want it more than anything, but I also want him to be positive this is what he wants," Rowan said. "What are you doing over there?"

"Trying to move a box of books that weighs about a thousand pounds," Belle said. "Hold on a minute."

Rowan waited patiently as Belle set her phone down with a clunk. She tidied up the dinner dishes from last night and listened to the faint sounds of Belle grunting. Rafe had left

460

half an hour ago to work at the Farthen's place, and she had immediately called Belle.

"Okay, I'm back," Belle said breathlessly. "But I gotta go. The stupid box is in my way, and I need Bennett to move it for me. He's out in the back yard, and I swear my cell phone loses its damn signal every time I walk through the west wing."

"Sure, I'll let you know in a few days what happens."

"Hold on," Belle said, "that's not what I meant. Come over for lunch – I'll text Ella and tell her to join us – and we'll talk more about it."

"Are you sure?" Rowan asked.

"Of course I am. I'll see you around noon, okay?"

"Yes. Thanks, Belle-baby."

"Anytime, honey."

Rowan hit the end button and shoved her cell phone into her pocket. She paced back and forth in her small kitchen, wondering for about the hundredth time if it had been a mistake not to let Rafe bite her last night.

It isn't. Rafe needs to be sure you're what he wants.

She sighed. Her inner voice was right, but she was a bundle of nerves. Rafe was adamant that he wanted to be with her, but his pack was important too and –

There was a knock at her door, and she headed toward it. She checked the peephole, her eyes widening with surprise, before opening the door. "Tagon? What are you doing here?"

"Hello, Ms. Jameson. May I come in?"

She cocked her head at him. "How did you know where I lived?"

He shrugged. "I Googled you."

"How did you get into the building?"

"One of your neighbours was leaving the building and

was kind enough to hold the door open for me. May I come in?"

She nodded and stepped back. "Yes, but Rafe isn't here."

"It's not Rafe I wish to speak with," he said before giving her a pleasant smile.

She gave him a suspicious look. "Why so nice, wolf boy?"

"Do I need a reason to be nice to my brother's mate?"

He sniffed at her, and she rolled her eyes. "You know I'm not technically your brother's mate yet."

"I imagine my brother has told you about my father's offer," Tagon said.

"He did."

"He was clear to my father that he would not leave his mate, yet he still hasn't bitten you. Does that worry you?"

"No."

Tagon smiled at her. "My father would like to meet you."

"Bring him by tonight. We can have tea and cookies," Rowan said.

Tagon shook his head. "My father is very ill and cannot travel."

"Fair enough. Tell your dad that Rafe and I will come by this evening."

"He wishes to meet with you alone."

"Why?" Rowan asked. "So he can convince me to convince Rafe to dump my ass?"

Tagon smiled again at her. "Surprisingly, no. He's missed Rafe very much and -"

"Then maybe he shouldn't have kicked him out of the pack," Rowan said.

The smile dropped from Tagon's face, and he cleared his throat. "My father wishes to meet you in the hopes that you can come to a truce that will allow Rafe to have you as his mate and be alpha of the pack."

"No offense, Tagon, but that sounds like a whole lot of bullshit," Rowan said.

Tagon bared his teeth at her, and she cocked her eyebrow at him before leaning against the wall. "Try again."

"I speak the truth," Tagon said. "But I don't care if you refuse to meet with my father or not. I'll tell him that you weren't interested in trying to help your mate. Goodbye, Ms. Jameson."

He stalked out into the hallway as Rowan bit at her lip. "Tagon, wait! I'll meet with your father."

Tagon turned to face her and smiled again. "Excellent. Come with me. I'll drive you there."

"You want me to go right now?" Rowan asked.

He nodded. "Is that a problem?"

She hesitated before shaking her head. "No, just let me grab my purse."

She ran into the kitchen and grabbed her purse before pulling her cell phone from her pocket. She quickly texted Belle and started to text Rafe when Tagon appeared in the kitchen.

"Ms. Jameson? I don't mean to rush you, but my father tires quickly these days. He's waiting for us, and I want to get back to him as soon as possible."

She shoved her cell phone into her purse without finishing her text and nodded. "Let's go."

RAFE'S CHILDHOOD HOME WAS LARGE AND SURPRISINGLY inviting. Bright sunlight poured through the living room window, and she set her purse by the door before wandering across the room. She studied the photos on the wall. Most of them were of Rafe and his brothers as children, and she smiled a little at the image of the three brothers standing in front of a large tree house, their arms draped over each other's shoulders and identical grins on their faces.

There was a noise behind her, and she turned and watched Tagon lead the old man into the room. He shuffled to the chair next to the fireplace and collapsed into it with a heavy sigh as Tagon draped a blanket over his lap.

Rowan studied him carefully. He was tall like Rafe, but his hair was a lighter brown, and he had bright blue eyes. She imagined in his youth, he had been a very handsome man but whatever illness had taken hold of him had etched lines into his too-thin face, and his skin was an unhealthy shade of grey. Still, his eyes shone with sharp intelligence, and he stared steadily at her even as his hands trembled.

"My name is Arone Taggert," he said.

"Hello, Mr. Taggert. My name is Rowan. It's nice to meet you," she said.

He studied her closely. "How old are you?"

"Old enough," she said. "Tagon said you wished to speak with me about Rafe."

"I do. Sit, please," he said.

She crossed the room and sat down in the chair across from him. She crossed her legs and folded her hands neatly in her lap. She was nervous, and she watched as the old man took a deep sniff in her direction.

"You're nervous," he said. "Why?"

"Maybe because I'm in a house with two wolves who aren't exactly my biggest fans?" she said.

He grinned, revealing white teeth. "Can you blame us? You're taking our son and brother away from us."

"No, you did that years ago when you refused to allow him back into the pack," she said.

He scowled at her, and she shrugged. "It's the truth, and you know it. Just because you don't want to hear it doesn't make it untrue."

"Are you always this outspoken?" he asked.

"Pretty much," Rowan said.

"What does my son even see in you?" he asked with mild disgust.

Rowan ignored his question. "I want to make this work, Mr. Taggert. I want to be Rafe's mate, and I want him to have his pack again. Tell me how we can do that."

"It's impossible. Rafe must choose," his father said.

Rowan glanced at Tagon. "Tagon said you wanted to speak with me about how Rafe could have both."

"I wanted to meet you to see what kind of woman has such a hold over my son. And to break that hold," he said serenely.

Fear bubbling up in her throat, Rowan shook her head. "We're done here. Goodbye, Mr. Taggert."

She stood and headed toward the door. Tagon stepped in front of it, and she gave him a cool look. "Get out of my way, Tagon."

He shook his head. "I can't do that. Sit and listen to what my father has to say."

She glanced at her purse, and he shoved it behind him with one foot. "You don't need your phone, Ms. Jameson. Speak with my father for a while, and I'm sure we can come to an agreement."

"When Rafe finds out you kidnapped me, he's going to kick your ass," Rowan said.

"He'll never know you were here," Arone said. "And since humans wander into the woods and die every year…."

He twitched in surprise when Rowan laughed. "Did you seriously just threaten to kill me?"

"Of course not," Tagon said hurriedly. "Father, don't -"

"Be quiet, Tagon," his father said. "No one knows you're here, human, and -"

"That's not quite right," Rowan said. "I texted Rafe before I left with Tagon."

Arone glanced at Tagon, who shook his head. "She didn't finish her text."

"There's no way you know that for sure," Rowan said.

"I know," Tagon said. "I have excellent eyesight."

Arone gave Rowan a bitter smile. "Human, you will listen to me and listen closely. Rafe belongs with his pack. He is meant to be alpha, and if you know what's good for you, you will not stand in his way. You will tell him that he is to return to us so that he may take his rightful place as alpha and find a nice bitch within our pack to mate and have pups with. Do you understand?"

"I think Rafe's old enough to make his own decisions," Rowan said.

"You're a stupid, stubborn little girl who has no idea how much trouble she's in," the old man snarled.

"And you're a dying old man who can't stand the thought of his child being in love with a human," Rowan said. "Just because your wife was an asshole who left you doesn't mean all humans are assholes. You're a giant dickhead, but you don't see me assuming that all shifters are dickheads, do you?"

Tagon's mouth dropped open as Arone stared at her in silent shock.

"I love Rafe, and he loves me," Rowan said. "Get used to it."

"He has not claimed you," Arone said. "He may call you his mate, but until he bites you, it's only words."

"He hasn't bitten me because I told him not to," Rowan said. "I told him to think about his decision for a few days."

"Why would you do that?" Arone asked.

"I love him, but if he wants to be with his pack, I will not ruin that for him. Of course, you could try not being a dickhead and let him have his pack and his mate."

"I will never allow humans into the pack again," Arone said in a low snarl. "And watch your tongue, or I'll rip it out of your head for speaking so insolently to me."

Rowan glared at him but kept quiet as Arone stared at the floor. Finally, unable to stand the silence any longer, she said, "Are we finished here? I'd like to leave."

"You will leave when I say you can leave," Arone said.

Rowan rolled her eyes. "What exactly is your plan? I can't do anything for you. Rafe is a grown man, and he'll decide if he wants to be alpha of the pack or not."

"You will stay here until you agree to tell my son you no longer desire to be his mate! Once you're out of his life, he will gladly return to his pack." Arone snapped at her.

Rowan snorted and dropped into the chair again. "Well, you'd better get me a drink because I'm going to be here for a long time."

"RAFE? HEY, WHAT'S UP?" BENNETT SAID AS HE OPENED THE front door.

"I need to speak with Belle," Rafe said anxiously.

"She's out back. We're having a barbeque with Ella and Duncan. What's wrong?"

Rafe shouldered past him and ran through the house to the

backyard. Belle stood on the deck with Ella and Duncan, and the three of them gave him a startled look as Bennett ducked out the patio door behind him.

"Rafe? What's wrong?" Belle asked.

"Do you know where Rowan is?" Rafe asked. "I've called and texted her phone repeatedly, and she hasn't answered. I've been to her apartment and Gaston's, and she's not at either place. I called her grandmother, but she hasn't talked to her since yesterday."

Belle stared at Ella, and the look on her face sent ice water through Rafe's veins. "Belle? Where is my mate?"

"I got a text from her earlier. She didn't say much – just that she couldn't make it to lunch because your brother was taking her to meet your father. Didn't she tell you? I texted her a couple of hours ago to find out how it went, but she didn't reply. I assumed she was with you." Belle said.

Rafe staggered back, his eyes turning bright green and his fangs popping out. He turned to leave, and Bennett grabbed him by the shoulders. "Rafe, wait!"

"Let go of me! My mate is in danger," Rafe snarled.

"You can't go alone," Bennett said. "Your pack is large, and you'll need help if they decide to be dicks. Duncan and I will go with you."

He glanced at the lion shifter, who nodded before kissing Ella. "Stay here, honey."

"No way, I'm going with you," Ella said.

"We both are," Belle said.

"No," Bennett and Duncan said in unison.

Ella glared at Duncan, and the lion shifter pulled her into her arms and kissed her forehead. "It's too dangerous for a human, Ella. We won't be long."

"What if something happens? What if -"

"Nothing's going to happen," Bennett said. "We'll find

Rowan and bring her home." He kissed Belle. "I'll text you when we have her."

"Be careful, Ben," Belle said.

"I will, Mirabelle. Don't worry." Ben kissed her again before he and Duncan followed Rafe into the house.

"Easy, Rafe," Duncan murmured as Bennett parked in front of the wolf pack's cabins. "Just wait a minute."

"Do not tell me to wait. They have my mate," Rafe growled. "I should have bitten her last night. With my mark, the pack would not have dared to touch her. Without it, she is defenseless."

"Not quite," Bennett said as she shut off the truck. "Rowan's tough, Rafe. She can hold her own."

"Against a pack of wolves?" Rafe said as he clawed at the door handle.

"Rafe, wait a minute. It won't do us any good if you go in there half-cocked and ready to murder anyone who -"

Rafe ignored Duncan and jumped out of Bennett's truck. He stalked toward his father's cabin, not waiting to see if Duncan or Bennett followed him. He kicked open the door of his father's cabin and stormed down the hallway. Tagon stood in the living room doorway, and Rafe, a thick beard growing on his face and his clothes straining at the seams, shot toward him and grabbed him by the throat. He slammed him into the wall and shook him roughly.

"Where is she?" he shouted. "Where is my mate?"

His face turning red and his eyes glowing a dark yellow, Tagon clawed at Rafe's hand.

"Brother! Enough!" Artemis said.

Snarling under his breath, Rafe dropped Tagon to the

floor. Ignoring his brother's gasps for air, he turned and bared his fangs at Artemis. "Where is she? Give me my mate, or I'll kill you, brother."

"Rafe, I'm right here."

He swung his gaze to the left. Rowan stood by the window, and his wolf howled happily at the sight of his mate. He ran toward her, she met him halfway, and he picked her up and kissed her frantically as Bennett and Duncan stepped into the living room.

"Rowan, my mate, are you okay?" He set her on her feet and cupped her face, examining her anxiously as she nodded.

"Of course I am, honey."

"When I heard Tagon had kidnapped you, I thought…."

Rowan squeezed his arms. "Kidnap is a strong word. I came with him because I wanted to, although he did lie to get me here."

She scowled at Tagon over Rafe's shoulder. The younger shifter returned her scowl, and Rowan stuck her tongue out at him before smiling at Rafe. "Everything's fine, honey. They didn't hurt me."

"Why did you bring her here?" Rafe glared at Artemis, who held up his hands.

"I had no idea, brother. It was Father who had her brought here."

"Where is Father?" Rafe looked around the room, growling under his breath, and Rowan slapped him lightly on the chest.

"Honey, calm down. Your father fell asleep three hours ago. I've been visiting Artemis and Tagon. Well, mostly Artemis. For some weird reason, Tagon doesn't like me very much."

She gave Tagon a saucy grin, and he sighed before walking toward the door. "I'm going to Sophina."

"You're not going anywhere," Rafe snapped. "You kidnapped my mate and -"

"Let him go, Rafe," Rowan said. "He was only doing what your father asked him to do." She grinned at Tagon. "You can grab my purse from wherever you hid it and leave it in the kitchen. I'll pick it up on my way out."

The shifter blushed slightly before nodding and leaving. Bennett glanced at Duncan. "We'll wait outside."

As the two shifters left the room, Rowan said, "Why did you bring Duncan and Bennett?"

"Because I thought... I couldn't get a hold of you, you weren't answering my calls or texts, and then Belle told me that you were meeting my father, and I thought the worst," Rafe said.

"I'm sorry," Rowan said. "Tagon confiscated my purse and cell phone earlier, and then I started visiting with Artemis, and I kind of forgot about it."

Rafe gave her a look of disbelief. "Please tell me what's happening here."

She led him over to the couch, and he sank beside her as she took his hand. "Tagon tricked me into coming out here to meet your father. He said your dad wanted to find a way that you could both be alpha of the pack and have me as your mate. But when I got here, it was clear that your dad wanted me just to go away. I refused to leave you and told him that you could make up your mind about what you wanted. That made him angry, and he said I had to stay here until I promised to tell you I didn't want to be your mate."

"He wouldn't let you leave. That's it?" Rafe said in confusion.

"Our father is not thinking clearly as of late. To him, it would make sense to force Rowan to stay here. Whatever illness he has is starting to affect his mind," Artemis said.

Rowan squeezed Rafe's hand. "After about an hour, your dad fell asleep in the chair, and Artemis showed up. He shouted at Tagon for a while, the two of them moved your dad to his bedroom, and Artemis said he would take me home. But then we got to talking, and I kind of lost track of time. I'm sorry, honey, I really should have called."

"You got to talking," Rafe said.

"Yes," Rowan said. "Tagon refused to join in, although he did skulk around the room the whole time, so I think I might be winning him over just a little, but Artemis and I are getting along just fine. Aren't we?"

Artemis grinned at her. "We are."

"Anyway, I'm ready to go home anytime you are," Rowan said. She stood up from the couch and walked across the room to take Artemis' hand. "It was so good to meet you, Artemis. You and Cassia will have to visit us."

"I have not won her back yet," Artemis said.

"You will," Rowan said. "I know it." She smiled at Rafe. "I'll meet you outside."

When she was gone, Artemis grinned at Rafe. "I like your mate. She has a fiery spirit."

"How did she know about Cassia?" Rafe asked.

Artemis shrugged. "She's easy to talk to. She loves you very much, you know."

"I know, and I love her. I'm biting her tonight, Artemis. Will you tell Father that I won't be joining the pack? I don't want to see him, not after he kidnapped my mate."

Artemis nodded. "I'll tell him. He's going to be unhappy with the both of us."

"What do you mean?"

"I have spent my entire life trying to make our father happy, Rafe," Artemis said. "Now I'm going to do something that makes me happy. I'm leaving the pack and will marry

Cassia if she'll still have me. Tagon will become alpha and will do well at it."

"What changed your mind?" Rafe asked.

"You," Artemis said. "Your human and the love you have for each other. I'll miss the pack, but I can't live without Cassia. Human or not – she's my mate, and I'd rather have her than my pack."

"You won't be alone," Rafe said. "You'll have me too."

"Thank you. I'll call you in a few days, all right?"

Rafe nodded, and the two men embraced before Artemis clapped him on the back. "Go on, brother. Claim your mate."

THEY WERE BARELY IN HIS DEN BEFORE HE WAS TEARING AT her clothing. Laughing, she poked him hard in his flat stomach. "Rafe, wait a minute."

"I don't want to wait," he growled before picking her up and carrying her into the bedroom. He set her down and quickly stripped off their clothing before pushing her onto the bed and covering her slender body with his. She hooked her legs around his hips and cupped his face.

"I love you, Rafe Taggert," she said somberly.

"I love you too, Rowan."

"Are you sure?" she asked. "Even with the age difference, even though I'm human, and even though this means you'll never be part of your pack again?"

He didn't hesitate. "Yes. Are you sure? If I bite you, you'll never get rid of me."

She laughed and kissed him hard. "That sounds perfect to me, honey."

He stroked her hair before licking a slow path across the sensitive skin on her throat. She moaned and arched her back when he nibbled at her collarbone, and he trailed kisses down her chest until he reached one stiff nipple. He circled it with the tip of his tongue as she buried her hands in his hair.

"Rafe," she moaned.

"Yes, my mate?"

"How much is this bite going to hurt?"

He sucked on her nipple until her hips rose and fell against him. "Only a little, I promise."

He switched to her other nipple, teasing it until its pink colour had turned to a deep rose, and her breathing was harsh pants. He traced her ribs with the tips of his fingers and let his fangs pop out before placing sharp little nips along her pale skin.

She moaned and pushed at the top of his head. "My pussy, Rafe. Eat it."

"Yes, my mate," he said with a slow grin.

He wedged his body between her pale thighs and kissed the cluster of freckles on the inside of her left one before nipping her with his fangs again.

She jerked and moaned again. "Rafe, now."

He buried his face in her pussy and pressed his big hands against her inner thighs, opening her wide to him. Her hands pulled and tugged restlessly at his hair as he licked her clit and slid two fingers deep into her warmth. He sucked at her clit, teasing it lightly as he thrust his fingers slowly.

She was moaning loudly, one hand still tangled in his hair while the other squeezed the sheets in a tight fist. Her body began to tremble, and he lifted his head and kissed the small patch of red curls.

"Look at me, my mate," he said.

She stared obediently at him as he lowered his mouth to her pussy and licked her clit with slow strokes.

"Oh God," she whispered. "Rafe, please, oh please...."

Her begging turned into a shout of pleasure as he sucked her clit into his mouth and her body shook with pleasure. He held her down, licking her clean and watching as she came down from the high of her orgasm.

Her hands were clenching and unclenching in the sheets, and he kissed one hip before sliding off the bed. He turned her onto her stomach and rubbed her smooth ass. "On your hands and knees, Rowan."

Her body still visibly trembling, she climbed to her hands and knees as he knelt on the bed between her thighs. He stroked her ass again before guiding his cock into her warmth. She arched her back when he breached her entrance and smiled at him over her shoulder. He gathered her hair in one hand and kissed the small of her back before moving in long, slow strokes.

"Love you," she panted.

"Love you too," he groaned.

He pushed in and out of her, the smooth, wet grip of her pussy moving him closer and closer to the edge. He reached beneath her and rubbed at her clit as he leaned over her and pressed a kiss against her right shoulder.

She was tensing in anticipation of his bite, and he licked the curve of her spine while he rubbed her clit firmly. His balls tightened, and he fought against his orgasm as she panted and moaned beneath him. Her small, tight ass slapped against his pelvis as she met each of his thrusts, and he licked her spine again as she relaxed and muttered his name in a low plea.

When he pinched her clit, she uttered a loud cry of pleasure and her pussy clamped down on his cock as she came. His orgasm washed over him, and he howled loudly before sinking his fangs into the back of her right shoulder. She cried out, her back arching, and he gripped her hip tightly with one hand as her pussy squeezed him exquisitely. He anchored one arm around her waist and withdrew his fangs. He licked the mark – her blood was sweet and delicious – until the small flow of red had stopped. She was shaking beneath him, and he eased out of her before lowering her gently to the bed. He curled on his side next to her, kissing the flesh around the bite and murmuring low words of comfort as she panted and trembled.

"I'm sorry," he said.

She rolled to her side to face him. "It's fine. It didn't hurt that much, or maybe I was coming too hard to notice."

He smiled and kissed her. "You're mine now, Rowan. Mine forever."

"And you're mine," she said. "I love you, Rafe."

"I love you, my mate."

Fifteen months later

"So," Belle sat at the kitchen table and grinned at Rowan. "How was the honeymoon?"

"Fantastic," Rowan said. "Fiji is beautiful, and the resort we stayed at was nearly empty. We had such a good time – thanks for recommending it, Ella."

Ella squeezed her hand. "I knew you'd love it. Duncan wanted to go to Hawaii for our honeymoon, but I convinced him to try Fiji, and we didn't regret it."

"I don't know," Belle said with a grin, "a Hawaiian honeymoon was perfect for Ben and me."

"I was a little worried that we'd miss Cassia giving birth, but Rafe talked to Artemis this morning, and poor Cassia still hasn't had a single labour pain," Rowan said. "She's almost four days overdue now. She's terrified the kid will weigh fifteen pounds when he finally makes an appearance."

Belle laughed. "I know shifters are on the large side, but I don't think that necessarily means they come out giant-sized as babies."

"You'd better hope not – your husband's a bear shifter and eight feet tall," Rowan said.

Belle glanced at Ella, who wiggled her eyebrows before clearing her throat. "Well, the both of us will soon find out."

Her cup of tea held halfway to her mouth, Rowan stared at Ella. "What did you just say?"

"I'm pregnant," Ella said.

"Me too," Belle said.

"Holy fuck," Rowan said.

She stared blankly at them as Ella said, "I'm thirteen weeks, and Belle is twelve weeks. I was going to tell the two of you together when you returned from your honeymoon, but, well...."

Belle giggled. "I dropped by to visit her one morning, and she was barfing her guts up in the bathroom. That made me throw up, and we both had to admit we were pregnant."

She glanced at Ella, and they both laughed. "Synchronized vomiting isn't something we ever want to experience again."

Rowan just stared silently at them, and Ella gave Belle a worried look before reaching for Rowan's hand. "Ro, honey, I'm sorry I told Belle before I told you. I did mean to tell the two of you together."

"I did, too," Belle said. "We weren't purposely trying to exclude you, honey."

"I know," Rowan said hoarsely. "I'm happy for you both. I swear."

"Then what's wrong?" Ella asked.

"There's nothing wrong. It's just…."

Rowan started to laugh, and Belle and Ella stared at each other in confusion.

"Ro?" Belle said. "What's so funny?"

Rowan laughed again, staring at her flat stomach, "I'm pregnant too."

Dead silence greeted her announcement, and she reached out and grabbed her two best friends' hands. "I'm eight weeks. I was going to wait until I was twelve weeks to tell you."

"Holy shit," Ella said.

"What she said," Belle said.

"You really are pregnant?" Ella said.

"I really am," Rowan said. "I'm cooking a little wolf baby in my belly as we speak."

Belle's mouth dropped open, and the three of them burst into simultaneous laughter. Bennett stuck his head into the kitchen. "Everything okay in here?"

"Yes," Belle said as she giggled again. "Everything's great, honey."

"Okay. Are you coming outside? The steaks are done, and Duncan and Rafe are starving and about to start eating without you."

"We'll be right there," Belle said.

As Bennett left the kitchen, she squeezed Ella's and Rowan's hands. "Come on, ladies. Our handsome mates are waiting for us."

EPILOGUE

"Ashley, hurry up!" The little girl planted her fists on her hips and blew a strand of her long red hair away from her face. "We need to get there before they do!"

"I know, Caitlin!" The dark-haired girl said. She scratched at a scab on her knee before adjusting her backpack. "My backpack is heavier than yours."

"That's because you put too many books in it." A blonde girl, her hair gleaming in the sun, said matter-of-factly. She opened Ashley's backpack and pulled out three books, shoving them into her pink bag before closing it and slipping her arms through the straps.

"Better?" she asked.

"Yeah, thanks, Krysten," Ashley said as they followed the redhead through the knee-high grass.

"I don't know why you brought books anyway," Caitlin said. "We're picnicking, not reading."

"Daddy likes it when I read to him," Ashley said defensively.

Krysten took her hand and squeezed it. "It's okay, Ash. I

brought my sketchbook because Papa said he'd teach me how to draw trees today."

"Boring," Caitlin said with a sweet grin. "Daddy's going to teach me to hunt rabbits." She suddenly bared her teeth, her small white fangs flashing at them as her eyes turned light green, and the other two girls giggled at her.

They were approaching the edge of the woods, and Caitlin made a squeal of excitement as she dropped her back-pack under a large oak tree. "We'll set the blanket here. It's the perfect spot."

The three little girls quickly set up the picnic. After arranging the blanket under the tree and carefully setting out the sandwiches and fruit in their plastic containers, Krysten peered into the trees. "They're late."

"Maybe Daddy stopped to pick a rose for Mommy," Ashley said.

"Or," Caitlin said, her eyes flashing with excitement, "maybe they're fighting a cougar or a bear!"

Krysten rolled her eyes. "There aren't any cougars left in the woods. You know that. They probably -"

She stopped, her eyes turning a dark yellow, as Ashley joined her at the edge of the woods. Ashley sniffed the air before growling happily as a thin layer of fur sprouted on her face. "Daddy!"

Bennett came striding out of the woods, and Ashley squealed with excitement when he picked her up and tossed her into the air. "Hello, baby bear."

"Hi, Daddy!" She hugged him, and he kissed her cheek before ruffling Krysten's hair.

"Where's Papa, Uncle Bennett?" Krysten asked.

"Right here, kitty-cat."

Krysten whirled around, a loud purr reverberating in her chest, and ran to Duncan. He picked her up, his own purr starting, and rubbed his nose against hers. "Did you bring your sketchbook, peanut?"

"Yes, Papa," she said as Caitlin, her tiny body stiff and her head cocked, stalked past them.

She lifted her head and sniffed the air before grinning at a large clump of bushes. "I can smell you, Daddy."

Rafe stepped out from behind the bushes and grinned at his daughter. Caitlin bared her fangs at him, and he laughed and scooped her up, tickling her gently before carrying her toward the others. "What did your mama say about baring your fangs?"

"That it's rude," Caitlin said. "But I'm only practicing for when I catch a rabbit this afternoon."

Rafe laughed again and carried her to the blanket to join the others.

"I made the sandwiches," Ashley said, "Krysten made the lemonade, and Caitlin cut up the fruit."

"It looks delicious," Bennett said. "Thank you for inviting us to your picnic."

"Thank you for coming," Krysten said in a serious voice, and the three men grinned at each other.

"Do you think Mama is lonely?" Caitlin asked Rafe anxiously.

"No, honey. She has your brother with her, and they were going to visit your Auntie Belle and Auntie Elle," Rafe said.

"Christopher and Eli wanted to come on the picnic, but I said no," Ashley said to Bennett. "I wanted you all to myself, Daddy. I'm your favourite, right?"

Bennett grinned at her. "I love both you and your brothers equally, baby bear."

"I'm glad I don't have a brother," Krysten said to Duncan. "Ash and Caitlin's brothers are annoying."

Duncan laughed. "Didn't you tell your mom this morning that Michelle was the most annoying baby sister ever?"

"Yes, but only because she shifted and clawed up my latest painting. Mommy made her go to her room, and she has to do all my chores this week," Krysten replied with glee.

Duncan kissed her forehead, and she smiled at him before saying, "Mommy was friends with Auntie Belle and Auntie Rowan when they were little, right?"

Duncan nodded. "Yes, peanut, they were."

"Best friends?" Ashley asked.

"Yes, baby bear," Bennett said.

Ashley glanced at Krysten and Caitlin before holding out her hands. The three girls held hands, and Ashley smiled happily at them. "We'll be best friends forever too. Right?"

"Right," Caitlin said.

"Forever and ever," Krysten said.

...and they all lived happily ever after

Keep reading for an excerpt from "Willow and the Wolf", Shifters Series, Book One.

WILLOW AND THE WOLF
EXCERPT

COPYRIGHT 2015 ELIZABETH KELLY

"I love your car." Willow smoothed her hand over the dashboard.

"Thanks," Mal said.

He opened the window and had to restrain himself from sticking his head out into the breeze. Willow's scent was everywhere, and he could barely concentrate on his driving. Her scent would cling to him for the rest of the day and drive his wolf absolutely mad with need.

"Maybe I could drive on the way back?" Willow said.

"No."

"Why not?"

"Because you're too little to handle this type of power."

She laughed and rolled her eyes. "Please, I've been driving cars like this since I was sixteen."

"Really?"

"Yup. My dad was a mechanic and a collector of fast cars." She stared out the window. "He taught me how to drive when I was twelve."

"Twelve?" He couldn't keep the disbelief out of his voice.

"Yes. Mama wasn't very happy about that. She gave

him the biggest lecture when she found out. She was worried I'd get in an accident. Of course, it was fine. Daddy was a very safe driver, and he taught me to be safe as well."

He grunted in reply, and she smiled at him again. "So, what do you say? Can I drive on the way back?"

"No."

She wrinkled her nose at him. "Meanie."

"Did you just call me meanie?"

"Yes. What? Is everyone too afraid of the big bad wolf to tell him the truth about his personality?"

"I'm not a meanie," he protested.

"Well, you're definitely a grumpy," she said.

"You don't know anything about me," he said.

"That's true. But whose fault is that? Not mine. I've been trying to get to know you over the last month," Willow replied.

"You don't need to know anything about me. You're my employee, nothing else."

"That doesn't mean we can't be friends."

She pouted adorably, and he had to clench his hands around the steering wheel to stop himself from pulling the car over and kissing away the pout. "It sort of does."

"Ridiculous," she snorted. "I think you just dislike humans."

"I don't dislike humans," he said.

"No? Then it's just me?"

"Ms. Tanner, I don't -"

"You know what I think? I think you just don't know enough about me. Once you get to know me, you won't be able to resist me, Mal." She wiggled her eyebrows at him, and he almost groaned out loud when she wet her bottom lip with her small, pink tongue.

"So, here are the facts about Willow Blossom Tanner. I'm twenty-five, I -"

"Your middle name is not Blossom," he said.

"It totally is. My parents were hippies. Did I forget to mention that?" She giggled.

He didn't reply, and she continued. "As I was saying, I'm twenty-five, single – but you already know that – and my best friend is Ava. What was up with Bishop and the sniffing, by the way?"

"Uh…" He didn't know how to respond.

"He certainly seemed to like her smell. Is that a bear shifter thing or a shifter thing in general?"

"Most shifters have an excellent sense of smell. They use it to figure out all sorts of things about other paranormals and humans."

"Like what?"

He shrugged. "Where they live, what they do for a living, how old they are, their emotions at the time."

"Really? How old they are?"

He nodded. He was suddenly sweating, and he hoped she wouldn't notice. Most shifters could tell from a single sniff if a person was hungry or happy, or frightened or – he swallowed thickly – aroused.

"That is so cool," she said thoughtfully. "Paranormals are so lucky. Imagine being able to sniff someone and know instantly if they were happy."

"Not all paranormals can do it," he reminded her. "Some have better senses than others."

"I suppose something like a penguin shifter wouldn't be able to smell your happiness," she replied.

"There is no such thing as a penguin shifter."

"How do you know?" She countered immediately. "Just because you've never seen one doesn't mean they don't exist.

They wouldn't live here, would they? It's much too warm for them."

"Penguin shifters do not exist," he said through gritted teeth.

"Do you believe in spirits?"

He blinked at the abrupt change in topic. "What?"

"Spirits? Do you believe in them?"

"You mean ghosts?"

"Ghosts, spirits, ethereal beings – whatever you want to call them." She shrugged.

"There is no such thing as ghosts."

She frowned at him. "You know, for being a paranormal, you have an awfully restricted view of the world."

He rolled his eyes. "I'm just not prone to ridiculous thoughts and ideas, Ms. Tanner."

"You think I'm ridiculous?" She gave him a hurt look.

"I didn't say that. I'm just implying that you have ridiculous *ideas*."

She mulled that over. "I suppose you have a point. To the unbeliever, I would come across as ridiculous."

"The unbeliever?"

"Yes. You know, someone like you. You're much too practical for your own good, Mal. You have to open your heart and your head to the possibility that there are things in this world that can't be explained."

"I prefer to be seen as normal, thanks. It's better for business."

She laughed. "True. I blame your upbringing."

"You know nothing about my upbringing," he replied.

"I know your parents aren't hippies like mine were."

"Were?" He glanced at her.

For the first time since he'd met her, the cheerful look on

her face dropped away. "My parents died two years ago in that plane crash. You know the one."

He nodded. It had been all over the news. One hundred and twenty-five humans and forty paranormals were killed instantly when the plane they were in had crashed into the ocean. "I'm sorry."

"Thanks. I miss them terribly. I'm an only child, and neither of my parents' siblings is still alive."

She stared out the window for a moment. "It gets pretty lonely, you know? Thank God for Ava."

She fidgeted with the buttons on her shirt. "I thought maybe I would see them again. Thought that maybe they would make an appearance just to say they loved me but that never happened. I shouldn't be surprised. Both my parents were extremely happy people. There was nothing left to keep them in this world. Still... I hoped they would want to see me one last time."

"What are you talking about?" Just when he thought she was normal, she threw out random crap like that.

"Nothing," she said cryptically. "Where was I? Oh yes, we were telling each other about our personal lives. It's your turn now."

He shook his head. "We weren't talking about our personal lives - you were talking about your personal life."

"Oh c'mon," she wheedled. "Throw me a bone, would you? I want to know something about the big bad wolf."

He snorted, and she grinned at him. "Maybe I can guess."

She studied him so long that he could feel a blush creeping up his neck. "Stop staring at me."

"I'm just trying to figure you out."

"It's rude to stare."

"I suppose it is. Maybe I should sniff you instead."

Before he could stop her, she had leaned over and nearly

buried her face in his neck. She inhaled deeply, and he stiffened and leaned away.

"It's even ruder to smell someone without their invitation," he snapped.

"Man, I've got a lot to learn about shifters. I thought shifters would be cool with the sniffing."

She sat back in her seat. "That didn't tell me anything, anyway. Other than you wear really great cologne."

He blushed, and she clapped her hands with unrestrained glee. "I made you blush!"

"No, you didn't!" he snapped again.

"Of course not. Your natural colour is bright red," she replied.

He stopped the car at a red light, and she grinned impishly. "Maybe you should smell me."

"Definitely not," he growled.

"Oh c'mon…it'll be fun!"

She unclicked her seat belt and leaned in until he could feel her small breasts pressing against his arm. He stared at her in panic as she tilted her head up.

"Go on, Mal. Sniff me," she said.

"Ms. Tanner, this isn't -"

"Are you a chicken?" She smacked him playfully on one broad thigh. "I've never seen you in your wolf form. Maybe you're actually a chicken shifter."

He growled angrily and pressed his face into her soft throat. He inhaled deeply, his cock hardening against the worn fabric of his jeans as her scent washed over him. He inhaled again and again as Willow waited patiently.

"Well? What can you tell about me?" she asked.

"You showered this morning."

"Obviously. I shower every morning. C'mon, wolf boy, tell me something you couldn't possibly know."

"You had strawberries and wine last night for dinner. You wear vanilla body lotion, but not this morning, you were excited by something last night, and you're twenty-six, not twenty-five."

She leaned back a little and stared at him in wide-eyed wonderment. "That's amazing! I did totally lie about my age!"

He could feel a grin creeping across his face, and her eyes sparkled happily in response. "Do me again, Mal!"

"I – what?" he croaked out. He couldn't stop the immediate mental image of yanking up Willow's skirt, tearing off her panties and making her straddle him while he fucked her senseless.

"Sniff me again! Tell me something else!"

"Uh, no, I don't think -"

He groaned out loud when she shoved her throat eagerly into his face. This time she rested one warm hand on his thigh, and he was helpless to stop from cupping the back of her head and holding her steady while he breathed in. His traitorous tongue licked her soft skin, his balls tightening when she moaned softly in response. Her hand clenched on his leg as he licked her again.

"Does – does taste tell you something as well?" she squeaked out.

"Yes," he muttered. Her arousal was strong and overpowering in the small car, and his wolf howled with delight when he nipped her neck.

"Oh!" She jerked against him, and he gripped her neck and forced her head to the side before licking from the hollow of her throat to her earlobe.

"What does it tell you?" she asked breathlessly.

"That you taste good," he whispered.

"Why do I get the feeling that the big bad wolf wants to eat me right up?" She laughed nervously.

He sucked on her earlobe. "Oh, he does, Willow. He wants to eat your sweet pussy until you're begging him for mercy. Until you've come so many times, you can't -"

The loud blaring of a car horn had them jerking apart. The light had turned green, and as the horn blasted again, he waved in apology and stepped on the gas.

He didn't dare look at Willow. His wolf was begging to be free, begging for him to pull over the car and take the little human who so obviously wanted him to. He controlled it fiercely, breathing in shallow breaths to try and avoid the smell of her need.

"So, um, that got a little weird, yeah?" Willow said.

"I'm sorry," he said hoarsely. "That was incredibly inappropriate of me, and I -"

"Don't worry about it," she said. "It was my fault anyway. I was the one who practically sat on your lap and forced you to sniff me."

He shook his head. "I want you to know that I understand how this must make me look and I promise you that I'm not the employer who – who hits on his staff."

"I know," she said. "Listen, if you keep my actual age a secret, I'll keep your inappropriate licking a secret. Deal?"

He stole a glance at her. She was acting calm, but he could still smell her excitement and see her flushed skin. If he wanted to, he could take her right now. She was wet and more than ready for him.

He growled and slammed his fist against the steering wheel.

"Hey, don't do that!" There was a thin thread of alarm in her voice, and she patted him on one broad shoulder. "Seriously, it's fine. I'm not going to sue you for harassment or anything like that."

He blew his breath out. He had licked Willow and, even worse, talked about eating her pussy. He didn't know what the hell he was thinking. He wasn't – that was the problem. His dick was doing all the thinking. Christ, he was in trouble. Willow said she would keep it quiet, but the girl never stopped talking. Kat and Bishop were going to find out, and he'd never live it down.

"Hey, Mal?" Willow's hand touched his tentatively, and he jerked it away.

"Yeah?"

"I meant it when I said I wouldn't say anything. I know I talk a lot, but I can keep a secret sometimes," she said.

"Yeah, I know. It won't happen again, I promise you."

ABOUT THE AUTHOR

Elizabeth Kelly was born and raised in Ontario, Canada. She moved west as a teenager and now lives in Alberta with her husband and a menagerie of pets. She firmly believes that a person can survive solely on sushi and coffee, and only her husband's mad cooking skills prevents her from proving that theory.

For more information about Elizabeth, check out her website at

www.elizabethkelly.ca

facebook.com/EKellyBooks

twitter.com/ElizabethKBooks

instagram.com/elizabethkelly_author

amazon.com/Elizabeth-Kelly/e/B00EOHZ0MS

bookbub.com/authors/elizabeth-kelly

ALSO BY ELIZABETH KELLY

Tempted Series

Tempted

Twice Tempted

Forever Tempted

Breathless

Tempted Trilogy (Books 1-3)

Red Moon Series

Red Moon

Red Moon Rising

Dark Moon

Alpha Moon

Pale Moon

The Recruit Series

The Recruit (Book One)

The Recruit (Book Two)

The Recruit (Book Three)

The Recruit (Book Four)

The Recruit (Book Five)

The Shifters Series

Willow and the Wolf (Book One)

Ava and the Bear (Book Two)

www.ingramcontent.com/pod-product-compliance
Lightning Source LLC
Chambersburg PA
CBHW050019030726
47506CB00001B/26